WAR AT THE EDGE OF THE WORLD

‒TWILIGHT OF EMPIRE‒
WAR AT THE EDGE OF THE WORLD
OF THE WORLD

IAN ROSS

HEAD
ZEUS

*Di boni, quid hoc est quod semper ex aliquo supremo
fine mundi nova deum numina universo orbi colenda
descendunt?*

Gracious Gods! Why is it that new deities, destined
to be universally revered, always descend from some
most distant edge of the world?

Panegyrici Latini VI

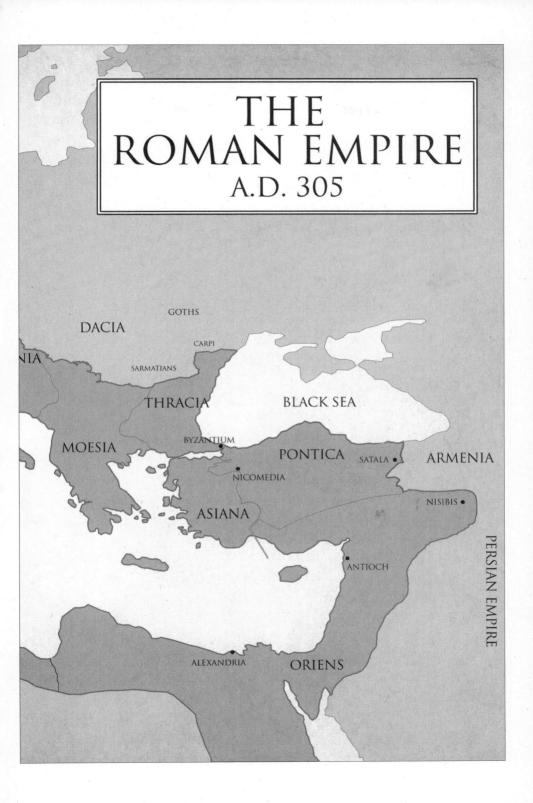

THE ROMAN EMPIRE
A.D. 305

GOTHS

DACIA

CARPI

SARMATIANS

THRACIA

BLACK SEA

NIA

MOESIA

BYZANTIUM

PONTICA

SATALA

ARMENIA

NICOMEDIA

ASIANA

NISIBIS

ANTIOCH

PERSIAN EMPIRE

ALEXANDRIA

ORIENS

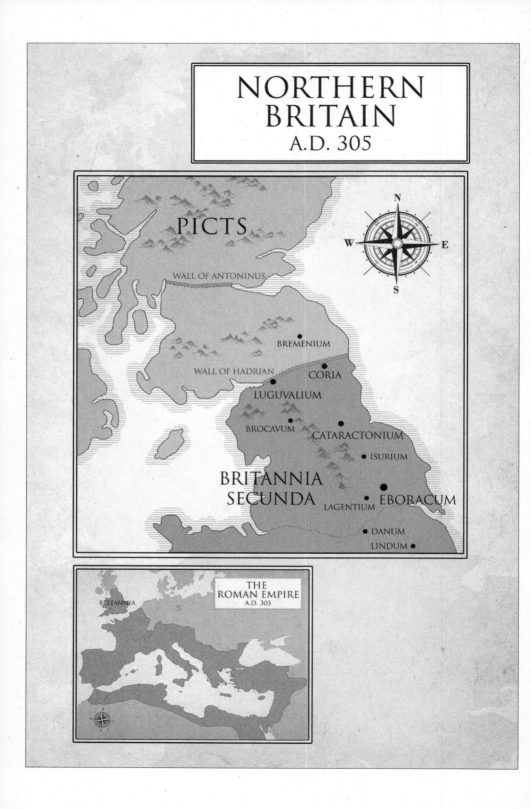

WAR AT THE EDGE OF THE WORLD

HISTORICAL NOTE

In AD 284, following half a century of crisis and civil war, military commander Gaius Aurelius Diocletianus (Diocletian) proclaimed himself supreme ruler of the Roman world. Realising that the empire was too large to be ruled effectively by a single man, he appointed Marcus Aurelius Maximianus (Maximian) co-emperor to administer the western provinces.

Eight years later, Diocletian once more reformed the system of government. He and Maximian remained as senior emperors, with the title *Augustus*. Each now took a junior colleague, Constantius in the west and Galerius in the east, with the title of *Caesar*. This rule of four was later called the Tetrarchy.

For over twenty years, the rule of Diocletian and his colleagues provided the firm foundation for a reborn Roman Empire. In time, however, the ambitions and rivalries of powerful men would destroy even the strongest union, and plunge the world once more into chaos.

PROLOGUE

Oxsa, Central Armenia, June AD 298

The army assembled before dawn. All night the legionaries had marched through dry ravines and across rocky slopes, stumbling in the darkness with muffled weapons, forbidden to make a sound as they flanked the enemy position. Now, as the first rays of sun lit the snows of the high mountain ranges, they saw the royal encampment of the King of Persia in the brown valley below them, with their enemies spilling from the gates in confusion. Already in their hearts was the promise of a battle won.

Twenty-five thousand men formed a battle line over a mile long. Massed squadrons of cavalry held the higher ground at the flanks: mailed Sarmatian lancers; Dalmatian light horsemen; mounted archers from Armenia and Osrhoene. Between them stood five thousand allied Gothic tribesmen in full barbaric array, fierce warriors from beyond the empire's northern boundaries. But at the centre of the line were ten thousand armoured infantrymen drawn from the crack legions of the Danube frontier. As the sun rose, the light gleamed off helmets of burnished iron and bronze, hauberks of mail and scale, the bristling tips of spears and javelins and the serried lines of oval shields. The sky-blue shields of Legion I Jovia bore the eagle and thunderbolt of Jupiter; beside them, the blood-red shields of II Herculia were emblazoned with the naked figure of Hercules with his club and lion-skin. To either side were the black shields of I Italica, the sea-green of XI Claudia, the white of V Macedonica and the tawny-yellow of IV Flavia.

Six months ago these men had left their garrison fortresses in Moesia and Scythia and marched southwards through Thrace and across the Bosphorus into Asia. At Satala on the upper Euphrates, they had been mustered by the Caesar Galerius, Commander of the East, before crossing the border into Persian-occupied Armenia. Through high mountain passes still bright with snow they had descended to the Armenian uplands, to face the expeditionary force of Narses, Great King of Persia.

And now the enemy was before them, shimmering in the dawn sun-haze. Impossible to guess the number of their host: forty thousand, or maybe twice that. The light caught the flash of their coloured banners, the heavy dazzle of their armoured horses.

In the Roman ranks, men shifted and spat as the sun mounted and the morning grew hot. The legionaries passed waterskins along the lines, tipping back their heads and swigging the cool liquid, letting it spill over their faces and down their necks. The front line was four men deep, spears and javelins readied behind locked shields. Behind them, the reserve cohorts formed another four-deep line, and in between were the tribunes and the standards, long funnels of purple and red silk streaming from the heads of gilded dragons. Dust fogged the air. The soldiers tasted it in their mouths; it gritted between their teeth. Sweat slicked their faces and poured down their bodies beneath the hug of their armour.

Back in the reserve lines, a bull-necked young soldier of II Herculia unlaced his helmet and pulled the hot iron from his head, scrubbing a palm through the short yellow stubble of his scalp. Sweat prickled between his fingers, and he blinked in the glare. A couple of his comrades were following his lead.

'Helmets *on*,' the centurion growled. He nodded away to the right. Along the front lines of I Jovia, a big man was approaching on a capering white horse, its trappings gleaming with gemstones. The soldier replaced his helmet and tied the laces beneath his jaw.

A sudden wave of cheering came from the ranks of the Joviani, the legionaries throwing up their hands and clashing their spears against their shields. The man on the white horse returned their salute. From down the line, the men of II Herculia could see him clearly now – his heavy red face and cropped black beard, his massive frame in a gilded breastplate, the purple cloak streaming behind him. Galerius, Caesar of the East. Their commander.

The emperor rode closer, the standards dipping as he passed. Behind him rode his senior tribunes and his mounted bodyguard; every man in the cohort tensed and craned forward, trying to catch the words of the address.

'Herculiani!' the emperor called, his horse backing and kicking dust, 'down there in the valley you see the last enemies of the Roman race!' His voice was high and straining, strange from such a big man, but thin and metallic, each word like worked brass. 'They think, these Persian slaves, that they've already defeated the flower of the Roman army! But it was only a small force that they met a year ago, from the eastern legions. Now, my brothers, they have you to contend with – Danubians! Herculiani!'

A massed shout from the ranks, the beginning of a chant, *Rome and Hercules, Rome and Hercules...* The soldiers shoved together, jostling, eager.

Galerius threw up his palm for silence. His voice cracked and snarled as he yelled to them. 'We've disturbed the Great King's breakfast!'

Laughter from the troops, a rattle of spearshafts against shield rims.

'Now... now this pack of yelping Babylonian dogs are coming up here to *demand an apology*!'

The laughter doubled, the clatter grew louder.

'Are you going to give them what they want?'

'NO!' A shout from massed throats.

'Are you going to send them crying back to their kennels?'

'YES! *Rome and Hercules, Rome and Hercules...*'

'When they come against us, brothers, remember you are men of the Danube! This scum of the Euphrates cannot stand up to you! Remember you are men of Hercules! Here on this hillside, brothers, we build the walls of Rome. Unbreakable!'

The chant grew to a wild cheer, a percussive tumult, men flinging up their hands in salute. The emperor turned on his horse, waving to right and left as his purple standard snapped above him, then urged his mount forward again.

Once more the quiet returned, the dust settling as the officers ordered their men back into formation. Clack and rattle of spear and shield, javelin and dart. The young soldier had seen the lie of the land as they had deployed: the slope dropped beneath them to a narrow stream, and then rose on the far side to the Persian camp. It was a good position – the momentum of the enemy charge would be broken as they crossed the stream, and then they had the slope ahead of them. All the Roman infantry had to do was stand their ground: against their solid anvil the swinging hammers of the allied cavalry would break the army of Persia.

Now the troops could hear the strange music from the enemy camp, the high metal screaming of Persian trumpets, the rattle and throb of drums so alien and unmanly to the Roman ear. Through the glare and dust they could see the banners racing forward and back as the mass of the enemy poured from their camp and assembled in battle formation. Heavy in leg and stomach, the soldiers waited in the sweating light.

'Steady, steady,' the centurion said. His face was impassive, sunburnt. Behind him, the big youth with the yellow hair stared into the middle distance, through the ranks of the forward cohorts and across the valley at the force gathering against them. He had served five years already in the legions, but this would be his first experience of pitched battle. The temptation to advance was strong – to close the distance with the enemy, bring things to a conclusion. To remain in formation under the coming storm would be a trial.

'Remember what the emperor said, boys,' the centurion said quietly. 'Hold firm, no buckling. If we're needed we'll move up, but not before.'

The soldier gripped his shield, the shaft of his spear; he put his trust in them, and in his brothers to either side of him.

The ranks of the forward line tensed, feet shifting in the dust. The front two ranks held the shield wall, spears levelled, trusting that the enemy horses would not charge into that barrier of bristling iron. The third rank raised javelins to their shoulders, while the fourth readied the throwing-darts that the Herculiani called 'wasps', cruel iron spikes each fletched like a short arrow, with a bulbous lead weight painted with stripes of yellow and black.

'Here they come!' cried a voice from the front ranks. The officers called for silence, but the men in the reserve cohorts needed no warning: already they could hear the rolling thunder of hooves, the braying of horses, as the Persian cavalry crossed the stream below them and powered up the slope towards their line. The stone-hard ground began to vibrate beneath their feet. Behind him the young soldier heard one of his comrades muttering a prayer. He spoke the words himself: '*Unconquered Sun, Lord of Heaven, Destroyer of Darkness, Your light between us and evil...*'

A high whirring and flickering above them now: slingshot and arrows arcing over their heads at the advancing enemy. The men of the forward cohorts joined the barrage, hurling their spiked darts and light javelins. Missiles filled the air like blown chaff at harvest; already the Persian light cavalry had closed on the front line, wheeling and shooting their powerful bows. Arrows clattered together in the air, battering down against the massed Roman shields. Screams of injured men rose into the dust.

'Keep your heads up,' the centurion called. 'They're not shooting at us – not yet.'

The fog of dust thrown up by the cavalry rolled across the hillside, staining the sky yellow and then brown, plunging the battle into an unnatural twilight. The noise of arrows against shields was like heavy rain on a tiled roof, as the Persian archers probed for a chink in the Roman line.

Then from the right there was an explosion of noise: the first wedge of Persian cataphract lancers had crashed against a weak point in the front rank of Legion I Jovia. Armoured men on armoured horses, each half a ton of flesh, iron and bronze. They pressed forward against the shields, trying to force their way through by weight and power, the riders wielding their long lances overarm as they struck down across the shield rims into the packed bodies behind.

From the reserve cohorts of II Herculia the young soldier could see little of the fighting, only the lances rising and falling, the sway of the Joviani standards. But he could hear it: a shrieking battering din like an armour workshop and an iron foundry combined, cut through with the screams of the dying.

He could feel the blood hammering in his chest and throat, and his body was liquid with sweat beneath the weight of his bronze scale cuirass. The desire to move forward and engage was almost unbearable, the only counter to the desire to turn and flee. Hold steady, he told himself. The air tasted of blood, dust and horses.

Cheers from the Joviani: the first cataphract assault had been driven off. But now horns were blaring from the left: the front ranks of II Herculia were under attack. A volley of shouts and screams, the thunder of armoured bodies in collision.

'The line's breached!' the centurion cried. 'Ready to move – follow my lead.' He turned to the big young legionary behind him. 'You, knucklehead,' he said, rough-voiced. 'Watch my back, and don't let any of those bastards get behind me!' The young soldier nodded, impassive. In his pale eyes was a look of slow dumb strength.

The centurion raised his spear and then swung it down to the left. The men of his century hefted shields and spears, gulped air, squared their shoulders. The furnace of battle was hot in their faces now.

'To the left – advance!'

Close-packed, the men of the reserve moved as one body, following the centurion along the rear of the front-rank cohorts. Now that they were moving the battle took form: there were men lying in the bloodied dust, wounded and dying where they had been dragged from the battle line, and the ground was littered with arrows and broken javelins, blood matting into the dirt. Heads lowered behind shield rims, the men moved at a jog trot as the noise of the fighting swelled around them.

Ahead, they could see the breach. The Persian horse archers had opened a gap between two front-rank units, and the cataphracts had smashed their way through and hurled themselves against the reserves. In the choking dust men and horses reeled together. Over the rim of his raised shield the young soldier saw a riderless horse, maddened and kicking, brought down by a flung javelin; an armoured cataphract turned circles, striking out with his lance at the infantry ringing him on all sides; more horsemen, massively encased in gleaming metal, forcing their way in through the breach; everywhere the slash and hack of blades, thrust of spears, battering of shields, men and horses screaming.

'After me!' The centurion's voice sounded distant in the dust and tumult. 'Wedge formation!'

Shields together, spears levelled, the century advanced into the mesh of combat. The young soldier felt his body burning with nervous energy; sweat poured into his eyes and blurred his vision. He was treading the dead underfoot now. An arrow thudded into his shield; another snicked off his helmet.

Edging forward, their feet sliding into the slime of mud and blood, the wall of men wheeled to close the breach. Then, as the dust cleared for a moment, they saw another wedge of armoured cavalry charging towards them, aiming to forge a path through the remnants of the front-rank men.

'Wasps!' shouted the centurion, and at once each man behind him snatched the weighted darts from the hollow of his shield. A moment to aim, another to throw. The darts pelted against the oncoming cavalry, iron spikes burying themselves in exposed flesh and catching in the bronze scales of their armour.

Still the cataphracts came on in a compact mass – at their head, a rider in silvered scales with green and scarlet plumes, angling his lance overhead in a double-hand grip.

'Form up!' The centurion's cry sounded distant through the churning dust. 'Lock shields – close the line!'

The battle had narrowed to only ten paces in each direction. The advancing horses came on at a heavy trot, blinkered and unswerving; they appeared unstoppable, an armoured avalanche.

Shields locked into a wall – thin, but enough to turn some of the cataphracts aside. Horses shied and stamped as they saw the row of bright ovals and the levelled spearpoints. The leader in the plumes and silvered scales dragged back on his reins, and his horse reared up. It towered above the legionary line, hooves striking at air. The young soldier saw the rider's face for a moment, bone-white with a flaring black beard.

Then the horse crashed forward again, one lashing hoof striking the centurion's raised shield. The centurion went down under the blow, and the rider leaned from the saddle as he drove the long lance over his head. With all the weight of horse and rider behind it, the lance sheared through the centurion's chest and pinned him to the dirt. Hooves kicked at the corpse, trampling it.

The young soldier hurled his spear into the advancing wall of horsemen, and it jarred against an armoured flank and arced away. Now the line was fractured, men bunching behind their shields and cowering back as the cataphracts once more urged their mounts forward. The soldier stood rooted, feet spread in the muddy dust, above the mangled body of his centurion. Without thinking, he drew the broad-bladed sword from his scabbard. He saw the plumed rider pluck an iron-headed mace from his saddle bow. He could almost feel the hot breath of the horse in his face, the rush of the mace as it swung down at him.

He raised his shield and caught the blow – the shock of it almost buckled him. The rim of his shield swung back and jarred against the nasal bar of his helmet, and he felt an explosion of pain between his eyes.

Blood was in his mouth. He saw the horse rearing again, the rider turning in the saddle with the mace raised for the killing blow. Feet grounded in the dirt, legs braced, he took a firm grip on his shield.

There is a hollow at the heart of fear; he was trained to find it and make it his own. The noise of battle fell away, the screams and the roar of combat, the blinding dust and the glare. The armoured horse turned against the brightness of the sky, its legs kicking, and as it fell forward he threw himself behind the shield, the muscles of his shoulder bunched against the wood – one solid lunge, all his weight behind it – and he felt the impact as a great punch through his body, a jarring shock that burst pain through his shoulder and across his ribs.

The horse staggered, reeling, the rider thrown off balance and pitching in the saddle.

His shield arm was dead, the pain a solid pulse, and his face ran with blood, but he held his ground and struck out with his sword, the long blade wheeling through the air in an overarm cut.

He felt nothing, no impact, and thought the blow had gone wide – then wet heat sprayed across his face, and when he blinked his eyes clear he saw something round and dark plummet heavily into the dust at his feet.

The horse shied back, kicking; the rider still straddled the animal's back, his arms loose and stiff, streamers of bright blood jetting from the hacked stump of his neck.

The soldier stared, uncomprehending at first. Pain filled his head and body, raw and brutal, but he was still on his feet, still alive. And now there were others alongside him, raising their shields beside his. Overhead flew the darts and the javelins. The panicked horse with its headless rider bolted forward, and the shield wall opened to let it through, still carrying its grisly trophy. The other cataphracts had turned as the momentum of their charge died under the hail of iron. Some were caught, ringed by Roman blades, and cut down. The wall of shields held; the gap in the line was closed. Then the horns sounded the advance, brassy and triumphant, the men of the legion stepped forward in unison, climbing over the bodies of the slain and the broken corpse of their centurion.

The young soldier felt only the pump of pain through his body. Time and distance had no meaning now. A wrack of broken weapons and bodies, tumbled men and horses, caught at his feet. Around him he could hear the victory chant, *ROME AND HERCULES, ROME AND HERCULES.* The slope was taking him downwards, through the battleground and into the area of scattered slaughter, where the allied cavalry had already cut up the fugitives. His head was ringing, his vision shrunk to a bright wavering funnel ahead of him. He saw Persian banners trampled in the dust, the stream running red with blood, corpses sprawled in the shallows. The water had widened and he could not think why, then he glanced to the left and saw the vast bulk of a dead elephant, fletched with arrows, blocking the stream. He took a few more staggering steps forward and collapsed. He barely felt the arms that caught him and eased him down onto the solid ground.

This is going to hurt,' a voice said, 'but not for long.' He felt a wrenching pressure in his shoulder and pain burst through him. He was awake, staring into the sweating face of a bearded army surgeon.

'Don't know how long you were walking around with a dislocated shoulder,' the doctor said, swabbing at his face with a damp rag, 'but that should fix it. You need to rest, though.

There's a lot of blood on you, but not too much of it's yours.'

'Did we win?' he heard himself saying. His tongue felt dead. The doctor grinned.

'Oh, yes,' he said.

Then he was on his feet again, his left arm bound up in a sling. Ranks of men opened before him, and a centurion he did not recognise was leading him forward. Teeth clenched, he tried to breathe slowly through his nose and not curse aloud at the fierce ache in his shoulder.

Noise of horns, and voices raised in acclamation. To his right he saw a raised mound heaped with Persian weapons and banners. A figure loomed up before him, out of the bright haze: he saw a glowering red face, a black beard above a gilded cuirass.

'Come on now, lad,' the centurion behind him said in a harsh whisper. 'Don't you know how to greet your emperor properly?'

'No need for ceremony,' the man in the gilded armour cried. 'We're all brothers here! Brothers in victory!' He raised his arm, and just for a moment the young soldier feared he was about to be clapped on the shoulder. Galerius, he remembered – this was the Caesar Galerius.

'Dominus!' the centurion said, with a slight bow. 'This is the soldier who stopped the cataphracts breaking though the front line of the Herculiani. He killed the leader – flicked off his head with a single blow! I saw it myself.'

'What's your name, soldier?' the emperor demanded.

He opened his mouth, but his throat was dry and he could not speak.

'His name's Knucklehead!' somebody called out, laughing.

'His name's Aurelius Castus. Ninth Cohort, century of Priscus.'

'Aurelius Castus,' the emperor called, almost shouting so all around could hear him. 'A true warrior of Rome! A true

Herculian! Tribune Constantine, present this man with the torque of valour.'

Cheers from the assembled soldiers. Another officer was stepping forward now, a tall young man with a raw flushed face and a heavy jaw. In his hands was a circlet of twisted gold with a clasp of linked horse-heads. The young soldier stood still, trying not to flinch, as the tribune fastened the torque around his neck.

Caesar Galerius had already moved away, congratulating other men, awarding further decorations. From the raised mound, surrounded by the spoils of war, he turned to address the assembled troops.

'Persia is yours,' he cried, in his thin metallic voice. 'The empire is yours! Joviani, Herculiani, Claudiani, Flaviani, victorious! Unbreakable!'

He slept for thirty-six hours, and missed the plundering of the Persian camp. But he heard about it later – the Great King's treasury, his priests and ministers, even the ladies of the royal Zenana were all in Roman hands now. The soldiers were glutted with gold. One man had found a tooled leather pouch full of round grey stones; he threw the stones away and kept the pouch, and became the laughing stock of his cohort. The stones he had discarded were pearls, lost in the dust now, but the soldiers were so rich that nobody cared.

Narses was beaten, a fugitive in his own domain, but still Galerius led his army onwards, east down the Araxes and then south across the border into Media Atropatene. Everywhere cities opened their gates, chieftains knelt before the conquerors from the west. Through Corduene and Adiabene they marched, down from the tight cold air of the highlands to the summer heat of the Tigris valley. The mighty Persian Empire, Rome's oldest and most implacable foe, collapsed before them.

Turning westwards, they forced a crossing of the Tigris above the ruins of Nineveh and marched out onto the plains of Mesopotamia. Then, after breaking the siege of Nisibis, they turned south down the wide flat valley of the Tigris. All the way to Ctesiphon, the young soldier marched with his comrades of II Herculia in the vanguard of the army. When the Persian capital surrendered, he joined them in their parade through the streets, their spears garlanded with laurel.

For the rest of his life he would have the memory of this victory. He kept that thought in his mind on the long hard march home, back up the Euphrates and across the Syrian plains to Antioch and the distant garrison forts of the Danube frontier. Surely nothing in the remainder of his days would match the glory of that campaign: into old age he would dream of it.

So he told himself. But he could know nothing of what his future held.

PART ONE

SEVEN YEARS LATER

CHAPTER I

Eboracum, Northern Britannia, April AD 305

By the time the walls of the fortress appeared in the distance the mist was thickening into rain. The line of soldiers on the road, thirty-eight men of Legion VI Victrix, increased their pace.

'Close up,' their centurion called over his shoulder, smacking his palm with the short broad-headed staff that marked his rank. 'Militar y step – let's try and look like soldiers, not a gang of labourers!'

The men grinned mirthlessly. They could see the scaffolding along the wall near the gate, the figures of other soldiers working to repair the old fortifications. Their new centurion wanted to give a good impression to his colleagues. But they closed up anyway, dropping into the accustomed regular pace, muddied boots crunching on the gravelled road. Centurion Aurelius Castus was a hard bastard, and an ugly slab-faced brute of a Pannonian too, but in the months since he had joined them they had come, grudgingly, to respect him.

They had been out all day, repairing a flood-damaged causeway on the Derventio road. All of them were tired and wet, hands blistered and legs aching from digging and shifting rocks and gravel. While the men of other centuries often marched out on work details carrying only their tools, Centurion Castus never allowed his men to leave the fortress without full kit. Each man, besides his mattock or muddied shovel, carried a sword and two light javelins, with a leather-covered shield slung on his back. They wore no armour or helmets – they were thankful for small mercies – but now as they marched they slung the tools and carried their shields and javelins instead. They were soldiers, they told themselves, not labourers.

The road ran straight, across a bridge and between the low warehouses towards the high double-arched gate of Eboracum fortress. Marching at the head of his men, Castus caught the smell of woodsmoke from the bath-house inside the walls. As his little half-century approached the scaffolding, some of the men up there called out to them – the usual obscene jokes.

'Castus!'

He rotated his head on his thick neck. Valens, a fellow centurion of the Third Cohort, stood on the lowest platform of the scaffolding, overseeing his men. 'Been admiring the British scenery again, have you?'

'No scenery around here,' Castus replied in a carrying growl. 'That's for civilised places. Out here on the edge of the world all you get's mist and mud.'

Laughter from the men on the scaffolding. Valens, hanging from the wooden beams, called back as Castus passed through the gate. 'The world has no edges, brother! It's a sphere, as everyone knows. Or is this information not current in Pannonia?'

As his men filed into barracks after kit inspection, Castus pulled off his round woollen cap and tipped his head back into the ache of his shoulders. The rain was slackening, but he enjoyed the feel of the cool water on his face and scalp. He looked up into the sky, iron grey, darkening. A deep sigh ran through him. Every evening he felt this way. Every evening the same dull torpor settled over him.

Twelve years in the army, and I end up rotting in this place…

Twelve months before, he had still been a soldier of II Herculia. Getting promoted to centurion before the age of thirty was a rare honour, won in the campaign against the Carpi on the great plains north of the Danube. But promotion had meant transfer – not only out of the elite Herculiani, his home since he had joined the legions, but away from the Danubian provinces, where he had been born, and across half the empire to this dull backwater of a frontier.

Fate had directed it – so he told himself. But that was little consolation. VI Victrix was an old legion, based here at Eboracum for nearly two hundred years. Few of the men in the fortress had ever seen combat, although there were many among them with grey hair. Ever since he was sixteen, when he had run away from home to join the legions, Castus had wanted only to be a soldier in the army of Rome. So he was still, but this life – work details, route marches and paperwork, overseeing building and road-mending, ordering his men to cut wood for the baths or whitewash the charcoal to stop the locals from stealing it – did not seem much like soldiering.

Back in his own quarters at the end of the barrack block, he threw off his swordbelt and hung it from a hook on the wall. Dragging his mud-stained grey tunic off over his head, he flung it into a basket for the laundry slaves to collect. His left shoulder ached – even seven years after that wound at the battle of Oxsa, damp weather gave him the dulled memory of pain. He wheeled his arm, stretching the muscles until the ache faded. Slinging a rough woollen towel and a clean tunic over his shoulder, he walked out bare-chested in his boots and breeches, into the rain again, heading for the baths.

Eboracum had been here even before the Sixth Legion had arrived in Britain. Most of the present fortress, like its crumbling walls, had been built by the great Emperor Severus, although there were parts of it that dated back to the distant days of Hadrian. They were just names to Castus, but they had a ring of ancient glory about them. Back in those days, so he liked to believe, the Roman army had still been the force that had conquered the world. Now they did their best to hang on to what they had.

As he paced down the lane between the barracks and crossed the wide central avenue, Castus saw decaying walls, peeling plaster, buildings that had once housed cohorts now empty and abandoned. The legion had shrunk since the great days of Severus – the fortress had been built for six thousand legionaries and a couple of auxiliary cohorts, but now housed barely two-thirds that number. The century he commanded, still officially eighty men, boasted only sixty-nine at full strength.

But it was easy to grow despondent, and it was not in Castus's nature to dwell on things that happened before he had been born. Let other men mumble about the past; he had known the might of a triumphant Roman army in the field, as he knew the great expanses of the empire, having marched back and forth from one border to the other. His experiences set him apart from the other men serving at Eboracum: few of them had even left Britain. They had been born here, sons of old soldiers of the legion, some going back generations. The distant affairs of empire, wars far away in the east or on the Danube, were as insubstantial to them as the mythic tales of Troy.

At first they had regarded Castus with suspicious awe, knowing that he had marched with Galerius against the Persians, all the way to Ctesiphon and the ruins of Babylon. The torque he wore around his neck was a rare distinction, proof of his valour.

Now they just joked about his background, and he had given up even mentioning the matter if he could avoid it. But he kept the memories to himself, to warm his blood in the cold and empty nights. A distant dream of heat and dust, the serrated shadows of the palm groves, the taste of fresh dates and wine, a girl he had known in Antioch, and another in Edessa... Above it all, the fury of battle and the triumph of victory.

Turning off the lane, Castus passed through the gate into the forecourt of the baths. Smoke swelled from the furnace room, beaten down by the persistent rain. Inside, the exercise hall was packed with noise, echoing under the high arched ceiling. Naked men ran laps, others squatted in groups playing dice or the twelve-lines game, and three or four leather balls were thudding between the walls. From the changing room Castus moved through the whooping mob in the cold plunge chamber and into the steam of the hot bath. Here and there one of his own men spotted him and touched a knuckle to his forehead in brief salute.

Stripped naked, he eased himself down into the hot water. The other bathers had moved aside to give him room: his bulk, the scars stippling his flesh, and the gold torque he still wore marked him out even for those who did not know his rank. Lounging in blissful solitude, he considered that he might have preferred the rough company of the common soldiers, but his promotion had also raised him above the pleasures of the crowd. A long soak, he thought, then a sweat, an oil and scrape, and a plunge in the cold bath to freshen up.

He stretched his heavy arms along the marble rim of the bath and closed his eyes. Steam filled his nostrils. His stomach growled, and he considered getting one of his men to fetch a couple of honey cakes from the stall under the portico outside...

'Centurion Castus? Is Centurion Aurelius Castus here?'

He opened one eye, staring into the fog. The caller was standing in the arched doorway, fully dressed. A military clerk from legion headquarters.

Castus lowered himself in the bath until his chin touched the water, willing the man to go away and leave him in peace. But already he could hear the others pointing him out and the scrape and tap of the clerk's boots on the tiled floor as he approached.

A voice through the steam. 'Are you Centurion Castus?'

Head back on the marble, Castus stared up at the man. Grunted.

'You're ordered to report to the praetorium,' the clerk said, with a cold smile.

Castus stretched his limbs in the water. 'Can't it wait?'

'The order comes from the distinguished Aurelius Arpagius. You're to come *immediately...*'

Sighing heavily, Castus closed his eyes again for a moment. A summons from the governor. Unusual, but he didn't let his curiosity show. The clerk tapped his foot on the tiles. Then, with a sudden movement, Castus pushed himself up and out of the bath. The water surged up with him, soaking the clerk's tunic.

'Right then, let's go. Unless you want to give me time to get dressed first?'

Back through the early evening gloom, dressed and scrubbing a towel over his damp bristling hair, Castus followed the clerk towards the praetorium, the governor's residence at the heart of the fortress. Unlike most other legions in the empire, the Sixth was still commanded by a civilian, the Praeses Governor of Britannia Secunda. Most of the time, though, Aurelius Arpagius concerned himself with administering his province, leaving the running of the legion to his tribunes and senior centurions. Castus had never spoken to the man – hardly even seen him, except at the triennial pay parades. He had no idea what such an exalted figure might want with him now – and in the praetorium itself as well.

At the corner of the headquarters building, a stooped figure stood in the rain. His damp tunic hung unbelted to his shins, and his hair was slicked flat. He pulled himself upright as Castus approached.

'Centurion!'

Castus paused, letting the clerk idle ahead of him. 'How long's it been now, Modestus?'

'Eight hours, centurion.' The man's head bobbed as he spoke, his jaw working.

'Remind me why you're here?'

'Drunk in barracks, centurion. Won't happen again.'

Castus snorted a laugh. Modestus was a repeat offender. But he could not remember how long he'd ordered the man to stand here on punishment.

'Get back to the barracks and dry off.'

'Thank you, centurion...' Modestus looked like he was about to say more, and Castus dismissed him with a slap on the shoulder. From the lane beside the headquarters, the clerk was clearing his throat noisily.

Around the corner, they reached the shelter of the praetorium portico. The clerk left him there, and Castus marched through the high, pillared doorway into the entrance hall. His boots clattered on the marble floor, and sentries to either side straightened to attention. At the far end of the hall, arched doors opened to a pillared garden at the heart of the building, lost in evening murk and rain. Between the doorways, lit by a flaming brazier, four statues stood in a raised niche.

Castus approached, bowing his head. The statues were near life size: four men in the gilded cuirasses and short capes of Roman military officers. Their painted faces were stern and blunt, with the heavy features of Pannonian peasant soldiers, just like those of Castus himself. The emperors, the four rulers of the Roman world: the Augusti Diocletian and Maximian, and the Caesars Galerius and Constantius. All of them looked alike, but each Augustus clasped his Caesar in a paternal embrace.

All his life Castus had known these men, the four of them in effigy, and Diocletian and Galerius in the flesh. Standing before them, he touched his brow in salute, as if to the images of the gods.

Steps led up from the entrance hall to the upper chambers – the clerk had told him that he was expected there. Along the painted corridor at the head of the stairs he reached a row of doors; a sentry outside one of them straightened to attention and gestured for Castus to enter.

The room beyond was large, but held a sense of privacy. Coals burned in a brazier, and Castus took in the three men seated around the low polished table before he snapped to attention.

'Domini!' he cried, loud enough to get an echo. From the corner of his eye, he was pleased to notice two of the men flinch slightly. Civilians, in his experience, always expected brutish rigidity in soldiers and it was best to flatter them. Staring at the far wall, he stood braced with his thumbs hooked in his belt.

'Our apologies, centurion, for calling you here at short notice.'

'Domini!' he shouted again, stiffening his shoulders.

'Yes, thank you. You may stand at ease, centurion.'

Castus rocked back on his heels, dropping his shoulders only slightly. The far wall of the room was painted with a landscape.

Goatherds, satyrs. It didn't resemble anywhere he had ever seen. Certainly not Britain. He lowered his eyes a little until he could see the men at the table. Castus had always possessed an odd intuition when it came to reading other men; he could quickly determine the subtle signs that showed character, mood and intention, while giving nothing away himself. A legacy of his childhood, maybe, and the need to gauge his father's violently veering moods.

The speaker was Arpagius, governor of the province and prefect of the legion. Castus knew he was from Numidia, a skilled administrator of some kind. A small man, his curled hair greying at the temples, he had a shrewd look, but he was uncomfortable beneath his appearance of dignified calm. The second man was one of the senior tribunes, Rufinius. He had a sour expression, as though he'd just drunk curdled milk. The third sat back from the table, against the wall, studying Castus carefully.

The governor turned now and addressed this third man, something almost deferential in his tone. 'This is Aurelius Castus, the centurion I told you about,' he said. 'He joined us quite recently, only last autumn, in fact, from the Second Legion Herculia at Troesmis.'

'He appears very young for a centurion,' the third man said, with an appraising air. 'Built like an ox, though... What are you, twenty-eight, twenty-nine?'

'Twenty-eight, dominus.' Actually Castus was not sure of his exact age, his father never having bothered to inform him of the year he was born. But he thought it better not to raise that fact now.

'So I expect you were promoted for bravery in the field?'

'Yes, dominus. By the Caesar Galerius, after the campaign against the Carpi.'

Arpagius stirred, clearing his throat and gesturing at the man who had asked the questions. 'This is Julius Nigrinus,' he told Castus, 'a notary from the imperial court at Treveris. He's on a tour of inspection here.'

So that explains the deference, Castus thought. He was not sure what imperial notaries actually did, but they seemed to inspire hushed tones. He gave a brisk nod. Nigrinus was wrapped in a cloak. His hair was dull brown, cut in a bowl, and his round smooth face displayed only bland enquiry.

'You have a Pannonian look,' the notary went on. 'Where were you born?'

'Taurunum, dominus, on the Danube. My father was a veteran of the Fourth Flavia Felix.'

'Ah, following in his footsteps, good...'

Hardly, Castus thought. His father had been invalided out of the legion before he himself had been born. He had taken up blacksmithing, but was a bitter man and a bad drunk, and had never wanted his son to join the army. *You're too stupid to be a soldier*, he had said, grimacing through another morning hangover. *What use would the legions have for you? I suppose they could use that great thick head of yours as a battering ram!*

'And you served for some time with the Herculiani prior to your promotion, I understand, in Persia and on the Danube?' the notary asked. Castus nodded again, staring at the far wall.

'Yes, dominus. First in the cohorts, then assigned to the *lanciarii*. I was draco-bearer of my cohort before I was promoted.'

'Ah, really?' The notary spoke quietly, and far too smoothly. He settled himself deeper into his cloak, although with the brazier glowing the room was not cold. 'Then you must know the condition of the Danubian army very well, I should say?'

Something in the man's tone was angling, ominous. Castus

30

felt a slight prickle of perspiration at the back of his neck. He nodded, staring at the wall and trying not to let his discomfort show. The noise of the rain outside was a steady rushing hiss.

'And how would you describe this *condition*? Are the troops... loyal?'

'Yes, dominus!' Castus declared, surprised. 'Of course... All soldiers of Rome are loyal to the emperors.' He had spoken loudly to cover his apprehension. His distaste as well: the suggestion that the elite Danubian legions might be less than loyal felt like a personal insult.

'To the emperors, yes. But are they loyal to *all* the emperors equally, would you say?'

Sweat broke on Castus's back and trickled down his spine. He had the bizarre sensation that he was being accused of something. What was happening here? What had these men been discussing before he entered the room? His sense of intuition had almost deserted him. Worryingly, he noticed that Arpagius was looking increasingly uncomfortable, dabbing at his brow with his cuff. The tribune, Rufinius, looked grimmer than ever.

'Yes, they're loyal to all the emperors. Dominus.'

The notary smiled and made a slight humming noise. 'That's good to know,' he said. 'But tell me – I believe the son of our western Caesar Constantius was on the Persian expedition. A man named Constantine. He would have been a junior tribune then. Did you happen to see him at all?'

'Yes, dominus. He led one of the allied cavalry squadrons at Oxsa. After the battle he... gave me this torque with his own hand.' Castus dropped his chin, feeling the clasp of the golden circlet at his throat.

'And was he popular with the troops?'

'Certainly. He was a good soldier.'

Tribune Constantine – Castus remembered him well enough, even years later. That long bony face and solid jaw, those deep-set, rather intense eyes. He thought back to a day in the south of Mesopotamia: the imperial party had gone to view the ancient ruins of Babylon, and Castus had been one of the guards. He remembered the young Constantine standing alone on a dusty mound, staring out across the burnt brown walls with a look of deep concentration. *Look at him*, one of the other soldiers had muttered. *Reckons he's Alexander the Great...*

'Perhaps,' said the governor, Arpagius, abruptly, 'perhaps we've questioned the centurion enough now?'

'Ah, yes, my apologies, I was only curious,' the notary said. He shifted forward a little, still gazing at Castus.

'The notary Nigrinus has brought a certain matter to our attention,' Arpagius went on. 'We considered that, since you have some experience of the, ah, the mood of the troops outside the province, we might share it with you, centurion.'

'A matter, dominus?'

'Yes. Some rather momentous news. But we must bind you with the strictest secrecy. What you are about to hear must not leave this room. Soon enough everyone will know about it, but for now we must keep it quiet. Do you understand?'

'I understand,' Castus said warily. He had no desire to know of any secrets.

'On the first day of next month,' Arpagius went on, 'our lords the Augusti Diocletian and Maximian will resign their imperial power at Nicomedia and Milan, and transfer supreme rule to the Caesars, Galerius and Constantius. New Caesars will be appointed to the junior positions. In this way the empire will be rejuvenated and stability maintained.'

Castus opened his mouth, but could not speak. His body

felt suddenly rooted to the floor. All his life, Diocletian and Maximian had been the rulers of the Roman world, akin to the gods. A cold sweat spread across his brow. How could men like gods simply resign? How could others replace them? He was dizzy, as if the world had shifted on its axis.

'The new Caesars', Arpagius said, 'will be Flavius Severus in the west and Maximinus Daza in the east.'

The names fell limply across the table. Castus was lost in shock.

'Are these men familiar to you?' the notary asked.

'No, dominus. I've never heard of them.'

'Hah, yes,' the tribune said, speaking for the first time. 'Neither have we!'

'Anyway, as you can imagine, we must handle the transfer of allegiance with the utmost care and tact,' Arpagius said. 'It may be, you see, that some of the barbarian peoples will see this as evidence of weakness, rather than of strength.'

'Strength?' Castus spoke without thinking. He noticed Nigrinus's quiet nod.

'Of course,' the notary said. 'To step down from absolute power, and peaceably hand the direction of the state to a chosen successor, surely demonstrates the stability and strength of the imperial system, wouldn't you say?'

'I suppose so, dominus. It's just... It's going to be a shock for the men.'

'Naturally,' the governor said. 'Which is why we're informing certain selected centurions of the legion well in advance. The news will be circulated in good time, so all the men are acquainted with it by the time of the ceremony. There will be, I need not add, an acclamation bonus for every soldier and officer.'

Castus raised his head. He had not even thought of bonuses.

'I can see you approve of that! Good. But for now, as I said, speak nothing of this to anyone.'

'Not a word, dominus.'

Along the corridor and down the steps, Castus thought back over what had happened. Already his memory of that short strange interview was becoming blurred. Had he imagined the odd insinuations in the notary's questions? Why had he asked about the Danube legions, and the tribune Constantine? Halfway down the stairs he paused suddenly. He had already forgotten the names of the two new Caesars. But neither of them was Constantine: the son of the current Caesar was being passed over. So why had the notary asked about the loyalties of the troops?

Shaking his head, Castus tried to quell the questions in his mind. He was a soldier, a simple man, and matters of politics were far above him. Still, he felt needled, apprehensive. Something had been going on in that room, and he had seen only a part of it, a brief glimpse exposed. Whatever it was, it was surely none of his concern, but he felt implicated anyway.

In the entrance hall he paused again before the statues of the emperors. Those mighty figures, rulers of his life, seemed different to him now. Sad, somehow, and lost, for all the strength of their mutual embrace. He touched his brow once more in quiet salute, then he marched out into the darkness and the rain.

A month later, on the first day of May, Legion VI Victrix assembled in full strength on the broad expanse of the parade ground outside the western wall of the fortress. Under a slate-grey sky, every man stared forward at the distant tribunal and the rising smoke from the sacrificial altars. They all knew what was happening now; there were no more secrets. But the promise of four gold pieces and a pound of silver per man had dulled the initial shock, and only the excitement of novelty stirred their ranks.

From his place in the Third Cohort, Castus watched the tribunes mount the tribunal, reverently removing the portrait images of Diocletian and Maximian from the legion standards and raising those of Constantius and Galerius in their places. Two new busts, two new Caesars, now filled the lower places. But all the busts looked similar, and from a distance it was hard to see any difference anyway.

Now the representatives of each cohort filed forward to take the oath of allegiance, the rest all following their words. It was a familiar ceremony, repeated every year. A festive mood spread through the legion: soon there would be fresh meat from the sacrifices in their bellies, and newly minted gold in their hands. The world might have tilted slightly, but only briefly, and now order was restored.

Castus tried to share their feelings. Still, as he stared at the standards, he felt a prickle of doubt. Why, he could not say.

But then the cheers of acclamation rang out, the troops throwing up their arms and yelling out the traditional cries, and the noise drowned out all further questions.

'Constantius and Galerius, invincible Augusti! Severus and Maximinus, most noble Caesars! Emperors! Masters of the World!'

Everything had changed, Castus thought. But everything had stayed the same.

CHAPTER II

'Shield... *wall*!'
Fifty-six shields clashed together in a rapid percussion, locking like tiles on a sloping roof. Fifty-six armoured bodies in four ranks, crouched and standing with spears levelled through the gaps. Each midnight-blue shield was painted with the emblem of the Sixth Legion: a winged figure of the goddess Victory with gold palm and laurel wreath. Castus waited for three heartbeats then yelled again.

'Half-step... ad-*vance*!'
The block jolted forward, the men moving together with shields tight. One step then pause, another step then pause, the low collective chant: 'Vic-*trix*, Vic-*trix*...' From the rear ranks Timotheus, who looked far too young to be an optio, kept the formation steady.

'Halt! By the right – open *ranks*!'
The block of men shuffled and then spread, the wall of shields opening into a skirmishing line with the second and third ranks moving up to cover the gaps. It was a difficult manoeuvre, and the century managed it well. Castus felt a brief warm glow of satisfaction. From the margins of the drill field, men and officers from other units had gathered to watch.

'From the rear – ready *wasps*!'
A hollow rattle as the rear-rank men plucked the darts

from behind their shields. The legion had not made much use
of the weighted throwing dart before Castus had joined them.
A hundred yards away across the drill field stood the row of
straw-stuffed practice targets.

'Loose!'

With a combined grunt, the rear-rankers hurled their darts.
Then, in practised sequence, came more darts from the forward
ranks, each volley arcing against the dull sky and raining down.
Castus flicked his eyes between his men and the targets – most
of the darts had fallen short or gone wide, but a few thudded
home into the straw.

Now a volley of javelins followed the darts, the century
advancing steadily by half-steps, kicking up the gravel of the
drill field. Then swords rattled from scabbards along the line
and the men halted, waiting for the order to charge. They could
see the straw targets bristling with darts and javelins.

Castus felt his chest swell with fierce joy. These were his
men; he had trained them and formed them, and he could
sense the pride they took in their abilities now, their collective
strength. He threw back his head to cry out the order that
would send the wedge of armoured men into a charge. Would
it be like this, he thought, in a real battle? Would they be so
determined then, so disciplined? And would he have the nerve
to command them effectively?

'You're showing me up, young man!'

Castus turned on his heel. Ursicinus, the legion's senior
drill instructor, stood with fists on hips. He was a wiry man,
and looked like an old grey rat. Castus was a head taller and
a foot broader, but the habit of deference was hard to break;
he straightened at once and touched his brow in rapid salute.

'Oh, don't let me stop you,' Ursicinus said, smiling sourly.
His own drills usually involved marching practice, and leaving

the men standing at attention for hours in the rain – the best way, he claimed, to instil a habit of patient obedience.

'Probably enough for today,' Castus muttered. He was tempted to continue anyway – order his men to charge, yelling, at the practice stumps with levelled blades. But Ursicinus was one of the highest-ranking veterans in the legion, and Castus knew enough not to try and antagonise him.

'Optio! Fall the men out.'

Timotheus raised his staff, then he barked the order and the formation broke apart.

'Impressive, I suppose,' the drill instructor said. He tapped Castus's mailed chest with his staff. 'Just don't think you're going to turn them into one of those crack Danube legions! There's not much call for them out here, y'know.'

'What would you know about that?' Castus said under his breath as the older man stalked away. Months of training his century whenever he got the chance – whenever they were spared from mending roads or walls or digging out latrines, or being sent off to guard the supply convoys – had turned what had been a shambolic set of men into something approaching soldiers. They had hated him for it at first, Castus knew that; he had beaten them hard, and managed to discharge some of the worst idlers into other centuries. But now he liked to think that they appreciated the distinction. Now it was only the disdain of the other officers he had to contend with: men like Ursicinus, forty years in the legion and never fought in battle, ground smooth by the routines of camp life and resentful of any suggestion that he might be wrong.

Pfft! Castus said to himself, and twitched an obscene gesture at the departing instructor. Optio Timotheus caught his eyes and grinned – the younger soldiers had picked up his enthusiasm much more quickly.

'Shall I take them back to barracks, centurion?'

Castus nodded. Young Timotheus was tough on the men, bit too much vinegar in his blood, but would make a good officer one day. As a deputy, he was perfect. His harsh yells drifted away over the gravel of the drill field as he formed up the men and set them marching back towards the fortress gates. He even got them singing as they left the field.

'You rile him up and he'll find some way to get back at you,' Evagrius said. 'Or make things hard for the rest of us.'

'I know,' Castus said. They were in the office room of his quarters, a whitewashed cell set aside for the routine administration that fell to every centurion's duty. Like most of the leaking old barrack block, it smelled strongly of damp plaster and mould. Julius Evagrius, standard-bearer and clerk, sat on a stool on the other side of the desk with a heap of wax tablets before him. Castus, leaning by the door, tried not to stare too dubiously at the documents.

'They don't mind it, though – the men. Ursicinus is a mean old goat, so they like it when you stick him one in eye!'

Castus grunted, shoving himself away from the door and looming over the table. 'You should know not to speak about another officer like that,' he growled. ''Specially not to me!' He jutted his jaw, giving his profile the look of a stack of broken bricks. But he was trying not to smile.

Evagrius assumed a grave expression and busied himself with his documents. 'Sorry, centurion.'

Standard-bearers, as clerks for their centurions, often had a slightly informal relationship with their superiors, but Evagrius more than most. Besides being a reasonable soldier and an excellent clerk, he also knew Castus's secret: his centurion could neither read nor write. In the years he had spent with II Herculia, Castus had barely spent six months under a roof, and there had been no time to learn even the basics of literacy. This was fine for a legionary, but since his promotion it had been a constant embarrassment, and one he liked to keep quiet. One of these days, he told himself, he would learn, but for now, squinting at the squirm of letters and figures covering the clerk's tablets made his head hurt.

'So what's the roster looking like?' he said, gazing out of the window into the darkening portico.

'Four men still absent on supply escort duty,' Evagrius said, darting his nib down the list of names, 'three men – Macrinus, Flaccus and Modestus – in the hospital, two more – Terentius and Claudianus – on leave. Macer detached to the river patrol. Aurelius Dexter still not returned from leave. That's ten days he's over now. Shall I mark him down as a deserter?'

'Better do that. Good riddance to him too. He's welcome to his flogging if he shows his face here again.'

'So that's fifty-eight men present for duty, centurion.'

'Right – sign that off for me.' Castus's own cramped scribble would never pass as a signature, but the standard-bearer had devised a reasonable-looking alternative.

'There's a memorandum here from Tribune Rufinius. Faulty brothel tokens are still turning up and they haven't tracked down the source. He asks all centurions to check before issuing new ones.'

'I'll leave you to see to that. Anything else?'

'That's everything,' the standard-bearer said. He closed the last wax tablet and slipped it in his pouch. Castus was sure that the canny Evagrius himself, together with his fellow clerks in other centuries and the merchants in the city, was behind most of the assorted scams and ruses in the fortress. Corruption was an institution in military camps all over the empire, and Eboracum had many a blind eye.

'Dismissed,' Castus said, although Evagrius was already on his way out, whistling.

The hospital building occupied almost a full block between the praetorium and the grain silos. Castus never liked going there – the dim complex of rooms contained a heady reek of sour vinegar that turned his stomach, and he had a suspicion that illnesses somehow travelled through the air – but owing to the legionaries' habit of constantly injuring themselves and picking up diseases, he was obliged to pay regular visits.

Now he followed the medical orderly along a corridor between starched drapes and into one of the wards. He was trying not to breathe too deeply, just in case.

'These three are yours, I think,' the orderly said. Castus merely glanced at the first two: they were legitimate enough. One had managed to impale his foot with the throwing dart on the drill field; the other had broken his leg falling off a horse. Both were eager enough to be discharged back to barracks: the hospital diet of herbal soup and blood pudding was designed to be unappetising.

'And this is Julius Modestus, who still has a fever.'

Castus stood by the bed, glowering. Modestus was looking more than usually sallow and sweaty. He opened his eyes and gave a weak cough. This was his third time in hospital since Castus had taken command of the century, and between his illnesses and his frequent punishments he had spent barely ten days on duty.

'What are you doing for him?'

'Oh, just herbal infusions and bed rest. A little light massaging of the limbs is often efficacious...'

Castus gave him a sideways glance. Medical orderlies were known to take bribes to keep shirkers in hospital, but this one looked sincere. He nodded, waited until the orderly had moved away, and then stooped over the bed.

'I want you back on your feet in two days, Modestus,' he said in a low voice, 'or I'll send Timotheus and Culchianus over here to give you the sort of massage you won't appreciate. Understood?'

'Understood,' Modestus croaked, then gave a few more coughs as Castus paced quickly back towards the fresh air.

'Ah, the terror of the Tigris is here! The despoiler of the Euphrates!'

'Watch what you say, Balbinus, or he may despoil you – he has that Herculian look in his eyes!'

'Only joking, my dear Knucklehead. Come and despoil a cup of beer with us!'

Castus tried to smile – how the unfortunate nickname from his old legion had managed to follow him across half the empire he had no idea. He sat down at the table, and the other three centurions shuffled along the bench to give him room.

The centurions' messroom was at the back of a small warehouse beside the main market. It was gloomy, and smelled of stale beer, but there was a fire burning in the brazier in the corner. The walls, painted with crude colourful murals of nude shepherdesses being chased by satyrs, were covered in scratched graffiti: the names of generations of centurions and tribunes of the Sixth, with accompanying obscene comments. There was a sense of heritage, if nothing else.

'Still enjoying life at the edge of the world, then?' Balbinus said, and stifled a belch. 'Or are you pining for the delights of Antioch, eh? The dark-eyed gazelles of Ctesiphon?'

'It's all right,' said Castus, and took a heavy slug of the warm sour beer. Balbinus was obviously drunk, but he barely understood most of what the man said at the best of times.

'Leave him be,' said Valens, the third man at the table. 'I smell the hospital on him.' For a moment Castus thought that the stale vinegar odour really had clung to him somehow; then Valens tugged at the end of his long nose and winked.

Of all the fifty or so centurions in the Sixth, Valens was only one Castus could consider a friend. Perhaps because he too was a relative newcomer – he had been transferred from one of the legions on the Rhine five years before. Although he had a wry sardonic air that Castus often found baffling, Valens at least had the bearing of a soldier. Not a stewed drunk and a gambler, like Balbinus and his friend Galleo.

'Man of few words, our Knucklehead,' said Galleo, scooping a fistful of coppers across the table. 'That's what they teach them out there on the Danube – *act first, speak later...* Mind you, with that barbarous accent he's got, you'd hardly know what he was saying anyway!'

Castus stared across the rim of his cup, unblinking. He kept his expression neutral, his hands loose. Let them think what they liked about him. Let them joke if they wanted. One swift jab of his arm and he could shatter the cup between Galleo's eyes, grab the other man by the hair and dent the table with his face. He enjoyed the bitter flavour of that thought, the intention idling in his mind.

When he first arrived at Eboracum, he had been given the usual initiation. In the corner of the messroom behind a barricade of benches and tables, they'd set upon him: he'd been expecting it, and managed to wrestle all six of the centurions in the cohort to surrender at the cost of a second broken nose and a cracked rib. Valens was the only one who took it lightly now – the rest all treated Castus with a sly mocking disdain. He had hurt their pride, he supposed, but they all knew he could beat them again if he wanted to – he was like a half-tamed bear brought to a feast, for the revellers to goad and dare themselves.

Still, he tried not to blame them for it. Service on the north British frontier held few rewards, and the centurions had little to boast about. So what if they mocked him for his military experience? So what if they laughed at the way he kept his boots and belts oiled and shining, his tunics cleanly laundered, his metal bright? He worked hard at training his men, and he drank little, and if they hated him for that he did not care. The army was his life, his only love. He had seen his father slump into indignity and be destroyed by it, and he would do anything to avoid that.

'Easy, brother,' Valens said quietly, leaning across the table. He nodded towards the door. 'I've got a couple of spare tokens for the Blue House, if you're interested.' Balbinus and Galleo were busy rattling dice in a cup. Castus drank down the rest of his beer and upended the cup on the table.

'Leaving so soon?' Balbinus cried, flinging the dice down. 'And you haven't even told us again how you beat the King of Persia at arm-wrestling!'

'You worry me sometimes,' Valens said as they walked together past the warehouses. 'You fall into one of your silences, and I think you're about to start breaking people's heads open.' The air was still, the crescent moon bright; it was as close to a pleasant summer's evening as Castus had known in this country. 'Mind you, I'm sure nobody'd think any the worse of you if you did...'

'They're just talking,' Castus said, shrugging lightly. 'Nothing better to do.' The mood of irritation still gripped him; but there was only one person he wanted to see now, and he knew where to find her. He could still taste the beer on his tongue, and worried that his breath might smell of it – cupping his hand over his mouth, he breathed and sniffed.

The sound of rapid hoofbeats came along the wide central street from the north-west gate. Both centurions stepped back into the shadow of the portico; a solitary horseman in a thick native cloak was riding hard along the street. He reined in before the gates of the headquarters building, shouted a reply to the sentries as he dismounted, and then ran inside.

'Looks like he's late for his supper,' Valens said as they continued across the street and down the broad colonnaded avenue towards the river gate. Knots of men passed in the darkness, some of them saluting when they noticed the centurions' staffs. A wagon loaded with barrels from the legion brewery groaned by, and then they were passing beneath the arches of the gatehouse and out of the fortress.

The road ran down from the gates to the stone bridge that crossed the river. On the far side, the lights of the civilian settlement spread along the banks. The colony of Eboracum, capital city of Britannia Secunda province, was almost as old as the fortress; Castus had been surprised at its size when he had first come here, although compared to the cities of the east it wasn't much. Tiled roofs caught the moonlight, and the smoke of a thousand hearths and kitchen fires rose towards the tattered night clouds. City and fortress depended on one another, but the soldiers of the legion did not mix much with the civilians on the other side of the river.

Crunching over the cobbles, the two men descended towards the bridge. Just before it, they turned off to the right along

45

another road that traced the strip of sloping ground between the ditch and wall of the fortress and the river. Along the riverbank there were low buildings: warehouses and shacks, crude taverns and brothels. Valens shoved a couple of staggering soldiers out of his path, while Castus paced along behind him, rolling his shoulders.

The Blue House stood at the far end of the row of buildings. Narrow and two-storeyed, with a rickety balcony overhanging the street, it was painted all over with a sky-blue wash. A side gate gave access to the yard, and a miserable-looking sentry was posted there to deny entry to anyone except centurions and tribunes. The Blue House was what passed for a high-class establishment in Eboracum.

An elderly eunuch in a blue chiton met them as they stepped through into the yard. Valens passed over his two tokens, and the eunuch held the leather discs up to the light of a lamp.

'Don't worry, they're genuine,' Valens said, and smiled over his shoulder to Castus. The eunuch made a weary bow and gestured them into the house.

'Welcome, welcome, brave and handsome centurions!' Dionysia, the madam of the house, was a woman in her fifties, wearing garish cosmetics and heavy earrings that chimed. 'Come in and be seated – you're our only visitors tonight! Sit down and I'll send for wine!'

In the blue-walled sitting room, Castus eased himself down onto a shabby divan and spread his knees. He always felt uncomfortable in brothels, even if Valens appeared entirely relaxed. A boy brought cups and a bronze pitcher of earthy brown wine. There was a thick smell in the air, like burnt flowers.

'The only visitors?' Valens said dubiously. He glanced up at the ceiling, as if he expected to see it shuddering.

A bell sounded, the beaded curtain across the inner doorway opened, and a group of girls filed into the room. Castus gazed at them: a couple were familiar from his previous visits, but the face he was looking for was not there. One of the girls, a skinny redhead who looked about fifteen, was trying to stifle a cough.

'Cleopatra!' Valens cried, getting up and seizing the hand of a tall dark-skinned girl. 'You're for me. Castus, which do you fancy?'

'Is Afrodisia not here tonight?' Castus asked, turning to the woman lingering by the door.

'Ah, Afrodisia,' Dionysia replied, rolling her eyes to the ceiling. 'Yes, but she's… she's *bathing* at the moment. Perhaps you'd like to wait?'

Castus nodded and settled back on the divan.

'Bathing!' Valens grinned. 'She's bathing in something, but I'll bet it's not mare's milk. Choose another one…' He gave the dark girl a slap on the buttocks and herded her out through the bead curtain, and the other girls followed behind him.

Afrodisia was really called Claudia Galla, but clients were supposed to use only trade names. Castus had met her only a month after arriving in Britain: a blonde woman, a few years younger than himself, with a soft womanly body and a tired ease about her that he found deeply attractive. Sometimes he had fantasised about marrying her, but the idea was absurd, the sort of misty notion that bored soldiers concocted when they spent too long in barracks. Even so, he wanted her now – wanted to see her and talk with her more than anything. The wine was stripping away whatever vague ardour he might previously have possessed.

Settling himself heavily on the narrow divan, he wondered at the gathering frustration he had felt these last months, the sense of barely tethered anger. Was it something he had inherited from his father? His promotion to centurion had seemed like a reward once, but now the fortress was coming to feel like a snare. He could lose himself here. All day he had been baited: by Ursicinus on the drill field; by Balbinus and Galleo in the messroom; by all the head-scratching routines of unit administration and hospital visits. He felt a raging violence inside him, a need for release. The disappointment at not seeing Afrodisia was just the latest of his vexations.

From somewhere upstairs he heard a man shout. Not Valens. A woman screamed – it was her, he was sure – and at once he was crossing the room: three long strides to the curtain with his centurion's staff gripped in his fist. Swiping aside the beaded curtain, he stared down the wooden passageway to the stairs: the big Frankish slave rising to his feet, Dionysia's startled expression through a doorway to the right.

'Centurion?' the madam said. 'Please, be calm... nothing is wrong!'

A woman's laughter came from upstairs. Castus lowered his staff and the beads dropped back into place, swinging and clattering. Embarrassment creased through him. A stupid mistake, that was all.

Another voice now, from out in the yard. Hurried words. Castus turned as the eunuch appeared through the doorway, stooping a bow.

'Would the dominus be Centurion Aurelius Castus?' he asked.

Castus glared at him, and the eunuch swallowed thickly.

'There is messenger for you, dominus. From the prefect. He claims it's an urgent matter.'

He stepped away from the curtain. Dionysia was still peering at him through the swinging beads, her earrings chiming.

Now what? 'All right,' he said. 'I'm coming.'

The praetorium was in darkness, only a few lamps burning in the upper rooms and the sentries at the door almost asleep against their spears. Two months had passed since Castus had last entered here, for his strange interview with Arpagius and the notary Nigrinus. This time things were different – the messenger had told him nothing, but had led him through the streets of the fortress at a rapid pace.

Up the stairs, he followed the corridor along to the same room he had entered before. The doors opened to orange lamplight and a huddle of figures around the central table. Castus took three strides across the floor, stamped to a halt and saluted.

'Dominus!'

'Yes, yes, quietly, please, centurion. Stand at ease.'

Arpagius had a creased look, as if he had been woken recently. A quick glance took in the other men in the room: two tribunes, Rufinius and Callistus; a long-haired man in a native cloak whom Castus recognised as the rider he had seen outside earlier; and a bearded balding man with a round face and startled eyes.

'What's the current duty strength of your century?' the prefect asked.

'Dominus! Four men still absent on supply escort duty, three men in the hospital, two men on leave, one detached to the river patrol, one absent without leave. Fifty-eight men present for duty, dominus.'

Arpagius raised an eyebrow. 'Impressively detailed,' he said. Castus suppressed a smile, and gave silent thanks to his standard-bearer.

'I want you to prepare those men you have available for immediate departure,' the prefect went on. Castus said nothing.

'You may want to sit down, centurion,' one of the tribunes

said, pointing to a stool. Castus winged his shoulders, then he sat down stiffly on the stool with his back straight.

'One of our frontier scouts,' Arpagius said, gesturing to the man in the native cloak, 'has just brought some potentially troubling information from north of the border. It appears that Vepogenus, who you may know is High Chieftain of the Pictish confederation, has died. Apparently a case of accidental food poisoning – he was feasting on mushrooms – but there are necessarily doubts about what's happened.'

Castus nodded, staying silent. He had never heard of Vepogenus, or the Pictish confederation. The Picts were a savage people who lived far north of the frontier, past the wall of Hadrian and the settled lands beyond, but he knew no more about them than that.

'Since the death is in dispute,' Arpagius went on, 'Vepogenus's military commander has declared himself regent until the tribal leaders can be gathered to select a new high chieftain.'

'The Picts have a multitude of leaders,' said the second tribune, Callistus, a solid military-looking man with hard eyes. 'But they've taken to… *electing* a chieftain to stand above the others. It's a new thing – easier for us when they just fought among themselves!'

'Vepogenus fought against us in the past,' Arpagius said, 'but he agreed to a treaty several years ago. He swore to keep the peace and not to attack the settled tribes to the south who are clients of Rome, and he's stuck to it. With him gone, there's potential for troublemakers to step in – the Picts are a very backward people, and believe treaties are made between individuals, not states. Therefore we must send an envoy, with a diplomatic party, to the tribal gathering and ensure that the old treaties are honoured by the newly elected chieftain, whoever he may be. I want your men to act as a bodyguard.'

'Prefect, with respect,' the tribune Callistus broke in, 'will a single reduced century be enough? Less than sixty men? We should send a cohort, surely...'

'No. This is an honour guard, nothing more. If we sent a whole cohort the tribes would suspect we were invading their land. Which we have no intention of doing.'

Watching the exchange, Castus was surprised by the change in Arpagius. On his last meeting the prefect had seemed worried, irresolute. Now he was much firmer, with a decisive note in his voice. Even so, the plan lacked appeal. Castus knew nothing of Picts or any other savages, and the notion of standing around acting as a ceremonial guard surrounded by howling barbarians tightened his stomach. He thought enviously of Valens, still at the Blue House with his dark-skinned Cleopatra...

'Would a mounted escort not be faster?' asked the bearded man. Castus had ignored him until now.

'Over that distance, no,' Arpagius replied. 'There's limited horse fodder north of the wall – the stunted little ponies the natives ride seem to live on air – and a cavalry force of that size would have to carry its own provisions or spend half their time foraging. Our soldiers can cover twenty miles a day on foot. Besides, I want legionaries there – the savages respect our legions; they fear them. They're Rome, to the natives' understanding. Centurion, you have a question?'

Castus paused, unaware that he had been staring quizzically. 'Dominus,' he said, 'I just thought... why choose my men for this?'

Arpagius gave him a thin smile. 'Because I warmed to you on our last meeting, centurion! You're the sort of plain, honest soldier I like. And because you've turned an unpromising crop of men into the smartest century in the legion. They look good and they march hard, and that's what I need at this moment.

Besides, I suspect you'll impress the natives. They're quite puny, on the whole.'

Nothing more to be said then, Castus thought. He recognised a foregone conclusion when he heard one. Standing up, he clasped his hands at his back, raised his head and stuck out his chest. 'Dominus! What are your orders?'

Arpagius nodded slightly, pleased. 'The decision of the tribes,' he said, 'is scheduled for the first light of the new moon, which is in fifteen days' time. The party will consist of one of my secretaries, Flavius Strabo' – he gestured to the bearded man, who bowed his head – 'and our envoy, to be collected from his villa a day's march north of here.'

'I'm not sure about that plan either,' the tribune said quietly, but Arpagius ignored him.

'Prepare your men to leave before dawn. I'll supply a docket to draw all necessary supplies from the commissariat, and eight mules to carry the baggage together with slaves to handle them. I'll also write an order to the commander of Bremenium fort to detach some mounted scouts to accompany you north of the Wall. I must remind you, centurion, that your force will *not* be expected to fight – they are an honour guard alone. Your first responsibility will be the protection of the envoy himself, then the security of your own men. You will have no say in any diplomatic negotiations, and should keep yourself and your men separate from the natives at all times. Do you understand?'

'I understand, dominus. We will do what we are ordered...'

'... *and at every command we will be ready,*' Arpagius said with a smile, finishing the customary soldier's pledge. 'Dismissed, centurion.'

CHAPTER III

Mile after mile, the road ran on across the open landscape, straight and true as a line scored on a surveyor's plan. The soldiers marched in open order, spread out along the road with the pack mules at the centre. As they passed the fourth milestone from Eboracum the sun rose, lighting the brown moors to either side and throwing their long shadows out over the gravel ahead of them.

Castus marched at the head of the column. Behind him came Evagrius, carrying a banner with the winged Victory emblem of the Sixth Legion, and after him the remaining fifty-seven men of the century. Each carried a full load – mail armour and helmet, shield and spear, sword, two light javelins and a sheaf of darts, plus a full canteen and hard rations for five days. Another twelve days' food per man was carried on the pack mules, together with the tents, cooking utensils, entrenching tools and fodder, and a sealed package of diplomatic gifts to present to the Picts. It was a heavy burden, but men and animals moved easily now, falling into the rhythm of the march. Castus had done his planning well.

It had been a different picture two hours before, when he had mustered his men in the pre-dawn twilight, just inside the river gate of the fortress. All of them bone-tired and aching from broken sleep, unwashed and unfed, none knowing where they were going or why. They had marched out in a ragged column, across the bridge and through the silent civilian settlement with their boots crunching loud on the cobbles. Castus had decided not to tell his men of the nature of the mission until they had a day's march behind them. He knew so little himself about what lay ahead.

But a winter of route marches had toughened the men up, and with the sun on their backs they soon picked up a good pace. The country to either side was open moorland, then at the seventh milestone they crossed a brook and moved into rolling cultivated hills. It was familiar territory to them all. Castus hung back every few miles and let the men pass him, swatting at his thigh with his staff as he checked them off.

'Atrectus! Get your spear up off the dirt – it's not a walking stick! *Shoulder!*'

'Sorry, centurion.'

Valerius Atrectus was a red-haired joker, and had often been on punishment back at Eboracum. Beside him marched Genialis, a slow, simple soldier who generally did whatever his friend told him. The worst men in the century for discipline, but Castus regarded them now with a contented smile. All of them were his brothers, his men, his command. He looked towards Evagrius, swinging along in the lead now with the standard over his shoulder, the hornblower Volusius marching behind him, Timotheus bringing up the rear with his easy stride. He checked his section leaders, each in charge of a group of eight: Culchianus, Attius, Januarius... All of them looked keen, disciplined and strong. Ready for whatever he might order. If Castus himself felt the tremor of uncertainty about what lay ahead, he was determined not to let it show.

Flavius Strabo, the governor's secretary, rode his pony along the verge of the road, remaining apart from the soldiers. Castus had hardly been aware of him when they had left the fort, and the man had said nothing to anyone since. Now, as he moved back up the line, Castus regarded him carefully, sizing him up. He was a smallish, fattish man, and sat badly on his pony, seeming to bounce up and down in the saddle as he rode. He probably only had a year or two on Castus, but with his shining bald forehead and trimmed beard he looked much older. Plainly dressed, but he wore an expensive-looking gold brooch securing his cloak. Castus had little experience of civilians, and little desire to expand on it – they were generally a nuisance anyway, interfering with the work of the professionals. Fine for selling beer or cattle, good at running inns, but little use for much else.

But as he dropped back into the rhythm of the march, Castus was aware that the secretary surely knew much more about the task ahead of them than he did. Stepping down off the roadway, he paced up alongside the man on the pony, trying to appear casual.

'So how far is this villa we're heading for then?' He was not sure how to address the secretary – *dominus* would surely be too deferential. As far as he knew, the secretary was only a minor functionary.

'Oh, quite a bit further. Three hours' march beyond Isurium, I'd say.'

Castus nodded. More or less as he had expected. They could break the march for a few hours at Isurium and make it to the villa before evening.

'And what about this envoy we're meeting?'

The secretary turned in his saddle and glanced down with a wry smile. 'The less you know about him the better, I'd say!'

'Fair enough.'

They moved on in silence, Castus falling in with his men again. He was sure now that Strabo knew something important about the mission ahead. Either he wanted to talk, but had been ordered not to, or he had been ordered to communicate something but was playing a waiting game. Either way, if the fat man wanted to be mysterious, he would let him. Castus could happily march twenty or more miles a day in complete silence with barely a conscious thought in his head, but the secretary appeared to be the kind of man who disliked silence. Give him a few more miles, Castus thought, and we'll see how well he fares with his attempt at secrecy.

He did not have long to wait. As they passed the eleventh milestone and trees closed around the road the secretary eased himself off his pony, wincing, and walked along with the reins in his hand.

'Do you think we might take a short rest, centurion? It's getting rather hot!'

'Don't worry about that. My lot can march five hours a day like this. They haven't even broken sweat yet. We'll rest when we get to Isurium, but if you want a lie down you can catch us up later.'

'Oh no, oh no...' the secretary said. He was kicking up dust as he walked along beside his horse. 'I'm sorry if I was a little short with you earlier. You must understand there are some things I can't openly discuss – or not yet, anyway.'

'That's fine. We've all got our orders.'

They walked on a little further in silence. The trees opened out, and the sun shone hot on their backs. Castus had been exaggerating about his men not sweating. He glanced at Strabo: the desire to talk, whatever prohibition might be on the man, was almost palpable. Fine then; he would draw him out gradually.

'Tell me about these Picts,' he said.

'Ah, yes, the Picts,' said Strabo, widening his eyes. They had drawn ahead of the marching men a little – Castus had not noticed. He reminded himself not to become complacent about this man.

'They live in the mountains and valleys, beyond the settled peoples to the north of the Wall of Hadrian,' the secretary said. 'Originally they were a collection of feuding tribes – Caledones, Miathi, Venicones and others. They fought many wars against Rome over the years, whenever they banded together and tried to resist us. Then the emperor Severus marched into the north with a huge army. You'll have read about Severus in the histories, I expect?'

Castus, of course, had read nothing at all, but he had heard of Severus. The emperor who had built the current walls of Eboracum fortress. He nodded.

'Severus campaigned against the tribes for three years, but failed to completely subdue them. His army burned and destroyed their homes and killed anyone they could find.'

Castus gave an appreciative grunt. He had always liked the sound of the emperor Severus: clearly a commander who knew the best way to treat savages.

'However, Severus died before he could finish the campaign. The tribes, though, had been driven back into the deepest and most inaccessible valleys of their homeland, and there they remained for most of the last hundred years, fighting among themselves, giving us no trouble.'

'Good result,' said Castus. As he had expected, the secretary had shrugged off his fatigue in his enthusiasm to talk. 'So then what?'

'Around twenty years ago,' Strabo said, 'there were reports of a new power in the north. The scattered tribes had banded together, to threaten the more peaceable tribes allied to Rome. They were led by the Miathi people, but their neighbours called them the Picts. A name to instil terror, it seems.'

'Doesn't sound very terrible,' Castus said. A thought struck him. 'Do they really paint themselves blue, these Picts, and ride around in chariots? That's what somebody told me...'

Strabo chuckled dryly. 'Oh, they do that on occasion, yes. You'll see for yourself soon enough. Anyway,' he went on, 'the Picts soon overran the settled tribal lands and threatened the northern frontier of the empire. At the same time, the Franks were raiding the coasts of Gaul and Britain too. So, as perhaps you recall, when Maximian was appointed co-emperor he sent a man called Carausius to deal with the situation.'

'Carausius,' Castus said. He recognised that name at least. The usurper who had seized control of Britain and the Gallic coast and declared himself emperor of the west. Even now, more then a decade after Carausius had fallen, the legions of Britain were still held in suspicion for their support of him. That, Castus had often thought, explained the poor condition of the province, the dilapidated fortresses, the demoralised troops.

'Shortly after this Carausius claimed the purple, he appointed one of his own officers, Aelius Marcellinus, to drive back the Pictish marauders. By this time they were under the leadership of a high chieftain, Vepogenus, of the Miathi royal house.'

'This is the one who's just died?'

'Yes – I'll come to that. Anyway, Marcellinus, a Spaniard by birth but married into the native British aristocracy, conducted a short but very effective campaign along the Wall of Hadrian. He broke the Pictish attack, and concluded a series of treaties with them to ensure peace. He also, ah... entered into what you might call a pact of brotherhood with Vepogenus.'

'A Roman officer did that? Not a good idea.'

'Well, it was effective. The Picts respect personal bonds much more than political treaties, you see. However, the following year Carausius was murdered by Allectus, one of his own ministers, who took over power, and soon afterwards seized Marcellinus and charged him with treason. Marcellinus managed to escape, crossed over to Gaul and surrendered to the new Caesar Constantius, giving him vital information about the usurper's forces. And then, as you surely know, Constantius led his army across the Gallic Strait and reconquered Britain for Rome.'

Castus nodded, trying to take it all in. He was aware that Strabo's story had strayed some distance from the matter of the Picts. Or had it? He was beginning to suspect that this man Marcellinus would become a lot more prominent very soon.

But Strabo had fallen back now, coughing and rummaging in his saddlebag for a canteen. Castus left him and marched on at the head of his men. Clearly the secretary felt he had said enough, for now.

Fields of young wheat edged the road, and from every copse rose the smoke of a hearth fire. This was rich farming country. Two miles further on, the men let out a ragged cheer as the town of Isurium appeared ahead of them. The walled settlement lay along the bank of a river, its tiled roofs bright in the morning sun. There was even an amphitheatre, the topmost tiers showing white above the trees.

The citizens were used to soldiers passing up and down the road, and few turned to watch as Castus led his century along the muddy main street and out by the far gate to the grassy bank of the river.

'Timotheus,' he called, 'fall the men out. We'll rest here for four hours. Set a sentry watch of ten men by rotation, and the rest can strip off and bathe in the river, eat and sleep if they can.'

The optio saluted and strutted away, already crying out the orders. Castus dropped down to sit in the grass. His feet were hot and sore in their binding of wool and leather, but he felt invigorated by the morning's march. The muscles of his legs were hard and strong, and he relished the prospect of another three hours on the road. Glancing over at his men, he was glad to see that they were eager too. They spilled into the river, shouting and kicking up spray.

Strabo was a different matter. The little secretary sat on a flat stone, pulling his boots off and examining his blisters.

'Better to keep them on,' Castus told him. 'They'll hurt more later, otherwise.'

'Too late,' Strabo said, before coming over and sitting beside the centurion. Together they ate cheese and hardtack and drank the watery vinegar wine, as the sound of splashing water and laughter came from the river.

'They appear so young, your soldiers,' the secretary said, squinting at the men in the water.

'Eighteen, the youngest,' Castus told him. 'Couple more nineteen.'

'And yet we train them to fight and to kill, and send them off to die for our empire...'

Castus paused, mid-chew, and stared at the man beside him. What could be wrong with that?

'How old were you, centurion,' Strabo asked, 'when you first killed a man?'

Castus swallowed. 'Sixteen or so,' he said. 'At least, I thought I'd killed him. Hit him over the head with an ironbound bucket and he went down like a sacrificial ox. It was half a year before I found out that he wasn't dead after all...'

Strabo had a pained expression on his face. He shook his head sadly. Castus just shrugged – he had not mentioned that the man he had hit with the bucket was his own father. He had been in Troesmis, a hundred miles down the Danube, and already signed up with II Herculia before he met a man from his home town who told him that the old man had survived. Good thing too – patricide was a terrible crime before the gods. Even so, he had never made any attempt to seek forgiveness.

The two men sat in silence as they finished their meal. The soldiers were climbing from the river and running on the bank to dry off. Castus wondered if Strabo had taken offence at his remarks – he had no desire to drive the man away from him, and still had much he wanted to learn.

'You were telling me about the Picts,' he asked.

'Oh, yes – I'm sorry...'

'After this man Marcellinus made his treaties and pacts and so on with them, what happened?'

'Yes, well. After the murder of Carausius, and the arrest of Marcellinus, the Picts believed that the treaties were invalid. When Constantius regained the province, he found that the Picts were once again raiding along the northern borders. In addition, a number of... shall we say *renegades*, officers of the former regime whose loyalties placed them beyond pardon, had fled into barbarian country and taken shelter there. These men were now aiding and directing the Picts in their assaults upon our territories.'

Castus sucked breath through his teeth. He had known of deserters from the legions, or criminals, crossing over to the barbarians. But never of Roman officers doing it. 'Treasonous bastards,' he said.

'Absolutely treasonous, yes. But for them, you see, the Picts were their only refuge. They hoped, I suppose, to regain their former lands and wealth with a Pictish army to support them. One can only marvel at their stupidity!'

'Something like that,' Castus said grimly. Once, in Persia, they had captured an enemy town and found three men with the garrison, former legionaries taken prisoner who had gone over to the Persians to save their skins. The men had been crucified on the walls that evening, and nobody had grieved for them. Traitors were no better than vermin.

'Anyway, faced with this threat, the Caesar Constantius in his great wisdom sent his Praetorian Prefect against the barbarians, assisted by Aelius Marcellinus. Between them they managed to repel the attacks and reimpose peace along the border. Marcellinus, by force and persuasion, restored his pact of brotherhood with the Pictish chieftain, Vepogenus. That was eight years ago, and ever since the peace has held.'

'But now this Vepogenus has died of eating mushrooms?'

'Died of something. We can only hope that mushrooms were involved, and not something less... natural. Despite the treaties, you see, there are many among the Picts who long to avenge themselves on Rome for their past defeats. Besides, one or two of those renegades I mentioned are still with them, and as you can imagine they still plot and scheme.'

'I don't have much of an imagination. Why weren't they surrendered to justice when the war ended?'

'Oh, well. The terms of the surrender were... difficult. In fact, you might better call it a truce. Since the few surviving renegades were present at the negotiations, and hold high rank among the Picts, it was difficult to... *apprehend* them, shall we say.'

'And what about Marcellinus? I've never heard his name before now.' Castus was developing a strong notion about the identity of their mysterious envoy.

But Strabo had got up and was heading for the river. 'Perhaps later,' he said. 'Just now I have a fierce need to wash my feet!'

* * *

Back on the road northwards from Isurium, the century passed across an open moorland of brown heather and wild grass. After five miles, Strabo turned aside from the road and led them off along a narrower track, due west into a broad river valley. The late-afternoon sun was warm and golden, and the feet of the marching men raised a low haze of dust over the road.

'Move up ahead with me a little way,' Strabo said, slipping down off his pony to walk beside Castus. 'I'll tell you more about Marcellinus, although I'm not sure it's safe for everyone to know, if you follow me.'

The secretary had a tired look now, and his face was dusty. He was developing a persistent cough, and swigged from a small bottle of medicine he kept in his saddlebag. All this way, Castus thought, the secrecy had been wearing away at him. Now he had to let it out.

'Nobody can hear us,' he said, glancing back. They forded a shallow rushing stream, the water soaking through their boots and leg wrappings. Strabo nodded, closing his eyes; the relief at being able to unburden himself was obvious. Not for the first time, Castus wondered just how much of the secretary's reserve had been calculated.

'I told you that Marcellinus led the treaty negotiations at the end of the last Pictish war,' Strabo said, quickly and quietly. 'There's a little more to it than that. Part of the talks involved an exchange of hostages – it's common among the native peoples, and Marcellinus understood their ways. As a token of his trust in Vepogenus, he sent his own son, a boy of fourteen, as hostage for our side.'

Castus whistled through his teeth. He had a bad feeling about the way this story was going. The shadow of a cloud fell over the road ahead.

'He died, the boy,' Strabo said. 'Murdered, probably by one of the renegades in an attempt to sabotage the peace talks.'

'And Marcellinus... forgave them?'

'He had to. Either that, or renew a destructive war and fight with rage in his heart. The murderer was never identified, needless to say, but I believe he had his suspicions.'

'Strong man.'

'Yes. Strong indeed. But the experience broke his spirits. He resigned his command after the peace was agreed, and retired to his estates. Few people have seen or heard from him since.'

But we will, and soon, Castus thought. He was grinding his molars as he marched. Savage barbarians, murderous renegade Romans – and an envoy with a killing grudge against both of them. He glanced back at the men behind him, marching along at an easy pace, spearpoints catching the lowering sunlight. Surely the tribune back at Eboracum had been right: they should have sent a full cohort, with cavalry support.

'He's still the most skilled negotiator in the province,' Strabo said quietly. 'And he understands the Picts, knows many of them personally.'

And wants to kill them, Castus thought. But he said nothing.

It was early evening by the time they reached the villa. The tiled roofs showed through the trees, then the white-pillared portico and the vault of the bath-house. Castus ordered his men into military step as they approached the gates with the standard proudly before them. Tenant labourers in dun tunics stood in the fields and watched them as they passed.

Aelius Marcellinus was waiting for them on the steps of the front portico. Castus knew him at once: his cropped greying hair and lined face contrasted with his muscular build and his upright military stance to give him a look of natural authority.

'Century – halt!' he called, and the soldiers behind him stamped as one man and stood in formation in the courtyard.

'Dominus, Centurion Aurelius Castus and century, Third Cohort, Sixth Legion Victrix, reporting for escort duty.'

'Welcome,' Marcellinus said. 'You may stand your men down, centurion. I've prepared billets for them in the stable block, and my people will send out food and beer.'

A fine parade-ground voice he had, Castus thought. Slight edge of the aristocrat, but nothing too refined.

Strabo had dismounted and stood to one side watching, unobtrusive. Now, as Castus relayed his orders to his optio, he saw the secretary approach Marcellinus and speak quickly and quietly. A look of sober consideration crossed the old soldier's face.

'Centurion,' Marcellinus said, coming over and placing a hand on his shoulder. The two men were almost the same height. 'I've ordered the baths heated for you and the secretary here. I hope you can join us for dinner this evening.'

'Oh, don't worry about me, dominus. Splash of well water and a bite of cheese is all I need. I'll stay with my men.'

'Brother,' the man said, smiling and showing his teeth, 'you're my guest. I get to hear so little from the wider world, and if we're to travel together for so long we should talk, I think.'

Castus shrugged, baffled. It felt strange and uncomfortable to be singled out for special treatment like this – it had never happened to him before. Then again, he had no real idea what the proper manner might be in these situations.

'I can see to the men, centurion,' said Timotheus, standing at parade rest just within earshot. 'You'd better find out all you need to know.'

'Right,' Castus replied, nodding. For a moment he suspected that Timotheus was winking at him. 'Right – get the men watered and foddered and see to their billets. I'll be back to check them over before they turn in. The watchword is *Sol Invictus*.'

The optio saluted, turned on his heel and marched away after the men.

In fact, Castus learned little over dinner. Washed of the road's dust and freshly dressed in his spare tunic and breeches, he reclined awkwardly on a couch in the gloomy dining room, listening to the two men talk. They were being scrupulously polite, even formal, discussing matters in Eboracum and the imperial city of Treveris in Gaul, where it appeared that Strabo had been living until recently. Nothing about the task ahead of them – Castus felt as though he was watching a strange ritualistic dance, the two men circling but never quite meeting. The meal was a simple feast but he ate little, and drank too much wine to hide his discomfort. His intuition told him that neither man trusted the other, and both had misgivings about the nature of their mission.

Towards the end of the meal a shadow fell across the mosaic floor, and Castus noticed figures in the hallway beyond the doors. He stood up quickly, swaying slightly with the effects of the wine.

'Relax, brother,' Marcellinus said. 'My family.' He gestured to the group in the hall. 'Please, come in and meet our guests.'

Two women entered, eyes downcast, with a pair of slaves trailing behind them. The older woman wore a dark, patterned tunic and shawl; her hair was almost white, and she had an expression of pained dignity. Marcellinus's wife, clearly. The other was maybe seventeen, with dark hair brushed into a circling plait. Her face was a pale oval, with deeply lidded eyes. When she glanced up, Castus saw the faint gleam of tears.

'My wife Claudia Secunda, and my daughter Aelia Marcellina,' Marcellinus said.

Castus, still standing, bowed his head to each lady in turn. He noticed Strabo doing the same from the dining couch.

'Husband,' the older woman said, 'we will retire soon. Please join us for a moment if you can.'

'Excuse me,' Marcellinus said, and swung himself upright. He left the room with the ladies following after him.

Strabo lay back on the couch, patting his stomach. He raised his eyebrows at Castus. 'So,' he said. 'That's our envoy!'

Castus drained his cup, and upended it by habit on the tabletop. 'I need to go and check on my men,' he said thickly. 'I'll be back later.'

Outside the dining room, he crossed the hall, conscious of the noise of his hobnailed boots on the mosaic floor. A corridor extended to his right, following the line of the front portico. As he moved along it, shuffling his feet, he saw lamplight from an open doorway.

He glanced quickly through the door as he passed: Marcellinus, with the women to either side of him, kneeling before an altar in a puddle of wavering light. A thin stream of incense smoke rose between them. Castus noticed the figure of the goddess in the niche of the altar: Fortuna the Homebringer.

Reaching the end of the corridor, he stepped out into the portico and then down into the courtyard. No sound from the stable block. He crossed the gravel, gratefully breathing the cool night air.

A sentry stood at the stable door, straightening up suddenly as he approached.

'Halt! What's the watchword!'

'*Sol Invictus*. It's me, Vincentius.'

'Sorry, centurion, all I saw was a shadow. So quiet out here.'

'Stay awake.'

The sentry moved aside and he entered the stable. His men lay stretched on the straw, many of them snoring deeply: the usual barrack-room chorus. The standard-bearer, Evagrius, stepped from the darkness and saluted.

'All well, centurion. Timotheus let them turn in early.'

'Good. They've given me quarters in the house, but I'll be up well before dawn. Make sure everybody is ready to move at sunrise.'

Another salute, and Castus went back out to the yard. The stars overhead were very bright and clear. He thought of Marcellinus and his family, praying for a safe return. The tears in his daughter's eyes... What did they think would happen? The wife had lost a son to the Picts already. Not surprising they were worried. Even so, he thought, perhaps they knew something he did not. In that case, better he never found out.

At the steps to the front portico he paused and breathed deeply, until his chest was full and he could feel the heavy beat of blood in his neck. *Your first responsibility will be the protection of the envoy... then the security of your own men.* So the governor had said. Marcellinus appeared to be able to look after himself, but those men snoring in the stable straw depended on him to lead them.

Castus exhaled slowly, but the burden remained upon him, the weight of command. He remembered something he had been told long ago by his first centurion, Priscus, who had died in the dust at Oxsa when the cataphracts had broken through the line. A stern man, hard and taciturn, but he had been drinking that day and he had grown strange, maudlin.

When they make you a centurion, they don't just give you a stick and a pay rise, boy, Priscus had told him. *They give you a new face too. A mask of bronze, riveted to the front of your skull. That mask is your duty, and you wear it always.*

Castus had not understood at the time; he had just nodded, frowned and tried to hide his dismay. *Because when you're up there in front of half a hundred frightened conscripts*, Priscus went on, *and the barbarians come screaming to cut them up, they'll be looking to you for strength. But it's not your face they want to see. Not a man's face. They want to see the mask, that bronze mask of command, hard and inflexible, without fear.*

Was that how Priscus had appeared at Oxsa as he had led them towards his own death? Castus could not remember now. But he remembered the trust he'd had for his centurion then, the belief in his strength. Would he be able to show that same conviction, when it came to it? All his life he had wanted to live up to that duty, to lead men in battle and take the challenge of command, but now he muttered a silent prayer that he would not be so tested, not this time at least.

Back in the corridor of the villa, he crept as quietly as he could towards his room. The lamps had all been extinguished now; everyone was preparing for an early departure. He was feeling his way along the wall when he noticed a movement from an open door and poised, muscles locked.

'Centurion,' a voice said. He could see her now, standing just inside the doorway. Her face was a pale smudge in the shadows, but he could see her large dark eyes, the intensity of her gaze. He stepped closer.

'My father trusts you,' the girl said, her voice little more than a whisper. She advanced into the corridor and stood before him – her head only reached his chest. 'He told me that, and he's a good judge of men.'

'Glad to hear it.'

'Promise me,' the girl said, eyes wide. 'Promise me you'll protect him and bring him home safely.'

'He'll be safe, domina. There's nearly sixty armed soldiers going with him, after all.'

'I need you to *promise*!' the girl cried in a hoarse whisper. She reached out and seized the neck of Castus's tunic. He felt her fingers, thin and hard against his skin. 'Swear to me that you'll look after him and watch over him at all times.'

'All right,' Castus said. He was not used to taking orders from women, but he could hear the desperation in her voice. 'I swear by the Unconquered Sun and all the gods of Rome that I'll watch out for your father, keep him safe and bring him home.'

She dropped her head, still clinging to his tunic. A moment passed. His arms hung by his sides, big and useless. He had no idea how to comfort her now.

Then, quickly, she raised her head, stretched on her toes and kissed him on the cheek.

'Thank you,' she said quietly, then she turned and went back into the consuming darkness.

CHAPTER IV

W e're going into Pictland? Just us – *on our own?*'
        'We pick up some mounted scouts at Bremenium,
but otherwise, yes, just us.'

'They'll cut us to pieces and boil our bones…!'

It was mid-morning, four hours of marching behind them
already, and now the men of the century were assembled at the
side of the road in the shade of the trees. Castus stood facing
them, his staff gripped level in both fists. He had not been
looking forward to this little address.

'Quiet in the ranks!' growled Timotheus, a moment too
late. Genialis's comment had already raised a stir of agitation.
Castus scanned the faces of his men: some looked shocked,
disbelieving; others apprehensive. One or two grinned in feigned
amusement. But a satisfying number just stared back at him,
neutral, trusting to the wisdom of their superiors. As do I,
Castus thought. For better or worse.

'We're not going to be doing any *fighting*,' he said, with
heavy emphasis. 'Our job is to escort those two over there' –
he jutted his staff towards Strabo and Marcellinus, waiting
with their horses on the far side of the road – 'up to meet
the Picts and talk things over with them in a *peaceful* and
friendly way.'

A few more grins now, the men nudging each other.

'So nobody's getting chopped up and eaten, unless I give you permission. We just march up there, stand around looking Roman, then march back home.'

'So long as we're not expected to dance for the Picts, or sing...'

'No, Atrectus, you're not. That would be counted as a just cause for war.'

The grins broke to laughter, and Castus allowed himself to relax a little, the tension easing from his shoulders. They were fine now, but they had ten more days of marching ahead of them. He would talk to Timotheus and Evagrius. Important to keep the rumours and the muttering in check, or he would be leading a very unwilling set of soldiers north of the Wall.

'That's all. Get into line and let's move – there's another four hours yet till we reach Cataractonium.'

They marched for the rest of the day, the road reeling on ahead of them and falling away behind, still straight as an arrow-shot. After a while it become hypnotic, the stretch of packed gravel always ahead, never ending, and the eye came to hunger for a bend, a bridge, anything to break the monotony. Castus didn't mind, though: easier to march steadily when you didn't have to think.

But it was impossible to banish thought altogether. He had slept badly at the villa; the bed had been far more comfortable than he was used to, and after a few hours he had got out and stretched himself on the hard tiled floor. The image of Aelia Marcellina had haunted him, the girl's pale face swimming in the darkness, the memory of her whispering voice, and the promise he had sworn to her. The lack of sleep was unsurprising.

Marcellinus and the secretary kept themselves apart, riding together along the verge of the road, often talking intently out of hearing of the soldiers. Good thing too, Castus thought: he had no wish to know any more about the mission than he had to. They were passing through farmland again now, and a group of field labourers straightened from their work and stood to watch as the soldiers went by. *They're like me*, Castus thought: *simple men with a simple job.* Two generations back he would have been the same as them. That was his blood, his heritage. He had no time for the intrigues of diplomacy.

As they approached Cataractonium, the end of the day's march, Marcellinus rode up alongside Castus. 'I believe my daughter spoke to you last night,' he said.

'She did, dominus.'

'I'm sorry about that. I had forbidden it. Oh, and you can drop the formal address now, brother!'

He slid down from the saddle and walked beside Castus with the reins looped over his arm. 'My daughter is an intelligent girl,' he said. 'But she's imaginative, and that isn't a good thing in a female. They can become fearful so easily. We only received word from the governor about this… *mission* a few hours before you arrived, so my family were still rather shocked by the news. Please don't let my daughter's words shadow your mind.'

'Of course not, domin… I mean, I'd forgotten them already.'

'Good, good. Do you have a wife yourself?'

'Never had the time.'

'Probably wise. I feel as I get older that we should live without too many attachments. But I love my family – my wife and my children.'

'You have other children?' Castus almost choked on the words – he hoped that Marcellinus was not referring to the murdered boy.

'Yes, I have a younger son in Eboracum. Didn't you know?'

Castus shrugged and shook his head. They walked on for

73

some time in silence, and Marcellinus took an apple from his haversack and fed it to his horse.

'You served in the east, so Strabo tells me. With Galerius in the Persian campaign?'

'I did,' Castus told him.

'That must have been something to experience. Galerius is quite the tactician, so I hear.'

'I suppose so.' Castus had little concern for tactics: going in hard and heavy, like a charging bull, was his favoured approach, and beating the enemy into the ground by brute force. But he had to admit that Galerius's planning at Oxsa had been very clever. The emperor had scouted out the terrain himself the day before the battle, so the men had said afterwards, disguised as a cabbage-seller...

'Tell me about it. It would pass the time.'

'Well...' Castus said. He had grown wary, since coming to Britain, of talking too much about his years in the Herculiani. Too many people seemed to think he was just boasting, or to feel lessened by the comparison with their own drab lives. Tentatively, he began to explain the positions at Oxsa, the night march that had brought them round the flank of the Persian royal camp, their battle line on the slopes above the valley. Then the Persian charge, the infantry taking the shock of it, the cavalry sweeping round from the wings... He was not a skilled speaker, and stumbled over the right words, but as he went on he saw the battle once more before him, heard the crash of impact as the cataphracts broke through the forward cohorts. Again he saw the horses rearing out of the dustcloud, over the bloodied wrack of bodies...

'... then after that we stormed their camp and took the lot – even the ladies from the harem, although Galerius ordered them to be treated with honour. I didn't see any of it, though.

I'd passed out from injuries by then. But I heard about it later.'

'Must have been a fine sight, a battle like that.' Marcellinus tipped his head back and closed his eyes, as if he could scent the blood and dust and hear the clash of combat. 'I would love to have been there.'

Castus glanced at him. His broad faced turned to the sun, his cropped iron-grey hair. This was a man who had commanded troops in battle, he reminded himself, and won great victories. It was strange to speak to him so frankly.

'I've spent my whole life in the western provinces,' Marcellinus said. 'Half of it in this damp borderland. Oh, I don't regret it – I'm rooted here now. But I wonder what I might have made of myself if I'd gone east. Another life, eh?'

'I suppose so. But you've done well yourself, so I heard.'

'Do you? And what exactly have you heard about me, centurion?'

Castus tightened his jaw, cursing his mistake. 'Oh, this and that,' he said. 'You… won a few battles against the Picts. Strabo told me.'

'Did he now?' The envoy's voice had dropped, grown colder. 'And how does he know, I wonder? He was in Gaul until eighteen months ago!'

'I suppose they told him, back at Eboracum.'

'Yes. I'll bet they did. Our friend Strabo seems very well briefed indeed.'

They were billeted that night at the town of Cataractonium, and then went on the next day to Vinovium fort. Soon afterwards they entered the hill country, and the road rose and fell across steep ridges and valleys. The sky was dull grey, spitting rain, but the troops marched with silent indifference. On the fifth day from Eboracum they arrived at the military supply depot of Coria, a few miles south of the Wall. Castus gave his men the following day to rest and resupply, and with a free evening ahead most of them filed off at once to the bath-house, the beer shops and the brothels.

The depot commander had allocated billets in a disused cavalry barracks inside the military compound. In his quarters, Castus pulled off his boots and lay on the bed. Evening light came in through the open window, and he closed his eyes and listened to the familiar sounds: soldiers arguing and laughing; the click and rattle of dice from the rough wooden portico; the creak of wagons; and the distant clatter from the armoury workshops. Almost like home, he thought.

Marcellinus and Strabo were accommodated in a house across the street from the compound, and it was a relief to be free of them for a few hours. For the last three days on the road he had watched them, trying to dull his curiosity. Something was going on between the two men, some strange tension that worried Castus like an itch at the back of his mind. Half the time they had ridden apart, as if deliberately avoiding each other, but then they would spend hours in close whispered conversation. Clearly there was little trust between them. It was none of his concern, Castus told himself. And yet... He had the safety of his men to consider, the success of the mission. He couldn't allow some obscure rivalry or suspicion between the envoy and the secretary to endanger that.

After five days of solid marching he was filled with a punchy energy, and the thoughts revolving in his head would not let him relax. Throwing himself up off the bed, he poured a cup of vinegar wine and drank it down. One of the slaves had left food on the table – fresh bread, pea soup and bacon – and he ate standing, pacing up and down the narrow room as the light faded outside and the first torches glowed in the portico. He cleaned and waxed his boots, then oiled his belts and other kit, and with the last of the light he burnished the rust spots from his helmet with a damp rag and ashes from the fire. Night had fallen, but he did not feel like sleep. He pulled his boots back on, shrugged a cloak across his shoulders and went outside.

Timotheus was under the portico, drinking wine with the sentries.

'Take over here for a couple of hours,' Castus told him. 'I need to stretch my legs.'

'You haven't stretched them enough today?' the optio asked with a smile. They had covered twenty miles since dawn, over steep roads from Longovicium.

'That was only a stroll,' Castus said.

Passing between the lounging sentries at the gate of the military compound, he walked out into the muddy central street of the civilian settlement. Dogs ran in the gutters, and light spilled from the open doors of the taverns. Grubby children begged for copper coins in the portico of the market building. It was starting to rain again.

Coria had once been a proper fort, but the ramparts had been torn down years ago and now it was a trading settlement and supply town for the Wall garrison. Beyond the military enclosure with its armouries and storehouses the town straggled along the road in both directions, the home of provisions merchants, craftsmen and prostitutes. Not a cultured or genteel place, but Castus liked the look of it well enough. He paced slowly along the street wrapped in his cape, only his swagger and his army boots marking him out as a soldier. He should check on his men, he thought to himself; there were off-duty cavalry troopers from the Wall forts in town, and plenty of potential for trouble.

By the time he reached the limit of the settlement it was fully dark, and the rain was thin and steady. He turned and looked back along the street. The massive grain warehouses by the market rose up black against the dull glow of the town. He was getting wet, and felt the first waves of fatigue in his blood. Back up the street towards the compound, he passed a group of his own men gathered in the lighted door of a tavern – Atrectus and Genialis laughing as they tipped back their cups, Culchianus playing dice with a group of cavalry troopers just inside – but he kept to the shadows and they did not notice him.

He was almost back at the compound gate when he saw the hooded figure on the far side of the street. There was nothing immediately significant about him – just another local tradesman in a waterproof cape, hurrying home – and Castus might have ignored the man, but there was something familiar about his build and the way he walked. A moment, and he recognised him: it was Strabo. Without thinking, Castus had stepped back into the deeper darkness under the buttresses of the grain warehouse. Where was the secretary going? His quarters had baths, a dining room, and there were slaves to run errands. There was no reason at all for Strabo to venture out into the town alone in the rain. Did he have some strange desire to go drinking with the soldiers, perhaps? Castus considered that he might be on his way to a brothel, but doubted that the dapper secretary would relish an encounter with the sort of hardbitten ladies available in a frontier town like Coria.

Already he was moving, tracing his way along the side of the street. The idea of following Strabo, skulking about after him like an informer, was repugnant; what the man did in his own time was his own business. But Castus had his duty to his own men to consider: if the secretary was doing something suspicious then he had to know, or the thought of it would eat away at him, and in time the men would notice his unease.

He shrank back into the timber portico of a tavern as the secretary crossed the street ahead of him. When he stepped out again the man was gone, but Castus saw the narrow opening of an alleyway. He paced quickly along the wall and peered around the corner. A stink of stale urine met him: the patrons of the tavern had been using the alley as a latrine. But there was the figure of Strabo, briefly visible where the alley widened at the far end.

Treading carefully, steadying himself against a crumbling wall, Castus moved along the alleyway. He had left his sword and staff in the barracks, and the only weapon he carried was a small knife in his belt; in street fights he preferred to trust his fists and physical bulk, but he doubted that Strabo was leading him into that kind of trouble.

He slowed as he reached the end of the alleyway. It opened into a wide courtyard, greasy with slops and ringed with low wooden buildings. At the far side, he could make out the figure of the secretary waiting at a door. A moment passed, and then the door opened: a brief gleam of lamplight as Strabo stepped inside, and then the door closed again behind him.

Castus leaned back against the mossy bricks. If the place was a brothel, it was a very unusual one. Perhaps the sort of establishment that catered for strange tastes? He had heard of such places, in Antioch and even in some of the western cities. But surely not in a rough frontier settlement like Coria? He belched quietly, tasting pea soup.

Crossing the muddy yard in six long strides, he stood before the door. There was no sound from inside, and he gave the planks a careful shove. Bolted, it seemed. As his eyes adjusted to the darkness he saw two symbols scratched into the wood of the doorframe: something that looked like a ship, and below it an X with a line through it, like a solar wheel. He stood breathing quietly, one hand on the door. Strabo might easily spend hours in there, and Castus did not care for the idea of loitering outside in the rain. He could barge the door down and demand to know what was going on, but that would involve crossing a dangerous line. So far, he had just been strolling in the public street. No, he thought, there was no more he could do, and he was feeling very weary now.

He pushed himself away from the door, negotiated the stinking alleyway and headed back towards the military compound, thinking only of the pleasures of sleep.

By the time he found Marcellinus it was the following afternoon. From the door of the storehouse, where Evagrius was arguing with the commissary about a consignment of hardtack, Castus spotted the envoy leaving the depot commander's residence. Abandoning the standard-bearer to his negotiations, he crossed the gravelled courtyard.

'Centurion,' Marcellinus said as Castus dropped into step beside him. Together they walked away from the storehouse into the open ground before the depot gates. Now that he had located the envoy, Castus found it hard to phrase what he meant to ask. Even to admit his suspicions seemed dishonourable, somehow unmanly: he would have felt more comfortable confronting Strabo directly. This kind of subterfuge felt alien to him, but his duty was to the security of the mission. He was just about to speak when Marcellinus cut him off.

'Are your men prepared to resume the march tomorrow?'

Castus gave a curt nod. Clearly the envoy had other things on his mind.

'Good. We'll be crossing the Wall then. First time beyond the frontier for most of them, eh?'

'There's a matter I need to discuss with you, dominus.'

Marcellinus paused, laid a hand on Castus's shoulder and steered him towards the gate of the compound. 'Very well, we'll cut the idle chat,' he said, and something in his tone told Castus that the man had merely been stalling – he knew very well what the question would be.

'What you make of the secretary, Strabo?'

Marcellinus's hand tightened on his shoulder, then dropped. 'I've been studying him these last few days,' the envoy said quietly. 'But I'm not convinced by what he says. What are your impressions of him?'

'Not much. He keeps himself to himself.' *Then again*, Castus thought, *so do you.* He did not wish to mention his brief espionage the night before, at least not unless he had to.

'He's strange, don't you think?' Marcellinus went on in a musing tone. 'Why was such a man sent on an assignment like this? He's not a native and he's only been in the province for a short time.'

Castus was not fooled. The envoy clearly knew more than he pretended, but he wanted to probe for a response without giving away his own position. Castus remained silent. Marcellinus waited a moment more, before turning suddenly, drawing himself up and tipping his head back.

'Centurion, I'm glad you came to me with your concerns. I wasn't sure, I confess, whether you knew about our friend Strabo or not... whether you were, shall we say... one of his *familiars...*'

Castus tightened his jaw at the implication, anger rising in his throat; he was satisfied to see the envoy flinch instinctively and step back.

'Forgive me,' Marcellinus said, inclining his head as if in apology. 'But it's reassuring to know I'm not alone in my suspicions. It seems I must go and talk to Strabo, man to man, and ask him to explain himself. I would like you to accompany me.'

'Why?'

'Because I want the meeting to appear more official than merely personal, perhaps. And because what he tells us might be of great importance once we travel into the north. Will you come with me?'

It was more an order than a request, but Castus nodded. 'Should I arm myself first?'

'I don't think that will be necessary. Hopefully we won't need to murder him.'

They crossed the street from the compound and entered the house opposite. There were two storeys, built around a little pillared courtyard; Marcellinus tossed his cloak to a slave in the entrance hall and then led Castus up the stairs to a door at the end of the corridor. He knocked and waited until they heard the voice of Strabo from inside.

'Gentlemen, come in,' the secretary said. He looked flustered, and quickly dusted the knees of his breeches, as if he had just been kneeling. 'Can I offer you some wine, perhaps?'

'No thanks,' Marcellinus replied. He seated himself on a stool by the window. Castus leaned back against the door.

'In what capacity were you sent on this assignment?' the envoy asked, hard and direct. Strabo raised an eyebrow, then he sat down on a divan piled with bedding.

'As the governor's representative, of course...'

'A position of great trust for a mere secretary, no? Tell me plainly, Strabo. What is your rank and station?'

As he watched, Castus saw a swift change come over the secretary: the baffled act fell away, and instead he appeared suddenly more controlled and focused.

'You tell me, envoy. Since you seem to have your suspicions already.'

Marcellinus smiled. He turned to address Castus now. 'Centurion,' he said, 'have you ever heard of the *agentes in rebus*?'

'No,' Castus replied, shrugging against the door. The title sounded so bland it could mean anything, or nothing.

'They're a corps of imperial messengers and investigators. They operate in great secrecy, and take their orders from the Office of Notaries and the emperor himself. One of their agents is placed in every provincial governor's staff.'

'Spies, you mean?' Castus pushed himself away from the door with his shoulders. The top of his head brushed the low ceiling. Strabo was smiling to himself.

'Not spies exactly, no,' the secretary said. 'But your guess is correct, envoy. I am an imperial agent, as you suspect. I was despatched eighteen months ago from the court in Treveris to investigate the loyalties of Aurelius Arpagius, governor of this province. Now I have been ordered to accompany you and... make sure everything proceeds in accordance with the emperor's wishes.'

'So why did you go to that house in town last night?' Castus demanded. He had taken a step forward as he spoke. Marcellinus frowned, raising a calming hand.

'So it was you that followed me?' Strabo said. 'I thought somebody did. But I guessed you would send one of your men, or a slave, rather than do it yourself.'

'Where did he go?' Marcellinus asked abruptly, confused. 'What is this?'

'He went to a house – I don't know why. There were symbols scratched on the door. Something like a ship, and a sun-wheel thing. An X with a line through it.'

Marcellinus paused, still frowning. Then he suddenly threw back his head and laughed. 'Oh, wonderful!' he cried.

'What I do, or believe, is none of your concern,' Strabo said quietly. 'My loyalties to the emperors are beyond question.'

'I don't understand,' Castus said.

Marcellinus was grinning, teeth clenched. 'Those were Christian symbols,' he said. 'Our friend Strabo is the follower of an *illicit superstition*!'

'Such a term proves your ignorance,' Strabo said, with more anger than his expression suggested. 'My faith is sincere, as are my loyalties!'

Castus knew little about Christianity. It was a secret religious cult, and its followers denied the gods and the authority of the emperors, and went into tombs to worship the ghosts of executed criminals and eat the flesh of the dead. More importantly, it was illegal. Shortly before the Persian war there had been an order discharging Christians from the legions without honour. Then, a few years later, an imperial edict had outlawed the practices of the cult entirely. But in the military fortresses of the Danube there had been little visible sign of it. Could there really be Christians in Coria? Castus felt a cold churning in his stomach. Such men were clearly deluded idiots, but possibly they were also traitorous, even dangerous. Being in the same room with one now was alarming.

'To be frank, I'm not too concerned about your faith,' Marcellinus said. 'You can believe whatever sordid fantasies you wish. Just keep it to yourself. I trust the centurion here is a tolerant man?'

Castus just grunted. He could only speak for himself, but he worried about the effect on his men if they found out.

'I'm not afraid of you,' Strabo said with a cool tone. 'Believe me, I've suffered more for the truth than you can know. But our Augustus Constantius is also a tolerant man, and has shown an inspired lack of the persecuting fervour so common in his imperial colleagues.'

'So he sent you here, out of the way? Very convenient for everyone. I had believed that the imperial service was purged of all your fellow cultists... But no matter. Now everything's out in the open. Or is there more you'd like to disclose?'

'No, nothing more. But, as for my role – we all have our orders. Just like you, envoy. And you, centurion. My own orders require me to keep silent on many matters. I hope you can respect that, as you respect the emperor I am glad to serve.'

'Very well,' Marcellinus said, standing up. 'I'm glad we understand each other, *Agent* Strabo.'

They reached the Wall of Hadrian at dawn the next day. It was misty, and the fortifications appeared suddenly ahead of them, a hard pale line of stone in all that empty grey. As they drew closer, Castus could make out the huts and sheds lining the road that led up to the single gate. The smell of cooking fires too – neither he nor his men had breakfasted yet, and his guts tightened.

Marcellinus rode forward and spoke to the decurion of the cavalry detachment on guard, while Castus and his men stood and stamped in the damp morning chill. Then the gates swung open, and they moved on along the road into the borderland beyond.

There was no change, at first, in the landscape. Fields to either side, and small farms or homesteads. All this country, Castus knew, had been part of the empire once. Now the tribes of the border were Roman allies, settled and peaceable – or so Marcellinus had claimed. He said that they would meet a party of these tribesmen a day or two further north, who would accompany them to the Pictish chiefs' meeting. Castus was wary of that idea – far better to keep themselves apart from the locals, he thought. Nobody outside the bounds of Roman control could be trusted. But Marcellinus understood their ways, and they would all have to trust in that understanding now. Castus would also have to trust in the interpreter that Marcellinus had hired at Coria, a weaselly Briton with a nervous twitch, named Caccumattus. The little man claimed to be of the Textoverdi tribe, and to speak the language of the Picts fluently, but his Latin was poor enough for Castus to be dubious of his value.

It was a hard day's march. The road ran straight as ever, but the horizons rose on either side to bare brown hills, craggy with rock outcrops. The farmland fell away behind them, and they climbed across windy uplands with the sky huge and tumbling with clouds above. At the day's end they reached the outpost fort of Bremenium, a white-walled bastion on the edge of nowhere. The garrison was made up of frontier scouts, tough wiry men on native ponies, most of them Britons from the mountains in the west of the province. Six of them were ordered by their commander to join the envoy's party – they would act as forward scouts and guides on the roads ahead.

At dawn Castus assembled his men in formation before the gates of the fort. Fifty-eight blue-black shields emblazoned with the winged Victory emblem. Fifty-eight armoured bodies, fifty-eight upright spears. He drew himself up stiffly before them, throwing his voice to challenge the breeze coming in across the hillside.

'Men, this is the last outpost of Rome!' He sounded hoarse, and the wind whined at his back. 'From now on, whatever you might have heard, we'll be in enemy country. Remember that, and act accordingly. We might run into some locals along the way, but don't forget they're barbarians. Treat them with respect, but keep your distance. And don't get any ideas about any blue-painted ladies you might happen to meet either – if you want to keep your balls where they're needed!'

A few smiles, a ragged laugh. Castus had overheard some of the men back in Coria debating the possible wantonness of the native women.

'We've got a hard march still ahead of us,' he said, raising his voice to reach the men watching from the fort wall. 'Five days at least. We'll be camping in the open, so we'll be making defensive enclosures every night and setting regular watches. You've been trained for it, so you know what to do. But keep this in mind, all of you: we're representing Rome from now on, and the honour of the Sixth Legion. Don't let your guard down. Don't get careless. I want you all as smart and tight as you would be on pay parade!'

Pacing before the front-rank men, he scanned their faces as he passed, trying to read their expressions. The optio, Timotheus, stern and alert. Evagrius, with the century standard across his shoulder. Atrectus looking half-asleep. The *cornicen* Volusius with his big curled horn ready to give the signal. Vincentius and Culchianus frowning beneath their helmets. All of them grey-faced, uncertain behind the mask of duty. Castus glanced away, composing himself. *Unconquered Sun*, he silently prayed, *Bringer of light and life, let me lead these men well. Let me return them all safely when this is done.*

'As I said, this is a peaceful diplomatic mission.' He smiled, and some of the men smiled with him. He was glad of that. 'But we're soldiers, and we're going into enemy country, so we're under war discipline from now on. Does everyone understand me?'

A chorus of dull mumbling from the assembled men. Castus slapped his staff into his meaty palm. 'Speak up!' he shouted. 'We're going to war. Act like it!'

'Understood!' the men called back, eagerly now.

A heartbeat's pause, a glance away at the empty hillsides, the brown heather.

'Sixth Legion,' he shouted, 'are you ready for war?'

'Ready!' the traditional cry came back.

'Are you ready for war?'

'Ready!'

'ARE YOU READY FOR WAR?'

'READY!'

The echo of their voices died over the hillside, into the wind.

'Optio, form up the men. Cornicen, prepare to sound the advance.'

Behind him, fifty-eight men assembled into marching formation as the slaves drew the pack mules together. The mounted scouts trotted forwards onto the flanks, edging the road. Marcellinus and Strabo nudged their horses into motion.

'Ad-*vance*!'

The horn rang out, a sustained double note, and a last cheer went up from the men in the fort as the century swung forward in march step.

They moved off, a small column in the great emptiness of the landscape, dwindling slowly until the sentries on the gatehouse saw them vanish into the far distance and the sound of their marching feet faded to nothing.

CHAPTER V

'Friends or foes? What do you think?'

'We'll find out soon enough,' Castus replied. Timotheus nodded grimly as both of them watched the scouts crossing the stream and galloping back towards them.

All day the conical hill had been visible on the flat horizon, the two blunt peaks to either side giving it the look of a misshapen head rising between massive hunched shoulders. Now they were close enough to make out the scattering of fires on the slopes below the hill, tiny sparks in the dimness of late afternoon, and the figures that moved around the fires.

Marcellinus spurred his horse forward as the scouts approached, riding down to meet them. Castus watched, dubious. Behind him, the men of the century waited on the ridge, shields readied, silent. Marcellinus galloped back.

'It's as I'd hoped,' he called out. 'Senomaglus, chief of the Votadini, with a party of his men. They'll escort us up to the Pictish meeting.'

'We don't need an escort,' Castus said. 'And neither do you, envoy.'

Marcellinus was grinning, leaning from the saddle. 'Don't worry,' he said. 'Senomaglus is a friend of Rome, a good man. I knew him well, many years ago. It's a mark of respect for his men to accompany us.'

'How many men?'

'Around a hundred, the scout said.'

Castus whistled between his teeth. 'Can't we keep our distance?'

'Not without giving offence. Form your men up and follow. There's a good camping ground two miles on beside the river.'

'Wait...' Castus called, but the envoy had already wheeled his horse and plunged away towards the stream, his cloak flying out behind him. Castus jutted two fingers at the pair of mounted scouts, then pointed away after Marcellinus. The two men saluted and cantered away again after the envoy.

'Form up,' he said to Timotheus. 'Double pace – let's go.'

If he had been expecting savages, he was disappointed. Senomaglus of the Votadini resembled a prosperous Gallic wine merchant, or even a retired legionary: clean-shaven, with close-cropped white hair and a tanned vigorous face. His clothes were neat and well cut, and there was a heavy gold torque at his neck, not unlike the one Castus himself wore. His warriors were a little more exotic: long-haired, some bearded, in long tunics knotted between the thighs, but they looked very much like the more rustic Britons of the Roman province. Castus had seen men like that every day in the fields and villages around Eboracum. These carried spears and small square shields, but there was little else to mark them out as barbarians.

The two parties faced each other on the level ground between the hill and the river. Marcellinus and the Votadini chief rode forward, met, and embraced from the saddle, both grinning like long-lost friends.

'Well, he is an allied ruler, I suppose,' Castus said. 'Timotheus, three times *long life* for the envoy's friend!'

The optio gave the order, and the legionaries threw up their hands in salute, crying out *vivat, vivat, vivat* in a martial yell. The effect on the Votadini was almost amusing: they fell back a pace, raising their shields, until they realised they were not about to be attacked. Castus hid his smirk as the barbarians, chastened, gave a ragged cheer in response.

The camping ground was rutted with the marks of old fortifications. Clearly Roman armies had passed through here before. There had once been a fort too; everywhere the turf and long grass was broken by chunks of moss-covered masonry. It wasn't surprising, Castus thought: it was an excellent location, and for the last two days they had been following the remains of the old road into the north. Strange to think of other men like him, other legionaries like his own, marching across this land generations ago. He wondered where their bones lay now – back home in a funerary urn, or lost somewhere in these dull green hills?

By evening they had set up the tent lines in an angle of the old fortifications, dug scratch trenches to mark off the defensive perimeter and sent a party of men with the slaves to the river to draw water. The cooking fires smoked, and the mounted scouts groomed their horses. Castus sat on a folding stool outside his tent, dictating the daily report to Evagrius: *Fifteen miles marched, direction north-west, no injuries, weather fair. Meeting with tribal host of Votadini.* The standard-bearer passed him the tablet, and he gave the indecipherable scribble scored into the wax a cursory glance and handed it back. He mused for a moment on all the other centurions who must have filled in their reports and muster rolls in this place, once upon a time. It was a comforting thought. Throwing up his arms, he yawned loudly and stretched, feeling the muscles of his shoulders bunch around his ears. The camp was filled with

91

a low golden light, peculiar to this country. Unfortunately it was also filled with tiny flying insects, which darted around his head, drawn to the sweat of his scalp. Swatting, cursing, he ate his cold meat and hardtack, drank his vinegar wine and waited for Marcellinus to return from the Votadini camp.

'Centurion? Do you mind if I sit with you?'

It was Strabo. The little secretary – *imperial agent*, Castus reminded himself – was considerably less dapper now than when they had left Eboracum together. His beard was wilder, and he had taken to wearing a native cloak of dogtooth checks. Castus had not spoken to him for the last three days, since the debate at Coria.

'I don't mind,' he said, and fetched a second folding stool from his tent.

'I wanted to apologise,' Strabo said, once he was seated, 'if I seemed rude back in Coria. I don't blame you for following me – you were concerned, of course, about the integrity of our assignment. Ironic, isn't it, that it should be *you* spying on *me*!'

He laughed, sounding ill at ease. Castus continued chewing his last hunk of hard bread.

'But I don't take you for a malicious man, centurion. Your intentions were good, you were not merely... *prying*. So, I'm sorry if I took it badly.'

Castus nodded, and then swallowed thickly. 'Tell me something,' he asked. 'This... religion of yours' – he glanced around quickly, but none of the men were within earshot – 'this *Christian* thing... What's it all about? I mean, what do you do?'

'What do we do? The same as any other men. We are not such strange beings. We believe in one God, and in the mercy of His son, who died for our sins.'

'Sins?' Castus said. He had a peculiar taste in his mouth, and took another slug of sour wine. 'Like what? I mean... is it true that you eat the flesh of the dead?'

Strabo threw back his head and laughed, genuinely amused. Castus frowned darkly. He had not been aware that it was a joke.

'You refer to the blessed sacrament of the *eucharist*,' Strabo said, smiling. 'No, it does not involve actual flesh-eating – that is an old, old calumny!'

'A what...? Well, never mind. But how can you serve the emperors when you don't believe in the gods?'

Strabo sucked his cheek, his beard twitching. 'My brothers have debated that question for hundreds of years,' he said.

Castus raised an eyebrow, puzzled. Had there really been Christians for hundreds of years? He'd had no idea.

'What I believe,' the secretary went on, 'is that our duties to the world of the spirit and our duties to the world of the flesh – the material world, I should say, to avoid misunderstandings – are quite separate. Where they do not contradict, we can give our allegiance and our service to the earthly powers. *To Caesar render what is his*, as our teacher said. In my case, I serve the Augustus Constantius willingly and with love. He is the only one of the emperors to have never seriously persecuted the faithful. A man of great wisdom and foresight. And so, by serving him I serve justice and truth, and by extension I serve God. As do we all.'

Castus felt unable to meet Strabo's inquisitive gaze. The conversation was unsettling his guts, and he wished he had not raised the subject.

'Is your god also in this place, then?' he said, flinging out a hand at the hills, the river, the broken turf.

'God is everywhere. His power is infinite. But surely you would agree – do you not worship one god yourself? The being you call the Unconquered Sun?'

'The Sun gives life,' Castus replied quickly. He touched his brow, as if to ward off an ill omen. 'The Sun is the chief of the gods. All the others draw their power from him. So I suppose, anyway. He watches over the soldiers – it's tradition.'

'And tradition is important to you?'

'Of course!' Castus glanced up at the man, baffled. How could he ask such strange questions? 'Tradition is all that makes us civilised. The old ways are always best.'

'Ah, yes, the old ways. And here we are, surrounded by them...' Strabo glanced away at the ruined fortifications in the grass, the layering of old ditches and walls growing indistinguishable in the dusk. 'Consider,' he said, 'how many Roman armies have passed this way, how many legions, all with their dreams of glory, their certainty of victory... What remains of them now? Maybe one day all our works will be like this. Nothing more than hummocks in the turf, for savages to wonder over!'

Castus snorted, deep in his throat. Fantastical idea, he thought. Then again, perhaps this man wanted the empire to fall? Perhaps he even prayed for it, in his secret gatherings...

'Aren't you afraid they'll punish you?' he said.

'Who? The law, or your gods? I have no fear of either. Death is nothing to one who believes, centurion. The grave is merely a gateway to resurrection, and the bliss of the hereafter. But what about you – what do you think lies on the far side of death?'

'Nothing much,' Castus said. 'Just darkness, forgetting. The end of light. It doesn't matter – it's what we do here that's important.' He stamped his foot on the turf. 'That's how people remember us, and that's how we're judged. Were we loyal and strong? Did we do our duty like men? Did we fight well when we had to? Anything else is vanity.'

'You're almost a philosopher, I think,' Strabo said. Castus stared hard at him, eager that he should not be mocked. But now Marcellinus was approaching, riding across the meadow from the Votadini camp, and Strabo was smiling, getting up and smoothing his tunic.

'I hope our talk has laid to rest any doubts you may have, anyway,' he said. 'My business is with the envoy, and the success of our mission. I hope we can strive together towards that end.'

Castus nodded, and the agent took his leave and walked away towards his tent. Night was falling, the perimeter of the camp lost in gathering gloom, and the smouldering fires were drawing masses of whirling insects. Timotheus would lead the first watch – Castus was glad of that. The talk of death, spirits, strange and secret beliefs had unsettled his mind, and the lonely darkness of the ruined fortification seemed a less comforting place now.

For two days more they crawled north through the hill country, still following the track of the old road. The men of the Sixth Legion marched in a compact mass, surrounding their baggage mules, with the scouts riding at the flanks. The Votadini warriors flowed around them in wild array, running on ahead and streaming to either side over the flanks of the hills. Some of them, mounted on their shaggy little ponies, rode alongside the Romans and called out to them; many of the soldiers knew the native British language, and some called back, but Castus soon ordered them to keep silence. The Votadini might be allies, but he didn't want his men striking up bonds with them.

At the end of the second day they reached the sea, the water spreading a sheet of dull silver in the low light. It was the mouth of an estuary, Marcellinus said, leading to the river that would take them to the Pictish meeting place. Here too there were old fortifications on the hill above the shore – this whole country was scarred with the welts of Roman camps and forts and roads – and once again the legionaries camped within the circuit of the fallen walls. The Votadini host whooped and sang from their own fires on the lower slopes of the hill.

'Why are they going to the meeting too?' Castus asked Marcellinus. They were sitting beside the fire in darkness, swatting at the insects. 'The Votadini aren't Picts, are they?'

'No, but they have treaties with them, as do we,' the envoy replied. 'They're brother peoples anyway – the Picts speak a dialect of the British language. They look different, but they have many links between them. Senomaglus is attending the meeting as a guest – he can't vote on the high chieftainship, but he's expected to approve it. As am I, of course.'

'They vote for their chiefs?' Castus asked. From the perimeter he heard the sentry's cry. The smell of the sea, rich and exotic, rose on the night breeze.

'Oh, yes. In fact, they have an odd system for it. A chief cannot be succeeded by his own son, only by a male relative from the female line. So a brother, for example, or a cousin on his mother's side.'

'Makes the women quite powerful, then?'

'Very astute! Yes, it does. They can't rule directly, but they have a lot of influence. But it's a good system, if an odd one. The Picts claim it avoids dynasties – they're very keen on their freedom, and don't like monopolies of rule – but more importantly it gives them a large number of mature experienced candidates to choose from. Rome has often suffered from underage emperors succeeding their fathers.'

'I suppose so.' Castus winged his shoulders. He remembered the governor, Arpagius, telling him that the barbarians may not understand the abdication of the old Augusti. Might take it as a sign of weakness. Perhaps they were more sophisticated than that after all?

'So what have you learned from our allies then?' he asked, poking at the fire with a stick. 'About what's going on. Did the old Pictish king die naturally, or what?'

Sparks rose, lighting Marcellinus's face. Since crossing the border, the envoy seemed to have shed part of himself – part of his Romanness. He looked more like one of the Votadini now than a former Roman military commander.

'We know nothing certain,' he said carefully. 'But there are suspicions. Vepogenus was a strong man, an honourable man. He was my friend and my brother by pact, and the news of his death genuinely pained me. But he had a lot of enemies among the tribes. There are also some others among them who… make it their business to stir old animosities.'

'The renegades.' Castus scowled into the glow of the fire.

'Yes. Strabo must have told you about them. There were three of them, but two killed each other and now only one lives that I know of. A former officer of mine, a Pannonian like you, I think. His name is Julius Decentius.'

'Was it him that killed your boy?'

Castus saw the envoy visibly flinch as his words registered.

'I don't know,' Marcellinus said quietly. 'I don't want to know either. But he could have been connected with the king's death. Not alone, though – he would need to work through the ambitions of others. Personally, I believe that the news of Diocletian and Maximian's abdication provided a spur to a plot against the king. This renegade convinced certain others that the empire would be weak, and this would be a good time to strike at us. Only Vepogenus's loyalty to the treaty stood in their way.'

'Any idea who the others might be?'

'Perhaps. A cousin of the king, named Talorcagus. I've met him, a very reckless man. He also has a nephew, Drustagnus, who if anything is worse. The king's own nephew, Vendognus, is a weak and stupid young man, but he has a strong-willed wife, a cousin of his, who may have plans for her own son in the succession. Perhaps all of them are working together. We'll soon find out.'

The list of unfamiliar and barbarous names clotted in the air, and Castus doubted he would ever tell one from the others. Back at Eboracum, he had made a few attempts to pick up the local speech, but he had no skill with languages. Latin, a bit of Greek: that was all he had ever needed, and the gargling vowels and slippery-sounding consonants of the British tongue meant nothing to him. But he gave an understanding grunt. Treachery and backstabbing deceit took the same form all over the world, after all, in any language.

The next morning Castus put his men through a full weapons drill on the grassy plain before the old fort, both to keep them in shape and to impress the watching barbarians. Formation march, shield wall, testudo and skirmish line, then dart and javelin release and charge in the wedge formation they called the boar's head. The legionaries responded well, still sharp after twelve days on the road. The Votadini seemed impressed too, whooping and yelling their encouragement at first, then falling quiet when they saw the disciplined force of the Roman attack.

As he formed up his men in line of march once more, Castus felt an enthusiastic energy charging his body. How many years had it been since this savage shore had witnessed Roman troops in battle order? Then he saw Marcellinus, watching from horseback with an appreciative smile, and remembered that this man too had brought an army into this land.

All that day they marched west along the shore of the estuary. Everywhere the ground rose and knotted into the traces of old fortifications, the marks of Rome. All of it lost in a wilderness now, fallen and forgotten. It was awe-inspiring, and somehow deadening. Castus remembered what Strabo had said in the camp beneath the three peaks: all this great work, all this effort, counting for nothing. By late afternoon they had turned north again, and towards the day's end they crossed a massive ditch and earth rampart, still clearly visible as it stretched away to the west.

'Do you know what this is?' Marcellinus called, sitting on his horse at the rampart's crest. 'This is the wall of Antoninus, or what's left of it. The furthest limit of Roman power, about a century and a half ago. Beyond this we're into Pictland!'

That evening they camped in the open, and the scouts brought in an ox and a pair of rams they had caught wandering near the old wall. Castus formed the men up at sunset, and they built a rough altar and gave sacrifice to Mars, Jupiter and Sol. Marcellinus took the priestly role, despatching the victim animals with careful dignity, then Castus led the men in the shouted acclamations as the smoke of the altar swirled the smell of fresh blood and cooking meat around them.

Strabo had not been present for the ceremony; Castus saw him shortly afterwards, wandering back into camp with a grave expression. He was angered by the man's attitude: whatever his private beliefs, surely he could see the need for unity at a time like this? But the ceremony had done what he wanted. They had asked the gods' permission to proceed, and no ill omens had been detected. The men's spirits were better, with the end of the road in sight.

* * *

'Roman friends!' the Votadini chief cried the next morning in his terrible Latin. 'You come! We go now. We meet Picti! Come – follow!'

With a wide sweeping gesture he turned his horse northwards. It was misty, and the pack mules stamped and shivered as the slaves secured the tents and kit on their backs. To the east the first rays of the sun were breaking the grey line of the horizon.

'Fall in – prepare to march,' Castus called. Then the horn sounded and the last stage of their journey began.

For six miles they followed a straight track across level country, water meadows and patches of forest. This was land long uncultivated, a true border. To the north and east the river looped and shone in the low sunlight, while to the west there were hills and high moorlands dark on the horizon. The Romans marched in close formation, weapons ready; even the Votadini had closed ranks, growing less boisterously confident now they had left their own territories and moved into the land of the Picts. Marcellinus was riding on ahead, tall and straight-backed on his black horse, with the Votadini chief riding at his side and his two slaves coming on behind with thick green branches raised over their heads. At Castus's back, every soldier's spear was tipped with a sprig of green leaves, the mark of peaceful intent.

'We've got company,' Timotheus said quietly as they approached a ford across the river.

'I've seen them,' Castus replied. For the last mile he had been noticing the figures among the trees lining the road: men in short tunics carrying spears, running. One of them dashed out onto the verge; for a moment Castus thought the man's face was heavily scarred, then he saw that the marks were deliberate, dark lines scored into his cheeks and forehead. The effect was alien, even inhuman. Castus fought down a shiver of superstitious dread. *They're only men*, he told himself. *Nothing we can't handle.*

The envoy splashed through the ford and rode up onto the track on the far side. A larger group of the tattooed men gathered on the road before him, parting as he approached. Where was Strabo? Castus wanted to look behind him, but feared that his men would notice his anxiety. Already they had begun bunching together, stumbling into each other.

'Order your ranks!' he called over his shoulder as they gained the dry ground on the other side of the river. 'Keep formation back there!'

The ground rose to the north-east, and a line of huge craggy hills sealed the horizon, brown and purple in the afternoon sun. From the woods to one side of the road dashed a small flimsy-looking two-wheeled cart of bent wood and wicker, drawn by a pair of shaggy ponies. A warrior stood upright in the back, brandishing a spear, his face fiercely scarred. There were more and more of these warriors now, lining the road, swirling around the marching column.

'This is looking bad,' Timotheus said through tight lips. Up ahead, Marcellinus was still riding forward, apparently unmoved by the Picts on all sides. Castus had assumed, back in Eboracum, that the tribal meeting would be a small gathering, a group of chieftains in a hut, or around some standing stone. Now things were beginning to look very different. The hills and woods to either side thronged with barbarians.

They crested a rise, and a wide valley opened before them, below the craggy hills. A river lined with trees rushed along the valley floor, with open slopes to either side. And the valley was full of men.

'Jupiter's cock and balls!' said Timotheus quietly. 'There are thousands of them!'

'Looks that way.'

The column had drawn to a halt on the road, the legionaries shuffling together, muttering and exclaiming. Before them, the encampments of the Pictish chiefs appeared to cover the far side of the valley, knots of warriors everywhere across the hills and waiting beside the road.

'We've got to stop Marcellinus,' Castus said quickly, 'before he leads us right into the middle of that lot... Culchianus! Jog on up to the envoy and tell him to wait. I need to speak to him.'

Culchianus saluted and ran down the slope after Marcellinus.

'Where's Strabo got to?' Castus demanded.

'Back with the mules, centurion, walking beside his horse. Reckon he wants to keep his head down!'

Up ahead, Castus saw the soldier catch up with Marcellinus. The envoy reined in his horse and looked back up the road.

'Vincentius, run back to Strabo and request his pony off him. If he won't ride, I will.' Castus called over the two nearest mounted scouts. He remembered their names now, Buccus and Brigonius. 'You two, stay with me. We're going down to survey that valley. Timotheus, keep the men moving, but slowly as you can.'

Vincentius came back with Strabo's pony, and Castus swung himself up into the saddle. Like all legionaries, he had been trained to ride, but had never been much good at it. Heavy and clumsy, his toes dangling, he jogged the animal into motion. It was an effort to stay upright in the saddle – don't slip now, he told himself, clinging grimly to the reins. Falling off his horse in full view of hundreds of barbarians would not be a good start.

'Centurion, why have you halted your men?' Marcellinus looked annoyed – Castus guessed that the delay did not suit his notion of diplomatic dignity.

'We need to find a secure defensive position on this side of the Pictish camp.' He was sweating heavily, struggling to stay on the pony as the animal tossed its head and tugged at the reins.

'The Picts have already assigned us a camping ground, over there on the far slope. We risk giving offence if we refuse it. Order your men on.'

Castus gritted his teeth, tried to keep his voice level. 'Dominus, with respect, that isn't a good idea. My responsibility is to the safety of my men. We need to keep them clear of the Picts and make sure we can hold our line of retreat.'

Marcellinus gazed down at him from his high horse, his expression darkening. Clearly he was not used to taking directions from his subordinates. The Votadini chief was watching with a look of veiled amusement.

'Very well,' the envoy said. 'You see to your men, and I will proceed into the camp and present myself to the chiefs of the assembly. I will rejoin you at your selected position before sundown.'

He jerked the reins and kicked his horse forward into a trot. Castus motioned for one of the scouts to go with him, then jogged the pony after them, cursing under his breath.

The track descended the flank of the hill and crossed the level ground before dipping again to a ford over the stream. Between the ford and the track there was a low steep-sided hillock, and Castus could make out what appeared to be a stone wall along the crest. Swinging his arm to the scout behind him, he urged his unwilling mount up the slope. At the top he slipped from the saddle and dropped heavily onto the springy turf.

'This looks like it,' he said as the scout cantered easily up behind him. The top of the hillock was dry and level, ringed with a knee-high oval of piled stones enclosing an area of about sixty paces by forty. A sheepfold, Castus guessed, but it had not been used for a long time. The wall had collapsed in places, and the ground inside the circuit was littered with stray stones and lumps of dried sheep droppings. He scanned the surroundings, assessing: level ground to the west and south, and a steep drop down to the bend of the stream and the ford to the north and east. No trees along the stream to provide cover for an attacking enemy. The ground on the far side of the valley rose higher, but it was well out of range of the longest bowshot.

Castus wiped his brow. He could make out the column of legionaries coming slowly down the flank of the hill to the south-west, the leaves on their spears giving them the look of a small copse on the move, and ordered the scout to ride back and tell Timotheus where to lead them. Then he stood in the centre of the stone enclosure, gazing at the surrounding land. From the top of the hillock he could clearly see the main Pictish camp on the far side of the stream, a few large huts surrounded by a mass of crude temporary shelters, fogged by the smoke of cooking fires. The little carts – chariots, he guessed – dashed out and back.

Now he had the chance, he was able to study the appearance of the Picts more closely. Many of them resembled their Votadini brethren, or the Britons from further south. But there were some among them who were clearly the elite warriors, the nobles and their retinues, and they looked quite different. They wore the same short tunics and heavy cloaks as the commoners, leaving their arms and legs bare, and carried small square shields, short swords and leaf-bladed spears with a round brass ball instead of a butt-spike. But their faces, and the exposed flesh of their bodies, were covered in scar-pictures, curling shapes and animal patterns, some picked out in bright colours dyed onto the skin. The older men wore spade-shaped beards and thick moustaches, and with their cheeks shaved they had the look of goats. The sides of their heads were shaved too, and the long hair at the top matted together with greyish clay into a stiff comb, which hung down at the nape of the neck.

Already Castus was assessing them with a soldier's eye, weighing up their strength and numbers. About two or three thousand in the valley, that he could see. Probably more in the surrounding woods and hills. They had no missile weapons that he could make out, aside from light javelins, and the little carts seemed to be designed more for transport than as effective fighting machines. For all their bold display, there was no apparent discipline amongst them; they had the numbers to be a formidable threat, but against even a cohort of trained soldiers the odds might be evened. He didn't have a cohort, but the thought was some comfort.

By the time his men had climbed the slope and crossed the low wall into the enclosure, Castus had recovered from the unfamiliar exertion of his ride. He stood with feet firmly planted, fists on hips, gripping his staff.

'Optio, form the men into fatigue parties,' he called. 'I want twenty men on sentry-watch around the position, the rest clearing this space of stones and sheep shit and piling the rocks back around the perimeter wall. Then six men down to the river to draw water and collect firewood, tent-lines and horse paddock marked out and fires lit. Have the slaves dig latrine pits on the south-east slope, downstream from our watering place. And get that shrubbery off the spears too. Watchword is *Securitas*.'

As Timotheus saluted and gave the orders, Castus turned to survey the Pictish encampment opposite. Whatever threat might come, whether these barbarians were peaceful or hostile, he was determined to be ready.

* * *

Marcellinus returned an hour later, as the evening shadows stretched long across the turf. The big leather tents were already erected, the fires smoked and spat, and the men of the Sixth Legion not on guard duty were busy cleaning their weapons and kit. Castus met the envoy outside his own tent, raised in the centre of the enclosure.

'An effective little fortress you have here,' Marcellinus said, swinging down from his horse. 'I'm sure the Picts are most impressed.'

They should be, Castus thought. *Most of the barbarians have surely never seen Roman legionaries in the field.* But he kept his views to himself.

'I've presented my greetings to the assembly of chiefs. We're just in time, actually – the first meeting is to be held tonight, an hour after sundown. There'll be a feast, and an initial discussion. I'll attend, of course, with Strabo. I'd like you and two of your men to come with me, centurion.'

Castus nodded, curt. This was Marcellinus's field, of course, and not his. Whatever his own views might be on the wisdom of walking into the heart of a barbarian gathering – especially one so filled with tension and grief – he knew he should keep them to himself. Marcellinus was the diplomat, after all.

'Vincentius and Culchianus,' he called, pacing across the camp enclosure, 'you're taking escort duty with me. No need for mail, but get the rest of your kit shined up nice.'

Back in his tent, he stripped off his sweat-stained red-brown tunic and changed to one of clean white wool. He cleaned and waxed his boots and belt, oiled and polished his sword and helmet. He fixed the tall crest of red horsehair to the helmet's ridge.

As the twilight gathered in the valley below the camp, and the last strokes of evening sun lay on the brown hillsides, Castus stood at the gate of his little fortification, flanked by his two men. Tension was massing in his shoulders, and his guts felt hard and tight. He eased the sword in his scabbard, raising the pommel and dropping it back. He flexed the muscles of his arms, stretched and breathed deeply.

Marcellinus strode towards him, followed by Strabo and the slaves.

'So, then,' the envoy announced. 'Let us go and present ourselves to the Picts!'

CHAPTER VI

In his years with the legions Castus had seen barbarians of many kinds: the long-haired howling Goths and the Carpi of the grasslands north of the Danube; the sinewy horse-archers that rode for the Persians; the Dacians and Iazyges he had seen as a boy in the muddy streets of Taurunum. But none of them had appeared as savage as the Picts, none so obviously glorying in their own barbarism.

Now, as the Roman party climbed the slope from the stream in the gathering darkness, the Picts were all around them. The encampment had no wall or obvious boundary; the gathering of men just grew thicker, until they walked along an avenue of warriors, some of them standing in carts, lit by the flames of fires and torches. Dogs snarled and circled between men's legs. Castus glanced back at his two legionaries and saw Vincentius staring at the barbarians in fearful wonderment.

'Eyes front,' he hissed through tight lips. 'Keep your heads up. Remember you're Roman soldiers.'

They approached the large structure at the centre of the encampment, a hut or hall, low under its roof of turf and bracken. Smoke swirled around it, and from inside came a guttural voice rising and falling in a kind of song. The figures on either side fell back, closing behind the Roman party to form a ring around the open doorway.

'Best leave your two men and the slaves out here,' Marcellinus said quietly. 'You can come on inside with Strabo and me.'

Castus gave his orders to the two legionaries, quickly and quietly. 'Remain here, don't move, don't talk to anybody and don't eat or drink anything they give you. Understood?'

'Understood, centurion,' Culchianus said grimly. Vincentius just nodded.

A loud voice cried out from inside the hall, then came a stir of other voices.

'We're announced,' Marcellinus said. 'Follow me.'

Ducking his head, Castus followed Strabo and the envoy through the low doorway of the hall. The smell hit him first, catching in his throat. A lifetime spent in the packed fug of army barrack rooms had deadened his senses to most bad aromas, but this was something else again: a concentration of bodies, woodsmoke and damp dogs, with something rotting underneath it all. A raw, animal stink that made his eyes water and his stomach clench.

He stumbled, caught at an upright post, and as he blinked the smart from his eyes he saw the rough oval chamber with the fire at its heart. It resembled a cave, with a ribbed ceiling of sticks sloping down on all sides. Around the fire a ring of men were seated on stools and log-benches, with others assembled behind them at the gloomy margins of the hall. Standing beside the fire was a ragged figure in a cloak, reddish twists of hair sticking up around his head like a rusty laurel wreath. He had paused as the Romans entered; now he went on with his cracked song, flinging out his arms, clawing at the air.

'What's he going on about?' Castus whispered, leaning forward. Marcellinus had taken a seat in the ring around the central fire.

'He's singing the praises of Vepogenus,' the envoy answered without moving his lips. 'Quite a lengthy saga.'

The assembled chiefs listened intently, rocking in their seats, gasping and sighing at particularly impassioned moments. Castus stood as far back as he could, his skull touching the low sloping ceiling. Strabo was beside him, pressing his chin down into the fold of his cloak, trying to look unobtrusive.

Eventually, the song died to a finish, the ragged bard clutching his hands to his face and twisting his body as he let out a last piteous moan, then dropping to sit on the ground. The assembly broke into wild applause, the chiefs shouting and clashing their drinking cups together.

'Went down well,' Castus muttered. He saw Strabo's neat smile.

Now Senomaglus of the Votadini was on his feet, calling out in a bold voice and gesturing towards the Roman party. Marcellinus got up, and the two men embraced beside the fire. Passing around the circle, the envoy threw his arms around each of the chiefs in turn, slapping them on the back. A boy appeared with three wooden mugs on a platter.

'Guest offering,' Marcellinus said as he sat down.

Castus took the cup that was offered to him. A dark scummy liquid filled it to the brim. 'What is it?' he said.

'Just beer. The Picts brew it themselves. Drink it down and try not to inhale.'

Strabo took a sip, and choked. 'Gah! It tastes like –'

'Yes I know,' Marcellinus said, smiling. 'They say the virgin girls of the tribe piss in the vats to aid the fermentation process.' Then he drained his cup in one long swallow, and threw it into the fire.

Castus raised the cup to his lips, trying to keep himself from gagging. Tipping back his head, he sucked the sour liquid down, and then hurled the empty cup towards the fire. Beside him, he heard Strabo coughing. The third cup thudded down into the embers, and the assembly gave wild yells of congratulation.

The brew was strong, and Castus took a deep breath to stop his head spinning, only to inhale even more smoky air. He shut his mouth and breathed through his nose, keeping one hand on the hilt of his sword and hooking his other thumb into his belt. This will soon be over, he told himself. The promise of fresh air and open space was painfully intoxicating.

Strabo had brought the bundle of diplomatic gifts, and now Marcellinus was unwrapping it. The chiefs gathered closer, craning to gaze at the gold and silver glittering in the firelight. There was a fine Roman *spatha*, the scabbard inlaid with gemstones, and a collection of silver cups and plates. Finest of all was a set of enamelled portraits of the four emperors on ivory panels framed in jewelled gold. Castus saw a couple of the chiefs passing the portrait set between them, twisting their lips and muttering as they rubbed at the gilding. Then it and all the rest of the presents disappeared into the murky depths of the hall.

'Four balls of Janus,' Castus said under his breath, 'not another song!'

But the man who now stood beside the fire, speaking slow gravelly words, was not a bard. He was older than the rest, heavily built, with a grey drooping moustache and a bare muscled chest heavily marked with scar-pictures and only slightly sagging with age. An impressive, commanding-looking man, Castus thought. He knelt down behind Marcellinus.

'Who's that?'

'Ulcagnus,' the envoy whispered back. 'The former king's armour-bearer and war leader, now acting as regent. Sensible man. With any luck he'll be voted in as high chief, and our job here will be done.'

'Who are the others?' As his eyes adjusted to the smoky light, Castus could better make out the forms and faces of the chiefs gathered around the fire listening to Ulcagnus's speech.

'The narrow-faced man with the dyed hair is Talorcagus, the king's cousin. He's one we have to be careful of. Impulsive, ambitious and no friend of Rome. The handsome young man next to him is his nephew, Drustagnus.'

Castus glanced at the two chiefs. He had noticed them before. Talorcagus had a look of fierce savagery about him even compared to the rest. His head was shaved almost to the top of his skull, with the remaining hair dyed reddish orange and teased up into a stiff crest like the bristles of a wild boar. The younger man beside him, Drustagnus, had a blunt face, black hair curled into ringlets and a hungry glare in his eyes. Castus knew the look. He would be tough contender in any fight, the sort with a lust for killing.

'Then that wiry young man opposite me is the old king's own nephew, Vendognus. He's weak and corrupt, but he was close to Vepogenus and stands a good chance of being voted in. I might be able to influence him, but he's a bad second choice.'

'And her?' Castus nodded towards a woman standing near the back of the room. She stood tall and proud, the only female in the gathering, and the men around her had drawn back slightly as if in respect. As Castus looked at her, the woman turned slightly and met his eye just for a moment. A strong face, bold, almost masculine.

But before Marcellinus could answer he stiffened abruptly, turning in his seat as another man entered the hall. The new-comer was dressed in native clothes, but wore no scars on his body, and was clean shaven.

'It's him,' the envoy said. 'The renegade. I did not think he'd show himself so soon.'

Castus felt Strabo's hand on his shoulder, drawing him back, and he stood and resumed his stance. The chiefs shuffled aside to give the man space at the fire. As he sat down, he looked up at Castus with a cold smile. Castus stared back at him, tightening his grip on the hilt of his sword.

Time passed, unguessable. One by one the chiefs got up to speak, their harsh gargling voices blending together in Castus's mind. He closed his ears to it, concentrating on taking in the details of the scene around him. Again and again his eyes strayed to the strong-featured woman at the back of the room. She was near his own age, he guessed. Somebody's wife – had Marcellinus not told him that? But whose? Her red-brown hair, the colour of a fox pelt, hung down her back in a thick plait. She wore a green sleeveless dress of heavy weave and a chequered cape secured at her breast with a massive silver brooch. A chain of thick silver links hung around her neck, and heavy silver clasps shaped like snakes circled her powerful arms. Staring at her, Castus willed the woman to look his way again, but her attention was held by the conference around the fire.

Talorcagus was on his feet, speaking in a low angry tone, stabbing his fingers. His orange brush of hair and long goat-like beard gave him the look of a fierce satyr, carved on a village gatepost. He sat down and Marcellinus spoke, his voice measured and slow, but Castus could hear the anger in the envoy's words.

Then, suddenly, the conference was at an end. The chiefs got up, flinging their cloaks around their shoulders, and stalked one by one out of the hall. Marcellinus followed them out, then Strabo, and Castus was just about to leave when he felt a touch on his arm. The renegade stood at his side, still wearing that cold, corrupt smile.

'Greetings, centurion,' the renegade said. 'My name is Julius Decentius. I believe you may be a countryman of mine.' He spoke with the trace of a Pannonian accent, and Castus felt a brief flare of nostalgia. But he stayed silent, drawing himself up to his full height.

'It's a pleasure to meet a Roman soldier so far from home,' the man went on, his hand still on Castus's arm. 'We should talk soon, you and I, when we have the chance.'

'I have nothing to say to you,' Castus said, trying to keep his voice level, his expression neutral. The man let his hand drop and took a step back.

'I was once a senior officer in the Roman army,' he said quietly. 'You should show more respect to me. We might have a lot in common, you know.'

'We have nothing in common,' Castus said. He gripped the hilt of his sword. 'I want nothing to do with you. And if you try and speak to my men or even approach them, you'll get a good Roman javelin through the gut.'

The renegade's expression shifted, his lips tightening. 'That would be very unwise,' he said, but Castus could see that he was shaken. Before the man could say another word, Castus ducked his head and strode out of the hall into the welcome chill of the night air.

Plunging his head down into the basin of cold water, Castus breathed out through his nostrils and then straightened. He shook his head and wiped the water from his eyes, then he scrubbed a palm over his wet scalp. It was morning, and the low hillock and the sheepfold were surrounded by a drift of mist that covered the Pictish encampment on the far slope. He had slept badly, dreaming of dog-headed yelping men capering around a fire, and a woman with fox-coloured hair who was trying to push him into a vat of foul scummy liquid.

Marcellinus had already left with Strabo for the day's conference, but Castus was glad he was not with them. Another session of incomprehensible ranting in the choking smoke-filled hall was more than he could endure. Besides, he had other things to worry about.

'Who were they?' he asked, rubbing a towel over his face and bare torso.

'Atrectus and Genialis,' Timotheus said. 'They went out with the water party at first light, but got separated down at the stream and haven't returned yet.'

Castus grunted. Typical that Atrectus and his slow-witted friend should be the ones to vanish.

'There were women down there, at the stream,' Timotheus said with a grimace of distaste. 'The others said that Atrectus was trying to talk to them.'

'I can imagine.' Castus pulled his tunic on over his head and buckled his belt. He wondered what effect a punishment flogging might have on the watching barbarians. Then again, the two men might not have gone off of their own free will...

'I'll mention it to the envoy when he returns, and he can ask the Picts to look out for them. Until then I want this camp under siege discipline. Nobody leaves without armed escort, and then only for essential duties. Double the watch at the perimeter, and keep another ten men under arms at all times in case of emergencies.'

'It's done,' Timotheus said. He saluted and strode away towards the wall. Sighing heavily, Castus noticed two of the

115

sentries apparently talking to somebody on the lower slopes. Their voices carried: British words with a Roman accent. A moment later, and the optio's yell silenced them.

Slinging his swordbelt over his shoulder and lacing his helmet straps, Castus began his morning tour of inspection. Many of the men appeared glum, wary now of the land outside the perimeter. *Good*, he thought, *that's how it should be*. But fear and suspicion worked against discipline, gnawing away at unity. The sooner he discovered what had happened to Atrectus and Genialis the better.

A watery sun was burning away the mist, and revealing the swell of the hills. Scanning the surrounding country, Castus saw Picts everywhere, groups of them with spears over their shoulders, some heading out into the hills and others returning. Many more just stood, as close to the Roman camp as they dared, watching the soldiers at the low wall. Castus suppressed a brief wish for a ballista or two. That would send them running back to their hovels quickly enough.

Along the valley, he saw a chieftain's party setting out on a hunting expedition, the nobles riding shaggy ponies with their dogs loping and yelping after them. With some surprise, he noticed the renegade Julius Decentius riding with them. Anger tightened his shoulders. If ever a man deserved crucifying...

'Centurion! Chariots coming!'

Castus marched quickly across the enclosure to join the sentry over by the gateway. He placed one foot up on the low stone wall and gazed down the slope towards the road. There were three of the little carts down there, the ponies drawing them along at a jog trot. The rear two carts held warriors with spears and javelins. In the leading vehicle was the woman Castus had seen at the gathering the night before. She stood up tall and straight in the rattling cart, her loose hair tumbling behind her. Her body looked sturdy, womanly but strong. She was staring back at him.

'Do you think they want to come up here?' the sentry asked.

'No, they're just scouting our position. They'll get as close as they can, though. Run back and tell Timotheus to send the reserve over. We might at least try and look formidable.'

The ten men came running back, clattering their shields and spears, and Castus formed them up along the wall and around the gateway. Below them, the chariots slowed at the base of the slope. Then the tall woman called out to the warriors in the other carts, and they turned again and headed for the ford across the stream.

Castus eased his foot down from the wall. He realised that he had been holding his breath.

Strabo returned early that evening, leaving Marcellinus back at the gathering.

'I couldn't stay,' he told Castus. He looked hollow, and had a haunted look in his eyes. 'There was some talk of... of bringing in a sorcerer, a witch doctor, to communicate with the shade of the dead king. They still think, you see, that he was murdered by poison, and cannot vote on a new ruler until his spirit is appeased.'

Castus felt the hairs on the back of his neck stir, and suppressed a shiver. It was a warm evening, but darkness was closing in, and the spirit world felt almost tangible.

'So I had to leave,' Strabo went on. 'Communicating with ghosts and devils is a terrible sin, and I could not be a party to it. I advised Marcellinus to retire with me, but he insisted on staying. He seemed... curious about what this witchcraft would accomplish.'

117

'His curiosity might become dangerous before long,' Castus said. The envoy's relish at being back among the native tribes had been obvious for several days now.

'I agree entirely,' Strabo said, and took another sip of chilled wine. For a while they sat in silence, listening to the muffled roaring from the Pictish camp, and the stamp and shout of the sentries calling out the change of watch.

'What sort of religion do these people have anyway?' Castus asked. 'Do they worship the same gods as the rest of us?' He caught himself, and felt an embarrassed flush on his face, but thankfully it was too dark for Strabo to notice.

'The same gods as *some* of us,' the other man corrected him dryly. 'To me, all of your various deities are at best myths, at worst devils. But we must not dwell on such things.'

Castus cleared his throat. He had almost managed to forget Strabo's own strange beliefs. Now the insult of them returned to him freshly. How could he talk that way? It was dangerously disrespectful, almost criminal... Then again, wasn't the man's religion actually a crime anyway?

'The Picts, though...' Strabo said, musingly. 'They are true heathens, of the worst sort. Their religion, if we can dignify it by that name, is nothing but childish superstition and bloody savagery. They worship certain groves and pools of deep water, and picture their gods as men with the heads of beasts and birds.'

Castus's skin prickled as he remembered his dream of the night before. He suspected that Strabo was enjoying his obvious discomfort.

'One of their gods, I believe, is the carrion crow that eats the enemy slain. Another is a faceless old hag who throws the valiant dead into a cauldron and brings them back to life. Such ideas are sent by the Devil, and grow in the minds of uncivilised men.'

118

'They don't scare me.'

'No? Even from my tent I heard you muttering and crying out in your sleep last night. Perhaps this place is affecting your spirits, for all the strength of your body.'

'Is it not affecting yours?' *You are the one who ran away from the witch doctor*, Castus thought.

'My faith is stronger than any barbarism,' Strabo said. He clenched his fist and pressed it to his heart. 'The Lord Jesus Christ watches over me and protects me. As He would protect you too, if you wished it.'

'I don't need your god,' Castus said.

It was nearly midnight by the time Marcellinus returned, and the envoy was in a grim rage. He summoned Castus and Strabo to his tent; the episode with the witch doctor had not gone well.

'And how do you think it looked,' he said, spitting the words, 'when *this one*, supposedly my assistant, went running off at the mere mention of divination?' He jutted a finger at Strabo, who sat in speechless anger on the far side of the tent. Castus was between them, his sheathed sword across his knees, saying nothing.

'They already think, most of them, that Rome was somehow behind the death of Vepogenus. The fact that this is entirely against our interests here seems to escape them! But then, when they call in their sorcerer, brother Strabo makes a quick exit! And what do you think the sorcerer said, after a great deal of moaning and shaking? *The killer was here with us, but is no longer!* Who does that suggest if not one of you two?'

'But that's absurd!' Strabo said angrily. 'None of us were here when the old king died! How can they think that any of us—?'

'Oh, you don't understand how these people's minds work.

They believe that poison can be sent by magic using bird droppings, or insects. I could tell them that Eboracum is thirteen days' hard march from this place and you were there all along, but why should they believe that? You're here now – so you could have been here then too, in *some other form...*'

Strabo threw up his hands, exasperated, and then slapped them down on his thighs.

'If that's how it is, I suggest we prepare to leave at once,' Castus said. 'Pull back to Votadini territory and wait to see what happens. There's nothing for us to gain here.' Except a cruel and sudden death, he thought.

'No, we stay,' Marcellinus declared. 'I still think I can bring the majority round. Ulcagnus is true to the king's memory, and our treaty. Even if he steps aside, the king's nephew Vendognus could be voted in. I need to be *here* to put what pressure I can on them.'

'What about the woman, the tall one who was at the gathering?' Castus asked. At once he wished he had stayed silent.

'What about her?' Marcellinus had a look of suspicious enquiry. 'Her name's Cunomagla, the wife of Vendognus. Ambitious in her own way, but mainly for her son to succeed rather than her weak husband. Has she spoken to you?'

'No. How could she?'

'She speaks a little Latin. A few of them do – they were taken as hostages when they were young. Drustagnus, the nephew of Talorcagus, does as well. Actually, they spent a few years at Eboracum. But don't imagine the experience made them love Rome any more. Personally I don't trust the woman, and neither should you.'

Castus nodded. But the envoy's words had covered some deeper uncertainty, he was sure of that. Marcellinus was hiding something.

'The decision of the tribal council is due the day after tomorrow,' Marcellinus said. 'So we only need stay until then. Courage, brothers – with luck we can pull victory from this yet!'

But the next day brought no luck. The two missing men, Atrectus and Genialis, did not return. Worse, one of the mounted scouts, a man named Bodiccius, also vanished. His five comrades appeared shamefaced and uncomfortable as they made their report: Bodiccius had gone off alone to hunt in the hills – perhaps he got lost? Perhaps his horse threw him? But Castus could read their faces: the missing man had deserted, most likely, and the rest of them knew it.

Standing at the wall, Castus looked out over an uncannily empty landscape. The native warriors and hunters who had filled their side of the valley and the surrounding slopes for the last two days had vanished, and there was only bare grass and silent woods to the west. But it was clear where they, at least, had gone: the great encampment of the Pictish muster on the far slope, where the chiefs would choose their new high chieftain that evening. All of them wanted to know which tribe, which family, would have the honour of leading their people, whether in peace or in war.

Marcellinus was already there, in the main council hut with Strabo. Castus had tried to talk him out of it: he did not get a vote in the council, and would learn of their decision quickly enough without needing to be present in the heart of it. But Castus had already realised that the envoy was acting under a strong personal compulsion, and could not bear to be absent when the decision was made. Marcellinus had also refused to take a bodyguard with him, saying that the chiefs trusted him now, and to bring guards would suggest that the trust was not returned.

Staring across the valley in the late afternoon sunlight, Castus wondered just how far the envoy's confidence had turned to dangerous hubris.

'Do you still want to take the midnight watch?'

Castus turned as his optio spoke. Both of them knew that whatever was going to happen would probably not begin until the night was well advanced.

'Best get some sleep if you do, brother.'

Timotheus was right; Castus slapped him on the shoulder and paced towards his tent. He tried to avoid glancing back at the Pictish camp. There was nothing more he could do now. Darkness, perhaps, would bring answers.

In the tent he stretched out on his bedroll, fully dressed, boots on. He had the ability, common to soldiers, to sleep at any hour of the day of night, whatever tumultuous noise was going on around him. Four hours, into sleep and then out again, without needing to be woken. Now, though, he lay awake staring at the leather of the tent above his head, listening to the subdued sounds of the camp outside. Nothing to be done, he told himself, and closed his eyes.

What was his friend Valens doing now, back at Eboracum? And Modestus, the shirker he had left in the hospital? He tried to picture the familiar route from the barracks to the bath-house, guiding his mind along it towards sleep. The Blue House appeared to him. Afrodisia coming down the stairs with a jug of wine. Then he saw another woman, her face a pale oval in darkness. *Promise me you'll protect him and bring him home safely...* No, he did not want to think about that. He thought of a bare white wall, the cracks in the plaster. The wall of his sleeping cubicle when he was a boy. His father's voice... Where was the old man now? Living or dead? But his mind wandered, deeper into sleep. He was walking across a dark landscape. Then there was a stag's head set on a pole, and it was talking to him...

'Centurion! Centurion, get up, quick!'

A hand on his ankle, pulling at his leg. Castus sat up, grabbing for the sheathed sword at his side. One forward lurch and he was out through the tent flap and staggering to his feet, swaying as the sleep flooded out of him. It was dark, and there was a strange noise, a buzzing and roaring carried on the breeze. He snatched the arm of the man beside him, pulling him almost off his feet.

'What's happening?'

'Look over there – it's the Picts!'

Throwing his swordbelt over his shoulder, Castus crossed to the eastern wall of the enclosure. Timotheus was there, with most of the rest of the century.

'It started just a few moments ago,' the optio said. 'There was a loud shout, maybe a scream, then they started up this wailing and drumming.'

Even from a distance and in moonless darkness, it was clear that the Pictish camp was in uproar. Sparks raced on the hillside: men carrying torches running or riding in carts. The noise was a steady throb, punctuated with wild cries and shouts. Castus grabbed Caccumattus the interpreter and pulled him close.

'What are they doing over there?'

'I not know!' The man shrugged. 'Maybe bad. Make sounds of anger!'

He didn't need a translator to tell him that.

'Brigonius, you and two other scouts ride over there to the Pictish camp and see what you can find out. Don't take any risks, just check and report back. But if you see the envoy or the governor's secretary and they're in trouble, get them out of there. Got it?'

The scout nodded and jogged away towards the horse lines. Castus glanced around him, the situation falling into focus. If Marcellinus and Strabo had managed to get clear of whatever was happening in the Pictish camp, they could be riding back even now and would need support. If not... Castus could hardly bear to imagine. They could be dead, or captured, or fighting for their lives. But he could hardly lead his whole force in battle formation into the heart of the enemy; they would be surrounded and cut off in the open country. *Think*, he told himself. He felt the pressure of expectation growing around him, the men looking to him for answers. *Think, decide...*

'I want sixteen men, fully armed,' he said, in as firm a voice as he could muster. 'Culchianus, your section, with Januarius's. Bradua, go to my tent and fetch my shield, mail and helmet. We're going down to hold our side of the ford until the scouts return. Timotheus, you have command of the fort.'

'Let me take the men out, centurion,' Timotheus said. 'You should stay here.'

'No – I need to be down there, not up here.' *Down there*, he thought, *where I can better decide what to do next.* 'With any luck the envoy and the secretary will be riding back that way soon and we can protect them.'

The runner came back with his kit, and Castus quickly shrugged on the heavy mail shirt, tightened his belts over the top and laced on his helmet. Around him the camp was in motion, men rushing to their own tents and arming themselves.

'Keep the hornblower at your side,' Castus told the optio. 'Sound a long blast every quarter-hour – if we get split up out there we'll need to find our way back in the dark. I want everyone in battle positions.'

'Don't worry, I understand,' Timotheus said.

124

The men were formed up, the three scouts already racing away down the slope towards the ford.

'What's the watchword?' the optio said as Castus made for the break in the wall.

'*Fortuna Homebringer.* May she protect us tonight!'

Down off the hilltop and away from the circle of fortifications, the night felt heavy and damp. The noise from the Pictish camp was muffled here, only the occasional shout or wail carrying across through the trees. Castus led his men at a rapid pace, the creak and clink of boots and weapons loud in the dead stillness around them.

Promise me you'll bring him home safely. Swear to me that you'll look after him and watch over him at all times... How had he failed? How had he managed to let Marcellinus walk unprotected into danger? There were so many things, now, that he knew he should have done. But none of that could change anything. Only the moment mattered, the blood pulsing in his neck, the sweat gathering in the small of his back, the fear of the men behind him like a charge in the air.

'Halt,' he called quietly. They were a few paces from the dip in the road that led to the ford, and through the trees he could sense the river flowing over the stones in the darkness. The men exhaled, leaning on their spears, hefting their shields. Not a sound now from the far bank. Only the lights of fires glinting from the hill slopes above them. Faint starlight picking out the glitter of moving water.

Then a cry, close and sudden. The scream of a horse, and the rapid battering of hooves on the packed dirt of the track.

'Close order – ready javelins!'

The legionaries shifted out of column and into formation,

sealing the neck of the road. The sound of horses drew closer, and then seemed to fade.

Suddenly they appeared from the trees on the far bank: two men riding at the gallop, one slumped across the mane of his mount, and a third horse following with an empty saddle. They surged down into the river and the water erupted into spray around them.

'Hold on! They're our scouts! Put up your javelins...'

The first rider cleared the river, and would have raced straight on up the track if Castus had not seized his bridle. The horse reared, stamped and shied.

'What happened? Brigonius, *report*!'

The second rider came up out of the river, the injured man sliding from the saddle with the shaft of a spear jutting from his side.

'They're dead – the two Pictish chiefs,' the exhausted scout gasped. 'Ulcagnus and Vendognus. Dead in their huts – poisoned...'

'Where are Marcellinus and Strabo?' Castus shouted, clinging to the bridle. 'Somebody catch that third horse...'

'Don't know... A party of warriors recognised us. They killed Buccus, and then attacked us.'

'Juno protect us,' Castus said. He seized the scout and dragged him off the horse. 'I'm going over there to find our men and bring them out if I can,' he called to the troops behind him. 'I need two volunteers who can ride.' *Better than me, that is*, he thought. Culchianus and Vincentius stepped forward, saluting. 'Get up on those other horses. The rest of you, take the injured man and get back to the fort, double pace. Tell Timotheus to prepare for attack, and if I'm not back in one hour, he should take command.'

He swung up into the saddle of the scout's horse. Even now,

he was not sure what he intended to do. All he could hear was the oath he had sworn to protect Marcellinus with his life.

'Don't stand there, go!' he shouted, and swept out his sword. He slapped at the nearest man with the flat of his blade, and all of them broke into motion at once, spilling back from the river and away up the hill towards the fort.

The river was quiet now, whispering over the stony bed. Castus turned in the saddle. The two soldiers were mounted behind him, spears in hand.

'You ready?' He caught Culchianus's answering nod. 'Keep close behind me and watch my back. Let's go.'

He kicked his heels into the horse's flanks, and the animal leaped forward into the water.

CHAPTER VII

Chaos ruled the Pictish camp. Figures ran and shouted in the firelight, brandishing torches, shadows racing and weaving, smoke hanging in the air. The three riders came up out of the trees at a hard gallop.

'Keep behind me,' Castus called back over his shoulder. 'Stay low and stay together.' He pulled off his helmet and slung it over the saddle horn; no need to draw attention to himself just yet. His horse was already panicking, and he kept a tight grip on the reins.

Into the light of the fires, they rode together. Figures scattered to either side, shouting, some of them raising spears. Castus could see the humped bulk of the great hut at the centre of the encampment – the mass of people was thickest there. He felt a plunging reckless fury running in his blood.

A javelin flashed past his ear; he ducked low over the horse's mane, and heard someone cry out behind him. Small bands of warriors moved in packs, angry and confused, but there were no clear allegiances between any of them. In a circle of firelight Castus saw a torn body sprawled on the turf, bright with blood: the scout Buccus, with four javelins stuck in his back. He saw a man in a chariot, one of the chiefs, screaming to the warriors gathering around him.

Dragging on the reins, Castus pulled the horse to a halt. The animal backed, circling, breathing hard. He was in the thick of the Pictish muster now, warriors all around him, women and children too. Scanning the faces, the massed shadows, he willed Marcellinus to show himself, or Strabo – as if by picturing them vividly enough he could cause them to appear. But the crowd had noticed him now, identified him as an outsider. Hoarse voices built into a chant – something like *Ladha Ruamnai*, but he could guess what it meant. *Kill the Romans.*

Culchianus was beside him, seizing the bridle of his horse. For a moment, lost in angry indecision, he could not tell what the man was shouting.

'… have to get away… Centurion, we'll never find them in this mess!'

He was right, Castus knew. At any moment the crowd would gather force and turn on them. But Marcellinus was still out there somewhere, maybe close. He twisted in the saddle, looking to left and right. Across the heads of the throng he saw a figure standing in a cart: a woman with a spear in her hand. Cunomagla. She raised her head as she noticed him, her strong jaw set, then lifted the spear and pointed away towards the river. *Go.*

'Ride fast, ahead of me, and don't stop.'

The two soldiers were already moving, and Castus hauled his own horse around and booted it in the flanks. The animal was sweating, half blown and terrified by the flames all around, but it leaped forward again and plunged towards the darkness of the riverbank. Castus just clung on as best he could.

Ahead he saw the two soldiers riding hard; Vincentius was hurt, slumped low over the saddle horns. A man stepped up ahead of them, and Culchianus drove his spear through him.

Movement to the right: one of the chariot carts, a spearman in the back and the driver whipping the ponies furiously.

'Keep going!' Castus yelled. 'Don't hang back!'

The cart veered, angling to cut him off, the spearman standing straight with feet braced and weapon raised in both hands. Onward, the vehicle closing in, then Castus dragged on the reins and jinked his horse round to the right. The animal slammed into the flank of the lead chariot pony, and the shock of the impact almost knocked him out of the saddle. Bent forward, he felt the spearhead slicing the air above his back. He swept his sword round, backhanded, and the blade sheared flesh and bone. Then he was clear, the panicked horse carrying him on as the cart veered away again.

Two men before him, raising shields, spears levelled. The first fell back as the horse kicked, and the second made a clumsy stab from his left. Castus swayed in the saddle, then he grabbed the shaft of the spear and wrenched it aside. He swung his sword across his body, down over the saddle horn to chop into the Pict's shoulder. The man howled and fell beneath the hooves, and Castus rode clear.

Trees to either side, then he was at the river and the water was bursting around him. On the far bank his two soldiers were waiting, and they turned together to confront their pursuers.

But the ford was clear behind them: figures on the far bank screamed from the darkness between the trees, and Castus could make out the cart circling back, the wounded spearman hunched in the back.

Riding again, the soldiers to either side, he urged his horse on up the dark slope towards the fort. The sound of a horn carried on the night air, then the calls of the sentries.

'Halt there! Declare yourselves!'

'*Fortuna Homebringer! Fortuna Homebringer!*' Castus heard his own voice shouting, hoarse, but felt only the burning pain in his throat and the heaviness of failure in his gut.

'I had the men light cooking fires,' Timotheus said, handing him a bowl of hot broth. 'Reckoned they might not get another chance for a while.'

Castus nodded, spooning up soup, then cramming his mouth with hard bread. Astonishingly, so it now seemed, he and the two soldiers had returned from their foray alive. Vincentius had caught a javelin in the shoulder, but it was only a flesh wound and he could still use a weapon. The wounded scout, though, had been dead before he was brought back into the fort.

'What's going on over there?' he said, his mouth full. 'Can you see anything?'

'Nothing very much. Just the usual clamour. The crowd's getting thicker around the main hut, by the pattern of the torches.'

Castus swallowed heavily and wiped his mouth. 'I ought to address the men,' he said. 'Form them up, but keep the sentries posted.'

'Centurion,' Timotheus said quietly, dropping to kneel beside him. 'The men all know what we're up against. They know what *you're* up against as well.'

Castus looked around him: the legionaries spaced along the perimeter, the others gathered in the glow of the cooking fires. All that they had feared these last fifteen days, all their worst and most horrible nightmares, were now coming true. Of course they knew what they were facing.

'All the same. It's only right.'

As the horn sounded the assembly he paced the line of the oval wall surrounding the camp, assessing what needed to be done. His thighs still ached from riding, and there was a cold trembling sensation in his legs. His hands too felt oddly loose and weak, and he clenched his right fist and smacked it into his palm repeatedly until he felt the strength in his arms returning.

This was what his centurion had meant all those years ago, Castus realised. The bronze mask of leadership. At the time he had thought that the mask just projected inflexible strength. Now he knew the truth: the mask concealed fear.

'Assembly ready, centurion,' Timotheus cried. Forty-six men stood drawn up in the last glow of the cooking fires, with the remaining ten still on watch around the walls. Castus strode forward and turned to face them, planting his feet firmly, hands clasped behind his back. He tried not to see them as an assembly of ghosts, of lost spirits, but the winged Victory figures painted on their shields appeared more substantial than the men themselves.

'Brothers,' he called, his voice low and steady, 'things do not look good. Two of our men are missing, along with one of the scouts, and two scouts are dead. The Domini Marcellinus and Strabo have either been killed or have fallen into the hands of the enemy. The Picts, for some reason of their own, have turned against us and will probably attempt an assault very soon.'

He waited a moment to let the words sink in. It was better that these things should be said out loud, before the contagion of unspoken fear could eat away at them.

'Some of you will be thinking we should pull out now, before the enemy muster against us. But that's a bad idea. Before we got two miles down the road the Picts would be all around us. Besides, we were sent here to protect the envoy, and we're not leaving while there's still a chance he's alive. The enemy outnumber us, but we're trained soldiers, well armed and equipped, while they're a spear-chucking rabble. We've got a strong defensive position here, and we can hold out as long as necessary. They hope, the Picts, that we'll break and run. They hope they can intimidate us with their numbers and their noise. But if we stick close together and hold these walls, we'll stand up to anything they can throw against us.

'An hour ago, I ordered the three remaining scouts to ride for Bremenium with a message for the commander there about what's happened. Any relief force could take days to arrive, but if we can hold off the enemy for only a day or two they'll realise our strength and we can negotiate with honour. They give us the prisoners back. We march out of here and go home.'

He let the stress fall on the last word. No need to raise false hopes; they all knew how steeply the odds were stacked against them. But it was something, at least, to believe in.

'Meanwhile, we've got work to do. Our current perimeter is too long to hold effectively – we need to shorten it. I want the wall to the south broken down and the stones carried back to make a new line *here*.' He swept his arm forward and back. 'Have the mules brought up into the enclosure and secured. Then six men fully armed to go with the slaves down to the stream with all the canteens and water containers. Fill as much water as you can carry. Two sections at a time can fall out and rest. Sleep if you can. The others will remain under arms at the defences. Optio, set the fatigues. *Dismissed!*'

As the assembly broke up, Castus went to the east wall and found Caccumattus sheltering there, staring out across the valley into the darkness. He had been surprised that the unimpressive little interpreter had not already made a run for it.

'Will they attack tonight?' he asked in a low whisper.

Caccumattus sucked his teeth, and then shrugged. 'No, I think. Picti no to fighting in night. Too much dark – only evil gods to see them!'

'Oh. Well, that's some comfort, I suppose.'

He would be prepared even so. It was still possible that the interpreter had stayed in the camp to deceive them into relaxing their guard. Distant horn cries came from across the valley, and the scattered fires had coalesced into one large blaze. A funeral pyre, perhaps? Impossible to tell at this distance.

A light rain was falling, but the night was warm. Castus watched the men building the new wall, and after a while fell to hefting stones himself, glad of the physical labour. The water party returned from the stream, and then the camp settled into a tensed quiet, every man wrapped in his cloak, gazing warily out into the night. Above them was the thin arc of the new rising moon.

'You see them? Down there to the right, in the long grass... There's another – he just moved.'

Castus followed the optio's pointing finger, but could see nothing at first. It was not yet dawn, but the light had increased to a damp greyness, and the surrounding plain and the slopes of the hills looked like heaped fog. His eyes smarted after eight hours staring at nothing.

'There! See, he moved again!'

This time Castus caught the movement: a man lying flat on the slope with a cape pulled across his head and body. Once he'd seen one he quickly spotted more: the hillside below the fort was covered in creeping cloaked men, edging closer now and again, crawling on their bellies.

'Think they might try and rush us?' Timotheus said. He appeared very young in the half-light, his cheeks covered with a downy beard, but his eyes were hard and sunken deep.

'No, we'd cut them down before they got close. They're just scouting us out.'

A dry snap came from the slope, and one of the men at the wall fell back with a grunt of pain.

'Heads down, shields up! Cover yourselves!' Castus shouted. 'What in Jupiter's name was that?'

'Lockbow,' Evagrius called. 'Native hunting weapon. I saw a few of them when I was in the Wall garrison. Like a short bow mounted on a stave. You can aim and loose them when you're lying down.'

'Shit of Hades,' Castus said.

A volley of snapping sounds came from the prone figures in the grass, the short arrows clattering against the wall and the raised shields or arcing overhead. The first shot had hit Culchianus in the shoulder.

'Any of you with slings – over here now!' Pointless to waste javelins on the skulking bowmen. Six men jogged across the enclosure, heads down, and dropped behind the wall.

'Whenever you see one of them move, crack him!'

Almost at once the first sling whirred and snapped, sending its stone flat and true to the target. A cry from the slope, and the men along the wall cheered. Another volley of arrows, and more slingstones hurled back, then the cloaked figures were getting up and scrambling back down the slope. Castus saw one, then two, knocked down by slingstones as they ran.

Behind them, the first sun was glinting through the ragged clouds over the mountains to the east. Castus turned, kneeling, and touched his brow. He muttered a prayer under his breath, and when he raised his head he saw most of the other men doing the same. Strabo, he reminded himself, was no longer here to disapprove.

He stood up, drew his sword and held the blade levelled above his head to reflect the light of the dawn.

'Unconquered Sun,' he cried out in his best parade voice. 'We devote ourselves to your glory. Send your light between us and evil, and give us victory this day!'

135

The shout of acclamation from the men around him was loud and sudden, spears clashing against shield rims. The long tense night was behind them, and they were drawing strength from the sun. Castus smiled as he sheathed his blade. So far, things were going well.

An hour later, the Picts began to gather on the plain and the surrounding hills. They came from the ford in massed columns, men on foot and on horseback, some riding in carts. Outside the range of javelin or slingshot they assembled in their warbands, sitting or squatting in the grass or leaning on their spears. Others appeared on the far side of the stream, where the ground rose towards their camp, many of them with light hunting javelins and the cross-shaped lockbows. The sky was heavy and grey, and a damp wind came down off the high hills.

'How many do you think, Evagrius?'

'Around two thousand, centurion. At least.'

'That's about what I make it.'

'Forty to one. Not bad odds!'

But now a horseman was riding slowly from the enemy mass, his spear raised and tipped with a leafy green branch. As he approached, Castus recognised the crest of orange hair, the goatlike scowl. Talorcagus, enemy of Rome.

'Caccumattus, to me.' The interpreter scuttled along the wall to kneel beside Castus. The Pictish chief drew closer, his horse mounting the lower slope. Another man rode behind him carrying a sack.

'*Ruamnai!*' the Pict shouted, punching his spear above his head. He began to call out his address, the words gnarled and ugly.

'He say: Romani kill Picti chiefs, Ulcagnus and Vendognus,' the interpreter said, translating rapidly. 'Try to make chief-talk to fail. But now Talorcagus – him – he high chief. King.'

'So I guessed.'

The Pict was still shouting, still brandishing his leafy spear.

'He say: Picti find killers, make punish. No want fighting with Romani soldier. He say you putting down weapon, go home in peace.'

Castus spat between his teeth. No doubt those among his men who understood the native language were already circulating the offer.

'Ox shit,' he said, and grabbed Caccumattus by the arm, pulling him close. 'You tell him this: Roman soldiers never surrender! And we didn't come all this way just to go home without a fight, either. Tell him his people must have short memories if they've forgotten what the Emperor Severus did to them a hundred years ago. We want Marcellinus, Strabo and our two soldiers back, *then* we'll think about going home.'

Caccumattus, released, stood up and called out the reply. There was something like defiance in his voice, quite unlike his wavering tone when he tried to speak Latin. Talorcagus circled his horse, and then shouted back.

'He say: You not Severus. You small silly man. Soon all to die, like... I no knowing what...'

But Castus could already see the second rider opening the neck of the sack. He lifted something out, drew back his arm and threw.

Two dull thuds from the grass; two heavy round objects rolling to a halt. A low anguished groan went up from the men along the wall. Talorcagus was stripping the leaves from his spear and throwing them aside, then turning his horse back towards his assembled warriors.

'So now we know where they got to,' Castus said quietly. One of the severed heads lay face down, but the other had the red hair and startled grey face of the legionary Atrectus. 'Get a cloth and jump down there, quick,' he said to Vincentius. 'Take Bradua with you. Wrap up the heads and bring them back – and try to handle them with respect.' The less time the grisly message lay in clear view of the other men, the better.

The ranks of the enemy shifted, warriors bunching and gathering. Some of them knelt down in the grass with wooden bowls before them – what were they doing, Castus wondered, eating breakfast? He reminded himself that his men had eaten nothing since the night before. But now he saw the kneeling warriors scooping handfuls of paste from the bowls and smearing it on their arms and bare chests. The paste left a vivid blue stain on their skin, around the scar-pictures of animals.

'What are they doing?'

'Blue make power of animals go into warrior,' the interpreter said. 'Call down sky, animal power free. Make very much brave.'

'Now I've seen it all,' Evagrius muttered, and gave a nervous laugh.

The blue-painted men stood up, throwing out their chests and flexing their arms, roaring through clenched teeth. From the ranks of the other warriors came a reverberating clatter and hum: they were beating the metal balls at the base of their spears against their shields. A strange ringing noise came echoing back off the hills.

Castus stood up. 'Everyone on your feet!' he shouted. The men rose together, shields up along the line of the wall. Castus glanced at the soldiers to either side of him, their faces pale with fear but tensed, straining with the anticipation of battle.

'Sixth Legion!' he cried out, raising his fist. 'Are you ready for war?'

'*Ready,*' the voices came back, uncertain.

'Are you ready for war?'

Again '*Ready*', stronger this time, the shouts joining in unison.

'Are you *READY* for *WAR*?'

'*READY!*' The last shout was loud enough to echo in the damp air. Castus could feel the energy of the men, the heat passing between them. Someone started clashing his spear against his shield rim, and the rest soon joined in. A great battering noise rolled down the slope towards the enemy horde.

A man scrambled up onto the wall: it was Vincentius, with his bandaged arm. 'Come on then, you filthy goatfuckers!' he screamed across the valley. Then, pulling up the hem of his mail and tunic, he jutted his hips at the enemy, sneering. 'Come on and *kiss this*!'

Wild laughter and cheering along the wall as Vincentius dropped back down. From the far wall Timotheus was calling for silence, but Castus gestured for him to stop. Let the men shout, let them laugh, if it gave them strength.

'Here they come!' somebody cried. The enemy horde gave a vast collective heave and began to surge forward, warriors howling as they advanced, punching their spears towards the wall above them.

Castus stood up again, drawing his sword and holding it high. '*Victrix!*' he yelled.

The men took up the cry, chanting it just they had on the drill field, drumming spears against shields. '*VIC*-trix! *VIC*-trix! *VIC*-trix!'

Castus wondered where the legion had won their title. Some long-forgotten war, back in the glorious ancient days. He had never bothered to ask.

Earn it now.

'Timotheus,' he shouted, cupping his hands to his mouth, 'keep your men watching the eastern slope. Culchianus, make sure they don't move round to the south. The rest of you, darts and javelins. When they get within thirty paces, stick it to them!'

But already the enemy tide was surging around the lower slopes, the painted warriors in the vanguard breaking into a run.

'Mouth of Hades, we're dead men now,' a soldier said. Castus clouted him across the back of his helmet. The rush of the enemy looked unstoppable.

'Ready darts!' he shouted. All along the eastern wall, the men flung back their arms to throw. Iron glittered in the low sun.

One...

Two...

Three... The first of the howling painted men was well within range now. Castus drew in breath, held it, and then shouted again.

'Loose!'

CHAPTER VIII

The missile volley broke the vanguard of the attackers, cropping down painted bodies under the hail of iron. But others were already leaping across their fallen comrades. Another volley, thrown flat and hard. Another ten or twenty enemy dead. Still they came on.

Castus stepped back from the wall, glanced to his left and then to his rear. Timotheus and Culchianus were still crouching: no attack from that side. The assault party were hurling all their strength against the western defences. All he could hear was the noise of his breath and his blood, the grunt of the men as they threw, the snarls and cries from the enemy on the slope below. He was shouting, but could not hear his own voice.

A javelin came in over the wall, and Castus saw one of his soldiers reeling back with blood spattering from a gashed throat. He dragged the man away and stepped up into his place, raising his shield just in time to catch a second missile ringing off the boss. As the Picts toiled up towards the wall the glare of the low sun struck them in the eyes; dazzled, reeling, they were easy targets for the legionaries. But the supply of darts and javelins was running short. Soon it would come to spears and blades.

'Come on then!' Castus yelled to the warriors on the slope, hammering the flat of his blade against his shield rim. '*Come on!'* The vigour of battle was in his blood, a clean and powerful tonic, erasing all other thought and feeling. His vision was clear, his heart racing, and he felt a wildness that was close to joy. But he held himself back; he was in command, he needed distance.

A knot of warriors surged forward, howling, and made a rush at the wall. Two were cut down by javelins, the third leaped up and punched overarm with his spear. The point thudded off a shield, then another javelin lanced him in the kidneys and he dropped heavily, without a sound. But all along the wall others were following his lead, bolting up out of the grass and running for the wall. Castus saw a painted chest, a snarling face, and swung his shield to catch the slash of a spear and flick it aside. He paused, blade levelled, just long enough for the Pict to step in close again, then he struck. His sword grated on bone, and he punched out with his shield boss and knocked the man back from the wall. Beside him, Evagrius speared a second attacker in the face.

The first rush had been broken, but there were still more warriors piling up the slope. One of them, massive and almost naked, paused ten paces from the wall and drew himself upright. He threw out his chest and spread his arms wide, displaying the fantastic tracery of scar-pictures bold on his blue-daubed skin. Roaring, he shouted up at the soldiers – challenging them, Castus guessed, to single combat. A moment later a flung javelin caught him in the chest and stuck, quivering. Castus saw the jolt through the man's muscles, the tightening cords of his neck; then his legs folded beneath him and the Pict fell, arms swinging, to sprawl on his back in the bloody grass. Something marvellous, Castus thought, in the mad bravery of savages. Almost a shame to kill them...

A horn blast from his left, and he swung round to see the flicker of spears along the southern boundary. Jumping back, he pulled Evagrius into his place at the wall, then cupped his hands and yelled across the enclosure to his optio. 'Timotheus! Ten men to the south wall. Follow me!'

Running, Castus leaped across the ashen scars of the cooking fires and slammed in among Culchianus's men. A body of Picts had angled around the slope and come up from the south, over the level ground where the previous boundary wall had been torn down. There were riders too, three or four warriors urging their shaggy ponies up and across the scree of fallen stones. Culchianus and his men had almost used up their supply of missiles already.

'Hold back!' Castus cried. 'Wait till they get close!'

The warriors advanced at a low jog, keeping silent, shields raised before them. They were learning already: they had seen that single men attacking the wall would be cut down, but a mass assault might break through. Behind them the riders had reached the level ground and cantered forward, urging on the footmen. A soldier stepped quickly up onto the wall, darting his javelin down into an exposed body, and then jumped back.

Timotheus and his ten-man reserve arrived just as the Picts made their rush. A volley of javelins flung at close range cut down the first of the warriors, but then the rest were up against the wall, striking with spears and swords. Roman blades lashed back, and the din of battered shields covered the screams and stifled gasps of combat. Castus saw a soldier fall, struck through the body, and jumped to take his place as the lead horseman was cantering in close, spear raised.

For a moment he remembered Oxsa, when the armoured cavalry broke through the front cohorts and crashed against the reserve line. But this horseman was no Persian cataphract. Castus stood his ground, the wall before him, and waited until the rider made his jump. The pony reared at the wall, and

143

Castus feinted at its head with his sword. Shying, the animal clipped the stones with its hooves and the rider was flung sideways; Castus seized his leg and pulled, driving the length of his blade straight up and into the man's exposed flank. Hot blood seethed over his hand and down his arm, and the rider fell heavily onto the parapet as Castus dragged his blade free.

'Get out of my fucking fort,' he said, and booted the body back off the wall.

The pony was cantering away, the other riders falling back, and the remaining warriors were retreating with them, demoralised by the stiffness of the defence. Castus turned and saw Evagrius waving from the western wall, and knew that the first assault was over.

'What's the damage?'

'Two men dead, Draucus and Jucundus. Three incapacitated by wounds. But we must have killed fifty of them, at least.'

Castus was kneeling at the centre of the enclosure, Timotheus and the section leaders gathered around him. Culchianus had his arm in a sling and a bandage around his head; Timotheus bled from a cut scalp, but his face was shining. Castus remembered that his optio had never been in battle before.

'Send out men to gather up all the javelins and darts they can find, and kill any wounded Picts out there too. Roll the bodies back down the hill a bit and heap them up like a wall. Then we need breakfast – just hardtack, cheese and water, but it should be enough. I doubt the men could stomach anything more.'

He got up, but then paused.

'That was well done, all of you,' he said quietly.

The eight slaves crouched by the eastern wall, with the mules in a frightened huddle beside them. They looked up, anxious, expectant, as their centurion approached.

'Listen to me,' Castus said, standing straight, thumbs in his belt. 'I want four of you to tend to the wounded. The other four take a spear or sword from the fallen and wounded men. Use them as best you can, when the time comes. Take helmets and shields too. I'll see to it that any of you who make it home are given your freedom.'

Arming slaves was strictly illegal, but he needed the numbers now. The slaves needed no further encouragement – anything was better than sitting defenceless and unarmed in the middle of a battle. They scrambled away at once towards the injured, and the stack of weapons laid beside the wrapped bodies of the slain. Four more men, Castus thought. Less the casualties so far, that gave him fifty-five with the strength to fight.

A harsh screech and a black flutter from overhead; Castus glanced up and saw crows rising up from the feast of carrion on the western slope. *Messengers of the gods*, he remembered, *or so the Picts believe*. A shudder ran up his spine.

Hours passed before the next assault. The horde out on the plain chanted and wailed, clattered their weapons, gathered around their shouting chieftains, then sat in the grass and waited, watching. The soldiers in the stone enclosure stared back at them, wary, fighting down nerves. The blast of horns and the cheer of the advance was almost a relief, when it came.

This time, the Picts moved forward in a mass, bunching together to the west and the south. There were fewer painted warriors among them now, Castus could see. Most were simple tribesmen in leather cloaks, but behind them were the chiefs and the nobles, on horseback or riding in carts, shepherding them forward. Far back on the north-west flank Castus saw the flash of silver ornaments, the fox-coloured hair hanging loose: Cunomagla, riding proudly in a cart with a spear in her hand. And beside her, a heavy fur cape over his shoulders, was the renegade Julius Decentius.

The Picts might not know the best way to attack a fortified position, but the renegade Roman surely did. Was he directing the assault now? Castus felt an ache in his jaw, and realised that he was grinding his molars. *Bastard*, he thought. *May the gods send a foul death upon him.*

Now a great collective roar came from the enemy ranks and they began to move up the slope with shields raised and weapons ready. The Picts gripped their spears far back towards the butt, Castus noticed, with the metal ball acting as a counterweight. It gave them a greater reach when they stabbed overarm, but weakened their thrust and spoiled their aim. He swigged water from a canteen, and then passed it to the man beside him. The lead-grey sky was beginning to spit rain, and the sun was gone.

The first charge came from the west, the Picts rushing up the slope behind their shields. As soon as they were in range, the darts and javelins bit, and a great wave of them dropped at once like grass swept down by the wind. For a long interval they lay among the bodies of their own slain, the dead warriors of the first assault still piled on the hillside. A horn wailed, and the mass of prone bodies stirred into motion.

'Light between us and evil!' Castus muttered. The dead men too were rising, their torn painted flesh and lifeless eyes lurching up from the beaten grass. He thought of the dark gods of the Picts, the hag who restores the dead to life…

Then he saw what was happening: the new attackers lifting the dead bodies and using them as shields, two men each lugging a corpse between them, chest to the enemy. Wounds showed

146

black in the dead flesh, mouths gaped, stiff limbs jutted. All along the wall, the soldiers were shrinking back from the ghastly vision below them.

'Centurion!' A hand clasped his arm – a runner from Culchianus at the south wall. 'Masses of them down there, centurion. They're not coming on, just hanging back below the ridge. But there must be a good few hundred.'

Castus grabbed at the back of his neck and squeezed hard. His mouth was dry, and he could not think. He glanced across the enclosure towards the east wall: two men of Timotheus's section were down, clutching the shafts of lockbow arrows, and the others were pelting darts and arrows onto the steep slope above the river. To the north the men at the all were crouched, waiting. No attack there.

'Evagrius, take over here,' he said. 'Don't let those walking corpses put you off – they're already dead!' The western attack was a feint, the eastern one a sniping distraction. The full assault would come from the south. He hoped he was right.

Crossing the enclosure at a run, he felt the fatigue aching in his limbs. He wanted water, but there was no time. By the time he reached Culchianus he could already see the ridge below the rampart boiling with Picts, all of them hunched together in the grass just out of range of the darts.

'If we had more men, I'd suggest a charge over there to drive them off,' Culchianus said.

'No. Let them come to us.'

He saw their strategy now, simple but effective. They were closing in from all directions at once, tightening a ring around the stone defences like a ligature. He gripped his helmet in realisation: the north, he thought. The main attack would come from the north, once the defenders had been drawn off to the three other sides.

But there was no time to react; already the Picts were rising from the ridge and dashing across the open ground towards the wall, a solid mass of them running behind their shields. They lacked the discipline to hold together as they ran, and their charge formed into a chevron as the stronger and faster men drew ahead.

'Lock your shields where they're thickest!' Castus yelled as the second volley of javelins arced out from the wall. A moment later and the first of the attackers flung themselves at the wall, Culchianus and his men slamming their shields into a solid barrier bristling with spears. Castus jogged to the left, sword drawn, and caught a solitary Pict scrambling in over the wall: a lunge and a stab, and the man fell back. Behind him he could hear the percussion of blades striking shields, speared men screaming, Culchianus yelling encouragement. He looked towards the north wall. Still no attack there.

The battle seethed along the line of the wall now, the Picts jostling together as their own first wave fell back from the barrier of shields. Soldiers flung javelins over the arched backs of their comrades, and could barely miss. Blades and spearshafts flickered and rang in the gap between the fighters: clash and scrape of iron, hollow thud of shields. Men screaming. Castus kept moving, ranging from one flank to the other, slashing out with his sword whenever an attacker broke through and tried to cross the wall. He listened to the noise of the fighting, waiting for the moment when the howls of attack and the desperate grunts of combat shifted to groans and wails, the noise of defeat. Or the cheer of impending victory.

But the noise, when it came, was from the other direction: a chorus of yells, a horn blast. He turned from the waist, mail shirt crunching, to see the scattered men along the northern wall wavering, a few even falling back.

'You! And you – with me *now*!' He was grabbing at men,

hauling them from the mesh of combat and dragging them after him. They stumbled together, still shocked by the ferocity of the fighting, confused now. 'North wall – run! *Go!*'

Then he was running with them, urging his heavy body on across the expanse of damp scrubbed turf, screaming to the men on the other walls to join him. Already he could see that he was too late: there were Picts swarming up from the northern slopes, beating aside the men at the wall and scrambling in over the defences. As he watched, a group of them kicked down the piled stones to form a breach.

'Orders, centurion?' Timotheus was at his side, bringing six men from the east wall.

'Shield *wall*!' Castus yelled, not even knowing how many were with him. Shields swung and battered together. Castus himself took the right wing, raising his shield before him.

'On my command, advance,' he said, and his voice grated in his throat. 'Ad-*vance*!'

It was only a ragged double line, but it moved together, shields tight, spears raised. Across the open space of the enclosure, the Picts were massing in front of the broken wall, shrinking back now as they saw the block of soldiers advancing towards them.

Castus felt a javelin jar off his shield, then another punched through the wood and leather and stuck, swinging wildly. Something else – a flung axe – wheeled through the air and he bashed it aside.

'Spears!' he called, and at once the men beside him canted back their arms and threw. The volley drove lanes through the Pictish mass.

'Swords – and *charge*!'

Blades rattled from scabbards as the formation broke into a run. Six paces, and they were kicking the bodies of the slain underfoot.

'Drive them out! Stick every bastard of them!' A crash and a jolt ran along the formation as the shields met the bodies of the attackers. Swords stabbed out between the shield rims, long blades aimed and reaching. The Picts were crumbling in the shock of impact, most of them fleeing back across the wall.

Castus saw the tumbled stones just ahead of him, the last few Picts turning at bay. Left and right, shield and sword: he turned a spearpoint, punched it aside and slashed the man down. Blood spattered his chest. He cut a second man across the face, then with all the strength of his arm he drove his blade up to the hilt in the belly of a third. He could hear himself yelling, a distant sound over the thunder in his head.

Breathless, reeling, he pushed the dead man down with his shield and hauled the sword free. Someone grabbed his arm and he spun on his heel, roaring – it was Timotheus, the optio falling back in fear, but then grinning. There was blood around his mouth.

'... out!' the man was telling him. 'Out!' Castus could not hear properly.

'South wall,' he tried to say. 'Get back there...'

'All driven out,' Timotheus said, his mouth working but only scraps of words audible. Castus felt a pop in his ears and the world rushed back. Pump of blood, cheers of the men around him.

Another attack like that, Castus thought, and it's over. He paced the circuit of the defences, jaw set, trying to keep the anguish from his face. Five more men and two of the armed slaves dead, and eight too badly wounded to fight again. Vincentius was among the wounded, as was Evagrius: the standard-bearer was tight-faced, lying with a smashed arm and a jagged gash in his side. But Castus smiled at the men as he passed, smacking them on the shoulders, clenching his fist. Another attack like that – he did not dare to think about it.

The ground below the southern wall was marshy with blood and heaped corpses. To the west it was hardly better; only a few of the attackers had dashed from behind their corpse-shields and made an attempt on the rampart, but the fresh bodies lying among the twisted slain had a ghoulish look. The dead Picts had been cleared from inside the enclosure and heaved back over the walls, the breach to the north repaired with piled stones. Now the light was coming in low from the west, under the dark lid of clouds.

'Vincentius is gone,' Culchianus told him quietly. 'There was a second wound – lung I think. He was choking on blood.' Ten men of his century dead, Castus thought. Ten wounded now. He bowed his head for a moment, nodding. Vincentius had never been a good soldier, but he and Culchianus had been close.

'Wrap him in his blanket and put him with the other slain.'

Forty men left, and the four unarmed slaves. When would the moment come that they could no longer hold the walls? When would he give the order to fall back and form a shield ring at the heart of the enclosure as their enemies swarmed in across the rampart? He gazed up at the sky and felt the steady drizzle flecking his face. Was this really their fate? What good would it serve, whose god would it benefit, for them all to die in this place?

The Picts attacked again just before sunset, rushing up out of the dusk. One group came from the east, up the steep slope from the river, while another band of them swung around to the south. But they broke and fell back almost at once, as if the ebbing light had stolen their courage, and left only one man dead and another wounded.

As night fell, the hillock was surrounded by a ring of fires. Torches moved like wandering fireflies between them, and from behind their rampart the Romans could hear the wailing sounds of lamentation, the rising and falling songs praising the great deeds of the slain. The fires burned until the third watch, then one by one all were doused and the smoky blackness closed over the plain and the hills. All night, strange and savage cries rose from the darkness below the walls, inhuman, unnatural.

Castus woke to the grey light of dawn. His blanket was damp with dew, and he threw it aside and stretched his aching back and shoulders. He rubbed his face with a damp rag – the water supply was too limited for washing – then he stumbled to his feet and began his tour of inspection.

'I hoped they might have all gone home in the night,' he said as he stood at the western wall. The Pictish horde was a huddled mass on the plain, stirring and shifting now.

Timotheus grinned, and the dried blood smeared around his mouth cracked. The optio's face looked as if he had been suspended over a smoking fire all night.

'Let the men sleep as long as you can. But make sure the sentries stay alert. The enemy may try and sneak up here while we're dozy.'

Castus crossed the enclosure to where the wounded lay. Evagrius was awake, but hooked and hollow with pain. He tried to struggle upright as his centurion approached, and Castus motioned for him to stay down. His wound was bad, but might not be fatal if it was properly dressed. Not much chance of that, though. Castus raised the man's head and gave him water.

The sudden brass yell of the horn jolted him back, the canteen slipping from his hand. Everywhere men staggered up from their blankets, thrashing from sleep, grabbing for shields and weapons. Castus had covered the ground to the western wall before he even realised he was moving.

'Messenger coming up!' the sentry cried. 'Least, I think it's a messenger...'

The plain in front of the hillock was still grey with mist, but Castus could see the Picts moving forward, gathering in their warbands. Ahead of them was a rider on a tall horse, with a man behind him carrying the green branch of parley. It was not a Pictish horse. The rider was not a Pict.

Julius Decentius rode closer, leaning forward in the saddle as the ground rose beneath him, the fur cape humped over his shoulders. Even from a distance, Castus could see the familiar cold smile. Worst time for this to happen, he thought, and surely the renegade knew that well.

'What does he want, do you think?' Timotheus asked, jogging up to the wall beside him. More men were crowding the rampart now.

'Think we can guess. Keep those sentries sharp on the other walls, though. Might be a ruse.'

Fifty paces from the wall the renegade drew to a halt. The stink of the dead was bothering his horse, and he kept a tight grip on the reins. For a long moment there was silence, only the cawing of the crows.

'Brothers!' Decentius called. 'You look tired!'

'Piss off, traitor!' a cry came back from the wall. 'You're not my brother!'

'Get back home to your Pictish bitch!'

Castus felt his chest swell and his throat tighten with pride. They had heart yet, even after the long night, the fierce day before. There was still fight in them.

'Centurion! I can see you there, centurion. Will you answer for your men?'

Castus jumped up on the crest of the wall, feet spaced wide. He hooked his thumbs in his belt. 'What do you want?'

'What I want...' the renegade replied, 'is to save your lives. We're all Romans, after all!'

'You don't look Roman to me.' Castus felt the press of men at his back, the raised shields, the ready javelins.

'You think...' the renegade called, raising his hand to address the gathered soldiers, 'you think the Picts are savages, but they're not! I've lived among them for over a decade, and see! I'm still alive! You've fought well – you've fought bravely. The Picts respect that. They respect *you*. They don't want to destroy you, but they will if you continue to resist. They'll kill you all and mutilate your bodies! Do you want that, centurion?'

'I can't hear you,' Castus shouted. 'Speak up or move closer.' Forty paces, he thought. Extreme range.

Decentius nudged his horse on up the slope a few steps. 'If you lay down your arms now, you can surrender with honour!' he cried, his voice cracking. 'You can march home with your wounded. Return to your wives. Your families. The Picts will let you go! Or – or you could stay here. Make your homes here. The empire has betrayed you, brothers!'

There was a long pause. A stir through the men along the wall. Whispers.

'What does he mean?' Timotheus asked. Castus hissed at him.

'It's true – you've been sent here to die! Your commanders want a cause for war, and your deaths will give them one!'

Castus glanced to left and right, scanning the men for signs of weakening, of wavering. But the grey faces along the wall were taut and defiant.

'Ox shit,' he shouted, and then leaned down to the man beside him. 'Pass me up a wasp.'

He held his hand behind his back, and at once the shaft of a dart slapped into his palm. It was still sticky with clotting blood. The renegade's horse blew through its nostrils and shook its mane, and Decentius urged it on up the slope another few paces.

'Romans! Brothers! Don't die for emperors who despise you!' His grin looked painted on his face. 'Come with me – live among the Picts! You'll have good lives, long lives here… You'd be treated as heroes, the pick of their women would be yours! Beautiful girls for brave warriors!'

'We've heard enough,' Castus cried. He held both hands clasped behind him, the dart point downwards. 'Get back to your friends, or that bit of foliage won't protect you!'

'Centurion, think carefully.' The renegade stretched out his hand, his horse climbed another few paces up the slope. 'I'm offering life, for you and your men! Lay down your arms now and your honour is secure…'

Castus waited, swaying slightly on his heels. Decentius stared up at him, his grin stretching into a sour grimace.

'Well? What's your answer, centurion?'

'Here's your answer, take it!'

Castus jumped back off the wall, braced himself on his right leg, and hurled the dart with all his strength. Decentius saw it a moment too late – his face blanched, and he hauled the horse's head round. Then the iron spike buried itself in his thigh and he screamed like a woman. The horse shied, reared, and he clung to the saddle as it bolted back down the hill.

Cheering all along the wall, spears clashing against shields. 'VIC-*trix*! VIC-*trix*! VIC-*trix*…!'

'Nice throw,' Timotheus said, grinning.

'No. I was aiming for his head.'

* * *

The attack came soon, and it was savage. The soldiers inside the rampart barely had time to eat and to clean their weapons before the first rush of the enemy surged across the plain and up onto the slopes. They came on slowly now, moving in a mass and pausing every ten or twenty paces to dress their ranks, howl their war cries and rattle their spear-butts against their shields. While the main body of them advanced from the west another band ranged around to the south, streaming up over the ridge through the scattered stones of the old wall.

The soldiers were silent at the defences, too hoarse, too worn with fatigue to shout back. Crouching behind their shields, they readied their javelins and darts, drew back aching arms and threw. Again the front waves of the attackers were felled; again the warriors behind them pressed forward.

Castus ranged across the enclosure, sword in hand, calling encouragement to his men. 'Mark your targets and aim high – the javelin will drop as it falls. Don't throw until they're in range. Keep to the walls – don't move back. Don't budge.' His mind was foggy with despair and fatigue, but his body still burned with sour energy. *This is how it is*, he thought. *We fight to the end, and then die fighting. We are soldiers.*

A wild yell and a clatter from the west as the first charge reached the wall. Spears and blades flickered against the dull sky. Castus ran, feeling as though he was swimming through thick fluid. He hurled himself between two of the soldiers, smiting down at once and bursting the skull of a Pict crouching beneath. The roaring noise was all around him. *If I feel like this*, he thought, *how must the others feel?* He stabbed out at a shouting face. The attackers had smeared themselves grey with the ashes of their mourning fires. He punched with his shield and knocked a man down into the bloody mess on the far side of the rampart.

The wave crashed and broke, then the attackers ebbed away. Soldiers pelted them with darts as they retreated. Their harsh cheer sounded more like a groan. Now there was fighting to the south as well – running again, Castus reached the wall just as Culchianus and his men threw themselves against the attackers. Shoulders behind shields, they shoved the Picts back and stabbed out with spears and blades, punching holes in the packed mass of bodies. The Picts dropped back, piling together, scrambling to escape. Castus was up on the wall, wheeling his arm, slashing down at the enemy below. His hand, his arm, his chest were bright and wet with blood. He could taste it in his mouth, and feel it in his eyes.

A dull bleat from the Pictish horns and the attackers turned and ran back, scrambling away and leaving their dead in twitching piles before the rampart. Castus sagged against his knees, gulping breath. For a moment he felt sick, but he swallowed the urge down. He had seen enough of the other men vomiting already.

'Centurion! Message from the optio – you'd better come quick.'

Castus grunted himself upright, wiped his sword on the hem of his tunic and slammed it back in his scabbard. Then he followed the runner back across the enclosure to the western wall.

'Looks like another parley,' Timotheus said. 'One of their chiefs, I think.'

There were five riders coming up the slope this time. One was Talorcagus, and behind him rode his brute-faced nephew Drustagnus. Castus was pleased to see that both men were bloody – they must have led one of the charges the day before. The third rider carried the swaying green branch, and the fourth was dragging something behind him. Castus stared.

At the back of group rode Senomaglus, the old chief of the Votadini. There were two men behind the fourth horse, led by a rope, staggering. Two men stripped to the waist, with sacks over their heads. His breath caught, and he gripped the wall. His leg trembled as he tried to climb.

'*Gods!* Timotheus, help me up here!'

Leaning on the optio's arm, lifting his massive frame onto the wall, Castus straightened his back and stood steady, glaring down at the approaching riders. Talorcagus pulled up just outside the range of the darts. Before him, the slope up to the rampart was clotted with his own dead warriors, their corpses flung on the dull red grass.

'Find the interpreter and bring him here,' Castus said. He had last seen Caccumattus the night before, down at the south wall, flinging javelins with a look of furious rage on his thin face. Culchianus had sent him back to tend to the wounded. Now the little man, more ragged than ever, came running across the enclosure.

'Centurio! I here!'

The Pictish chief had already started to bellow out his message. As he spoke, the two bound captives were marched up the slope and made to kneel. Their captor ripped the sacks from their heads. Marcellinus and Strabo, gasping and blinking in the daylight.

'He say: Romani fighting well. Too much bravery! His heart wanting for to make deal.'

Castus stared down at the two captives. They knelt in the grass, the corpses spread before them. The man behind them had a short-bladed knife in his hand.

'He say: Picti let Romani soldiers to go. March with weapons. Picti no to attack – he make promise word. Senomaglus of Votadini go with Romani, guide them to safe country.'

Castus stood on the wall, swaying slightly. His body felt as thin and light as a lath-wood mannequin, but sweat was pouring down his back beneath the hug of his armour. All along the wall behind him he could hear the other soldiers translating for their comrades. A steady stir of whispers. Senomaglus wore a look of humiliation, and did not glance up.

'What about the prisoners?'

'He say: If you no say yes to go, he make to kill prisoner mans.'

The guard stepped around behind Strabo, dragging his head up by the hair and placing his blade against the stretched column of his neck. Strabo rolled his eyes, terrified. The cross of hair on his bare chest was slicked with sweat. Marcellinus, kneeling beside him, was saying something... *Accept? Don't accept?* Castus could not make out the words.

But now Talorcagus was speaking again, stretching up from his horse and raising his finger. He was pointing straight at Castus.

'He say: Also *you* must go. Centurio – he say you go to prisoner. Then prisoners live and all others Romani march to home.'

'Don't listen to him,' Timotheus said. He seized Castus's leg, his fingers tight on the muscle of his thigh.

Promise me you'll protect him. Swear to me that you'll look after him... Castus felt his head empty. The men behind him were silent, watching. How many of them were left now? Something between twenty or thirty still fit to fight. Another attack would break them, and all would die. They, Strabo and Marcellinus too. Already his fingers were unbuckling his belt.

'What are you doing? Centurion?'

He slung the sword baldric from his shoulder and jumped

back off the wall. He passed his sword and belt to Timotheus and his helmet to Culchianus.

'Keep these safe for me.'

'No! You can't do this…' Timotheus was grey-faced, stammering. The other men crowded behind him, some of them reaching out to their centurion, others hanging back, hiding the shame of hope.

'Get into rank!' Castus bellowed at them with all the parade-ground brass he could muster. He stooped, shrugging the mail shirt off over his shoulders. The links clashed around his head and then dropped heavily to the ground before him.

'Take that with you as well… Optio Timotheus, I'm handing command of the century to you. Form up the surviving men with all their kit, and load the wounded who can't walk onto the mules. You'll march out of here and keep going till you reach the river. Fill canteens, wash your wounds then keep going. Keep close to Senomaglus and the Votadini, and don't let your guard down till you reach Bremenium.'

'Centurion,' Timotheus said. There were tears in his eyes, and Castus could not bear to look at him.

'Somebody needs to tell what happened here,' he said quietly.

'We'll come back for you,' Timotheus said, and then grabbed Castus in a firm embrace. Culchianus stepped up and did the same, other men gripping his shoulders and arms.

'We'll come back – and we'll bring the whole legion with us. We'll scythe those bastards down – every fucking one of them!'

'Do that,' Castus said. With his unbelted tunic hanging below his knees he stepped up onto the wall and jumped down on the far side. Open-handed, he walked steadily down the slope, stepping over the crumpled bodies on the blood-damp grass. Behind him he could hear Timotheus shouting the orders to form the men up.

Twenty paces, then thirty. The Picts gathered on the plain were making a noise now, a rising hiss and then a gathering roar. He kept his breath steady. He kept walking.

PART TWO

CHAPTER IX

It took five of them to wrestle him to the ground and strip him of his tunic, and he fought them all the way. He dropped one with a kick to the groin, head-butted another and broke his nose. Then they began clubbing him with spears and the flats of their swords, until he was kneeling with his arms bound tightly behind his back, and Castus felt them wrench from his neck the gold torque he had won at Oxsa.

This is what surrender feels like, he thought. But he was oblivious to the pain and the humiliation. Slaves have no feelings, he told himself.

He was dragged to his feet and made to stumble forward with a spearshaft pressed to the nape of his neck to keep his head down. All he could see was the dirty turf, and the bare feet of his guards scuffing along beside him, kicking him sometimes when he struggled. Then they got into the mass of the Pictish gathering, and there it was worse. Women screamed at him and threw stones and clods of earth: he was the leader of the soldiers that had slaughtered their sons, their brothers, their husbands. He felt their spit flecking over his bare back, until the guards drove the women away from him.

'Castus!' He twisted his head against the spearshaft and saw Marcellinus beside him, in the same wretched condition.

'I'm sorry,' the envoy gasped, 'it wasn't...' One of the guards struck him with a spear-butt, and Marcellinus was silent.

They passed through the stream, the water splashing up into Castus's face. Then they were moving up the far slope into the main Pictish encampment. The two prisoners were thrown together onto the dirty straw of a wattle-walled enclosure – a pigsty, Castus guessed, by the smell. He rolled onto his side, then he knelt and flexed his shoulders, trying to break the cords that tied his wrists.

'Don't,' Marcellinus said. 'They're damp rawhide – you'll just pull them tighter.'

The envoy lay on his side, his skin very pale and grey. Castus could see the welts of a beating across his shoulders.

'What happened?'

'They took us just as we were going into the council hut,' Marcellinus told him. 'We heard shouts from across the camp, then we were surrounded by armed warriors – it must have been planned that way in advance. Then we learned that Ulcagnus and Vendognus had been found dead in their huts by their own men. We were treated well at first, Strabo and I – put in a hut by ourselves, with a guard at the door. Later, I suppose once Talorcagus had taken control and they'd started the attack on your position, they dragged us out and beat us, then tied us with sacks over our heads...'

'Why did they think you'd done it?'

Marcellinus just grimaced, shaking his head against the dirty straw. The gate was dragged open, and another body was thrown into the pen beside them: Strabo, with a purple bruise across the side of his face.

'My men,' Castus said. 'Have they got away yet? Did either of you see them go?'

Both shook their heads. 'Senomaglus promised me he'd protect them,' Marcellinus said. 'I think I believe him. I hope

I believe him. But there was nothing else you could do. You fought well, but it was over.'

Several hours passed before the guards returned. Rain fell, and Castus tipped back his head and opened his mouth and tried to drink it from the air. Then the wattle gate was flung open again and the guards were among them, dragging at their aching arms, threatening them with spears.

Heads down, they were led across the encampment, between low huts and shelters and the walls of other animal pens. Castus fixed his mind on the knot of pain between his shoulders; his hands and arms were numb, and he stumbled as he was dragged along. He heard Marcellinus cry out beside him, and then he was forced down to kneel.

'No, this is barbaric!' Marcellinus hissed between his teeth. The envoy was struggling against his guards now, trying to break away.

Castus raised his eyes slowly, wincing against the ache in his neck. Before him was a low mound surrounded by open space, and on the mound was a single tree. The bark had been stripped away to the bare white wood, and the branches lopped off close to the trunk leaving long spikes sticking up. Marcellinus was shouting in the Pictish tongue, oblivious to the guards around him.

'It's a triumph tree,' he cried out. '*Cran na buadag...* Don't look at it!'

But Castus continued to stare, dazed. Groups of warriors were gathering around the mound and the stripped tree. With a lurch of horror, Castus recognised what they were carrying. Heads – severed human heads, some carried by the hair, others with a thumb hooked inside the jaw. The heads of Roman soldiers.

Beside him, he heard Strabo muttering prayers to his Christian god. He wanted to pray himself, or shout out in rage, but his throat was locked and he could not make a sound. He watched as the warriors climbed up to the tree, some of them clambering on each other's backs, and one by one stabbed the severed heads onto the spiked branches. Five heads, then ten, then twenty... Castus watched and counted, sickened and dizzy. He saw the face of Vincentius staring back at him. Then Brigonius and his comrades, the three scouts he had sent to summon help from Bremenium. One of the slaves he had armed and offered freedom. Draucus and Jucundus...

No Timotheus, no Culchianus. The heads had been taken from the fallen soldiers left lying in the compound wrapped in their blankets. All of them decapitated after death.

Marcellinus was shaking his head fiercely. 'I'm sorry,' he said. 'I'm sorry.'

Now the last of the warriors climbed down from the mound, leaving the tree adorned with thirty human heads budding like terrible bulbous fruit from the bare branches. Around the base of the trunk the Picts had stacked the broken shields and shattered weapons gathered from the battle site. The warriors stood in a massed circle around the mound, raised their own weapons in salute and howled out their chant of victory.

Castus had seen many strange and horrific sights in his life, but the stripped tree with its ghastly trophies left him sick and weak. They were his own men, those pale bobbing heads, men he had trained and led in battle. Men who had trusted him to command them. *If they murder me now, I deserve it.*

But the warriors were falling back from the mound, joining the vast throng that filled the open space all around. A line of carts drawn by shaggy ponies turned between them and began to circle the tree. In the lead cart, Talorcagus stood up tall and proud, raising his spear to the shouts of victory.

'Look at him,' Marcellinus said. 'He's sealed his rule in blood already.'

Behind the new king rode his nephew Drustagnus, then the other chiefs of the Picts. Only the woman, Cunomagla, was not among their number. Castus felt glad of that – he could not bear the idea of seeing her gloat over his slain. The carts drew to a halt, the chiefs dismounting. Now a strange figure was moving between them, an ancient woman dressed in grey tatters, carrying a leather bag.

'The witch,' Strabo said, with a hissing intake of breath.

The chiefs and their warriors moved behind the witch as she advanced, shambling, towards the bound prisoners. Beside him, Castus saw Marcellinus give a sudden lunge and try to get up. The guards wrestled him back to his knees.

'That's my saddlebag,' Strabo said quietly, in dawning horror. 'She's got my saddlebag...'

The witch halted, throwing the bag down; Castus recognised it now, a square satchel of tooled Roman leather. He had seen Strabo carrying it on his pony. Throwing up her arms, the old woman let out a long keening wail. She reeled in a circle, and then dropped forward to scrabble at the bag. The chiefs and the warriors drew closer around her.

Castus felt the tip of a spear pressing at the hollow of his throat, another at his back. He could not breathe, could not move.

The witch-woman knelt upright with a cry of satisfaction, holding up a small brass bottle with a stopper. The assembled Picts fell back, gasping and shouting.

'Cough medicine,' Strabo said, with a despairing grimace. 'It's only cough medicine...'

But now Talorcagus stepped to the front of the group and raised his arm, pointing at Strabo. Guards to either side seized the imperial agent by the elbows and started to drag him forward.

'No, surely not!' Marcellinus cried suddenly in pained disbelief. 'They're saying it's poison… they're saying he murdered the chiefs with it…!'

They don't care, Castus thought. Everything now had a terrible sense of inevitability. Marcellinus made another sudden lunge, slipped from the grasp of his captors and leaped to his feet. He managed two long strides towards Strabo before one of the guards smashed at his leg with the flat of his sword. Castus heard the sharp snap of bone, and then Marcellinus was sprawled in the dirt, writhing and choking.

Strabo was made to kneel before the assembled chiefs. He looked very calm now, his face pale but clear and his eyes shining. One of the guards gripped his hair and drew back his head, raising a short curved knife to the sky. Castus could hear the chanting and the yells, but could understand nothing. His gaze was fixed on the kneeling man.

'I am a soldier of Christ!' Strabo shouted, suddenly and very loud. 'Oh, Lord God, I commend my soul to you!'

The chanting grew louder, the chiefs stepping away from the pinned captive as the guard lowered his cruel blade.

'In the name of the Lord Jesus Christ,' Strabo cried through clenched teeth, his face shining with fierce defiance, 'I offer my soul to God in hope of salvation…'

Then the voices rose to a great shout, and Castus looked away quickly as he saw the knifeman move. When he glanced back, he saw the blood spraying across the bare earth, Strabo's half-naked body tumbling sideways, the knife raised once more to the sky, shining red.

* * *

They freed his wrists, and he snarled in pain as sensation returned to his trapped hands. Before he could struggle, they dragged up his arms and tied them once more to a baulk of wood pinned behind his neck.

For the rest of that day they marched, up the hill from the encampment and on over high desolate moorland. There was only a small group of guards, twenty or thirty warriors with spears, and they moved at a steady lope, dragging Castus along with a halter around his neck. Marcellinus they carried on a crude stretcher, his broken leg wrapped in fleece.

Whenever he could, Castus straightened his back against the wood at his neck and gazed around him, trying to pick out landmarks he might remember, trying to gauge distance and direction. The sky was overcast, but as the day wore on he saw his shadow before him and slightly to his right, and knew they were travelling north-east-by-east. They crossed the mountain flank and descended, following a rushing stream into a broad valley that stretched almost to the northern horizon.

As evening came on he saw fires on the hilltops: beacons, and here and there the walls of small forts. Smaller fires moved in the valley below: lines of men with torches, streaming westwards towards the tribal muster. One small victory over Rome was not enough for them, Castus realised. Now the whole nation of the Picts was rising. He thought of his men, Timotheus and the rest, marching at full pace towards the frontier, with the Pictish horde surging behind them. He could not afford to think about these things. Only survival mattered now. Survival and, one day, vengeance – for Strabo, for the dishonoured bodies of his fallen soldiers, for the jubilation of the barbarians around their trophy tree. One day, he thought – and the hunger for that vengeance drove him on.

* * *

171

When night fell the guards led them up to one of the hill forts, a ring of stone set on a spur above a valley cleft into the mountainside. At the centre of the fort was a broken tower of massive masonry, and they built a large fire against the wall of it. The flames curled up over the mossy stones, throwing huge rearing shadows onto the surrounding hillsides. Castus lay at the edge of the light, chewing a hank of dried meat, with Marcellinus on his stretcher beside him.

'Stupid of me,' Marcellinus said, 'to try and intervene like that. I couldn't have done anything to stop them.'

'Suppose not,' Castus said. He would have done the same, he knew, if he hadn't had a spear pressed into his throat.

Marcellinus was silent for a while. His broken leg was clearly paining him, but he was trying not to let it show.

'So it was Talorcagus and his nephew,' Castus said, 'who poisoned the other chiefs.'

'Almost certainly. And they probably killed Vepogenus too. And now they have the power to kill anyone who accuses them of it.'

'And what about the woman... Cunomagla, you called her. Wasn't she the wife of Vendognus?'

'She was. Now his widow. But there was no love between the two of them. I wouldn't be surprised if she was part of the conspiracy as well. With her husband gone she's free to advance her own son as future king... Which puts her in competition with Drustagnus, of course...'

'If they start fighting among themselves,' Castus said, 'all the better for us. What about Decentius, the renegade? Did you see him? I stuck a dart in his leg.'

'You did? *Good...*' Marcellinus managed to smile. 'I didn't see him, no. He'll be around somewhere, though, if he lived. He's sure to be involved in the plot.'

Castus frowned, remembering something he had forgotten in all the confusion of the last twelve hours. 'He said... Decentius, I mean... he said something about the empire betraying us. Sending us to die deliberately. What did he mean?'

Marcellinus lay still. Perhaps thinking, Castus told himself. Perhaps trying to frame an acceptable answer.

'I don't know,' the envoy said at last. 'I confess I heard something similar from Strabo – he was taken away to meet with Decentius during our captivity.'

Castus decided to ask no more about it, for now. He gnawed off another bite of the dried meat and squeezed it between his molars. Whatever might have happened – or not – in the muttered conversations of conspiracy was nothing to do with him.

'Can I ask you something?' Marcellinus said.

Castus nodded. The meat was sticking his teeth together.

'Why did you agree to surrender back there? I mean – what was going through your mind?'

The meat came free, and Castus swallowed it. He took his time before answering.

'Your daughter... made me swear an oath. To protect you.'

'Marcellina? She made you do that?'

'Yes. To protect you and bring you home safely.'

Marcellinus tipped his head back. '*Ha, aha!*' he said, gasping against the pain as he laughed. '*Ha ha ha!*'

In the grey of morning they set off again, moving north-east along a narrow track between the mountain slopes and the wide plain of the valley. The sky had cleared, and the sunlight came down in bright torrents, lighting the landscape to grey-green and golden brown. The hills and the plain below were striped with the rolling shadows of clouds and, in the far distance, the northern horizon was lined with bare blue mountains.

After five or six miles they forded a wide stream; then the trail swung eastwards. There were settlements of clustered huts across the plain, and the coils of a winding river glinting in the sunlight. The baulk of wood chafed against Castus's neck with every step, and he could no longer feel his hands, but he kept marching.

Finally, as the sun set behind the hills, the trail curled around into a narrow valley and began to climb. The slope rose, until Castus could barely stagger upwards with his shoulders bent. He glanced up and saw a wall of massive stones looming above him in the twilight, almost twelve feet high with a wooden palisade along the top. The guards led him around the base of the wall, then up into a narrow opening between the rearing ramparts. A stone-lined passage, open to the sky above, sloped on upwards. The guards cried out to the men on the wall above them, and a heavy wooden gate opened.

Fatigue coursed through his body as Castus climbed from the entrance passage into the enclosure of the fort. Round huts with conical roofs of straw and turf packed the raised terrace inside the stone rampart and palisade. Dogs barked from the darkness and torches flared bright in his face. Still he was led onward, between the huts to a second, higher wall that lay within the first. Another narrow cleft led upwards; goaded with a spear at his back, Castus stumbled through the gap and climbed towards the upper terrace of the fort.

Three or four large huts and a cluster of smaller ones stood at the centre of the enclosure, with smoke rising into the still night sky. Castus snatched a look back over his shoulder at the darkened landscape to the north, the wide spread of the valley, but rough hands pushed his head down, and he felt himself shoved forward into a low confined space. Behind him he heard Marcellinus cry out in pain; then he was wrestled off his feet and his hands were untied from the baulk of wood. The ground seemed to vanish from beneath him, and for a moment he was falling, before hard stone rushed up and struck him in the back. He lay still, breathing quickly, blood pumping through his body. Stone all around him – hard and cold and deep. He took a deep shuddering breath as the dread crawled through him. Then he began shouting.

'Are you awake? Can you hear me?'

'Yes... Where are you?'

'Over here – I can reach your ankle... Do you feel that?'

'Where are we?'

'Underground. A storage chamber in the fort. You're safe, don't worry. Just don't sit up – the ceiling's very low and you'll hit your head again. That was quite a clout they gave you when you started yelling. You've been unconscious, I think.'

Castus was lying down in total darkness, and when he raised his arms his knuckles grazed stone to either side. The chamber was more like a tunnel, barely four feet across and lined on all sides with heavy slabs. *Like a sewer*, he thought. *Like a grave*.

'There's water here, and food. And a straw mattress beside you somewhere. Here – I'll pass the jug.'

Castus stretched out his arm, reaching blindly in the constricted space. His fingers hit something and water slopped over his hand. He found the rim of the earthenware jug and lifted it carefully to his mouth, drinking deeply.

'Centurion,' said Marcellinus's voice from the darkness, 'I have some bad news.' Castus stiffened, placing the jug down. The use of his rank title seemed ominous.

175

'What is it?'

'When they were carrying us in, I heard them talking. Some of the Picts – Drustagnus was there, I think. They said... I'm sorry, brother... they said that your men did not reach the frontier.'

Castus raised his head slowly, reaching up to the stone overhead, the stone on either side. He pressed his feet against one wall and his back against the other. Fists clenched, he tried to slow his breathing, his blood.

'What happened?'

'The Picts attacked them as they marched – only a few miles south of your position on the hill. They didn't have a chance. The Votadini fled at once and your men were cut down before they could get into defensive formation. Not one of them escaped. I'm sorry.'

Castus could feel the roar gathering deep in his throat. His shoulders knitted, and he punched with both fists against the wall. Punched and punched again, pressing with his back against the stone. He clenched his teeth, pummelling himself backwards, his fists and feet forwards, as if he could burst open the walls that surrounded him and fight his way out – as if he could destroy this whole fort, tear it apart with his hands and kill everyone... The shout burst from him, ringing in the confined space.

'Stop! This won't help us...'

Flinging himself sideways, Castus thrashed his arms out in front of him. There must be a door; there must be a way out of this tomb... Then he felt Marcellinus gripping his shoulders, pushing against him.

'Back! *Down!*' the envoy said. 'Centurion! I'm ordering you! You'll kill us both like this.'

His head scraped on the low ceiling as he recoiled into a crouch. He pressed his fists to his eyes, then to his gaping mouth, his furious rage turning to hard black grief inside him. His men – the century he had trained and led, were destroyed to a man. Timotheus, Culchianus, Evagrius – even the wounded men butchered.

'*We will do what we are ordered,*' he said quietly, his voice dull and edged with iron. '*And at every command we will be ready.*' The soldier's oath. He had lived by it all his life. Even death is a command, he thought. Even death an order, to be obeyed.

'Stay calm, brother,' Marcellinus said. 'Any sudden move and we both die.'

The wooden ceiling-grating at one end of the narrow subterranean chamber had been raised, and bright daylight beamed down from above. Harsh Pictish voices as Marcellinus was lifted up through the opening. Castus crawled after him, and when he raised his arms his wrists were seized and tied. Squinting in the light, he climbed up into a ring of spears.

Surprisingly, he was not under the open sky but inside a round hut. The daylight that had seemed so blinding after his hours in darkness came from the open doorway, and a fire smoked in the hearth at the centre. Three of the guards squatted around Marcellinus as he lay on the ground; the envoy's face was deeply lined, greyish, and Castus could see the bandages around his injured leg were swollen and black. The other guards kept their weapons levelled at Castus, forcing him down to kneel beside the open grating to the chamber below.

One by one the visitors filed into the hut. First a group of noble warriors, their arms and faces heavily scarred with beast pictures, their heads shaved at the sides and their hair matted into thick hanging pelts. After them came Cunomagla, widow of Vendognus, wrapped in a dark cloak with her fox-coloured hair bound in a plait. She had a child with her, a delicate-looking long-haired boy of nine or ten years, and held him before her as she stared down at the prisoners.

Then, stooping as he entered the hut, Drustagnus, the brute-faced nephew of the new Pictish king. Castus tensed, flexing his arms against the bonds tying his wrists. He set his jaw, glaring.

Another man entered then, older and rather small, with a hunched back, carrying a wrapped bundle. He approached Marcellinus and knelt beside him, and Castus shuffled forward on his knees with warning in his eyes.

'Don't worry – he's a herbalist,' Marcellinus said quickly. His voice was hardly more than a gasp. 'I know him – he served Vepogenus well. He needs to look at my leg...'

The little man was peeling away the bandages. The sour smell of mortifying flesh made Castus's stomach tighten and he looked away. The boy was gazing at the injured man on the floor with a mixture of fascination and repulsion. Something familiar in his face, Castus thought. Something he had seen before.

'You,' said Drustagnus suddenly, in Latin. 'Your name?' He was sitting on a stool beside the hearth, holding an apple. Castus remembered that the man had learned Latin as a hostage in Eboracum. He and Cunomagla too. He drew himself up straight.

'Aurelius Castus, Centurion, Third Cohort, Sixth Legion,' he said, trying to keep his voice level. Trying to keep the murder from his eyes.

Drustagnus smiled, and bit into the apple with his blunt yellow teeth. He spoke again as he chewed. His Latin was heavily accented and barbarous.

'Soon, I go with my uncle. Talorcagus. Pict King. We make

war on Romans. Then I return here. You – brave warrior. You teach me and all warriors skill of Roman fighting. Then, when Rome king come here, we fight. We kill him.' He made a casual swiping gesture with his hand. 'Then Talorcagus king all Britannia. And after him – *me*.'

Not a chance, Castus thought, but said nothing. Marcellinus had already told him of the preparations for war, the Pictish host assembling from all directions. Twenty thousand spears, or so the guards had claimed, and Marcellinus had said this was plausible. Warriors had come from Hibernia across the sea, and from the Attacotti of the far north. Even many of the Votadini and Selgovae tribesmen had thrown off their allegiance to Rome and joined the uprising. In his mind, Castus had seen them scythed down by the legions, falling in screaming waves before the iron storm of the ballistae and the javelins. But then he remembered the triumph tree with its gory harvest of heads, his men lying dead and mutilated on the road...

Drustagnus stood up suddenly, tossing the apple core into the hearth. He swept his fur cape over one shoulder, baring a scarred sword arm, and then snapped out a question to the herbalist. The little man was busy mixing a paste of herbs and fat in a pestle and spreading it on Marcellinus's leg. He answered, quiet and deferential. Drustagnus nodded, grunted, and strode out of the hut.

'He says your friend recovers soon.'

Castus blinked, unsure at first who had spoken; then he saw the woman, Cunomagla, looking at him. For the first time he noticed the fine tracery of markings on her skin, her bare upper arms and forehead inscribed with swirling shapes more subtle than those worn by the warriors. She spoke more fluently than Drustagnus, still with an accent, but her voice was low and rich, almost the voice of a man.

'Thank you,' Castus said. She looked him in the eye, her expression hard and unmoving. Assessing him. Was she too his enemy?

'It is dark in the pit,' the woman said. 'I send light.'

Then she turned, urging the boy ahead of her, and made for the door. As he left the hut the boy glanced back, from under the hem of his mother's cloak, and Castus realised where he had seen those features before. An oval face in darkness. Marcellinus's daughter.

The light was a small oil lamp with a twisting flame that threw their shadows back into the reaching darkness of the chamber. They sat together beneath the wooden grating, so the oil smoke could rise and they could breathe the faint damp freshness of the outside air. It was night – Castus could not judge how long they had spent together locked in the pit. Three days, or four? The herbalist had come and gone several times, applying more of the foul-smelling paste to Marcellinus's ruined leg. The envoy's face had a sunken look as he lay back against the wall.

'The boy, Cunomagla's son,' Castus said to him. 'Yours?'

Marcellinus nodded, and the shadow of his head swept up and down. 'Yes. You guessed. After my last campaign against these people, when I made the treaty with Vepogenus, it was sealed with a pact. A pact of brotherhood, but also of marriage.'

'She's your *wife*?'

'Not by our terms. Only by native custom. She was fourteen or fifteen then, the king's niece, a girl of the royal household. I thought little of it at the time, but later she was sent down to Eboracum with the other noble hostages. Drustagnus and some others. It was inconvenient – I had a Roman wife, and a family, of course. But I... well, the child was conceived. And soon afterwards I was accused of treason and imprisoned. You know the rest of that tale.'

Castus nodded, remembering what Strabo had told him, in what seemed a previous life. The escape to Gaul; the return with Constantius.

'Does the boy know who you are?' he asked.

Marcellinus just shrugged. 'Two years had passed by the time I came north again,' he said. 'Cunomagla had returned to her people, and been married to her cousin Vendognus, who claimed the child as his own, though all knew otherwise. Perhaps the boy himself knows, perhaps not. She avoided me then. She's a proud woman, and ambitious. That was the last I saw of either of them, until I returned here with you.'

Castus narrowed his eyes as the lamp-smuts began to smart.

'I once thought,' Marcellinus said, 'that she might have been responsible for the murder of my son, my legitimate son, when he was held as a hostage. She might be capable of that, to revenge herself on me. But I think not. It would not have availed her anything. She was loyal to Vepogenus then. Now, I'm not sure where her allegiances lie...'

'With Drustagnus, it looks like.'

'I don't know. And perhaps I don't want to know.' Marcellinus closed his eyes, head back against the stone slab of the wall. 'You have to escape this place, brother,' he said quietly.

'We will. Both of us.'

'Not me,' Marcellinus said, smiling grimly. 'With this leg, I'd just slow you down...'

Castus gripped his shoulder. 'I'm not leaving without you. I swore an oath to protect you.'

'An oath to my daughter! Very conscientious of you. She is little more than a child. Do you know, she was betrothed four years ago, to a cousin of her mother's who lives in the southern province. But the wedding has never been arranged. Why...? My *reputation*. I'm still seen as suspect. And my family suffer for that. Marcellina has lived all her life at my villa – barely even been to Eboracum more than once or twice. What does she know of the world, do you think?'

'Doesn't matter. An oath is an oath. I swore to the gods.'

'Well, then,' Marcellinus said, almost under his breath, 'May the gods forgive you.'

He woke suddenly, disorientated. The air was thick and greasy with the smoke of the lamp. Raising his head from the straw mattress, he saw Marcellinus sitting back against the wall of the chamber with the wavering flame before him. He held a wooden bowl between his palms.

'Sorry to wake you. I have something I need to tell you.'

Castus raised himself on one elbow, blinking in the smoky glow. Marcellinus lay back against the stone slab, smiling, his eyes only half-open.

'I am leaving you soon,' the envoy said in a low, quiet tone. He no longer sounded pained or anguished. 'I release you from your oath.'

'What do you mean? Leaving how?'

'This bowl contains a toxin made from the extract of a certain root. The herbalist smuggled it to me, at my request. He will be gone from here before morning, and so will I, by a different route.'

'No, I can't allow it...' Castus stretched forward, still groggy from sleep, but Marcellinus raised a palm in warning. After so many days as an invalid, he had suddenly regained his look of authority. Sitting back against the wall, he was once more a Roman commander, a leader of men.

'Do not try to stop me, brother. This is my choice. It is the honourable way. I have made too many mistakes in my life, and returning to this country will be the last of them. I will not be a valuable hostage to them any longer.'

'Then give me the poison too.'

'I'm sorry, there is only enough for one. Besides, in releasing you from one vow I must ask of you another. *Escape this place...* Return to my family and tell them what happened to me. Tell them that I died by own hand and by my own will. You must do this – it is my last order to you.'

He was speaking slowly, deliberately, and Castus realised with a shock that he had already drunk the poison and the bowl he held was empty. In the lamplight he could see the sweat forming on the envoy's brow, the twitch in his jaw as his teeth clenched and relaxed.

'Promise me!' Marcellinus said. The bowl fell from his hands, and he wrenched a heavy ring from his finger. 'Take this – my seal. Return it to my wife, and she'll know that I sent you.'

He tossed the ring, and Castus caught it in his fist. There was nothing he could do to stop this now. Marcellinus's throat was tightening, his eyes flicking open and closed. Castus moved closer, but once more the man motioned him away.

'You may not... want to watch this,' he said, with difficulty. 'I'll extinguish the lamp in a moment... Just a little *more light...*'

Hardly able to breathe, Castus lay down again and rolled on his side facing the wall, the ring held tight in his hand. He heard Marcellinus gasp and retch, his foot kick against the wall; the lamp was snuffed out. A long-drawn breath in the darkness, shuddering, then the wet rattle of death.

Castus lay still, waiting, counting his heartbeats. When he reached one hundred he sat up and groped in the dark for the body slumped against the far wall. He found the neck, checked for the pulse and felt nothing. The solid smoke-smelling blackness was all around him and he felt the dread of death crawling across his skin.

He waited as long as he could bear, and then he dragged himself to the grating and started hammering at it, yelling for the guards.

CHAPTER X

The music was strange, barbaric, unearthly: thudding drums, wailing pipes and voices, rhythmic shouts and screeches. Castus pressed his cheek to the rough wood of the door and squinted through the crack between the boards. Firelight dazzled his eye; then he saw capering figures in black silhouette, reeling shapes against the blaze, sparks shooting into the night sky. He saw manlike figures with the heads of animals and cruel birds, and felt the sweat freeze on his brow.

But these were men. Men wearing bird-headed masks, dancing around the fire with crooked steps, hands clasped behind their backs. He shuddered, fearful of the strange noise, the dark alien gods, the breath of magic and superstition. On his hands and knees he backed away from the door into the dank gloom of the hut.

Three days had passed since they had taken him from the pit where Marcellinus had died. He had been brought out by night and seen little of his surroundings, but had noticed the half-moon between the clouds, and realised that it must have been ten days since the battle. Ten days for the Picts to muster their forces – Aurelius Arpagius would not be expecting his delegation to return until the end of the month. Only then would he realise that something was wrong, and by that time the Picts could already be assaulting the Wall. Perhaps, he thought, the barbaric celebration outside marked the beginning of their campaign, a ritual declaration of war against Rome?

He sat on the floor of the hut and fed a few twigs and some dried moss to the meagre fire in the central hearth. This hut was his new prison: a circle of massive stones enclosing a space only five paces across, containing a straw mattress and a central fireplace. The walls rose to waist height, and above them was the sloping conical roof of smoke-blackened timbers and heavy old turf. Castus had already tested the strength of the ceiling – it would be possible for him to break a hole large enough to clamber through, but the noise of the cracking wood would surely alert the guards outside, and they would be waiting for him as soon as he emerged.

Twice a day the guards removed a slat of wood near the bottom of the door and slid a wooden tray of food and a beaker of water through to him. He could hear their voices outside sometimes, but aside from that he was kept in total solitude. Again and again the images of the battle returned to him: the fury of the attack; the faces of his men as they waited at the wall; Timotheus and Culchianus embracing him before he left them... Hunched on the floor, head lowered, he clasped his fists at the nape of his neck, as if he could press the memories from his mind. Then he stretched on his toes until he could grip the topmost roof beam, and began furiously pulling himself upwards, touching the beam with his chin each time, until the muscles of his arms and stomach burned and he felt the sweat tiding down his back, and dropped lightly to the floor again. Other times he ran on the spot, or whirled and dodged around the narrow circuit of the hut, scuffing up dirt, keeping his reflexes sharp, guarding his strength until he had a chance to use it.

The sound of the music died away outside into a vast muttering hush, then a last cry sounded and he heard the assembly break up. Crawling to his mattress in the dark, he lay on his back and waited for sleep. Soon, he told himself – soon he would find the chance he was waiting for, and somehow make his escape, or die in the attempt.

Battering at the door woke him, and he sprang up. Daylight showed between the slats, and he pulled on the rough sleeveless tunic they had given him and stood ready beside the hearth.

The door opened, and the scarred face of the guard appeared as he stooped into the hut, the stiff comb of his hair brushing the low lintel.

'*Ech! Deugh umlaen!*'

Castus nodded, and paced towards the door. As he stepped outside he met an arc of levelled spears, and stood passively as the guards tied his hands behind his back. Then they prodded him forward.

It was the first time he had properly seen the fort in daylight. Beneath the heavy sky he saw the flat summit of the hill ringed by the crest of a broad stone wall and a waist-high palisade. The ground fell away on all sides, dropping to the lower surrounding compound. Within the upper enclosure were ten or eleven huts, some animal pens, and at the centre the big firepit from the celebration of the night before, still sending up thin grey smoke. As he passed between the huts Castus saw the dark slopes of mountains on either side, and to the north a wide river estuary gleaming dull silver.

'Centurion!'

Castus halted, and the spear jabbed against his back. In the doorway of one of the huts he saw Julius Decentius, the renegade, leaning on a stick. The man's leg was heavily bandaged above the knee.

'I'm sorry about the way things have turned out,' Decentius called. 'Most regrettable. I did all I could but—'

Castus snarled, cutting the man off; anger bulked his shoulders and he started forward, fists clenched. Two spears knitted across his chest, holding him, but the renegade had already cowered back into the doorway. His expression was flickering between naked fear and a sickening attempt at a smile.

'You must believe me, I tried to help you…' Decentius said, his voice strangled in his throat.

'I don't need your help,' Castus hissed back. Then the guard shoved at his shoulder and he walked on. He could sense the renegade staring after him. Could it be true, Castus thought, that after all his betrayals the man still believed they were allies, fellow Romans? The thought soured his mouth, and he spat.

They reached one of the larger huts at the far end of the compound, and the leading warrior stepped forward and banged on the door with the butt of his spear. The door swung open, and the guards moved aside, gesturing for Castus to enter.

Warmth met him as he stooped through the door, and the smells of cooking food and damp greasy wool. Something else as well: a high keen scent. It took a moment for his eyes to adjust to the gloom, and he stood up straight as he felt the bonds slipped from his wrists.

'The men outside think you are a wild animal, and must be kept tied at all times. But I trust you can behave like a human.'

Castus recognised the voice, that low and heavily accented Latin, before he made out the figure of Cunomagla herself, seated at the far side of the hut. He took a few steps from the door towards the central hearth. There were several others in the room: women in plain gowns kneeling on the floor. One of them worked at a spinning wheel, another at embroidery. All seemed carefully oblivious to his presence.

'Sit,' Cunomagla commanded. Castus lowered himself onto a stool beside the hearth. The walls of the hut were hung with woven pictures showing the figures of animals and men locked into a strange stiff frieze. Pale skulls of horned animals were mounted around the slope of the ceiling, and a bronze cauldron hung suspended by a long black chain above the fire. Castus leaned down to rub the ears of a lean yellow dog lying beside the hearth; the animal flinched and bared its teeth at him.

'I was sorry for what happened to your envoy,' the woman said. Castus tried to judge the woman's expression. Nothing in her eyes or her voice suggested that Marcellinus had been important to her, once. The boy, his illegitimate son, was sitting on the floor beside his mother.

'He chose his own way out,' Castus said. He could see Cunomagla more distinctly now. She had thrown off her cloak and wore only a sleeveless green dress that gathered in her lap. Her heavy ornaments – the chain of double silver links at her neck, the massive snake-head bands on her arms – caught the glow from the hearth fire. Behind her, Castus could see a broad hunting spear leaning against the wall. He had no doubt that she would use it if he made a step towards her or her son.

But what, he wondered, must he look like to her? His hair and beard had grown out into an unruly yellow-brown scrub, and in his native tunic he could easily pass as some kind of barbarian himself. Only his army boots marked him as a Roman. The Picts went barefoot, and had no need to take them.

'What do you want with me, lady?'

'Just to talk. Do not worry – none here understand Latin. We can be plain with each other.'

'This is your fort, then? You rule here?'

'No,' she said. 'This is Drustagnus's place. I am his guest… or maybe his prisoner. But Drustagnus has gone to make war

189

on the Roman lands, with his uncle the king. You think they will be... victorious?'

Castus thought for a moment. He remembered the sneering attitude of the young Pictish chief when he had last seen him. *Be careful*, he told himself. *This woman too is one of them.*

'At first, perhaps,' he said. 'But later – no. Once the Roman forces rally against them, your people have no chance. The legions will march north and destroy this country.' He tried to keep the vengeful anger from his voice.

'I think so too,' Cunomagla said quietly. She held his eyes across the glow of the embers. 'I was two years in your city, your Ebor-acum. Drustagnus also, but he was too young to know what he saw. This city is not the greatest of your empire, I think?'

'Far from it.' Castus almost smiled, thinking of Antioch, Nicomedia, even the cities of Pannonia.

'Yes. And Romans have many legions. This I learn when I live at Ebor-acum. This, and this language, and the stories and customs of your people.'

'What stories?'

'I learn that Romans are vicious and cruel, and crush their enemies without mercy. I learn that their armies can be destroyed, but more armies always come after them. I learn that emperors can be murdered by slaves, and can rise from nothing. Your customs are very strange to me.'

'Some of these stories are strange to me too.'

She smiled a little at that, just the slightest flicker. The glow from the hearth was very warm, and Castus felt a slow drowsiness creeping through him, a sense of intoxication like the first effect of strong wine.

'If the armies of Rome destroy the new king, and his nephew Drustagnus too, my son will be one of the few in my land with the ruling blood, of female line. He could become king.'

'If there's anyone left for him to rule.'

Cunomagla closed her eyes for a moment, as if gathering her thoughts. 'There are stories my people tell,' she said, 'of when the Romans came to our land, many fathers ago. Your emperor, Sey-verus. We ran from him, to the high mountains, to live like animals in that country. In my father's father's time we struggle and fight, all against all, and make ourselves human again. Now we return to our land, and we are strong. We are free, not like Romans. You understand this?'

'You don't look like free people to me.'

'You are Roman,' Cunomagla said with a dismissive smile. 'You don't know what is freedom! But you know we fight for this – our land and custom.'

'That I can understand, yes,' Castus said. He had seen it many times before, after all. Seen that determination smashed by the legions, and only the dead and the burning villages left.

'My son is too young now to rule as king,' Cunomagla said. 'But *I*... I could rule in his name until he was of age. If I had a husband to stand beside me.'

'Take one then,' Castus said. The woman was staring at him, proud and direct. It was an unfamiliar sensation to him. She laughed.

'If I take a husband, *he* will want to be king. Drustagnus wants this. Then my son could never rule.'

Castus felt his mouth drying. The mysteries of Pictish royalty were beyond him, but now he was beginning to see the connection. Marcellinus, he thought, was supposed to be here instead of him.

'But only if your husband was a Pict,' he said.

Cunomagla nodded slowly. 'You,' she said, 'are a brave warrior. I have seen you, strong in battle. All my people know this.'

191

She stood up, and in the firelight she seemed to tower beneath the blackened roof. She picked up the spear from behind her. She had never looked as powerful, or as commanding.

'You... can be my husband. When Talorcagus and Drustagnus are dead, we both rule, in my son's name. My people are wild and fierce and love freedom, but we could govern them. Make treaty with Rome – peace between Roman and Pict. When they have seen the Roman war, they will understand this.'

'*Peace?*' Castus said, sneering. The word sounded incredible, impossible. He felt stunned and angry; the thought of surrendering himself to be the consort of a barbarian woman, of the race that had slaughtered his men, was repulsive. But there was another feeling inside him too, almost nauseating in its intensity. Desire, like something slowly uncoiling in his belly. Had Marcellinus killed himself so that he did not have to make this choice?

'Better to rule over living men than dead,' Cunomagla said. 'Better to rule than to die.' She lowered the spear until the blade pointed at Castus.

'Why not Decentius? He's a Roman.'

'This man is not a man. He is a traitor to his people. He is less than vermin.'

But would I not be a traitor too, he thought, *if I did what you want?*

She raised the spear again and placed it back against the wall.

'Go now,' she said. 'Think on what I say. Soon I call you again.'

Outside the hut, the cold fresh breeze caught in his throat. Castus coughed, and then breathed deeply, letting the clean air wash over him as the guards tied his hands again. He tried not to meet any of their eyes as they marched him back towards his hut. But he saw Decentius, the traitor, watching him from a far doorway with a sly and calculating grimace.

Castus lay on his mattress, staring into the gathering darkness as the hearth fire died down. He could hear the calls of the guards from outside, a doglike yapping and a cackle. The earthy taste of barley porridge was thick on his tongue, and sleep was far away. His body was alive with angry frustration. He was not a slave, to be commanded by savages, or a beast to be driven by the goad. He was a Roman soldier. He told himself that, but what did it mean now? Already Talorcagus could be leading his tribal horde against the Wall. If he had half the numbers that Marcellinus had suggested then the garrison would be overwhelmed. And then what? If Arpagius assembled the legion in time he might defeat them in the field, but if not...

Set against that, what happened to Castus himself seemed utterly unimportant. He was a dead man already, in the eyes of everyone he knew. So what, if he became Cunomagla's consort? A slave and a prisoner, pretending to rule over savages? But, no, he could not allow himself to do that. He could pretend, until he had a chance to break free, but subterfuge was not in his nature and the idea disgusted him. Better to die, then. He could pound at the door or rip his way through the roof, and throw himself at the guards outside to die under their spears. Maybe even take one or two of them with him. He sat up, determined to do exactly that. But then he remembered the promise he had made to Marcellinus. To escape, and carry word to his family. He still had Marcellinus's seal ring, concealed in the toe of his boot. A promise to a dying man had the force of a sacred oath.

Castus got up and paced circles in the darkness. It was hot and stale in the hut, and his beard and hair prickled with sweat. Scrubbing at his head, he flung himself down on the mattress again and pulled the coarse blanket over himself. He felt his mind, exhausted with tumbling thoughts, slowly lurching towards sleep.

It was a sound from the door that startled him fully awake again, the rattle of the locking bar and the soft grunt of the rope hinges. An hour had passed, maybe more; he could not tell. He lay still, eyes wide, trying to guess the shapes around him in the dark. Cold night air flowed in from outside. Then a figure entered the hut and the door was closed once more.

'Who's there?' he said, low in his throat, and felt more keenly than ever his lack of a weapon. But only a single figure had entered the hut – and with a quick sense of inevitability he realised who it was.

'Be still,' she said, crouching beside the embers in the hearth and feeding them sticks until the fire crackled back into life. The glow lit her face, her thick hair. 'It is the custom of my people', she said, 'that a woman of royal blood can choose her men. Any that she desires can be hers.'

She stood up, a column of shadow above the fire.

'Do I get to choose as well?' Castus said.

Cunomagla dipped her head and her face dropped into the shadow of her hair. She lifted one hand and unpinned the brooch that fastened her dress at the shoulder. The dress fell, and she stood naked in the firelight. Castus stared at her, transfixed: all over her body, her powerful arms and broad shoulders, her heavy breasts and wide hips, the flesh was marked with a tracery of scar-patterns. She paced across the hut and knelt beside the mattress. Heavy silver glinted at her throat and on her arms. Then she laid her hands on his shoulders and pushed him down onto his back, straddling his hips and pressing her breasts against him. Her scent was raw and heady: smoke and meat and sweat.

'Choose, then,' she said.

They let him out of the hut the next day, and allowed him to walk with hands unbound. The warriors would not look at him, but Castus caught their scowls and sneers, and saw the way they fingered their spears and the hilts of their short swords. One of them, a man with a long-toothed doglike face who seemed to be the leader, threw off his leather cape and walked with chest bared, as if to show off the pictures gouged into his skin. Castus remembered Cunomagla's skin the night before, the softness over the muscle, and the delicate welts he had traced with his fingers in the darkness after the fire had died down. He could still smell her musk all over him, and knew the guards could smell it too.

He walked a short circuit around the upper enclosure of the fort. Seabirds wheeled over the estuary, catching the level silver sunlight as they turned, but the mountains were black. He checked the position of the sun. The estuary lay to the north, and to the south was high desolate moorland. A crooked valley descended from the high ground, curving around below the north-eastern gate of the fort – Castus could make out a hunting party returning, mounted men with dogs. He glanced around for Decentius, but could not see him.

As he reached the south-western end of the fort enclosure, he became aware that the number of men around him had increased, more warriors joining those that escorted him, a gathering throng of them trailing behind. He tried to appear oblivious, keeping his movements slow and careful, but he could feel his shoulders bunching and tightening under the coarse weave of the Pictish tunic, and the hair that had grown across his scalp and jaw prickled with fresh perspiration.

The men ahead were leading him between the last two huts and the wattle-walled pigsties to where the ground sloped down towards the wall and the palisade fence. There was an open area here, of short springy grass, and as the crowd behind him passed between the huts they spread out to either side. Castus looked at the wall; it was only waist-high, and he could cross the palisade with a spring. To run at it, to jump: the temptation was almost too much. But what was on the far side? A steep drop, and a further compound below. For a moment he imagined himself doing it, but he knew that the moment he moved he would die, his back quilled with Pictish javelins. Perhaps, he thought, they were hoping he would make such an attempt and give them the excuse they wanted to kill him.

Now the leader, the dog-faced man who had cast away his cloak, was facing him. Castus stood at ease, feet spread, waiting. The crowd of other men encircled them, and the leader bared his teeth and winged his shoulders, flexing his chest muscles and biceps so the animals gouged into his flesh seemed to writhe.

'*Umdaula!*' the man said. '*Deugh en-ray!*'

A thirsty hiss went up from the spectators as their champion dropped into a wrestling stance, arms raised and hands spread to grapple.

Castus shifted his feet, backing slightly. His opponent lacked his weight and muscle, but had a look of wiry strength and agility; he would be fast, no doubt. There were fresh wounds on his body too – he had been injured in the battle on the hilltop. Most of the other warriors bore the same scars; they were veterans, Castus realised, left behind here to guard the fort while the younger men joined the attack on the Roman frontier.

Pulling off his tunic and throwing it aside, Castus faced his opponent bare-chested. The Pict was speaking under his breath: taunts or insults, Castus assumed. He had an urge to leap in close and swing a punch at the side of the man's head, but something told him that this was what his opponent was expecting. Instead he kept shifting his stance, backing and circling, keeping his fists close to his body. The crowd were spitting hatred.

Let him win, Castus told himself. Nothing to be gained from victory here. This was about pride; they wanted to humble him, show him they were the masters now. Either that or provoke him – most of the onlookers carried weapons, and he could never take them all on empty-handed. Fine, he thought. But he could not make it look too easy.

'Come on then,' he said through his teeth. He could feel the heat of the crowd at his back. 'Come on, you bitch's bastard!'

The Pict darted forward suddenly, dodging in under Castus's reaping swing and driving a shoulder against his sternum. Castus staggered, breath bursting from his lungs; his opponent was quick and fierce, hooking a leg behind him to kick at the back of his knee and bring him down. Castus locked his thigh muscles, fighting just to remain standing, and the two of them grappled together, stamping and swaying. The Pict's body was smeared with some kind of grease; he was eel-slick and hard as a whip.

All around the crowd pressed in, their harsh voices building to a chant. *Ladha Ruamna*. Castus knew what that meant: this was no friendly wrestling bout. They wanted him dead. His enemy's teeth grated against his cheek, and Castus drew back his head and butted it forward. A crunch of cartilage, and there was blood spattered over his face. The Pict yelped in pain, and drove his heel in a hooking kick. Pain, then a crippling weakness shot up Castus's side.

Overbalancing, he crashed over onto the turf. His enemy was on top of him, grasping and pinning him; a sinewy arm snaked around his neck and tightened, twisting. All around were feet stamping, faces contorted in savage relish. Castus got a knee beneath him and pressed upwards. The tendons in his neck burned.

Ladha Ruamna! Ladha Ruamna…! Their bodies twined together, the two men wrestled in a half-crouch. Castus swung his arm back, grabbing for the Pict's hair, but felt hard fingers inching across his face. He tried to twist his head further away, but the Pict could almost reach his eye sockets. Already the fingers were hooked, to gouge and to blind.

A sudden twist of the neck, and Castus opened his mouth and seized the man's thumb between his teeth. He bit down hard, using the arm locked around his neck as a fulcrum, until he felt bones crack and tasted blood. The Pict screamed and released his grip, staggering away.

Kneeling on the ground, Castus spat the blood from his mouth. Sweat was in his eyes. The crowd of warriors surrounding him had drawn back, and his adversary, panting breath and clutching his injured hand, stood before him with his face seething. He snatched a spear from one of his comrades, lifted it in his left hand and aimed it.

Castus stared at the point of the spear. This was his death.

Then a sharp cry came from up the slope, between the pigsties. The crowd broke apart. There between the huts stood Cunomagla, wrapped in her rough-weave cloak with her hair loose and anger in her eyes. Her voice again, commanding – Castus could not even try to understand her, but knew her meaning.

The warriors fell away. Even the leader, clutching his bloody hand to his chest, slunk back. Cunomagla directed a level stare at the gathering, nodded imperiously, turned and stalked away. Behind her, lingering by the pigsties, was the renegade Decentius.

Castus got up, slow and careful, feeling the pain in his limbs but not wanting to show it. Keeping his head straight, he walked back up the slope towards the main compound. Decentius stepped forward as he passed.

'I called her as soon as I heard the shouting,' the renegade said. 'You could say I saved your life...'

Castus glanced at him without expression. He could see the despair in the man now, the desperate need to reach out to a kinsman. Almost understandable, trapped in this savage place. But a traitor could never win his gratitude. He narrowed his eyes. Then he shrugged and walked back towards the hut.

That evening he sat alone, staring into the bright heart of the embers and trying not to think. His body was still bruised and aching from the fight. He was not waiting for her, he told himself that. His only desire was to escape this place. But later, after several hours lying sleepless on the bare mattress, he sat up at the sound of the opening door.

She came to him, as she had before, but they did not speak. That previous time he had been worried about the noise, fearful that someone outside would hear them – he had even put his hand over her mouth to try and quieten her, but she had shoved him away laughing, as if he were childish to care about such things. This time, he knew that it did not matter who heard them. The sex was fast and fierce, and she matched him in angry passion. Only afterwards did she lie still, almost tender in her contentment. He ran his palms over her body, the cold hardness of the barbaric ornaments and the coarse curling lines scored into her flesh with a blade. He was fascinated and repulsed, and filled with a strange warmth beyond simple desire.

'Thanks for saving me from your friends outside,' he said. 'I think they'd rather have killed me.'

'They would not dare,' she said. 'They are afraid of me. Drustagnus is their master, but I am of the royal house, and they would not deny me.'

'Even so. I'm still an enemy to them. How long will they keep on following your orders?'

'Orders?' she said, smiling. 'You talk so much like a Roman. Here there are no orders. My people do as their rulers direct from love, and respect.'

Castus stifled his laugh. There had been little of love or respect in the way the guards had looked at her earlier. Just a cowed temporary deference. He wondered what sort of game Cunomagla was playing: setting her own authority against Drustagnus, perhaps? Demonstrating that she too could rule men? Either way it was dangerous, and he was the one who would pay the price if she lost.

'What will you do,' he asked her, 'if the Roman army comes here?'

'Fight them,' she told him. He felt her body tighten, muscles hardening. 'I will never be a slave, or run like a dog.'

She raised herself on one elbow, and her hair fell across his chest. 'And what would you do?' she said. In her voice Castus thought he could hear a softness, even a sadness, that he had never heard before.

'If the gods allowed,' he said, 'I would be marching in their ranks.'

For three more nights she visited him, coming after dark when the fort was silent and leaving again before dawn. Castus never knew whether she had guards or attendants of her own, who waited outside while she was with him. With every passing day the idea of escape, like the idea of home, the memory of the legion, seemed more distant.

On the fourth night she seemed changed. Castus had little experience of the moods of women; Cunomagla, he had decided, was more than just a woman anyway. She was a barbarian first, a war-leader second, and female third. Even so, he could tell that something was troubling her. After they had lain together, almost before their breathing slowed, she pushed herself away from him and sat back against the stone wall of the hut. The last glow of the fire lit her broad face, the set of her jaw.

'The men here have sent word to Drustagnus that I consort with you,' she said. 'They think I make plots with you to go against their chief.'

Castus sat up. 'What will Drustagnus do?' He thought of Strabo's death, the jerk of his body as the knife slashed his neck, the pump and spatter of blood, and suppressed a shudder.

'Order them to kill you, I think,' she told him. 'Me, they would not hurt. But I can protect you, I...' Already she was sounding less certain; the true price of her bid for authority was becoming clear.

'If Drustagnus commands it,' Castus said between his teeth, 'I'll die. Things won't go so well for you either. But if I was not here... If I escaped...'

She seized his arms, fingers digging into his biceps. 'No! I cannot allow that,' she cried.

Castus's heart kicked at the meaning of her words, the strength wakening again inside him. He rolled forward suddenly, breaking her grip on his arms as he lunged against her. Before she could fight back he had her pinned against the stones of the hut wall, one forearm braced beneath her jaw, her right wrist gripped tight.

'You can't protect me from Drustagnus,' he said in a harsh whisper. 'You know that. So set me free… or give me a way to free myself.'

'Never!' she spat back at him, alive with sudden fury, and he saw her teeth gleam in the darkness. 'You're mine… I own you!'

He felt her body flex and writhe against him, the heavy links of the chain she wore at her throat pressing into the muscle of his arm.

'Think again,' he said. 'The Roman army owns me, body and soul – and I'll never submit to you. If that makes us enemies then so be it.'

A sudden prick of pain against his belly: a knife, held low in her left hand. She registered his flinch, and smiled in bitter triumph. 'Do you really think', she said quietly, 'I'd come to you unarmed?'

They paused, locked together and breathing hard, the unseen blade held between them. Castus felt the warm weight of her hair falling over his arm. He felt his anger shifting; death stood on all sides. Only this woman could help him now. *Think*, he told himself.

'You say you had no part in these killings,' he told her, measuring his words. 'No part in this war. You say you're a friend to Rome… Help me get away from here and I can tell my commander that. If I die here, you and your son will both be marked as enemies.'

For a moment she glared at him, still holding the blade against his skin. Then he felt her shoulders drop, and the knife was gone. He eased himself back, releasing his grip on her.

'You can tell your commander this, in Ebor-acum?' she said quietly, as if to herself. 'I and my son both?'

'Yes. But I can't do that when I'm penned up here.'

'You tell them, then,' she said, staring at him in the darkness.

'Tell them I am no enemy to Rome.'

'Prove it,' he said.

She threw herself against him, kissing his mouth hard.

Later, as he lay in half-sleep, he felt her get up from the mattress. He opened his eyes. The fire was almost gone, and she was a dark moving shape in the deeper darkness of the hut. He saw her stoop, and then fasten the dress at her shoulder. Stoop again, and a faint metallic clink came from the hearth.

'Cunomagla?' he said in a low whisper. For a moment she seemed to look at him, but all he caught was the movement in shadow. He heard the door creak open, and thud closed. The faintest breath of night air lingered in the darkness.

Up off the mattress, he felt his way across the dirt floor to the hearth, running his fingers over the cracked and sooty stones of the rim. He touched cold iron, then his hand closed around the haft of the knife. He picked it up carefully and ran his fingers over the blade. Six inches long, triangular and single-edged, with a cruel point.

He kissed the black iron blade, and then grinned with clenched teeth.

CHAPTER XI

Crouched beside the door, Castus gripped the knife in both hands, trying to fight down his nervous impatience. A whole day had passed since Cunomagla's visit – a day of waiting, of pacing circles around the hearth, exercising, pointlessly turning plans around in his mind. He would know nothing until he got outside the hut, outside the fort, and that alone was going to be difficult.

The guards brought him food twice a day, once a little after sunrise and again in the evening. That morning he had eaten, but the evening meal he had ignored. The wooden platter and bowl of gruel sat beside him now, on the worn stone sill before the slat in the door where the guard had placed it. *How soon,* Castus thought, *before the guards peer through the slat and see the food untouched?* He had rolled the straw mattress and wrapped the blanket around it: with the fire burning low it might look like a man's body lying in the shadows at the back of the hut. He prayed they would not summon help – two men, even three he could deal with, but any more and he would be dead within the hour. His stomach clenched, and he felt the pulse jumping in his neck. The black iron knife was an anchor in the darkness, and he clung to it.

Footsteps and voices from outside, and he gently eased himself up to stand pressed against the wall. The door would open towards him, and anyone standing in the doorway would not see him. Or so he hoped.

The slat rattled open, and faint dusk light shone across the sill; a long arm, corded with muscle, came through the gap and took up the wooden platter. Then the platter fell, the bowl tipping and spilling cold gruel. The voices outside grew urgent. The guard was only a foot or two away now, crouching outside the door to peer through the open slat – Castus could smell the rank fat the Pict warriors smeared on their bodies. He tensed, holding his breath, muscles burning.

A rattle as the heavy oak locking bar was lifted from the door. Then the wooden boards swung slowly open. Castus waited, gripping the knife – he had seen how the guards had to stoop as they passed beneath the low stone lintel. He drew a sharp silent breath. Then he flung all his weight against the door.

The heavy boards crashed hard against the man in the doorway; then Castus spun on his toes and threw the door back open. The guard was reeling, pitching over against the frame of the door. Castus grabbed him by the hair and flung him down on the floor behind him. The second guard was standing just outside. He was holding a sword, but his face was blanked by surprise. Castus saw the man's chest rising as he drew breath to shout; he launched himself through the doorway, raising his elbows with the knife levelled. The short stiff blade rammed into the guard's throat, stabbing through his windpipe. Castus threw his arm around the man's waist to catch him as he fell, dragging him back into the hut and kicking the door closed behind him.

For a moment he stood breathing hard. The first warrior was still on the floor, moaning and struggling to rise onto hands and knees. Castus stepped across him, locked his elbow beneath the man's jaw and tightened his muscles, pressing down on the spine with his free hand. The warrior struggled, kicking out; then his neck twisted and snapped and he went limp.

The knife made an ugly sucking sound as he dragged it from the second man's throat. Blood gushed and pooled, black in the shadows. Wiping the blade, Castus wrapped it in a rag and slipped it into the waistband of his breeches. Then he took the short leather cape the first guard had been wearing, put it on and picked up the fallen sword. For a few moments he crouched, waiting for his heartbeat to slow, the energy of killing to ease. He needed to be calm now, he told himself. Calm and quick.

He cracked open the door again. It was almost fully dark, and the compound was deserted. No other warriors in sight, none drawn by the brief bloody struggle at the hut door. Castus concealed the sword beneath his cape, and then opened the door wide enough to slip outside. The air tasted like cold clean water, or the most refreshing wine.

There were animal pens to either side of the hut, and behind it a short slope down to the wall and the palisade that ringed the upper compound of the fort. Castus edged along the wall; then he crouched beside the wattle fence of the animal pen. He drew up the hood of the cloak, hoping that in the darkness he might resemble a Pict to any distant watcher. But there was blood all down his right arm and splashed over the chest of his tunic. He had not noticed it before. He scanned the line of the wall, and saw a single sentry standing on the parapet behind the wooden palisade, about a bowshot distant. The wall on this side was only shoulder height, but Castus knew that it fell away much further on the far side, as the slope of the hill descended.

Turning, he stared back across the compound; there, on the far side, not fifty paces away, was the hut of Julius Decentius. How much time, he thought, before the other warriors noticed that the guards were missing? How much time before they went to investigate? Quickly, before caution gripped him again, he shoved himself away from the wall and began running, head down, across the compound.

As he neared the hut he heard a burst of laughter, and saw a spill of firelight from an opening door. He threw himself down beside a pen on the far side of the compound, but it was only a woman coming from one of the other huts with a bowl of cooking scraps. She flung them into the pen, and Castus heard the grunt and shove of pigs. He waited until the woman had returned inside, then scrambled up and ran to the door of Decentius's hut.

He did not know how many people might be inside. Decentius may have warriors with him. He may even have a wife and children – Castus had not considered that. But he could not turn back now. A glow came from inside, showing between the boards of the door. He rapped on the boards with his fist, and heard a voice from within.

As soon as the latch was raised he threw himself against the door. The figure on the far side reeled back, saying something in Pictish; then Castus punched him hard on the jaw and he fell. Closing the door behind him, Castus drew the sword from beneath his cloak. Decentius was sprawled on the ground beside the hearth, an upended stool beside him. There was nobody else in the hut, and Castus stepped away from the door with the sword held low.

'Centurion,' the man said, holding his jaw, 'what are you—?'

'I've got a message for Aelius Marcellinus,' Castus said in a low whisper. He was standing close to the fallen man, close enough to strike. Decentius managed to sit up. His eyes flicked across the room to the Roman cavalry sword on the far side of the hearth.

'Aelius Marcellinus is dead.'

'That's right. And you can give him the message when you meet him in the land of Hades. Tell him: *Aurelius Castus sent me to follow you.*'

He drew back his arm to strike, but the man raised a hand, imploring.

'Wait!' he said. 'Please... you're mistaken!'

'Mistaken how?' Do it now, Castus told himself. Strike, and get it done. But then he remembered the renegade's words at the parley before the besieged fort. *The empire has betrayed you... Don't die for emperors who despise you!*

'I...' Decentius said, kneeling now. 'I am a loyal servant of Rome.'

'You're a renegade and a traitor. Now you'll die.'

'I'm not a traitor, no! I've been an exile for ten years, that's true. But my loyalties have always been to the emperors.' He was speaking quickly. His eyes still flickered towards the sword. 'I have... I've been in communication, these last two years, with agents of the imperial government, a very highly placed officer of the Notaries, from Treveris...'

Castus felt his brow cool suddenly. His arm ached from holding the sword. He remembered the strange subtle man in the praetorium at Eboracum, months before. His questions about the loyalties of the army. *Nigrinus.*

'He came here?'

'No. No, we communicated by messenger. I have documents, coded documents – if you'll allow me to show you...'

'I've got no use for documents. Explain quickly.'

'I was promised,' the man said. 'Promised a full pardon, the restoration of my military rank and honour, my ancestral lands... I would have done anything for that, centurion. All these years exiled in this place, living in a hovel surrounded by savages. What would I not have done?'

208

'What *did* you do?' Castus growled. He stepped closer and seized the man by the shoulder. Decentius hung limply from his fist.

'I was ordered... to provoke the tribes into an uprising against Rome. To arrange the deaths of the king and his supporters.'

'Balls! Why would Rome want a Pictish uprising?'

'So the new emperor could bring an army to Britain, and his son too. The emperor... is a sick man. He needs military victories, acclamation for his son, before he dies...'

'Don't believe you,' Castus said. He flung the man down, and stood breathing hard above him.

'Oh, it's true.' Decentius was smiling now, that same sickly grin Castus had seen before. He remembered the renegade calling out his offer of surrender to the besieged soldiers in the fort. His arm tightened.

'I am a Roman soldier, just like you,' the renegade said. '*We will do what we are ordered*... But, you see, once you light a fire it is hard to control. This uprising... is greater than I'd anticipated. I have done my work too well, you could say!'

'You could say that.' Castus felt doubt pooling inside him like cold oil. The urge to strike, to kill, was almost instinctive. But he could not – the man's words had gouged at his determination. What could he believe now? Decentius stared up at him, mouth open, his face sick with fear but emptying now, resigned.

Keeping his eyes on the crouching man, Castus moved carefully around the hearth. He took the cavalry sword from where it was leaning against the wall and threw it down before Decentius.

'If you're a Roman,' he said, 'die like one.'

He stepped back, and Decentius picked up the weapon and reversed it with trembling hands.

'Thank you, brother,' he said quietly. He lowered the pommel until it rested on the floor, and placed the point beneath his breastbone. 'Could you look away for a moment while I do this? It's hard to die well.'

Castus turned only slightly. From the corner of his eye he caught the sudden movement, the man on the floor springing up with the blade turning in his hand. He wheeled, bringing his own weapon up to block the attack. Iron clashed and whined as Castus parried the blow, then Decentius collided with him, pinning his sword arm against his side. He could feel the renegade trying to turn his blade and stab it into his back. They wrestled together, standing, feet scuffing.

'Bastard!' Decentius hissed through his teeth. Castus dropped his sword and shoved against him. Reaching blindly with his left hand, he found the hilt of the iron knife in his waistband, pulled the blade free and punched it between Decentius's ribs. The man jerked, let out a single cry. Then his legs gave beneath him and the sword fell clattering from his hand. Castus hurled the dead man backwards, and he fell sprawling into the hearth, scattering sparks.

Snatching up the fallen weapon, Castus dragged the largest brand from the fire and ran from the hut. Panic beat in his head, the fighting energy, the killing energy, powering him now. He took four long strides and hurled the burning brand over the wattle fence into the animal pens. Pigs shrieked and scrambled, butting against the fence as the flames ripped and crackled across the dry straw. Castus was already around the far side of the hut, in the shadow, staring at the parapet of the wall. The sentry had seen the fire: Castus heard his shout, and then saw him jump from the wall and run towards the animal pens. The snap and hiss of the flame was loud now, and the screaming of the pigs was louder still. Castus dropped his head and ran, down the short slope and then up, springing to catch the lip of the wall and pull himself up to lie across the walkway.

Other figures were running towards the fire, and the wall was clear in both directions. The wooden palisade was only chest high here, made of laths woven between timber posts. Castus got up and stuck the sword through his belt. Then he snatched at the top of the palisade and leaped up and over into the darkness.

He turned as he jumped, grabbing the palisade on the far side and letting himself drop, bringing his feet up beneath him. A heavy thud through his legs as he struck the wall and hung, clinging to the outside of the palisade. The wooden laths creaked under his weight, bulging outwards. Men were running in the lower compound, and he hoped they would not look up. Twisting his head against the bunch of his shoulder muscles, he could see the dark humped turf of a hut roof below him. It looked empty; no smoke came from inside.

For a moment more he clung on, then he eased his legs down, kicking his toes at the wall for grip. He released his hands and began to slide, the stones grating against his chest; then he pushed himself away and let himself fall, turning in the air. The turf rushed up beneath him and he crashed down onto his back on the slope of the roof, feeling it creak and give slightly beneath him. Drawing the sword from his belt he scrambled down off the roof and dropped to the ground.

Castus circled around the curve of the hut wall, keeping below the eaves. He vaulted a fence, stumbled through the mud of an animal pen, and then saw the outer wall of the fort before him. A dog leaped up from a hut doorway; he heard the bark, then the snap of the rope halter as it lunged. He pushed himself up and ran for the wall.

Two men appeared in front of him, and he rushed them. The first he caught off guard, slamming into him and knocking him down. He dodged the spear of the second man, and swung the flat of his sword at his face. The man flinched back, and Castus kicked his leg from under him, stabbed down and felt the blade sink into flesh. He slashed the first man over the back of the head and ran.

Swerving between the huts, he reached the wall in six long strides and jumped onto the parapet. No time to glance at the drop on the far side. A flung spear darted past his head as he grabbed at the palisade and pulled himself over it. He was falling at once, the ground yawning away beneath him into darkness. Throwing out a hand, he caught at the rough stones of the wall and clung on for a heartbeat before letting himself drop again. Air rushed around his head. Then the ground punched up at him and drove the breath from his body.

He had fallen onto a slope, and as soon as he got his legs beneath him he toppled forward again, rolling and scrambling. Stones and dry thorny scrub beat at his face and arms. He lost his grip on the sword and caught himself on a grassy outcrop, reaching back until he felt the hilt in the darkness. Shouts came from the wall, and another spear flicked past and buried itself in the turf. Then he pushed himself forward again, half running and half tumbling. The ground levelled beneath him, and he was on the side of a hill below the fort with the horns blaring above him.

His elbow was skinned and bleeding, his face felt raw and swollen and his chest and flank were covered in bruises and scratches, but he was free and running with the night huge and cold around him. The slope fell away to his left, into the crooked valley that led down to the plain before the estuary. But the track from the gate of the fort led down there – already he could hear the yip and yelp of the hunting dogs from the lower compound, the shouts of the hunters as they spilled forth after him. Ahead and to his right the ground rose towards the high moorland, with mist rolling between the ridges. He began to climb the slope, making an oblique course towards the nearest hillcrest. He held the sword before him, spiking it into the turf and using it to pull himself up. His legs were burning and he was fighting for breath, but the thought of the dogs behind him drove him on.

Up the exposed slope, scrabbling for handholds as it steepened, he did not look back. He gained the ridge, and began to run. In the darkness he had no sense of direction, but he could see the smoke and the distant hearth fires of the fort up on the hilltop and kept them behind him. Further along the ridge he dropped down onto the far slope, running in bounding leaps between the tummocks and the thrusting thorn bushes. The ground levelled again and grew wet and soft beneath him, and he was running and stumbling across a boggy valley. Coarse grasses grabbed and swiped at his ankles, and he could see nothing in front of him, only the dim flank of the hills to his right. The wet ground sucked and hissed with every step.

Now he heard the dogs barking away down the valley, the cries of the hunters as they rode in pursuit. How long could a man on foot outrace trained hunting hounds and horsemen? He dared not look back, and flung himself onwards. Something tripped him and he fell face-first into damp earth and black water, but clawed his way up and ran again. He could feel the strength leaking from him like blood flowing from a wound.

He began to climb again, the ground drier and more solid underfoot. Above him, through the mist, he could see a rocky hillcrest lined with trees like the bristles on a hog's back. Every drawn breath punched at his lungs, and he stared only at the ground immediately ahead of him, trying to force himself on, trying not to think about the beasts racing after him. The sword in his hand was soft iron, the blade blunted and bent where he had used it to pull himself up the slope. It was little more than a metal club now, but it was the only weapon he had. Grabbing at the brambles and thorn bushes, he dragged himself towards the rocks. The mist thinned here, and he could see the bulge of the land, the bare slopes of the moors. He came to a patch of level ground below a wall of exposed rock, black twisted trees hanging over the brink, and turned at bay.

There were two dogs after him, huge grey beasts galloping up the slope. A single rider he could see, some way behind them coming up out of the mist. Castus tried to straighten the blade of his sword against a rock; then he pulled off his leather cape and wrapped it tightly around his left arm.

The first dog was already bounding over the lip of the level ground. It was almost the size of a man, with powerful legs to spring and powerful jaws that could rip out a victim's throat with one bite. Castus planted his back against the rock. The dog snarled and then crouched back to leap. Castus threw himself forward, feinting with his bound left arm, and as the animal sprang forward he dodged sideways and swung the sword. The flat of the blade smacked against the hound's snout, breaking its jaw.

The second dog was already springing: Castus turned just in time and the heavy body struck his shoulder, claws gripping the leather cape that wrapped his arm. He shoved against it, keeping on his feet, and for a moment he heard the jaws crunch close to his neck, felt the rank rotten meat-breath filling his face; then he punched low and level with his sword. The dull blade grated against the animal's hairy ribs, and he struck again and again as the claws mauled at his shoulder. Then he shoved again, knocking the animal back off him. A wheeling stroke with the sword, and he heard the snap of bone and the spatter of blood.

Already the horseman was surging up the last slope towards him, cloak swinging behind him, spear raised in his fist. Castus stamped down on the neck of the wounded hound, scrambled across the level and dropped down onto the stony slope below a thicket of thorn bushes. He heard the pony blowing hard as it cantered up onto the level, the harsh grunts of the rider urging it on. He raised his head a little and saw them standing above him, the rider bare-chested under his cloak, spike-haired, craning from the animal's back and staring into the darkness. The pony shied as it scented the blood of the dogs, and the rider kicked at it and pulled the rope reins. Around the lip of the level ground they came, until they were almost directly above where Castus lay, only the thorny scrub between them.

Come on, Castus prayed silently. *Don't stop there. Don't wait for the others*. Already he could hear the cries and whoops of other riders down in the valley, the bray of hunting horns. He shrugged his left hand free of the cape and closed his fingers around a fist-sized rock. The horseman above him had no horn, but turned and shouted, waving his arm. His voice was swallowed by the mist.

The pony moved forward again, hooves kicking loose stones down over the lip and through the twisted branches to where Castus lay. He waited, flat on his back, breath held tight in his chest, until the Pictish rider had moved across the level ground above him. Then he tossed the rock out into the darkness down the slope, and heard it thud and crackle through the scrub. At once the rider cried out and urged his mount forward, down over the lip of the level ground and past the thorn bush towards the dark slope where the rock had fallen.

With his head turned to his shoulder Castus could see the pony kicking down over the lip, its hooves almost close enough to reach out and touch. He stayed lying still until the animal had almost passed him. Then he rolled up off the ground with the sword in his hand. In one forward lunge he seized the rider's hanging cloak and dragged him backwards, striking up with the blade of his sword. The rider only managed a single strangled gasp before he tumbled off the pony with the blunt tip of the blade jabbing hard into his kidney. He fell heavily, the cloak flipping over his head, and Castus slammed the sword down over the top of his skull and then flung the bent blade aside. The pony had carried on down the slope a short way, but it tried to rear back as Castus bounded out of the darkness. He paused to snatch up the leather cape and the fallen man's spear, then he caught the pony's bridle, dragged its head down and managed to vault up onto its back.

The rider was on his feet again, bleeding from the head, reeling on the slope. Castus pulled back on the reins, turning the pony and kicking at its flanks. As the rider staggered closer, blinded and yelling, he stabbed the man in the chest with his own spear and then booted him down.

'*Yah!*' he said through his teeth, screwing the pony's head round and directing it at the crest of the ridge to his right. '*Yah! Come on!*' He kicked his heels into the animal's flank again, but the pony was terrified, backing and shying. He could hear the pursuing riders coming up the valley behind him, their cries gaining volume as the mist thinned. The pony had no saddle, and Castus felt himself sliding on the coarse blanket across its back. He pulled up his aching legs and slapped the pony's flank with the shaft of the spear. Still it refused to advance – rather it was trying to turn on the slope and gallop back into the valley. *This*, Castus thought, *is why I was never a cavalryman...*

'Have it your way then.'

He pulled the hood of the leather cape back over his head, swung the pony round and let out the reins. The animal leaped at once, and Castus locked his thighs tight around its flanks and leaned back as it plunged down the slope, hoping that in the gloom he could pass as a Pict. The mist rose around them, and he could see the forms of the other riders coming up from his right. He swung the spear flat, gesturing away to one side; then he kicked at the pony again and let it carry him on across the head of the valley.

The riders cried out in triumph, their dogs bounding along beside them as they cut left up the slope away from him. Hardly daring to believe that his deception had worked, Castus drew in the reins, turning the pony as gently as he could and urging it upwards away from the hunting pack. He kept his head down, hunching against the pony's braided mane as the land rose again beneath him. Back on the far slope he could hear the shouts and yells of the hunters: they had found the butchered dogs, he guessed, and their speared comrade.

'*Come on*,' he was whispering, '*come on*,' shunting against the pony's spine, and this time the animal responded to his commands. They gained the ridge, dropped down the far side, and then the mist swept over them and the sounds of the hunt died suddenly into the silent dark.

CHAPTER XII

All night he rode, across the bare hills and the boggy moors, splashing through streams and skirting tangled woodlands. The mist receded as he moved away from the estuary, and between the clouds he saw the moon just past full. At times, when he dismounted to rest his legs and let the pony drink water or crop at the tough spiky grass, he tried to work out the direction he was travelling. Southwards, roughly, he guessed. Now and then he thought he heard the sound of dogs, or the distant horns of the hunters, but he saw nobody. By the time the moon sank and the sky lightened to the east, the shore of a vast body of water lay ahead of him, the far side still lost in night. He secured the pony to a low tree, lay in the grass at the waterside and slept.

Bright sunlight woke him, and he opened his eyes to a clear blue sky. It was soon after dawn, and the lake was ice blue to the black mountains on the far shore. Castus dragged himself to his feet. He felt skinned all over, his bones bruised, his shoulder aching with the welts where the dog had clawed him. Stumbling across the shingle at the edge of the lake, he plunged his face and arms into the cold water.

He rode through the day, hardly daring to stop and rest, keeping well clear of inhabited places. The pony carried him westwards through the hill country, then across into the deep wooded valley of a rushing river. Castus looked down through the trees and saw the white haze of a waterfall, the torrent spraying between high rocks. He found wild blackberries growing along the valley side, and ate until he was sick of the taste and the sweetness.

Towards evening the valley curved south, and Castus saw the broad silver loops of a wider river, with gulls circling in the last light of the sun. Squinting, he remembered this landscape: in the middle distance was the dark line of the road he had followed with his men on their last march to the Pictish meeting ground. The wall of Antoninus was only a few miles to the south. He slept in the bushes above the muddy riverbank, and at dawn stripped off his clothes and held them bunched above his head as he swam beside the pony, kicking and thrashing across a bend of the river until he staggered up on the far shore.

There were warbands moving on the road. Castus saw one of them as he made his way from the riverbank: twenty or thirty warriors with spears and pack animals. But they were a mile in advance, and did not look back as he rode, crouching low, over the flat ground towards the road.

A mile further across the plain, a vast number of crows were circling over a thicket of woods. Castus dropped down off the pony and secured the reins. He walked, legs numb. As he moved around the edge of the thicket the smell came to him, and his stomach tightened with dread. Dead flesh, old slaughter. Around the last tangled branches of the thicket, he saw the open ground beside the road, and the single stripped tree with its harvest of rotting heads.

He walked closer, feeling his empty guts beginning to heave. The heads were blackened, pecked and gouged by birds. But he made out the face of Culchianus, the features of Timotheus. Then he could look no more, and turned away with a low anguished groan. His shoulder buckled and he pressed his clenched fists to his head. Sickened anger boiled inside him, and a terrible wrenching despair that brought him close to tears. He forced himself to turn and look again, burn the terrible image into his mind. *Remember this*, he told himself.

Away from the road, he moved up into the reaching moorlands to the west. Across foot-sucking bogs and heather-covered hillsides, rushing streams and spills of dry scree, he traced his way southwards until he made out the overgrown ridge of the old wall of Antoninus. At the mouth of a valley beyond another slow stream, he saw the line of the ridge knot and curl, weathered stone showing through the grass and moss, and rode his pony through a gateway in the long-abandoned fortification.

A little further up the valley he came to a small settlement, just three humped huts with a wicker fence around a yard and some animal pens. The men in the yard did not look like Picts, and Castus kept his spear pointing to the ground as he rode closer.

They gathered at the gate as he approached, and a woman came out of the largest hut behind them. Castus halted, dismounted. The smell of woodsmoke and cooking food reached him. None of the people were armed, and they watched him warily. He considered how he must look to them: big and bruised, stubble-bearded, with fresh scars on his face and arms. He was riding a Pictish pony, and wearing a Pictish cape. It occurred to him that he could probably walk right in and take whatever he wanted, and they would not try to stop him.

He stuck the spear in the ground, trying to smile without baring his teeth. *I don't want to harm you*, he wanted to tell them. *I've killed about six men in the last few days, but I won't kill you if you let me.* He raised his hand and mimed eating, and the woman backed away and hurried inside the hut. One of the men opened the gate and gestured towards a log, worn by much sitting.

Castus eased himself down onto the log, keeping his eyes on the men until the woman returned with a wooden bowl of barley porridge and a cup of water; then he ate fast, unable to hold himself back. He grinned and nodded, and set the bowl down. Vast contentment washed through him. He heard the sounds of cattle, and for a moment remembered something from his childhood: the dairy behind his father's workshop, and drinking warm milk from a ladle.

The woman pressed her palms together and laid the side of her head upon them. *Sleep.* She pointed towards one of the smaller huts with the question in her eyes. Evening was coming on, the light mellow and granular now, but Castus stood up and shook his head. He wished he had something to give in exchange for the food, and thought of Marcellinus' seal ring, still concealed in the toe of his boot. But that would be worthless to them, and if any Roman ever found it they would suffer. He pressed his palm to his chest, over his heart, and backed away, and all of them smiled.

As he rode away up the valley he wondered who or what they must have taken him for. Doubtless they were glad to see him gone, but in his weakened state their simple frightened charity seemed a gift from the gods.

For another four days he pushed on southwards, taking his directions from the position of the sun, resting in thickets of trees with the spear lying beside him. Sometimes when he slept he dreamed of Cunomagla, and woke to imagine her musky scent around him, caught between angry desire and longing for her. At other times he saw the foul trophy tree in his dreams, and started awake in a sweat of terror.

Twice more he managed to beg food from isolated settlements; on his third attempt, men came running from the huts, shouting, with bows and javelins in their hands, and he rode clear before they got within range. After that he avoided human habitation. He found an orchard of wild apple trees, and devoured the small tough fruit ravenously.

On the third day he met a broad track that ran straight across the hills and the valleys, and recognised an old Roman road. He followed it on southwards, alert for warbands, and later that day he met the trail of the devastation.

From across the hill he smelled the burning, and rode warily until he could see the blackened walls of a village on the low bluffs above a river. Crows circled, but there was no triumph tree here. Was this a Roman settlement north of the Wall, Castus wondered, or had the inhabitants merely been loyal to Rome? The dead lay where they had fallen, hazed with fat black flies. Castus gazed at the corpses, their wounds black and clotted. Several days had passed since they died. There were no survivors, and the stink gripped him by the throat, and he retreated.

He rode on, more slowly now, expecting to see the warriors ahead of them. There were bodies beside the road in places, cut down in flight, men and horses left to rot. A few of the dead wore the tunics and breeches of Roman soldiers. Once Castus thought he saw a woman's body with a dead child beside it, a bloodstained blanket thrown over them, but he passed on. A few miles further was the burnt ruin of another village, and he looked away from the charred black corpses strewn among the roofless huts.

Towards evening on the fourth day he crested a ridge and saw the wide river estuary and the salt marshes, and knew that he had arrived at the western coast. There was hard-packed gravel underfoot and the margins of the road were cleared of scrub, and then he saw before him the white line of the Wall of Hadrian drawn across the low landscape like a streak of chalk. In the far distance long trails of smoke rose, and Castus rode with gathering anticipation: he was almost home, almost within the boundary of the Roman domain.

Oblivious to all but the road and the gateway ahead, he did not hear the riders behind him until the hooves of their horses battered on the gravel of the road. Four of them, and two more charging up out of the woods ahead. Castus reined in the pony, canted the spear back overarm. There were too many of them – he would die, he realised. Icy shock held him immobile. Then as he opened his mouth to shout his last battle cry he saw the sun glinting off the riders' helmets and mail, the emblems on their shields.

'Wait!' he tried to shout, but he had not spoken aloud in six days and his voice was a strangled gasp. The riders came on, spears levelled, faces glaring beneath the rims of their helmets. Castus threw down his own spear, raised his arms above his head, managed an inarticulate shout.

The horsemen drew up suddenly, kicking dust, and then circled with the spears pointing. Castus grinned, coughed, and found his voice.

'I'm Roman! I'm a Roman soldier!'

Flavius Domitianus, Prefect of the Petriana Cavalry, was a large harried-looking man in late middle age. 'They came upon us four days ago,' he said, gazing out of the window towards the smoking ruins of the town of Luguvalium, half a mile away behind the Wall. 'The scouts reported a large mass of them moving down from the north-west, and I sent four squadrons out onto the road. They scattered ahead of us, but it was just a feint and the main body crossed the wall a mile or so east of here, then swam the river and circled round behind us. They fell on the town that evening. We managed to get most of the people back here into the fort, and cut the bridge behind us, but they burned the town. I've lost three hundred men, killed or missing. The gods know how many civilians are dead.'

They were sitting in an upstairs room of his headquarters, in the fort of Petrianis. Through the open window Castus could hear the familiar sounds of army life, but also the groans of wounded men, weeping women, the slow stir of despair. The relief he had felt at being surrounded by solid Roman walls again had not lasted long.

Domitianus lifted the cavalry sword from the table and weighed it in his palms. 'Do you know, centurion, how many times in the last four days I've thought of falling on this blade, from shame?'

Castus remained silent. Only an hour had passed since the scouts brought him into the fort. He was tired and filthy and dazed, but Domitianus looked much worse. Grey stubble was dug into the prefect's hollow cheeks, and his eyes were bloodshot and smudged.

'Ten years I've commanded this fort! Ten years of patrolling, gathering taxes, supervising the natives, and never once a sniff at action. And when it comes – within six hours everything collapses around me! I've lost a third of my strength, the town's burned and the enemy have slipped past me – and now I've got two thousand civilian refugees to look after.'

He slammed the sword back down on the table, the blade ringing. 'It's disgusting,' he said. 'But somebody's got to command this mess.' His voice choked off as he turned quickly back to the window. Castus could not tell whether Domitianus was more angry at the enemy, his own men, or himself. He sat silently at the table, drinking heated wine and eating bread and beef stew.

'At least I managed to fire the message beacon before we were cut off,' the prefect said grimly. 'Since then I've been sending out patrols to scout along the roads and cut up any stragglers they can find. You were almost one of them, centurion. So what happened to you?'

Haltingly, Castus told him the story. It seemed an impossible tale now, and the further he got into it the harder it became to tell. He mentioned nothing of the death of Marcellinus, or the renegade, or Cunomagla.

'And you got away and made it all the way back here?' the prefect said, and grunted. Castus could not tell if the man believed him or not. 'Well, you'd better get washed and get into some clean clothes, then I'll see what I can do for you. My patrols have reported the roads clear to the south – it seems most of the enemy have moved off south-east, towards Eboracum. Hopefully our governor Arpagius will be dealing with them even now, if they get that far.'

'You think they'll just raid and then return north?'

'You think not?'

Castus shook his head. 'I think they'll try for as much as they can.'

Domitianus touched his brow. 'Pray to Jupiter they don't get it,' he said.

Bathed, shaved, rested and dressed in a clean white military tunic and grey breeches, Castus joined the prefect and two of

225

his decurions for dinner later that evening. They ate sitting in the records room of the headquarters: Domitianus's own rooms were being used by the curiales and wealthy families of the burnt town. It was a grim and subdued meal, and Castus said little but only listened. His own adventures north of the wall seemed of little interest to the men of the Petriana, compared with their own recent disasters.

'I'm sending twenty of my men on a long reconnaissance tomorrow, to Brocavum,' Domitianus said. 'I need to check if the roads are clear. You can ride with them, and pick up another escort there. I'll issue you with a horse to replace that barbarian pony thing you were riding, and you can collect a sword and anything else you need from the armoury. You can take four days' marching rations too, which should be enough to get you to Eboracum. I can't spare more.'

Castus thanked him.

'Well then,' the prefect concluded. 'I'll have the orderly show you to a bed. You leave at dawn.'

Two days later, Castus rode down off the high barren moors towards the rich farmland north of Eboracum. He was mounted in a proper saddle, on a broad-chested Roman cavalry horse, with a good Roman sword slung over his shoulder, and he had made good progress south from Petrianis and up across the high country. The weather had been foul across the moors, and the commander of the little fort up on the pass had refused him an escort.

'As far as I'm concerned,' the commander had said, gesturing out to the east, 'all that country belongs to the enemy now. I've only got a hundred men here, and I have to hold this pass. If you want to go that way, you're on your own.'

226

'I have to go on,' Castus had told him, leaning on the parapet above the eastern gate.

'Well, the gods be with you. I'd keep off the roads if you can. We've had reports from deserters fleeing the Wall garrisons that the barbarians are swarming across the countryside unchecked. They've already plundered Cataractonium and they're moving south. If I were you, brother, I'd stay here.'

But the morning was bright and clear and the road straight, and after five miles Castus reached an abandoned village and customs station at a river crossing. A little way further he turned off the road and headed southwards, following farm tracks and woodland trails. There had been no sign of the enemy for the last two days. The attack that had breached the Wall at Petrianis had swung left, rolling along the rear of the fortifications towards the rich settled lands to the south-east. After eight days in the saddle Castus was weary and sore, the motion of the horse beneath him a torment, but he pushed on, urging the animal to a canter whenever he found level ground and an open track. It would be a day or more before he reached Marcellinus's villa, and another half-day to Eboracum.

The country was deserted here; the inhabitants must have fled to the hills in terror of the enemy. Castus did not blame them – it was illegal for private citizens to own or carry arms, so they would have had no way of defending themselves – but it felt eerie to find this settled country so empty. He skirted the silent villages and passed the shuttered farmhouses, riding slowly with sword in hand. But still there was no sign of the Picts – they must have kept their force together, aiming for larger targets.

He travelled more slowly after that, watching the trees and the fields, wary of ambush. It occurred to him that he had no idea how to find the villa without getting back onto the main road and retracing his steps to the turning. Evening was coming on when he reached a small village in a fold of a wooded river valley, houses of wood and stone and thatch around a large central tree with broad-spreading leaves. From one of the houses, vague in the dusk, Castus could make out a rising thread of hearth-smoke. He rode closer, sword in hand, watching the other buildings. The silent empty village was unnerving, and as the light faded the surrounding woods appeared ominous.

'Hey!' he called as he sat his horse beneath the tree. 'Come out! I'm a Roman soldier.'

The door of the house opened a crack, then wider, and a woman stood on the threshold. She was old, around fifty, with a creased face and grey hair, but her back was straight and she stood proudly, almost defiant.

'Thanks be to Brigantia Dea,' the woman said. 'Are you with the relief force?'

'I'm not with anybody, I'm by myself.' Castus glanced around at the other houses. All were closed up, no smoke rising.

'They've all gone away,' the old woman said coldly. Her voice was tightly clipped, her Latin fluent, with only the slightest taint of accent. 'Off to the hills when they heard the news of the battle. I told them I wasn't leaving – I won't abandon my hearth and the shrines of my ancestors. Are you a deserter?'

'No,' Castus said. He eased himself down from the saddle and stretched his aching legs. 'I'm a centurion of the Sixth Legion. I'm trying to get back to Eboracum.' A sudden weariness came over him, and he stretched his mouth in a yawn.

The old woman turned and called out to somebody inside the hut in the British language. 'Come inside,' she said. 'The slave will see to your horse.' A tangle-haired boy with a slack smiling mouth came from the house, took the reins and led the horse gently towards the drinking trough.

'What battle?' Castus asked, as he followed the woman through the door.

'You haven't heard? It was two days ago, outside Isurium. The barbarians fell upon a column of the Sixth and destroyed them utterly. They say two thousand men died, and the survivors fled back to the walls of Eboracum.'

Castus felt his head reeling. It was not possible... but the woman had spoken plainly and did not seem the sort to believe the stories of cowards and liars. For a moment he stood in the doorway, feeling the weight of the news sinking through him.

'How far is Isurium from here?'

'A good day's walk. Only four or five hours for a horseman. But it's too late for you to travel now, if that's what you're thinking.'

Numbed, Castus stepped inside the hut. A plain room, white-washed walls and rushes on the floor, hearth at one end and a living space at the other, with curtained alcoves for sleeping. Neat and homelike, but he drew his sword and placed it on the table as he sat.

'There's no danger here, not now,' the woman said quietly. At the hearth, a slave girl squatted in the ashes preparing a meal; she looked like the twin of the horse-boy outside. 'My father was a soldier of the Sixth,' the old woman said, 'and my son serves with them now.' A slight catch in her voice as she spoke. 'Perhaps you know of him? His name is Valerius Varialus, of the Fifth Cohort.'

'I don't, I'm sorry. I've only been with the legion a short time.'

'Ah. I thought your accent sounded strange. You're a foreigner then. Well, no matter.'

She sat at the far side of table, and in the last light through the narrow window Castus saw her face lined with unspoken grief. A soldier's daughter, a soldier's mother. Alone in this abandoned place, too proud to leave or to admit her anguish.

'I'm searching for a villa near here,' he said as the slave girl brought food and a cup of beer. 'It belongs to a Roman named Aelius Marcellinus. Do you know of it?'

The woman frowned, considering, but then shook her head. The slack-mouthed boy came in from the darkness of the yard, and the woman called out a question to him. Her voice was harsh, demanding, and the boy made a strange gesture, half a shrug and an expressive flutter. Then he held up his fingers, counting and pointing. A mute, Castus guessed.

'Tasca here knows the place you mean. It's about six miles south and east – but it'll be dark soon, as I say, and the country isn't safe. Stay with us tonight and the boy will take you in the morning.'

For a moment Castus wanted to refuse. The thought of further delay now, when he was so close, was almost maddening. But he knew the woman was right: unless he forced the mute boy to guide him at swordpoint, he would soon lose his way and be prey to any danger. Besides, he was tired. Too tired to think properly, or to act effectively.

Once he had eaten he allowed the slave girl to lead him to a dark corner of the room piled with blankets. He lay down, lulled by the hushed voices of the old woman and the twin slaves talking beside the hearth. At the edge of sleep a face appeared to him: Marcellinus's daughter, speaking silently. Her eyes held the same quiet anguish as the old woman of the house. Another soldier's daughter, Castus thought as his mind slipped into darkness. Could the girl somehow know that her father was dead?

The sky was light but the sun was still below the trees as Castus prepared to depart. He plunged his head into the horse trough and then flung himself back, spattering water. Wheeling his arms to ease the cramps in his shoulders, he watched the boy saddle the horse and fetch a mule from behind the house. The old woman stood in the doorway with the slave girl.

'Take this,' the woman said, passing Castus a bundle wrapped in greased rag. 'Hot barley cakes, for the journey.'

'Thanks,' Castus said, and swung himself up, wincing, into the saddle.

'If you get back to Eboracum, please look for my son. Varialus, remember. Tell him Adiutoris and Jucunda, his mother and father, are safe.'

'I'll tell him.' Castus paused, gave a brief military salute, and then turned his horse.

'May the gods protect you,' the woman Jucunda called as he rode away.

The mute boy led at a brisk pace, bouncing along on his mule, and soon the sun was striking down through the trees and lighting the strips of tilled ground beside the path. At times the boy turned and twisted his mouth, gesturing and making sounds that Castus could not interpret. He wanted to tell the boy to go faster – now it was daylight he felt the urgency of the situation more clearly. He hardly dared think what he hoped, or what he feared, to find ahead of him.

They followed the loop of the river, keeping to the high ground above the trees on a dirt trail. A mile more, then two, and as they crossed a broad marshy sward Castus looked up and saw crows wheeling over the trees. Then the boy gave a strangled cry, pointing: a body lay in the grass beside the trail. A young man, wearing the clean white tunic of a house slave. Flies gathered on his lips.

Castus kicked his horse forward, swerving around the boy on the mule and galloping on up the trail. Alone now, he rode on between the trees until they broke. Then he saw the villa before him.

The roof had fallen in, the walls were smudged with black, and a thin mist of smoke still rose from the gaping doors and windows. Castus stared, breathing hard, tasting ash in the back of his throat. For a moment he wanted only to die – the shame of the delay, the failure – but he could see no flames, and he knew that the burning had happened more than a day before.

Slowly now, he nudged the horse forward through the last of the trees and across the open field at the back of the villa enclosure. There was an old rampart, a ditch and a wooden palisade that circled the compound, but the palisade was neglected and broken down in places and the ditch overgrown. Scanning the woods, the circuit of the rampart, the ruins, Castus let the horse carry him closer. When he reached the ditch he dismounted and tethered the horse to the broken palisade, then climbed across into the compound with his sword drawn.

Nobody in sight. The scene was almost peaceful, with the slow curls of grey smoke, the sunlight heavy on the grass and the gravel of the forecourt. But the air stank of burnt timber and plaster, and the memory of violence seemed to shimmer in the still air. Castus paced across the herb garden at the back of the house. Tensed, muscles tight, he climbed the steps to the porch. Broken tiles cracked under his boots. The air was charged with soot here, and he pulled up his neckscarf to cover his mouth.

In through the blackened doorway, he clambered over the wrack of charred timbers and tiles from the fallen roof. He could still feel the heat of the fire radiating from the walls. Clambering over collapsed beams, he reached the corridor at the front of the house. Misted fragments of broken glass ground and crunched beneath his feet, and looking down he could make out the pattern of the mosaic floor through the thick coating of burnt debris. He moved to the right, towards the wide doorway of the dining room where, just over a month before, he had eaten dinner with Marcellinus and Strabo.

Sunlight came from the shattered roof, lighting the haze of smoke and soot. Flies were already circling, and a stench caught in his throat and churned his stomach. Castus stood in the doorway, pressing the scarf over his mouth. For a moment he saw only the burnt wreckage. Then what had seemed a charred timber became the stump of a reaching arm. Teeth showed between shrunken black lips.

He stepped back into the corridor. Nothing could have survived here. Any that escaped would have been hunted down, like the dead slave out on the track. Backing away further, scuffing his feet through the debris, Castus emerged into the shadow of the front portico. Pulling the scarf down from his mouth, he took great heaving lungfuls of air. His head was spinning, and his stomach crawled. Marcellinus's wife and daughter, with their whole household, were as dead as Marcellinus himself, and for all his vows Castus had not been able to protect any of them.

Then, as he stared into the bright daylight of the forecourt, he saw the pony. A native pony, tethered beside the stable block, head down and cropping grass. He stepped quickly behind one of the standing columns of the portico, but before he could look again he heard a sharp cry. He knew it at once: the cry of a man at the point of death.

Flinging himself away from the pillar he jumped down into the yard and sprinted across the gravel with his sword held low. The cry had come from behind the stable block. Breathing hard, Castus threw himself against the wall of the stable and turned, scanning the yard behind him. Empty. He doubled the corner and saw another building before him, a disused bath-house with the door hanging open. The cry had come from there. Warily, he advanced from the stable wall towards the open door, dropping into a fighting crouch as he paced forward. Flies whirled around his head, and he heard birdsong from the trees beyond the boundary fence.

Four paces from the door he paused, squinting into the darkness of the building. A body was lying face down just inside the threshold. A man, in native cloak and tunic, with a bloody wound in the centre of his back. Castus moved closer, breathing slowly, glancing to either side. He reached the doorway and studied the body – quite dead, not a twitch of movement. It looked as though a single blow had felled the man. Castus winged his shoulders, feeling the sweat of his palm as he gripped the sword, then he leaped forward, across the body and through the door.

Sudden movement from his right, and he ducked just in time. The heavy head of a mattock swung across his back and buried itself in the wall beside the door, spraying plaster. Twisting on his toes, Castus came back upright with his sword levelled, elbow drawn back to strike.

For a moment in the thick darkness he could see nothing, just the tool stuck in the wall with the haft jutting out into the sunlight. Then he heard a hiss of breath, and saw the movement of a body shrinking back from the doorway. He growled, edging forward, and at that moment a spear slashed in through the doorway and a man's body blocked the light.

Castus moved without thinking. He dropped, turned and punched out with the blade in one swift movement. The sword caught the man as he came through the door, stabbing up under his ribs. Castus stepped in close, into the body-smell, the blood-smell, slamming into his attacker and grappling his neck as he drove the sword in up to the hilt. The body slumped against him, twisted and fell, and Castus dragged the blade out of the wound.

Blood was on his face, hot on his right hand and up his arm, and he felt the energy of battle pulsing through him as he turned again to confront the person sheltering inside the door. A lunge and a stab and it would be finished.

As his eyes adjusted to the darkness, he saw her crouching in the deepest corner of the room. Castus eased down his blade. 'Marcellina?' he said.

The mattock fell from the wall and clattered on the tiled floor.

CHAPTER XIII

'It's me. Aurelius Castus. The centurion who went north with your father. Do you remember?' It was hard to get the words out. His throat was still tense from the fight.

He laid his sword down, stretched out his hand to her. But his hand was covered in blood; his whole arm was spattered with it. Now he could feel the ringing in his ears, the aftershock of combat. His heart was still beating heavily, and his hand trembled.

'Look at me,' he said, trying to soften his voice. 'Look at me – I'm Roman. I'm a friend... You understand?'

The girl stayed crouched in the corner, drawn tight, shuddering. She wore a long tunic of fine light-blue wool, a coral necklace and pendant earrings, as if she had just walked out of the house, but her hair was hanging loose. How long had she been hiding like this? And what strength must it have taken her, Castus thought, to swing the heavy mattock hard enough to kill one man, then swing it again as he had stepped through the door himself?

'I'll get you water,' he said. Picking up his sword he backed away from the girl, stepping over the bodies sprawled inside the doorway. The man he had just killed lay on his side, eyes open, with a lake of blood spreading around him. His hair was cropped short with a tuft at the back, and his sparse beard was trimmed around his mouth. Not a Pict, Castus reckoned; the man was from one of the southern tribes perhaps. Votadini or Selgovae. A scavenger dragging through the wreckage of war.

Castus looked up from the corpse, into the sunlight, and stopped still. Two ponies were tethered at the back of the stable.

Two at the back, one at the front. *Three.*

'There's another one,' Castus said quietly. He listened into the silence, hearing the ticking of the roof beams overhead, the trickle of plaster from the wall where the mattock had struck. Then – just at the edge of hearing – the slight shuffle from outside, the rasping intake of breath.

The third man was pressed against the outside wall, edging towards the door.

'*Stay quiet,*' Castus whispered to the girl. '*Don't move.*' He could feel the pool of wet blood spreading around the soles of his boots. No sound from outside; the man was not moving. If he ran now, he could reach the ponies and ride for help before Castus could catch him.

One long breath, then he leaped through the doorway and into the sunlight. He spun immediately to face the wall, and the man was there, braced. Castus noticed that he was holding a Roman spatha – battlefield loot. For a heartbeat they stared at each other.

Then the man cried out, feinted to the left and jumped right, flailing his spatha in the air; the long blade was unfamiliar to him, and he did not have the balance of it. He was running, trying to swerve around the limit of Castus's reach. Castus stamped forward, slashing his sword in a wide low arc and cutting the man on the back of the knee as he ran. The man screamed and fell, hobbled, into the dust.

Two steps, and Castus stood over him. The man rolled onto his side, lips drawn away from his teeth. His weapon had fallen and he lunged for it, fingers scrabbling in the dirt, snarling a curse in his own language. Castus trod on the man's shoulder and forced him onto his back, reversed his grip on his sword, raised it in both hands and plunged it down.

Marcellina screamed as he stepped back into the bath-house. She was still crouching in the corner with a dirty shawl pulled over her head.

'I got him, don't worry. He's dead now. But there might be others around – we have to leave.'

The girl flinched back as he approached her. She seemed to have forgotten who he was.

'Juno preserve us,' Castus muttered. He wiped his sword on a dead man's tunic, sheathed it, and then came back to kneel beside Marcellina. She was crying, or trying to, just tight little stabs of breath. He slipped his arm beneath her knees and she started to struggle against him, but he held her tight, got his other arm around her shoulders and lifted her. She went limp in his arms, and he realised that she had passed out.

They rode until evening, south-west away from the villa and through the hill country onto the flanks of the high moors, far from marauding bands. Castus had tried to put the girl on one of the native ponies, but she was even less of a rider than he was, and short of tying her to the beast's back he knew she would never manage the journey. So he carried her before him, perched across the saddle bow with her legs dangling over the horse's flank, supporting her with his left arm. Not an easy or comfortable ride, and they made slow progress, but at least she had stopped trying to fight him.

There was still light on the western horizon, and Castus could make out the silhouette of a rocky tumulus on the high ground. At first there seemed to be giant carved figures standing on the hilltop, but as he got closer he saw that they were strange formations of rock, towers and piers, and boulders piled into stacks. Once, when he was marching across Asia with the Herculiani, he had seen something similar in Cappadocia; somebody had told him that the shapes were carved by the wind, but Castus could hardly believe that was possible. It was a strange sight, unnerving against the glow of sunset, but he needed a secure refuge, and there was no sign of human habitation up there.

As he rode up off the slopes of the moor, the rock towers rose all around him, with wild grass and heather between them. The wind was strong up here, whining and blustering around the tall stone masses, and Castus steered the horse to a sheltered place in the lee of one great stack, where a hollow at the base created a shallow cave, before dismounting.

'We'll stay here tonight,' he said to the girl, helping her down off the horse. She went at once to the cave and sat inside it with her back pressed to the stone. She had been completely silent since they left the villa. Castus took the saddle from the horse, rubbed the animal down as he had seen the troopers of the Petriana cavalry doing, and then tethered it in a patch of grass between the rocks. When he returned the girl was still sitting as he had left her, with her knees drawn up, staring at nothing.

'No fire,' she said suddenly as he started piling sticks and dry bracken. He glanced at her – she was remembering the burning villa, he guessed – then shrugged, kicking the little heap of kindling aside.

'Fine. We'll eat cold food then.' He placed the remaining barley cakes and a canteen of water beside her, then sat chewing at hardtack and dry cheese. Night had fallen between the stones, and the girl was almost invisible in her little cave.

Castus had seen the effects of shock many times before. Most men, after their first experience of battle, had that glazed look, that distracted air. But with Marcellina it went much deeper. Once, in Antioch, Castus had met a Greek doctor who told him that the mind, like the body, can be wounded by violence. Perhaps even destroyed. For Castus himself there had always been the legion, his brothers around him, their common purpose and duty. The shock of combat was a shared thing, easily digested and soon just a part of life. For the girl, though, there was none of that. Everything she had known, all family and sense of the world around her, had been destroyed.

'Where is my father?' she said, and her voice echoed slightly off the hollow rock. 'Why did he not return with you?'

'Ah,' Castus said. He had tried several times, in the preceding days, to compose in his mind a suitable speech to explain what had happened. But he had always imagined himself sitting in the villa, with Marcellinus's wife and daughter before him, both mutely composed, demure, accepting. Now, instead, the villa was burned and the mother butchered, and there was only this dark windy wilderness of rock and heather, this unhinged girl, and he could think of nothing to say.

He took Marcellinus's heavy gold signet ring from his belt pouch, knelt beside the girl and took her hand. He placed the ring in her palm, closed her fingers over it and sat back again.

Marcellina opened her hand and looked at her father's ring, rolling it on her palm. She drew a long shuddering breath.

'I remember you,' she said, and Castus could make out her raised face in the moonlight. 'I remember – you're the centurion. You're the one who promised… You promised to protect him and bring him home…' There was a curious wandering note in her voice, as if she was waking from deep sleep. 'You promised,' she said again, with more emphasis. 'You *promised*!'

She threw the ring violently at Castus, and it hit him hard on the forehead and dropped to roll against the rocks.

'*Why?*' she cried out in a great rush of anguish and realisation. 'Why are you here? Why did *you* come back and not *him*?'

'I'm sorry, domina. It was his own wish – I...'

'*Quiet!* Don't talk to me! Don't come *near* me!' The girl was on her feet now, crouching back against the curve of the rock wall, gasping back tears. Castus remained seated. Anything he tried to say now would be wrong.

'You... *stupid-headed liar*! You *bastard*! Why did you come back? Why did you break your vow?'

She bent to snatch up a handful of small stones and threw them at Castus. He swatted them away with his forearms, but now she was grabbing larger stones, pelting them at him, spitting breath.

'I curse you!' she cried. 'The gods curse you!'

Castus rolled his back to her, covering his head, feeling the stones cracking off his shoulders. He was about to get up and restrain her when he heard the last stone fall and the girl drop to her knees, sobbing. He turned and watched her; she looked so small in the moonlight, so weak and broken. Wincing, he clambered to his feet.

Standing up straight, hands clasped behind his back, he addressed the girl. 'Your father and I were taken captive by the Picts after a battle. Your father was injured, and his status placed him in an impossible position. He chose death as the honourable way, and charged me to return here and find you. To tell you what happened.' He glanced to his left, and saw the gold ring catching the moonlight; he picked it up and put it back in his pouch. 'I'll keep this for you,' he said.

But the girl was hunched over on the ground and did not look up. Castus unpinned his cloak and draped it over her body.

'Stay here,' he said. 'Try and sleep if you can. I'll be back soon.'

Moving around the flank of the rocks, Castus peered upwards into the darkness and saw a crevice running towards the summit. Grunting, he pulled himself up, his boots grating against the gritty rocks, until he could raise his head over the top of the stack. The western sky behind him was still luminous blue with the afterglow of sunset, and he did not want to present a silhouette to anyone watching from the slopes below, so he pulled himself up over the lip of the rock and crawled forward on his belly until he could lie flat on the warm stone summit, looking eastwards into the night.

The sight took his breath. The dark land spread away for miles to the flat horizon, and all across it there were fires burning. Some of them were little sparks, flickering, but others were great scars and lines of flame traced across the landscape. The Picts were burning the villages and the crops in the fields. The wind was behind him, but even so Castus thought he could smell the distant conflagration.

He lay still, transfixed, until the last light was gone from the western sky, and then sat upright on the smooth stone. Eboracum was out there somewhere in the darkness, over on the furthest edge of the plain. Was that too burning? Had the enemy destroyed everything?

For a long time he sat still, staring. Then he felt the chill of the wind on his back, and the cold in his bones. He rolled off the rock and began slowly edging his way back down.

At first light, Castus collected kindling and lit a fire in a hollow of the rocks out of sight of the cave. He boiled water in his mess pot, and crumbled half of his hardtack into it with some bacon fat and cheese to make a thin savoury gruel. He was cleaning and sharpening his sword when Marcellina found him.

'I apologise for being impolite to you last night,' she said. Castus turned and saw her standing by the rocks with his cloak wrapped tightly around her. The girl's face was very pale, and there was darkness around her eyes. She looked older in the daylight, no longer a child.

'Impolite?' he said, and raised an eyebrow.

'I was... distressed. Please forgive me.'

He sniffed, and lifted the pot of hot food from the fire. She squatted, took a wooden spoon and started to eat, blowing on each spoonful to cool it. When she had finished eating she stood up again, away from the fire.

'I want you to take me to Eboracum,' she said, not looking at him. Castus kept working on his sword, drawing the whetstone along the blade. 'My brother is there... my younger brother. He's the only family I have left now...'

'That's where I'm going,' Castus said.

'I'll... I'll see to it that you are rewarded for conveying me safely...' Her voice caught, and when Castus glanced at her he saw tears on her cheeks.

'I don't need a reward,' he said. 'It's my duty to protect you.'

He stood up and slipped the sword back into its scabbard. Then he kicked out the fire.

Braced against the charred and sagging thatch of a barn roof, Castus craned his neck upwards and squinted into the level sunlight. The grey horizon was broken by trees and rising trails of smoke, but he could make out the distant smudge of the city in the distance. The barn had been half burned – one end of it was in blackened ruin and the other barely standing – but it was the highest vantage point he could find, and as close to Eboracum itself as he dared to go in daylight. Beneath him the thatch shifted, and he heard wooden laths splitting.

Sliding down the steeply pitched roof, he dropped from the low eaves and landed heavily.

'What did you see?' Marcellina said.

'Not much. Couldn't get high enough to see over the trees.'

'I'm lighter than you – help me up and I'll look.'

All the way down from the moors, Marcellina had ridden behind Castus, sitting across the rump of the horse and gripping his belt. Her mood had shifted: from being stunned and subdued that morning she seemed determined, assertive and even reckless. Castus had to remind himself that she was still in shock, the wound in her mind still gaping. They had talked little; they had a shared purpose now. But first they had to be sure that the city still held out.

Castus crouched, and the girl climbed up onto his back. The skirts of her tattered blue gown were pulled up around her hips, and as she clambered up onto the thatch Castus saw her slender legs, long and bare and white. He looked away again quickly.

'What can you see?' he called. The girl had climbed right up to the ridge poles and was standing, her hair loose in the breeze, gazing east.

'I can see the city,' she cried out. 'There's smoke... but it's only from this side of the river, not the fortress. There's something against the walls – something wooden, and that's burning... but there's no smoke from inside.'

'You've got sharp eyes,' Castus said.

'Wait, there's... There are lots of men, barbarians. All over the country between here and the city.'

Castus nodded. They had seen several small parties of Picts

and other barbarians on their ride down from the moors, all intent on plundering, and had managed to avoid them all.

'They've encircled the fortress,' he said. 'Otherwise they'd be inside it, not out here... They don't have the strength or equipment to attack the walls, but if they can keep the remains of the legion trapped inside they can plunder all they want.'

The girl was already sliding back down the roof, kicking burnt chaff over the eaves.

'Let's go then,' she said. She jumped from the roof and Castus caught her. 'We can ride straight through the enemy and into the city if we're fast enough...'

'Not in daylight,' he said. 'They'll have pickets on all the roads stopping anyone going in or out...'

The girl pushed herself away from him. 'I need to get into the city,' she said. 'I need to find my brother, and I don't want to wait any longer.'

'Domina!' Castus called to her. 'I told you we won't get through them in daylight. We'll have to cross the river upstream and circle round from the north-west, but we need darkness for that.'

She turned on him, suddenly furious and petulant. 'I'm not one of your soldiers!' she said. 'You can't give me orders! I demand we go to the city now!'

Castus pulled himself up onto the horse. He took a drink from the waterskin.

'I'm not ordering you to do anything,' he said. 'I'm trying to protect you. If you want to die, go ahead.'

For a few moments she stood her ground, glaring at him, her shoulders set. Then she exhaled loudly, stepped towards the horse and allowed him to draw her up behind him.

* * *

There was thunder that evening, then heavy rain. Castus and Marcellina sat together in a low hut near the river, listening to the water gushing down over the domed reed-thatch of the roof and spattering from the eaves. They had no fire, and the hut had been plundered of whatever poor furniture and utensils it might once have contained. But at least it had not been torched – this damp settlement among the reed beds beside the river was too small and mean to bother burning.

'How long must we wait here?' Marcellina asked, squatting against the wall, trembling slightly at the sound of the rain.

'We'll cross the river an hour before dawn. The fortress is just over a mile away, so we should try and reach it at first light. Don't want to try creeping up on a guarded gate in the dark.'

She nodded, preoccupied. They were eating the last of the hardtack and marching rations, although neither felt hungry.

'Your brother should be in the fortress,' Castus said. 'He'll have been evacuated there with of the rest of the citizens from the town. He'll be able to look after you, I expect.'

'Oh, yes,' Marcellina said bitterly. 'He'll look after me. He has to – he's the head of the family now. Even if he is only thirteen. But now Father's… gone he'll have no trouble marrying me off to some cousin or other from the south. He won't have to give much of a dowry.'

'Is that what you want?' Castus asked her.

'I'm seventeen years old,' the girl said with a sour irony that startled him. 'I should have been married years ago. What I want doesn't matter.'

The rain had eased outside, and Castus got up and crawled towards the low door of the hut. Marcellina grabbed his arm – her touch was unexpected, and shocked him.

'Where are you going? Don't leave me!'

'I need to check on the horse, then do some other things.

246

I'll be back in an hour or two. Stay here. Don't go outside.'

'Take me with you!'

Castus shook his head, tugged his arm away from her and went out into the wet dusk.

It was fully night by the time he returned, and the rain had stopped. He stamped back into the hut and tossed two damp Pictish cloaks down on the floor. One of the cloaks was stained with blood, but he hoped the girl would not notice in the dark.

'Where did you go?' she asked quietly.

'Just along the river. There's a bend to the north of here where we can cross, but we'll have to swim with the horse – can you do that? If we wear these cloaks we might pass as Picts till we're close enough to the walls, then we'll have to ride hard.'

'You killed some more of them, didn't you?'

'A couple. Hard work – I nearly slipped on the wet ground.'

'But you're hurt – you're bleeding.'

Castus grunted, seating himself against the wall. The second Pictish sentry had gashed his arm with a spear. Marcellina crawled across the hut on her knees and knelt beside him. He could see her face in the shadows, her smooth cheek and the curve of her lips, her large eyes watching him as he tore the ripped sleeve of his tunic from the wound and washed away the blood.

'I need a strip of your shawl,' he said, 'to use as a bandage.'

For a moment she drew back, uncertain, maybe disgusted, but then nodded quickly and ripped at the hem of the shawl. She passed him the torn strip and watched again as he wrapped it around his biceps and tied it, one end gripped in his teeth.

'Tell me what happened to you, back there at the villa,' Castus asked her as he flexed his bandaged arm. He saw her flinch at the memory. 'No – maybe I don't need to know,' he added.

Marcellina sat with her knees drawn up and said nothing for a long time, but in the half-dark Castus saw her expression shifting, her lips opening to speak and then closing. He wished he had not asked, but still he wanted to know.

'They came very suddenly, the Picts...' the girl said at last. She spoke in a calm, measured voice. 'We were in the dining room, just lying down to eat, and we heard the shouting from outside. They must have come from the back of the house and surprised the watchman... Mother told me to hide in the large closet.'

Castus saw her eyes closing, her throat tightening. She was gripping her knees in the circle of her arms. 'I heard... but I didn't see,' she said. 'Mother tried to talk with them. Tried to order them away. Then I heard... I think they killed the slaves first. I was too terrified to think about what was happening. One of them opened the closet door but didn't see me. It seems impossible – some god protected me...'

Castus touched his brow, and saw the girl do the same.

'Then I looked out, and saw Mother and Brita the maid dead on the floor. Their clothes were gone, they were... there was a lot of blood. Several others dead, and the roof was burning... I just stayed where I was, hiding. I couldn't breathe because of the smoke. When I looked again the whole room was on fire, the whole villa... I wrapped myself in a blanket and ran outside...'

'You were brave,' he said quietly, and the sound of his voice was harsh and rough compared to hers. She was shaking her head, the pendant earrings swinging.

'No. Just scared. So scared I didn't know what I was doing. It was... maybe a day I was hiding in the old bath-house, or two. Then I heard those men outside, talking and laughing. I found the tool, the pickaxe thing... One of them came through the door and I just hit him as hard as I could.'

'Hard enough to break his spine,' Castus said. 'Not bad. And you'd have brained me too if I hadn't seen the body on the floor and been on my guard.'

'But there were three of them. If you hadn't come...'

'Don't think about that. Just thank the gods it happened as it did, eh?'

'How can I thank the gods for anything? My family are dead. My home is destroyed. I have nothing left. Maybe it would have been better if I'd died.'

'You're still strong,' Castus told her. 'Think about what happens next, not what might have been.' He felt the same sensation he remembered from their talk in the villa long before, when the girl had made him vow to protect her father. A desire to comfort her somehow, or ease her distress, but no idea how to do it. He felt clumsy, untrained in kindness. Strange, he thought, that he should find killing two men in the darkness quite easy, but talking to a frightened seventeen-year-old girl so hard. Perhaps for other people it would be quite the reverse?

'Anyway,' he said, 'I promised your father I'd protect you.'

'You did?' In fact Castus could not remember if that was the promise he had made – but it was in the spirit of it, he was sure.

'Yes. So sleep now, and in a few hours we'll move.'

He spread his own cloak on the floor for the girl, then took the less bloody of the Pictish capes and, wrapping it around his shoulders, lay down on the other side of the hut. His wounded arm stung, but he could ignore the pain.

For a while he lay still, eyes closed, thinking back over what he had seen on his reconnaissance foray earlier: the bend in the river screened by trees, sixty paces, more or less, to the far bank with trees and then flat meadows on the other side. A mile to the walls of the fortress... His mind clouded, dulled by sleep, and he thought he was back in the Pictish hut, waiting for Cunomagla to come and join him. Warmth spread through his body at the recollection. *If I die in the next few hours*, he thought, *will that be the last sensation I remember?*

A slight noise, a shuffle and a step from the darkness, and Castus opened his eyes as Marcellina eased herself down beside him. He felt her body against his, her arm wrapping his chest.

'Let me stay here,' she whispered. 'I don't feel so scared now.'

He made a sound, low in his throat, and tried to resist the urge to move and embrace her. She was unmarried, he reminded himself, and a virgin. She was stunned, and not in control of herself. The girl's head lay against his shoulder; then she was pressing her face into the hollow of his neck, her breath on his skin.

'Wouldn't it be good', she murmured, 'if we could just stay like this? Not go back to the city... just go away somewhere safe, into the hills...'

'We both have our duty,' he said quietly.

In the darkness he saw her raise her head and look at him for a moment.

'It's a shame,' she whispered. Then she lay down beside him again.

Four hours later, they were riding along beside the river. Willows grew close to the banks, trailing foliage into the slow water, the moon was screened by cloud and in the thick darkness Castus could barely see anything. The river was a moving grey shape to his left, the trees a spreading blackness all around. Behind him, Marcellina rode with her legs astride, like a man, clasping his waist. Both of them wore Pictish capes of dark tanned leather, and Castus had removed his boots and breeches.

The horse moved slowly, ears back, nervous in the dark with the sound of the flowing water. Castus knew this stretch of river well – the soldiers used it for swimming practice – but in the darkness it was an alien and uncanny place, almost supernatural. The willows creaked and hissed as they passed beneath them, and the sound of the river was unnervingly like voices. The spirits of the wood and the water felt close, and not comforting.

'Here's the place,' Castus said, and turned the horse towards the water. In fact, he could see almost nothing, but the sound of the river had changed, and he guessed that this was the wide shallow bend where a spit of mud and sand spread from their bank and another lay on the far side. The horse splashed forward into the water, Castus nudging it repeatedly with his knees and heels. The surge of the river was loud at first, and then the water rose around the saddle girths and the knees of the riders.

'Slip down on the other side,' Castus whispered, 'but keep a tight grip on the saddle horn or you'll be pulled under.' Then he dropped into the water, and felt the cold striking into his chest. Marcellina gasped, and the horse kicked between them as it swam. Moonlight flooded through a rip in the clouds, and the river was suddenly bright, the spray glittering. Castus glanced back, and swallowed water, but saw only the blackness of the reaching willows and Marcellina's hand pale on the saddle horn.

Then the horse rose as it reached the ground on the far bank, and Castus hauled himself across the saddle and pulled Marcellina up behind him again. Water streamed from them as the horse climbed the last distance from the river into the darkness beneath the trees. No sound came from the meadows beyond, no shout or flare of light. Castus reined in the horse, then turned to check that the girl was secure behind him. She was soaked, and beginning to shiver in the damp night breeze.

'You ready?' He saw her nod, the peak of her hood dipping. He nudged the horse forward again, out through the trees and across the low water meadow towards the fortress.

A mile, he thought, more or less. Some way to his left, north-east, was the line of the paved road that led directly to the gates. The temptation to goad the horse into a gallop was almost overpowering. Already Castus could see the growing paleness in the sky, the first suggestion of dawn. He kept his head down, the hood pulled over his face, and let the horse walk slowly forward. At a stand of trees he halted again, scanning the surrounding country as it emerged slowly from the night.

'There are men behind us, in the meadow,' Marcellina said in a tight whisper.

'I've seen them.' They were going down to the river on foot. Not a threat.

The horse stamped and snorted, shaking its head and tugging on the reins. The bridle clinked. Ahead of him Castus could make out the mass of the Pictish force camped in the open ground on either side of the road: bodies huddled in blankets or crude leaning shelters, fires still smoking from the night watch. Impossible to judge their numbers. Beyond them, in the far distance, the wall of the fortress showed as a pale line against the retreating darkness. There was not enough cover for a slow approach, unless along the riverbank, and then they would be easily trapped if anyone discovered them.

'Hang on tight,' Castus said. He felt Marcellina press herself against his back, her cheek against his shoulder, arms clasping his waist and fingers gripping his belt. He leaned forward over the horse's mane, and dug his heels into the animal's flanks.

For a few moments there was only galloping motion, the noise of the hooves dulled by the damp ground, and Castus heard the breeze rushing around his head and driving cold through his wet clothes. He looked up as a man rose from the darkness and then fell back with a cry. Castus kept the horse's head straight and kicked wildly. He could hear shouts from all around, and he drew his sword and swung the flat of the blade back against the animal's hindquarters. The charge seemed unstoppable, impossibly fast, straight through the Pictish encampment and out into the open ground beyond. When Castus looked again he saw that the light had grown and the encampment was gone, but the fortress wall was still far distant and now there were riders coming along the raised causeway of the road to his left.

He snatched a glance behind him: more pursuers, riding up from the riverbank, legs splayed from their galloping ponies, spears raised, shouting. Marcellina's cape had slipped from her shoulders, and her hair streamed out wet and dark. The horse leaped a muddy ditch, and the jolt as it landed almost threw Castus from the saddle. He screwed the reins around, angling sideways, towards the road. There was no point in caution or concealment now.

Up on the causeway, the horse swerved and skidded on the gravel. Staggering, it charged forward again. The gate was dead ahead now, and Castus could see the watchfires burning between the crenellations. The noise of the hooves on the paved road was thunderous, but the Pictish riders were only a few paces behind. Castus heard Marcellina scream loud in his ear, and a javelin flashed past his shoulder and clattered against the road ahead. The powerful cavalry horse could outdistance the smaller Pictish ponies, but there were other riders ahead, angling up from the river to cut him off.

Castus raised his sword, yelling furiously across the horse's bent mane. The leading rider was coming up the causeway, raising his spear; he threw, but the missile fell short. The horse charged closer. To hang back now, Castus knew, would mean encirclement and death.

Suddenly the rider was beside him, swinging with his sword. Castus parried the blow, kicked out with his leg, and the pony reared back. Then they were through, and the road was open right up to the gates. Teeth clenched, back arched, Castus drove the horse onwards – only a few hundred paces remained.

Figures were moving up on the wall, shouts echoing out into the damp dawn air, then a harsh ratcheting noise. A loud sudden snap, and Castus glanced up just in time to see the jerk of the released catapult arms. He threw himself forward, and the yard-long iron-tipped ballista bolt cut the air just above his head.

'Don't shoot!' he yelled. 'We're Roman! I'm a Roman soldier!' But his voice was lost in the rush of the wind, the roaring of his blood, the noise of the hooves.

Another ratcheting click, another snap. Veering left and right, Castus saw a second bolt flicker past and spike the road behind him. He stretched himself up, hood thrown back, yelling to the men on the wall. Fifty paces from the gate – the bolts could not miss now – but he did not slow down.

He heard a scream from away behind him, and turned his head. A laugh burst from his throat: one of the pursuing Picts was stretched on the road, his pony capering away. The artillerymen had realised their mistake at last and adjusted their aim.

Now he saw the great gates cracking apart and slowly draw-ing open, armed men rushing over the threshold. The horse gave a last surge of strength, in under the shadow of the walls.

Then the stone arches were above them, and Castus heard the welcome voices of soldiers around him.

Through the echoing stone-paved tunnel beneath the gate, he slowed the horse to a walk and then to a halt. The animal was soaked in sweat, shuddering and tossing its head. Castus dismounted, and then helped Marcellina down. He turned to confront a ring of shields and levelled spears.

'Who are you?' demanded a face from beneath a helmet rim. Castus could not stop grinning. The ground felt loose and unstable beneath his feet.

'Aurelius Castus,' he gasped. 'Centurion, Third Cohort, Sixth Legion.'

'Is this woman a prisoner?' Two of the soldiers were leading Marcellina aside by the arms. She stared back at Castus, breathless and confused.

'No... no, she's the domina Aelia Marcellina, daughter of Aelius Marcellinus, envoy...'

The circle of men broke, and Castus saw an officer, a tribune. He did not recognise the man. A cold shivering sensation rose from his gut.

'Where have you come from?' the tribune said in a low hard voice. Castus told him – the north, Pictland – but he was stammering the words, exhaustion fighting through the energy in his blood.

'You're under arrest, centurion,' the tribune said. 'Surrender your belts and weapon.'

Two soldiers seized his arms. Castus stood passively for a moment, baffled. Then he shrugged the soldiers roughly away from him.

'Arrest? On what charge?'

'Desertion in the face of the enemy,' the tribune said. 'The penalty is death. Take him away!'

CHAPTER XIV

'Over forty days ago,' the governor said, 'you left this fortress in command of a century of men, with orders to escort an envoy and my secretary into Pictland. Now you return and tell me that all these men are dead and you alone have survived. In the meantime, the Picts have crossed the Wall, devastated my province, defeated my legion in the field and surrounded my capital. It doesn't look good, does it?'

'No, dominus,' Castus said. He was standing at attention, tunic unbelted, still bloody and unshaven after three days in the guardhouse.

Aurelius Arpagius, governor of the province and prefect of the legion, paced across the mosaic floor of his private chamber in the headquarters building. His beard, once so neatly groomed, was now wild and ragged. His eyes were sunken, and his dark skin had a yellowish tinge from lack of sleep.

'Do you know how many deserters have flooded into this fortress in recent days?' he asked. 'Half the Wall garrison fled when the enemy first raised their heads above the horizon! My troops at Isurium broke after the first engagement! Panic, centurion, is eating through this whole province. It must be *stopped* – discipline must be restored. That's why I've ordered the arrest of any further deserters who come through the gates. And that's why I've ordered the execution by stoning of any officer, centurion or above, found to have deserted his command.'

Castus nodded. He had already given his report, in as simple and soldierly manner as he knew how. He had told Arpagius almost everything about what had happened: the Pictish muster, the capture of Marcellinus and Strabo, the defence of the hilltop fort. He had told him of his own surrender and imprisonment, Strabo's murder, their captivity and Marcellinus's death, his escape. All he had left out was the involvement of Cunomagla; he remembered his promise, but this was not the moment to mention her.

'Your duties,' the governor said, 'were to protect the envoy and the safety of your men. You have failed utterly in both. Understand?'

'Yes, dominus.'

'But... bearing in mind the circumstances, I am prepared to suspend the sentence of death for the time being. You will remain under arrest and confined to quarters until I have time to decide whether you should be discharged without honour or reduced to the ranks...'

Castus kept his shoulders straight, his chest out, but anger was boiling inside him and he could feel his face reddening. He could hear the scratching of the clerk's stylus on the wax tablet. The soldiers at the door were already pacing forward to lead him away.

'Dominus!' he said, tight-throated. Arpagius glanced up at him sharply. 'Dominus... the Roman renegade I mentioned...'

'Yes?' The governor's eyes narrowed, and his face grew still. 'You put the man to death, you said?'

'I did. But before he died, he told me... certain things.'

A long pause. The tribune Victorinus, perched at the end of the couch, looked at the governor and raised his eyebrows.

The clerk paused in his writing. Then they all looked at Castus.

'*Things?*' Arpagius said. He cleared his throat quietly. 'Victorinus, Proclinus, leave us and take the guards with you.'

The tribune and the clerk stood up, saluted, and then paced out of the room. The guards closed the door behind them. Arpagius circled the desk and leaned back against it. The governor was a head shorter than him, but Castus felt the searching pressure of the man's gaze.

'So – tell me,' Arpagius said quietly.

'Dominus, the renegade and traitor Julius Decentius claimed that he had been acting under imperial orders to raise a rebellion among the Picts. He claimed that he was receiving instructions from an imperial agent in the province, who had come from Treveris, and had promised him a pardon for his crimes. He said... that my men and I had been sacrificed by our superiors.'

Arpagius was silent for a long time. He tugged at his beard, and Castus noticed that the man's forehead was beaded with sweat.

'Did you believe him?'

'Dominus... it's not for me to believe or disbelieve. I can only report what he said to me.'

'Well, I know nothing of it. The words of a renegade – a man you describe as a traitor? A man trying desperately to talk his way out of a just execution...? It seems to me this sort of man would invent any plausible excuse, no?'

Castus looked directly at the governor for the first time. 'I would have killed him anyway. He knew that.'

The governor held his gaze, the silence bristling between them, and Castus felt the anger rising in him again.

'Who have you told about this? Anyone?'

'No, dominus.'

'What about that girl you brought in with you. Marcellinus's daughter. Did you mention this to her?'

'I did not.'

'Good... I've got twenty thousand civilians sheltering in this fortress, centurion. The last thing I want is for evil rumours to start circulating amongst them. The same goes for the troops, of course. I would strongly advise you to say nothing of what this renegade told you to anybody. Is that clear?'

'Quite clear, dominus.'

'When I received warning of the enemy attack on the northern forts,' Arpagius went on, pacing back to the couch and sitting down, 'I at once sent an urgent message to the Augustus Constantius in Gaul. As we speak, he is assembling a field force and preparing a rapid march to relieve us. When he gets here... I will perhaps raise the matter with his staff. Meanwhile, I order you to put it out of your mind. Do you understand?'

'I understand, dominus.'

'Good. As far as you or I are concerned, whatever happens beyond the Wall *stays there*.'

Strong hands gripped and lifted him, and he fought against them, still lost in the fevered dreams of grief. In his mind he saw again the grisly tree, and he thought the voices were Timotheus and Vincentius, calling to him from the far side of death.

'Easy, brother, easy now,' one of them said. The hands were dragging him up off the cold flagstone floor. He lashed out, but somebody caught his wrist and held tight.

'How long's he been like this?'

'Two days, centurion,' said another voice. Castus knew this one: the thin-necked youth with a frightened stare who had been set as sentry outside his door. Castus had never seen him before. The other speaker was his friend Valens.

'Get him up, careful now. By the gods, he must weigh twice what I do!'

The world swung, and Castus let himself swing with it. His head reeled with the fumes of the wine; his mouth was dry with the taste of it, and his eyes felt gummed shut. He had never drunk to excess before – that was his father's weakness.

A bolt of cold water struck him in the face, splashing down his chest, and he gasped and cried out as he opened his eyes. Valens and two guards stood before him. Castus aimed a kick at the man with the bucket, but missed. His head was screaming and his hands ached.

'Look what he's done to the wall!' the sentry said. Above the bed Castus could see the plaster cracked and broken to the brickwork. That explained his battered fists, he thought. The painful grazes on the forehead too. Between them the guards dragged him up to sit on the bed and gave him water. He gulped back three large cups of it.

Officially, he remembered, he had been forbidden to leave his quarters, but he had been granted a trip to the baths and to the hospital to have his wounds dressed. Then they just gave him a big clay jug of wine and left him to it. How long had he spent like this, drunkenly raging or sprawled on the floor? He could no longer properly account for the time that had passed, nor did he want to remember.

Valens ordered the other men out, kicked a stool over to the open window and sat down on it. 'You look disgraceful, brother,' he said. 'Still, you should be grateful you were out of this. It hasn't been warming to the heart, these last ten days.'

Castus had not seen his friend since returning to the fortress. Valens looked as worn down as everyone else in Eboracum, his expression soured with a mixture of anger, fear and shame at what had happened.

'Arpagius even neglected to tear down the scaffolding where we'd been repairing the walls,' he said, lowering his voice. 'The Picts made a rush at it when they first got here – almost got inside too. We had to burn it ourselves in the end to keep them back. It was chaos – half the centurions and tribunes dead or missing after the battle, refugees pouring in. The enemy destroyed all the buildings along the river – they even burned the Blue House! But don't worry, everyone escaped, except that old eunuch doorkeeper – the Picts killed him. And since then we've been stuck in here and they've been out there.'

'What happened at Isurium?' Castus asked, squinting against the light from the window, the thunder and flashes of lightning in his head. He had been unable to find anyone willing to tell him about the defeat.

'Bloody shambles,' Valens said, worrying at a stalk of grass with his teeth. 'The enemy had us flanked before we'd even deployed from line of march. Arpagius ordered us to form square, but the baggage train was still spread out along the road and the Picts fell on it before we could form up. Everyone giving different orders. No discipline. The First and Sixth Cohorts managed to put up a fight and withdrew intact, but for the rest of us it was just a rout. Balbinus and Galleo died. Ursicinus saw his battle at last, after forty years of service. Last thing he'll ever see. I don't mourn them exactly, but... The legion's in rags, brother.'

From outside came the sound of horns, and then the shout and stamp of the watch being changed. The usual female screechings from the married quarters at the end of the barracks. Most of the women would be widows now. Castus felt a roll of nausea in his gut; he was glad he had managed to avoid facing them.

'There'll be a forced conscription levy on the civilians,' Valens went on with a weary sigh, 'and we'll enlist any of the men who retreated from the Wall garrison that don't have standing cohorts left. But it'll be months before we can take the field again.' He swabbed at his brow, and then smiled ruefully. 'And what about you?' he asked. 'Adventuring in Pictland? Picking up stray women?'

'I don't want to talk about it,' Castus said, more sharply that he had intended.

Valens's smile slipped. He gripped Castus by the shoulder. 'Sorry, brother,' he said quietly. 'At least we're alive, though. Thanks be to the gods.'

Castus nodded, and planted his thumb and finger upon his brow.

'Valens,' he said as his friend turned to go. 'The woman who came in with me. Aelia Marcellina. Do you know what happened to her?'

Valens sucked his cheek, shrugging. 'Probably given a billet somewhere. Half the barrack blocks have been turned over to the refugees. I'll ask around.'

'Thanks, brother,' Castus said. He waited until Valens was gone, and then closed the shutters and threw himself down on the bed in the welcome darkness.

Summer passed to autumn, and the rains turned the packed streets of Eboracum to mud. Castus remained in his quarters, pacing the narrow room, sleeping as much as he could. Valens came by once or twice a day, bringing news: the prefect was sending out patrols into the surrounding countryside to try and break through the Pictish blockade. A party of the enemy had been surprised while swimming in the river, and forty or fifty cut to pieces, naked and unarmed. But food was running short, and everyone was on half-rations of barley and water. The civilians were rioting, and there was still no news from the south, and the expected relief force led by the Emperor Constantius.

There were other visitors too. The ten men who had been on leave, sick or on detached duty when Castus had taken the century north had straggled back to find their comrades dead and their centurion under arrest, but they presented themselves outside his window, in twos and threes, and reported themselves fit for duty. Even Modestus, the habitual shirker, who had been discharged from hospital in time to fight at Isurium. He had somehow managed to distinguish himself in the rout; Castus thought he looked more wretched than ever, but the man wore a bandage around his head like a gold crown for valour.

'No fear, centurion,' Modestus said. 'You'll be out and in command again any day now. Me and some of the others are putting together a petition to the governor, asking him to release you.'

'Don't bother,' Castus said, but he was pleased. Even small scraps of mercy were a blessing to him.

It was the fourth day of September, a grey and blustery morning, when Valens banged on the door and leaned into the room.

'They've gone,' he said. Castus sat up from the bed.

'Who?'

'The Picts! They left in the night, and the patrols report them heading south. The emperor has his field force at Danum, and they've gone to try and hold the river crossing at Lagentium against him. Least, that's what I've heard...'

Danum was only three days' march south. Castus dashed his face with water from the bowl beside the bed.

'Oh, and another thing,' Valens said with a sly smile. 'You're released from quarters. Forbidden to leave the fortress, though – in case you were thinking of running off after them...'

The Emperor Flavius Valerius Constantius, Pius Felix Invictus, Augustus, Ruler of the West, Restorer of Britain, Conqueror of the Franks and the Alamanni, arrived at Eboracum on the fifteenth day of September, riding in through the ruins of the city and across the bridge with his mounted bodyguard all around him.

It was a drizzly afternoon with a cold breeze from the river, and Castus stood with the gathered soldiers on the wall rampart near the Praetorian Gate. He leaned across the parapet, gazing down, and picked out the emperor among the mounted men: a stooped figure on a large grey horse, riding with his head lowered, wrapped in a purple cloak. The gates opened, the governor Arpagius marching out with his tribunes and the city notables to greet the imperial party, and as the horns blared from the gatehouse the assembly along the walls, soldiers and civilians, threw up their arms and cried out the salute. *Ave Imperator! Ave Imperator!*

They had already heard the news of the battle at the Lagentium river crossing. The vanguard of the imperial field force had met the Picts and won a swift and bloody victory over them, the enemy breaking almost at once and fleeing in a ten-mile rout, cut down in their thousands by the cavalry. Already the emperor had declared himself Britannicus Maximus – Conqueror of the Britons.

'Look there,' Valens cried, seizing Castus by the arm. 'The black shields – that's the First Minervia, my old legion! And the red shields behind them are the Thirtieth Ulpia. Those are some real soldiers...'

The imperial party had passed beneath the gate, and now the troops of the field force were swinging across the bridge and crossing the burnt ground before the fortress walls. Two thousand armoured infantrymen from the legions of the lower Rhine, a thousand cavalry of the Equites Dalmatae and Mauri, and eight hundred fierce Alamannic tribesmen from the forests of Germania. With that small force alone Constantius had beaten the Picts in the field and sent them fleeing back to their wilderness, and there were more troops on the way. Castus felt a sinking sensation in his gut – the failures of the Sixth Legion appeared all the more glaring now.

Cheering and the noise of horns came from inside the fortress, from along the colonnaded Praetorian Way that led to the headquarters building. The colonnades were thronged with civilians, refugees from the plundered city and the surrounding countryside, barely held back by a cordon of soldiers. Castus stared down from the wall and wondered whether Marcellina was anywhere among them. In the four days since he had been released from confinement he had failed to find any trace of her: there were more than twenty thousand civilians in the fortress, billeted in the abandoned Eighth and Tenth Cohort barracks, the market, the tribunes' houses, the baths' porticos... Over fifty families named Aelius, and Castus had no idea of Marcellina's brother's full name. The stewards and city curators had no accurate list of the refugees anyway. At least he had been able to locate Jucunda's son, the soldier Varialus; wounded now, and soon to be honourably discharged. He was one of the lucky ones.

Castus trailed Valens down the steps from the wall rampart and made his way slowly back to barracks, shouldering through the crowds. There would be a full parade later that day, with the remains of the Sixth and the men of the newly arrived detachments drawn up to salute the emperor. But Castus was still officially in disgrace, and could attend only as a spectator. He preferred to remain in his quarters, waiting. Very soon, he suspected, the attention of the imperial party would swing his way.

He did not have long to wait. Two days later he stood stiffly in the portico of the praetorium, dressed in his best and cleanest tunic and breeches, belts oiled and gleaming, face pink from the razor. Governor Arpagius and his household had been ousted to one of the tribunes' houses, and the old praetorium redesignated the Sacred Palatium, until the long-neglected imperial residence in the city could be cleaned and repaired and made habitable for the emperor and his retinue.

Castus tried not to consider how much depended on the events of the next hour – his military career, his future, perhaps even his life. The summons had addressed him only as *soldier*, a man without rank or position. He shifted on his heels, but the tight knot of anxiety in his belly remained. The guards at the door wore the silvered scale armour and gilded helmets of the Praetorian Cohorts: hard-faced battle-scarred men, most of them former soldiers from the German and Illyrian legions. They did not meet his eye.

Then his name was called from within, echoing through the marble halls, and Castus marched through the portal and across the mosaic floor of the vestibule, pausing to salute the freshly painted statues of the Augusti and the Caesars standing in their alcove.

Guards led him from the vestibule and around the colonnaded walks of the central garden. In an antechamber with deep red walls, four men of the Corps of Protectores stripped him of his sword and shoulder-belt. As they patted him down for concealed weapons, a eunuch in a starched and gold-embroidered linen tunic spoke in a flat metallic monotone.

'On first passing through the veil and beholding the Sacred Presence, you will render your salute and acclamation. You will then advance six paces, halt and perform the genuflection.'

Castus nodded, dumb with nerves. The eunuch did not glance at him, but went on with the instructions.

'You will not speak, nor will you raise your eyes. You will only stand when you are bidden. You will only address the Sacred Presence when questioned directly. Are these protocols understood?'

Another nod. The eunuch closed his eyes. 'Any infraction of protocol will result in your immediate removal from the Presence,' he intoned. 'You may proceed.'

His boots crunched loudly on the polished floor as Castus followed the guards through a doorway, across a corridor and into a large hall. A purple drape was drawn aside, and he walked forward into the smell of incense. Something else, he thought. Something medicinal, like the smell of the hospital wards.

He stopped, saluted. 'Ave, Augustus!' he cried, and the echo crashed back from the high marble walls. Six stamping paces and he dropped to one knee, head lowered, heart kicking in his chest.

The sound of his voice died into silence. A cold breeze was sweeping across the marble floor. At the periphery of his vision Castus could make out the guards lining the walls, their boots and their grounded black and gold shields. 'You may rise,' a dry voice said.

Castus stood to attention, thumbs hooked in his belt. Now he could see the edge of the dais at the far end of the hall. The feet of the seated emperor, his red leather shoes sewn with pearls, jewels on the straps. He remembered the aftermath of Oxsa, seven years before, Caesar Galerius appearing before him out of the fog of dust and pain. This was quite different: this was how emperors were supposed to be experienced by their subjects.

'Aurelius Castus, formerly Centurion, Third Cohort, Sixth Legion,' the dry voice said. A herald, Castus realised. The emperor had not spoken. He dared to raise his eyes slightly – he could make out the figure on the dais more clearly now. Constantius sat in a high-backed chair, still wrapped in his purple cloak. His head hung forward, his nose jutting like the beak of a bird of prey, his lean heavy jaw set firmly. Castus tried to hide his shock: even from the edge of vision he could see how tired the emperor looked. His skin was yellow-grey with fatigue.

'Yes,' the emperor said. The single word hung in the air for a few moments. 'You're the one who went north with the envoy, got captured, then escaped.' His voice still had a distinct Pannonian accent, much like Castus's own. The emperor had been born only a hundred miles or so from the town where Castus had grown up.

'The praeses Arpagius has informed us of your exploits,' the emperor went on. 'It all sounds very... *unusual*. Were you given any help in your escape from the barbarian citadel?'

Castus felt his throat lock. A direct question – he had to answer. He not had told Arpagius about Cunomagla or her role; he had not trusted the man with that information. But now, alone in the centre of a marble hall surrounded by armed guards, in the presence of the emperor, he felt he could say nothing about it. Sweat rolled down his forehead.

'No, dominus,' he said.

'I see,' the emperor said. He paused. 'Then you were daring indeed. We commend you on your actions.'

Castus took a long slow breath, and tried not to exhale too visibly. Shame stirred in his belly; he had promised Cunomagla, but he must find another opportunity to honour that debt.

'Our secretaries inform us that you previously served with the Second Legion Herculia, against the Sarmatae and Carpi and on the Persian campaign. Is this correct?'

'Yes, dominus.'

'I remember him, Father,' a second voice said. Castus glanced up, surprised, and met the eyes of the other figure on the dais, who stood beside the emperor's chair. A man in his early thirties with a raw ruddy face, he was dressed in the white uniform of a tribune of the Protectores, but the resemblance to the emperor was obvious. The same beaked nose and lantern jaw, the same intense stare. But while the emperor appeared tired and ill, this man stood straight-backed, his eyes burning with effortless authority. Constantine, Castus remembered. The emperor's son.

'At Oxsa, dominus,' he heard himself saying. 'You gave me a gold torque for valour.'

'I did!' Constantine replied with a slight smile. 'But you do not wear it now.'

'The Picts took it from me, dominus. When I was captured.'

'And you would like the opportunity to win it back, I expect?'

'Yes, dominus. Or to earn another like it.'

A stir came from the assembled guards and secretaries, and Castus flinched. Had he overstepped the bounds of protocol? But a moment later the emperor too smiled, and gave a short cough of laughter.

'Your attitude pleases us,' the emperor said. 'It's good to meet a Pannonian soldier who knows his business in this place. We order that you be restored to your rank as centurion, with immediate effect. We need all the skilled men we can find, eh?'

'Thank you, dominus,' Castus said with lowered eyes.

'You will make a further and more detailed report to my notaries,' the emperor went on, in a harder, brisker tone, 'giving all pertinent information on the Picts, their forces, their leaders and their strongholds. Centurion, you are dismissed.'

Castus saluted, then paced backwards until he reached the purple drapes and passed out of the Sacred Presence. He dared not breathe until he reached the fresh air of the garden colonnades.

He was halfway across the vestibule to the main doors when he heard his name called again. The eunuch in the embroidered linen tunic gestured to him.

'Centurion Castus,' the man said again, in that same flat voice. 'You will now make your report to the notary. Come.'

Already? Castus thought, with dull foreboding. He had been looking forward to finding Valens and drinking a cup of good wine, in celebration. The eunuch nodded, as if in answer to the silent question. Foolish to imagine, Castus told himself, that he had escaped with such ease.

He followed the eunuch down narrowing corridors, away from the palatial wings of the praetorium and into the administrative area. The eunuch paused at an open door, and motioned with his palm. The room beyond was a small dining chamber, the couches moved back to the walls and a couple of chairs placed beside a low table in the centre. A man in a plain blue tunic sat waiting. Castus recognised him at once. That bland face, the skinny throat, the ugly bowl-cut hair. Julius Nigrinus, Tribune of Notaries.

Castus felt an uneasy pressure growing at the nape of his neck. The door was closed, and they were alone.

'Please be seated,' Nigrinus said. 'Take some wine, if you like.'

Castus sat down. The notary had a waxed tablet open in his hands, and was passing his eyes over the written text.

'This is the report you gave to Arpagius,' he said. He closed the tablet and dropped it on the table. 'A fascinating document. Is it all true?'

'Of course,' Castus said. He could barely hear the notary's quiet laugh.

'Stirring stuff!' Nigrinus went on. He sipped wine. 'Of course, I'm saddened to learn of the death of Aelius Marcellinus. And Strabo too, particularly. Strabo was one of my most effective agents in this province.'

'Your agents, dominus?' Important to retain the correct address, Castus told himself. This was not personal.

'Yes, mine. I've been in charge of all the intelligence operations in Britannia Secunda for some years now. So, as you can imagine, centurion, I'm very interested in what you can tell me of... *affairs* in the north.'

His voice was too smooth, too subtle. Castus tried to remain impassive. The man was goading him in some way. But to what end?

'Was there anything, do you think, that you failed to mention when you made your report?'

The line was before him now. Castus dared himself to step across it. Nigrinus was an imperial officer, a tribune, and it was his duty to tell him everything he knew. Had Cunomagla not asked him to do just that? Tell the imperial command about her support for Rome, her innocence in the deaths of the king and the others? Yes, Castus thought – but whom was he to tell, and when? He stayed silent.

'Arpagius tells me', the notary went on, 'that you did mention something to him, subsequent to your official report. He tells me you claim to have spoken with a renegade Roman officer named Julius Decentius. Shortly before putting him to death, of course... He tells me that this Decentius made certain allegations about imperial involvement in the uprising. Do you have anything to say about that?'

'I told the governor all I know... dominus.'

'Indeed.' Nigrinus picked up a gold stylus and circled it between his fingers. 'Well, it's an extraordinary story.'

'So is it true?' Castus felt the heat rise to his face as he spoke. The notary put down the stylus. When he spoke again his voice was stony cold.

'True?' he said. 'Is it true that the emperor planned to provoke an uprising among the Picts? What do you think, Centurion?'

'I... I don't know. Dominus.'

'The emperor,' Nigrinus said, leaning forward, 'does not *plan* anything! The emperor merely *wishes* for certain things to be. It is up to others to plan – others such as me, centurion. And others still to carry out those plans.'

Castus clamped his jaw shut and spoke through his teeth. 'My men died!'

'They were soldiers. Dying is *their job.*'

A long moment passed, glaring. Castus had already been threatened with death for desertion – what would the punishment be, he wondered, for murdering an officer of the imperial household? Perhaps one day he would find out. But not yet – not with the balance so steeply set against him. He breathed out, tried to ease his shoulders down from their aggressive hunch.

'But of course,' the notary said, in a mild tone, 'the story isn't true at all. Merely the rantings of a condemned man. I don't blame you for being troubled by it – in those circumstances, who wouldn't be? But I happen to know that this whole sorry episode was planned and directed by somebody else.'

'Somebody else?'

'Hmm. In your report you mentioned several of the Pictish chiefs and leaders – one Talorcagus... Drustagnus... But it turns out that the conspiracy to assassinate the old king and several others and create a breach with Rome was led by a woman!'

Castus said nothing, but his heart was beating fast.

'Yes! Who would credit it? A barbarian Cleopatra. This woman, Cunomagla is her name, was the wife of one of the murdered men. Apparently she wanted to use a war with Rome to extinguish the entire royal bloodline and leave the succession open to her own bastard offspring. So this unsavoury bitch, this *harlot princess*, arranged the poisoning of the king, his chief supporter and her own husband and fixed the blame on... well, on you and your party.'

Stunned, Castus sat with his jaw hanging loose. The man was lying – of course it was not true. That was his first reaction. But then, he thought, but then... He remembered those nights in the hut, when Cunomagla had come to him. Her offer of marriage, then her demand that he carry her promise of allegiance back to his commanders. If the other leaders were slain in battle, she would be left in control and Rome would not act against her. It made terrible sense. But everything inside him revolted against the idea.

'I dare say,' Nigrinus continued, 'that the renegade Decentius was probably part of the plan himself. Apparently he was a former paramour of this Cunomagla woman. Oh, they're most profligate, the barbarians – they wrestle in their kennels with anyone, their women fuck without thought or feeling. But soon enough she and all her people will suffer a just punishment.'

'Dominus?'

'It's too late in the season now. But next spring the Augustus Constantius will lead an army into the north to harry the

273

Picts and destroy their lands and homes. They must learn that they cannot rise against Rome with impunity! Then, no doubt, their leaders will die or be delivered up to us, and pay with their lives for their crimes. Your men, centurion, will be avenged.'

Castus managed to nod. A fierce anger was boiling in his throat. Anger against this sly officer and his duplicity; anger against the Picts. Anger against fate, and against Cunomagla for involving him in something he could not hope to understand.

'Tell me something, centurion,' the notary said. 'Do you believe in the gods?'

'Yes. Of course.'

'And you believe the gods direct our fate?'

Castus blinked, uncertain. His anger had chilled into a glazed loathing.

'Our friend Strabo had his own faith, did he not? His belief in that single all-knowing, all-loving deity. Do you think it was a comfort to him, his *Christianity*, when he died?'

Castus remembered the secretary's death, the cruel knife, the blood. He remembered the look of fierce pride in his eyes.

'He went to his god like a soldier.'

Nigrinus raised an eyebrow. 'I'm glad of that,' he said. 'As for myself, I do not believe in gods. Not those of the heavenly realm. I tend to believe that we make our own fate. We make our own gods too, here on earth. And in time, if we prove faithful to them, these new-made gods, they may reward us. Do you understand my meaning, centurion?'

Castus held the man's gaze for several heartbeats. He had the sudden unnerving sensation that the notary knew everything, could look into his mind and see revealed there every thought, every misgiving. That the man knew all that happened in the north; even, somehow, that he had directed it himself...

274

This was a battle of wills, Castus realised. Just as he could read the inner feelings of other men by the signs they gave away, so the notary was reading him. He would not allow himself to be drawn out so easily.

'I just follow orders, dominus,' he said.

The notary's lips formed the shape of a smile. 'Oh, but of course,' he said. 'And our emperor appreciates that. He is inclined to take your word that everything happened as you say it did, and not to look further into the matter. Not to consider any failures of judgement, or of courage, or any disreputable negotiations with our enemies, perhaps...'

'I know nothing of such things.'

'No, I'm sure you don't, centurion. But you must see that you have a certain debt to pay, no? A debt of honour, of loyalty? And perhaps in the coming months you will have an opportunity to repay that debt.'

Castus swallowed down his anger, kept his expression neutral, but he knew that his eyes had turned cold and hard.

'I hope so, dominus,' he said. Then he stood up sharply and saluted.

'One more thing before you go,' the notary said. 'This strange story the renegade told you – this *lie*, I should say. I hope you will forget it. I most certainly hope you will not relay it to anyone else. Because, you see, if it should come to my attention – and I am a very attentive person – that you've been telling anyone at all about this matter, I will arrange for you to be silenced. Understood?'

'Yes, dominus,' Castus said in an ashen voice.

CHAPTER XV

'Look at those barbarian bastards! They're *laughing* at you!'
The twenty-eight recruits grounded their heavy practice
shields and gazed across the puddled gravel of the drill field.
At the far perimeter stood a group of Alamannic tribesmen,
heavily bearded men in striped tunics and bright red leggings.
At this distance, Castus could not tell whether the men were
laughing or not, but he was angry enough not to care.

'Back to your positions!' he yelled. The recruits wearily
hefted their shields and formed up in two facing lines. Castus
stalked between them, brandishing his staff.

'This time, stand your ground! Keep your formations and
push... You're not children! GO!'

Again the lines slammed together, the recruits grunting
with the impact, leaning into their shields, each line trying to
drive the other back. After only a few heartbeats the whole
mass collapsed into confusion.

'Gods below,' Castus said under his breath. Cold October
rain was falling steadily, running down his back, but his face
was red and his neck swollen from shouting. This kind of
angry display did not come naturally to him – most of it was
just performance. But it was genuinely infuriating, after all
the work he had put in over the last year training his previous
century, to have to start from scratch all over again.

'Pick yourselves up,' he growled. 'You'll keep doing this until you can hold the formation and stand your ground. We can carry on all night if we have to.'

From away to his left, Castus could hear his new optio's cracked scream. He had the rest of the men at the practice posts, doing *armatura* sword drill. The clack and smack of the weighted wooden blades against the wooden posts had been constant for over an hour. For the last month, this had been the routine: weapons training all day; drill; and running and marching with loaded packs. Route-marching every ten days, with entrenching practice. Horse-riding and swimming could wait. They had practised the regular formations: the testudo of locked shields, the attack wedge and the shield wall to oppose cavalry. Already six of Castus's new recruits had been invalided out, too injured or exhausted to continue. Of the rest, there were eight broken noses, several cracked ribs and sprained ankles, two broken arms, and a great deal of near-mutinous resentment.

It was not their fault, Castus told himself. Half of them had never wanted to be soldiers anyway. They were labourers and potters, butchers and stable boys, farmers and dock workers: anyone who was neither a slave nor a member of the civic council had been called for conscription. A few were keen to revenge themselves on the Picts, but the majority had no desire to spend the rest of their lives under arms. The wealthier citizens had found ways to wriggle out of it, of course, and many others had fled to the fields, or even mutilated themselves to avoid enlistment. Only the unlucky, the poor or the genuinely vengeful remained. The rest of the new men were from disbanded cohorts of the Wall garrison. Some were reasonable soldiers, but most were older men in their forties or even fifties who had long ago forgotten the military disciplines. Together they made up a poor-quality stew. The only good men were the ten from the old century who had been away when Castus had marched north and had survived the battle at Isurium. He used them now as substitute trainers.

'Macrinus, take over here,' he said to one of these, and the man stepped promptly into place. Castus's throat hurt, his head was aching, and he was tired of raging at the recruits. With no surviving training officers, the centurions and optios had to do almost all the bullying themselves. It would be a hard autumn, and a harder winter ahead.

Then again, Castus thought as he strolled over to the practice posts, *you never know how a man will turn out*. Take his new optio, for example. Four months before, Castus would have discounted Claudius Modestus entirely – a shirker, a gambler and a drunk, a hospital-malingerer, a complainer... But Modestus's brief brush with combat had changed him utterly. He was still far from perfect – Castus had smelled stale beer on the man's breath several times – but he was showing himself to be a tough and enthusiastic deputy. *Give a man some prestige and some responsibility*, Castus reasoned, *and he'll either rise to it or break*.

'Come on, you cocksuckers! Come on, you fuckers! *Kill* them, don't stroke them – that's your *enemy*!' Modestus's voice had risen to a cracked screech. The recruits under his supervision were sweating heavily, labouring at the practice posts like slaves at a quarry face.

'*Stab* with the point, you arse! Don't wave it about! Do you wave your cock like that, Priscus, when you're *fucking*? Eh? Put some balls behind it!'

Castus hid his smile. The same obscene words, the same threats and insults, in every legion's camp all over the empire. He had heard them before so many times. Far away on the other side of the drill field, the Alamannic spectators were wandering off towards the beer shops and the brothel shacks that had sprung up among the ruins along the riverside. The rain was getting heavier now, and they had seen all they needed to see of the might of the Roman army for one day.

Back in his quarters that evening, Castus stripped to his loincloth and stretched to ease the tight ache in his muscles. He was bent double, clasping his ankles, when Valens walked in.

'Message came for you earlier,' the other centurion said, dropping onto a stool by the open window. Castus eased himself up, grunting, and heard his back click.

'What was it?'

'I don't know, do I? It's a written message… on a very nice quality tablet too.'

Castus winced, not just from the ache in his back. Valens knew well that Castus was unable to read, although neither man ever mentioned it. Sitting on the stool, he smiled slightly and fanned himself with the sealed wooden wafer.

'Better read it to me,' Castus muttered, pulling on his tunic. 'You're… closest to the light.'

Valens slid his thumb down the side of the tablet, breaking the wax seal, and then unfolded the two leaves.

'*Aelia Marcellina to Aurelius Castus, greetings,*' he read. He glanced up, his smile broadening, one eyebrow raised.

'Just *read it.*'

Valens shrugged, went on. '*If you are well I am well. I regret that our parting was abrupt, and I never had the…* what does that say?… *the opportunity to thank you for your assistance…* Nice handwriting this girl's got – she must have written it herself… Oh, don't glare at me, brother! Very well… *My recent circumstances have not allowed me to communicate, but if you have a moment spare of your duties tomorrow I would be pleased to receive you at my lodgings and render my thanks in person...* She gives the address: the green portal, in the street of the glassblowers, left from the forum baths... Oh, there's a postscript. *If you still have my father's signet ring I would be very grateful if you could return it...*'

Valens turned the tablet over, holding it up to the light. 'No sign of secret messages,' he said. 'No imprint of loving lips...'

Castus lobbed one of his boots across the room, and Valens dodged it.

In the autumn sunlight the city of Eboracum appeared a less desperate place than it had for a long time. The scars of war and plundering were everywhere, of course: blackened walls; broken timbers; shattered plaster. But the burnt debris had been cleared from the streets, the houses and shops patched up and reoccupied, and it was a living city once more, a place of civilisation rather than wreckage and despair.

It was Dies Solis, the Day of the Sun, and the men of the legion were allowed the afternoon free for the baths and kit repairs. Crossing the bridge from the fortress, Castus picked his way along the colonnades lining the main street of the city. Everywhere was activity: men unloading sacks and amphorae from wagons; men climbing scaffolding with hods of bricks or wet plaster. Anyone working in the building trade had been exempted from the military draft, and there were more than enough hands to help with the reconstruction. Merchants from southern Britain and Gaul had sent their barges up the river, bringing grain and wine and woollens, and luxury goods too. The space beneath the colonnades was crowded with flimsy stalls. Castus passed a herbalist's and a shop selling hair tonics. The air smelled of cooking smoke and brick dust, cut wood and horse sweat.

There were plenty of soldiers in the streets too: many of the men of the field army had been billeted in the city, and all along the streets there were swaggering legionaries from the German detachments. Foreign troops too: bearded Alamanni with dyed red hair lingering outside the taverns and staring at the women; dark Mauretanians squatting around the public fountains. After centuries of slow provincial decay, Eboracum was once more looking like the vigorous frontier settlement it had been in the great days of the empire. And with the emperor himself in residence, it was also one of the centres of the Roman world.

Maybe it was just the sunshine, Castus thought, but being in the city raised his spirits more than anything else these last months. There was a sense of hope here, of pride and of activity. For all his instinctive dislike of civilians, it was good to see them putting their city back together again. He paused for a while in the forum, beside the blackened pillars of the temple of Neptune, and watched the huge temporary wagon park that filled the open space heaving with life.

The prospect of seeing Marcellina again perplexed him. He had been ready to assume her gone and put her from his mind completely. She had no connection to him, beyond the chance accidents of war that had thrown them, briefly, together. And how would she appear now, recovered from her ordeal, composed? Would she too blame him for what had happened? The note had given no clue. But beyond his misgivings, Castus knew that he wanted to see the girl, even if only once. The memory of her had haunted him for too long, the sense of things unspoken and unresolved, and now he needed to lay it to rest.

He found the address soon afterwards, without difficulty. It was only a hundred yards or so from the forum, down a narrow street past the baths: a large house with tall blank walls. The glassmaker's shop opposite was still a gutted shell glittering with broken shards, but the green doors were hard to miss, standing between their tall masonry columns. Castus knocked, and then stepped back into the sunlight and waited.

A slot in the door opened, and an eye stared out, ringed by wrinkles.

'Aurelius Castus, Centurion, Sixth Legion,' Castus declared loudly. 'Come to pay respects to the Domina Marcellina, as she requested.'

The slot closed, and Castus heard the thud of a bolt and the rattle of a chain. Then the door swung back, and he stepped in over the threshold.

Beyond the door was a large vestibule. The room still smelled strongly of stale urine, and there was a large black scar in one corner where a cooking fire had burned. The painted walls were scratched and gouged all over with crude Pictish-looking shapes that could have been drawings or words. The old door slave bobbed around Castus, staring at him.

'The domina is… indisposed,' he said. 'But the dominus will receive you, with his guardian. Please… allow me to take your cloak.'

Further into the house there were more signs of the destruction. The vestibule opened to a garden portico, but the pillars were pitted and chipped and the garden itself a rutted mess. It looked as if somebody had dug it up looking for buried valuables. The mosaic floor in the portico had been smashed too, apparently with a hammer. Castus rubbed his boot over what looked like a scrubbed bloodstain.

'They killed the cook,' the slave muttered. 'Please – this way...'

The slave led Castus down a short passage from the portico to a room at the rear of the house. It must have been a pleasant chamber once – the walls painted with scenes of flowering shrubs and fruit trees. Castus remembered that this house had belonged to Marcellinus. He wondered whether the envoy had spent time in this room. He would not have liked the look of it now.

'Greetings,' said the boy in the embroidered robe sitting in the middle of the room. 'Please sit. I am Aelius Sulpicianus, son of Aelius Marcellinus. We were expecting you.'

Castus lowered himself onto a flimsy-looking cane chair. The shutters were closed and the room was quite dim, but he could make out the features of the boy sitting before him. Something of his father, and of his sister too – the same delicate oval face, the same large dark eyes. He was about thirteen, Castus remembered.

'This is my tutor, Aristides,' the boy said, gesturing to the other man in the room, loitering on the couch. Aristides was balding, with a sour mouth and a badgerish beard. Expensive rings on his fingers. Probably handy with a cane, Castus thought.

'I got a letter from your sister,' he said to the boy. 'She asked me to visit her here.'

'She wrote to you without the permission of the dominus Sulpicianus,' the tutor said. 'As Sulpicianus is now head of the family, this was an error.' Clearly he was the one in charge here.

'Your slave said she was... indisposed.'

'Yes, my sister is unwell,' the boy said. His expression did not waver. He had something of his father's nerve at least. 'The shock of her experiences has wounded her deeply, and she is still not in a state to receive visitors.'

IAN ROSS

'She has lucid moments,' the tutor said. 'But they soon pass. She faints and sweats, cries out, forgets things...'

'I'm sorry to hear that,' Castus said in a level voice. A moment passed, and he heard birds singing from the garden courtyard.

'You are the centurion who was assigned to protect my father,' Sulpicianus said. 'Is it true you were with him when he died?'

'Yes, dominus.'

'Then... did you not think it was your duty to keep him alive, and not let him fall into the hands of the barbarians?'

Castus took a sharp breath, sitting up straight on the creaking chair: the boy had been schooled in what to say. He glanced quickly at Aristides, but the tutor looked away. Castus felt angry for a moment, but then remembered. Sulpicianus had lost his entire family. He had a right to judge poorly those who had survived. *Say what you need to say*, he told himself. *Then get out.*

'Your father died by his own hand,' he said slowly, feeling the clumsiness of his words, 'and by his own will. If I could have saved him, I would have done it. I would have given my life for his if I'd had the chance. But we were betrayed, and your father chose the honourable way out. He charged me to bring word of his fate to you... and to return this.'

He reached into his belt pouch, fingers fumbling, and found the heavy gold signet ring. Leaning, he placed it on a side table.

'Thank you,' the boy said coldly.

'Your father was a good man. A good soldier. He was thinking of you, at the end. His last words to me were to convey his love to you, and to your sister.'

The boy closed his eyes, and Castus saw his jaw tremble. He was close to tears now. Castus stood up.

'I will give sacrifice to the gods for your health and the good fortune of your family,' he said. 'And please greet your sister for me.'

He caught the tutor's wry nod as he left the room.

Outside in the cool light of the portico, Castus winged his shoulders and felt a cold shudder running up his spine. He exhaled, letting his anger subside. His shame was harder to be rid of. Surely there was more he could have said? Something noble, or meaningful? But he was a soldier, not a diplomat. He shook his head. There was nothing more he could do for this family now.

As the slave went to fetch his cloak, Castus glanced back across the garden. There was a window high in the far wall, giving light to one of the inner rooms, and Castus saw a movement there. Marcellina, gazing back at him from the darkened chamber. He held her eye for just a moment, and then she was gone.

CHAPTER XVI

'Name?'
    'Julius Stipo, centurion.'
'What was your profession?'
'Fullery assistant, centurion.'

Stipo was a short lad, little more than a boy, but his shoulders were broad and he had an open, unintelligent face. Castus grunted and tapped him on the shoulder with his cane.

'You're in with Remigius. Cell six. Go.'

The laundry boy picked up his bag of possessions and crossed to the barrack portico, where his future comrades were already waiting. Remigius, an experienced soldier whom Castus had appointed leader of the eight-man section, looked coolly unimpressed with the newcomer.

Standing in the lane between the barrack blocks, this last batch of new recruits were still dressed in civilian clothes, although each already wore the lead disc at his neck that signified enlistment to the legion. Castus glanced down the line: a sorry set, the last scrapings of Eboracum's conscriptable civilian population. But they would bring his century up to something near its old strength, at least.

'Name?' he said to the next man.

'Claudius Acranius, centurion.'

Acranius was a former scenery-painter at the theatre, or so he claimed. Actually, he looked like a drunk, and had a nasty inflammation around one eye. Castus looked over at the barrack portico, crowded with idling men. After only a month, the new soldiers had formed their tight bonds, their networks of allegiance and distrust. He struggled to remember all their names. The pressure of keeping control of them all, keeping them knitted into a unit and not letting the bigger mouths and the fiercer tempers dominate the rest, was a burden.

'You're with Placidus. Cell eight. Go.'

Placidus was badly named. A squat and thickly muscled Gaul from a disbanded cohort of the Wall garrison, he had already stamped his mark on the men in his section. They were his gang now, and poor Acranius would have a hard time of it for the next few days, until he buckled under. It was not, Castus told himself, his concern. Anyone joining the legion would have to fight his space, until he had won some respect. It wasn't pretty, but it was the way of things.

'Name?'

'Musius Diogenes.'

Castus cleared his throat, and leaned forward from the waist until the man flinched. 'You address me as *centurion*,' he said.

'Sorry... *centurion*. No offence intended!'

'What was your profession?'

'Elementary schoolteacher... *centurion*.'

Castus drew back, staring down his nose. Diogenes was probably his own age, but looked older. His hair was fuzzy and receding from a domed forehead, and his bulging eyes and weak chin gave him a startled look.

'You make good money as a schoolteacher?' he asked roughly.

'Oh, yes, centurion! Fifty denarii a month for every pupil.'

'So what happened?' Anyone earning that amount could surely have bought his way out of the draft – many others had done just that.

'I… have no pupils… centurion!' the man said, shrugging.

Castus tightened his lips to hide his smile. The man was completely unsuited to the army, but at least he was amusing.

'You can read and write then, and do arithmetic?'

'Oh, most certainly, centurion! With a high degree of aptitude!'

Castus frowned heavily, alert for any sign of humour. But the man appeared earnest. He tapped him on the shoulder with his staff.

'Cell six. Remigius. Go.'

He could already see Remigius shaking his head with a disgusted expression. The schoolteacher too would have a hard time ahead of him. But, well – *sink or swim.*

Standing braced, staff clasped behind his back, Castus watched the men filing back into the barrack cells. At the end of the portico was a small group of women sitting with their bags and bundles, a few with small children. Nearly half of the new recruits had brought wives with them – more trouble for the future, no doubt. No matter, Castus decided. He would let them jostle and squabble for now, and bawl them out later.

'Modestus,' he called. 'Take over here.'

The optio nodded smartly and marched across to the portico, already shouldering his staff.

Six months, Castus thought, before the emperor would be ready to take the field. Would that be long enough to beat and bully these men into a soldierly shape? It seemed impossible. He stifled a long yawn, turned on his heel and marched towards the centurions' messroom.

'Brother,' said Valens, coming up behind him. 'Walk with me over to the drill field, will you?' With all the confusion in the fortress, Castus had not seen his friend in days. The other centurion fell into step beside him and they strolled together down to the main street and turned right towards the gate leading to the drill field.

'Have you heard the latest?' Valens said, speaking from the corner of his mouth. Castus turned his head and pressed his chin into his shoulder – he had never been able to speak sideways.

'What?'

'Arpagius is gone. Sent off back to Numidia to add up his sums! Apparently the city council wanted to prosecute him for failing to protect their property adequately. And after the fiasco at Isurium he didn't smell good to the bigger chiefs either. Tribune Rufinius has been promoted to prefect of the legion.'

Castus nodded. He was not sorry that he would never be seeing Arpagius again, and Rufinius seemed a competent officer at least. But that was not what Valens had wanted to discuss.

'What else?' he said.

'There's talk going round the centurions' messes,' Valens mumbled. 'You saw the Augustus – up close, I mean. How did he look to you?'

'I only really saw his shoes.'

'But did he look… healthy?' Valens was barely even moving his lips now, and Castus had to stoop towards the smaller man to catch his words.

'Healthy?' he said, and glanced around quickly. They were walking in the centre of the street. From their left came the thunderous clatter of the armoury workshop, working to produce weapons, shields and body armour for the new recruits. The air reeked of hot iron and forge smoke, and nobody could possibly hear them over the din of hammers and anvils. But still Castus felt a cold stir at the back of his neck. Discussing the health of emperors was treason. 'Be careful what you're suggesting,' he said in a low rumble.

'Don't worry, brother! I'm just concerned. A sense of loyal regard for our domini.'

They fell silent for a few moments as they passed the tall portals of the headquarters building.

'You saw his son, too? Constantine?'

'I saw him,' Castus said. His discomfort had not eased, and he wanted to step away from Valens, as if the mere suggestion of treasonous talk might be contagious.

'There were a couple of Protectores down at the Blue House the other night. The new one, I mean, in the old Tenth Cohort barrack... They told me that Constantine had only joined them at Bononia on the Gallic coast, just before the crossing to Britain.'

'What of it?'

'Well – do you know where he'd been? Apparently the son of the Augustus has been in Nicomedia these last eight years, at the court of the *other* Augustus, the senior one, Galerius. In a sort of gilded captivity, so they implied. When the news arrived of the uprising here – by express messenger, as you'd imagine – Constantine petitioned Galerius for permission to go and join his father on the expedition. Galerius could hardly refuse, but he'd barely given his nod – while he was drinking over dinner, so they say – before our Constantine was off. He rode all the way from Nicomedia to Bononia by post relays in just over ten days, mutilating the horses as he went so he couldn't be followed by a countermanding order!'

'Is that even possible?' Castus had travelled most of that route himself when he had come to join the Sixth, and it had taken him nearly three months.

'Seems so. He's here now, anyway. And you know that quite a few in the army think that Constantine should have been made Caesar after the abdications? Apparently the mint in Alexandria had already started turning out *Constantinus Caesar* coins when they heard the news – they had to recall them and break the dies. These two Caesars we have now, what are they? Flavius Severus is a drunk and a gambler who can't control himself, let alone the empire. Maximinus Daza's a common soldier with no more experience of commanding armies than... well, than you!'

This time Castus really did step back, and gave his friend a hard appraising glare. Valens looked away, as if conscious that he had said too much.

'Don't tell me these things,' Castus said, cold and level.

'You'd hear the same in any officers' mess, brother. Here, in Gaul – all across the empire, probably. If you weren't too thickheaded to listen when you're off duty you'd have heard much the same.'

'But I don't *want* to hear it!'

Politics, Castus thought, was a stinking mire. Nothing to do with him. The emperors were to be revered, whatever their personal failings. They were beyond mere men; the purple robe elevated them to stand beside the gods. It pained him – quite literally burned in his guts – that the circles of supreme power were just as foul with intrigue and suspicion as the mortal world far below. Because if the emperors could not be trusted, could not be wholeheartedly admired and obeyed, where was loyalty? Where was honour?

In his mind he heard the voice of the notary, Nigrinus, and his subtle threats and insinuations. *We make our own gods too, here on earth.* Then the panicked stammer of the renegade Decentius, just before Castus had killed him. Both men had been sucked into the intrigue: one prospered by it; one had died of it. The muck of politics was corrosive. It rotted morals; it made men weak and terrified, or turned them into monsters. Castus shuddered, hunched his shoulders, tried to ignore Valens's disapproving stare.

They were passing beneath the north-west gate now. The sentries gave their salutes, and Castus remembered, with sudden startling clarity, the early dawn when he had ridden in through those gloomy arches with Marcellina. Barely three months ago, but it seemed like years. Valens was marching on, head down, and Castus took three long paces to catch up with him. They emerged from the dark tunnel beneath the gate into the sunlight, and turned left into the drill field.

'There he is,' Valens said, nodding away into the middle distance.

A crowd was gathered around the margins of the field, most of them soldiers and centurions. In the centre of the field straw bales had been set up for cavalry practice, and a troop of the Equites Mauri, light horsemen from North Africa, were wheeling and darting their javelins at the gallop. It was an impressive display, but the crowd was not watching the Mauri. Constantine, the emperor's son, was riding with them. Mounted on a powerful grey mare, and dressed only in a quilted white linen corselet, he rode hard at the bales, flinging his javelins with great grunts of effort. Each one flew straight to the target, punching into the bale and hanging slack as Constantine spurred his horse away.

'You brought me here to see this?' Castus asked.

'He comes down every afternoon. Sometimes with the Mauri, sometimes the Dalmatae or the Scutarii. Joins in their practice, at all arms. Quite a performer.'

'Just for show, you think?'

'Could be. Letting the army see who's going to be leading them.'

They had dropped their voices again, as if by instinct.

'The emperor leads the army,' Castus said quietly. 'Nobody else. This man's just a tribune of the Protectores.'

'The emperor is *sick*...' Valens said, almost under his breath. 'If we're going to war in the spring we ought to know the facts, do you agree?'

'I don't care. All that matters is that we go. We have reason enough.'

'Well, as to that,' Valens said in a brisker tone, 'it's not exactly certain if we go or not... There are new detachments arriving from the German legions. The Eighth and the Twenty-Second. And two cohorts of the Second Augusta from the southern province are camped just south of the city, did you know that? The Sixth might just be left here in the spring after all, holding the fort.'

Castus frowned. Surely that could not happen? He remembered the emperor's words, in the audience hall. *We need skilled men like you* – was that it? Not, surely not, just to work at training recruits at Eboracum either.

They walked back to barracks in silence.

Saturnalia, and the dark wintry streets of the fortress were loud with the noise of riotous celebration. Released for the period of the festival from the bounds of military discipline, the soldiers roared and laughed from the taverns and the baths' porticos, rampaged around the colonnades, climbed onto pedestals naked, oblivious of the freezing drizzle, to yell bawdy songs at the moon.

Leaving the centurions' messroom, where most of his fellow officers had barricaded themselves in for the night, Castus flung a common soldier's cloak over his head and paced warily back towards the barracks. He had drunk a few cups of beer, and he was still alert but tired. Parties of men gathered on the street corners, fighting and singing. Now and again one of them recognised him – the cloak did little to hide his bulk – and flung a half-mocking salute. Castus stepped aside as a naked man wearing an ivy wreath came charging down the main street, riding bareback on a terrified cavalry horse, screaming, '*Io Saturnalia…!*'

Another few days and the celebrations would be done. Then it would be the Day of Sol Invictus, the birthday of the sun – by then the men would be sobered up, kit cleaned and polished, all of them dressed in their best clothes for the dawn parade to salute the rising sun. After more than two months of training, Castus was beginning to have a little more regard for the men of his century. Countless days on the drill field had battered the inert matter of their civilian selves into shape, at least to some small degree. Perhaps, he thought, by the spring they might be fit to call themselves soldiers.

Some of them were still causing problems, Castus thought as he turned into the barrack lines. Placidus, the burly Gaul from the Wall garrison, was one of them. A braggart and a borderline insubordinate. The scenery-painter Acranius had lived up to expectations, and contrived to get himself admitted to hospital three times already. But, despite his appearance, the schoolteacher Diogenes had proved surprisingly able. He stuck up for himself, had a tenacious sort of stamina, and gave a fearless performance on the drill field. His eccentricities were accepted now, even respected, by his comrades – but Castus still found him bafflingly peculiar…

As he moved towards his own quarters at the end of the block, Castus caught a movement in the darkness: two figures, heavily cloaked, standing in the doorway of his rooms. At once the lingering effects of the alcohol were gone. His hand went to his belt, but he had left his sword back in his quarters and had only his staff.

'Who's there?' he said, clear and loud.

'Centurion Castus,' a woman's voice said. 'I'm sorry – I know it's late. I hoped to find you at home.'

Castus recognised the voice at once, but could scarcely believe it. The second figure, a tall man, drew a lantern from under his cloak and uncovered the light.

'Domina Marcellina,' Castus said. 'Why are you here? You shouldn't have come – it's Saturnalia. This is no place for you.' He was pacing closer as he spoke. The man in the cloak was the big slave from the house.

'I know... As I say, I'm sorry. But I wanted to see you.'

Castus unlocked the door and ushered them both inside. He lit the lamp in the vestibule as the two of them shed their cloaks, and the big slave squatted down at once just inside the door, with a heavy club across his knees.

'I'm here without permission, you see,' Marcellina was saying. 'My brother and his tutor have forbidden me to leave the house, but they gave the slaves the night off duty, and I was able to persuade Buccus here to accompany me.'

Even so, Castus thought. It was less than a mile from her house to the barracks, but this was the rowdiest night of the year. Anything might have happened. He felt angry, but did not know why. Instead he went through into his private rooms, and Marcellina followed behind him.

'I know this is... irregular,' the girl said. She sounded unsure of herself. 'But after you came to the house and I was forbidden to speak with you, I... What my brother said was unforgivable. His accusation that you had failed in your duty, I mean. His tutor put him up to it...'

Castus set the lamp down on the table and glanced around

his quarters. Weapons and kit hung from nails on the walls; bowls were stacked on the table. Dirty boots and muddy tunics in a pile in the corner, and the tatty blanket that screened his sleeping alcove thrown back to reveal a mess of bedding. The whole place stank of stale clothing, lamp smoke and army life. Marcellina caught his look of dismay.

'Don't worry,' she said with a slight smile. 'We've both known worse.'

She seated herself on a stool beside the shuttered window. Now, for the first time, Castus looked at her properly. His memories of her were conflicted: the strange self-possessed child he had seen at her father's house during the long march north, and the shocked and ragged fugitive she had later become. Now she was something more than both, it appeared: a grown woman, quietly confident and collected, dressed plainly in a dark wool gown. Only her pendant earrings and coral necklace showed that she came from wealth.

'I wanted to thank you,' she said. 'In person, rather than by letter. I realise that you didn't have to come back for me like that. You could have just left me at the villa. And you were... very brave too. I'm sure I wouldn't have survived without your help.'

'You were brave too,' Castus told her. 'Hanging onto the horse like that. I'd have jumped off if I was you.'

She smiled a little again. A slight twitch of her lips, but there was a sense of shared warmth in it.

'I wanted to thank you as well for your... restraint,' she said, and dropped her gaze as she noticed his jaw tightening. 'You know what I mean, I'm sure,' she said, almost stammering the words. 'I was... in a state of distress when you found me. Not myself. I know I acted in an immodest way, and I'm sorry. I'm glad you acted with honour, and did not... take advantage of my situation.'

'What did you *expect*?' he asked, unable to keep the low anger from his voice. She was blushing, twisting the hem of her shawl in her hands, but when she looked up at him again he caught a glimmer of challenge in her eyes. A more knowing, adult glance. Once again he had that sense of physical clumsiness he had felt before with this woman.

'You're not the way you appear, are you?' she said. 'I mean, it's not for me to say – I hardly know you... But you put on an act, I think. Always appearing the strong obedient soldier, unthinking. Like a dumb animal, almost...'

Castus rocked back against the table, trying not to frown too heavily.

'No, I'm sorry,' she went on quickly, 'I don't mean to offend you. It's just... I don't think you're really like that, are you? You do it on purpose. You appear that way, so people underestimate you. I'm not very good at expressing myself...'

'That makes two of us.'

She smiled at that. 'You're a good man, centurion. That's all I'm trying to say.'

For a few moments they remained silent, each avoiding the other's eye.

'There's something else.' She looked up again. 'A man came to the house, asking questions about you. He had two bodyguards with him – I think they were Praetorians.'

'What sort of man?' Castus asked warily. He already had a good idea of his identity.

'Thin, dry-looking, the way he spoke was... not pleasant at all.' Marcellina twitched her shoulders, uncomfortable with the memory. Castus started forward from the table.

'He threatened you?'

'No, no...' she said, eyes wide at the sudden vehemence of his words. 'He was not aggressive, but his questions were strange, his manner cold. He was asking about what had happened, after... after you found me at the villa. What you'd told me, and whether we'd discussed my father.'

Castus blanked his face, tried to keep his tone neutral. 'What did you tell him?' he asked her, aware of the tightness in his chest.

She shrugged. 'I told him that I had been too discomfited by my experiences to notice anything of what was happening. Besides,' she went on with a quiet smile, 'why should I have paid any attention to you? You are just a simple soldier, after all.'

How much easier it would be if I were, Castus thought.

'You did the right thing,' he said. The idea that Nigrinus was still stalking around, that he had deliberately sought the girl out, both chilled and angered him. Marcellina too had been in danger, although she surely did not know it. But she was safe, they were both safe, for now at least; he eased out a held breath, unclenched his fists and smoothed his palms along the edge of the table.

'What will you do now?' he asked her.

'Oh, my future has been decided,' she said. 'By my brother and his tutor between them. The house is being sold and we're moving to the southern province. My engagement to my cousin Felicianus had been resumed, and we are to be married in the spring.'

Castus remembered her anger when she had spoken of this before, in the marsh hut. There was none of that now, just a calm, sad resignation. It was like duty, he supposed.

'When are you going?'

'In two days' time. My brother wishes to leave the house as soon as possible – he dislikes the bad spirits there, he says. We'll go to Danum first and spend the winter there. So we won't meet again, I'm afraid.'

Castus felt a dull ache in his chest. He had almost entirely forgotten about this girl, or so he had thought. Certainly he had never considered that she might mean anything to him – just a civilian he had saved, a vow he had broken. The memory of her had stayed with him all this time, without his realising it. But it would be safer for her to be far away from Eboracum.

'I wish you well,' he said.

For another moment there was silence, broken only by the wild, distant cries of the revellers in the street. Marcellina looked at him, as if she were daring herself to do something, or say something more. As if she were waiting for him to act. A moment passed, and then she gathered her dress beneath her and stood up.

'I should leave you in peace then,' she said. 'I too wish the fortune of the gods upon you and your future life.'

She moved towards the door, and Castus followed after her. At the threshold she paused suddenly, hunching her shoulders and shivering.

'No,' she said, and turned. 'I didn't mean to leave like this.'

Castus moved a step closer. The lamp was behind him, and darkness fell between them. Marcellina took a long breath.

'Except for my father, you're the only man I've known who's ever done anything for me,' she said. 'The only man I've... respected. And you're not my father.'

'No, I'm not.'

She moved, stretching quickly up on her toes and sliding her arms around his heavy shoulders. He felt her body pressing against him, then her lips on his. He did not move.

'May the gods protect you, Aurelius Castus,' she said as she dropped back.

'And you,' he said.

He waited in the doorway as she went out to the vestibule, then he heard the slave opening the door and both of them leaving. The door closed again.

For a few heartbeats more he waited; then he snatched up his cloak and went outside. Just a girl, he thought. And gone now.

He threw the cloak around his shoulders and stalked away between the barrack blocks. The Blue House would be open late tonight. Afrodisia might be there. It had been a long time, but he needed her company now.

Four months later, the full strength of Legion VI Victrix was drawn up on the drill field. A bright spring day, and the new prefect, Rufinius, climbed the tribunal and stood before the standards of the legion. In front of him, four thousand men waited in rank and file, dressed in parade white with their spearshafts and shields freshly painted, their helmets and corselets of mail and scale polished and gleaming. Castus stood with his men in the ranks of the Third Cohort, all of them listening, expectant.

'Brothers,' Rufinius cried into the thin cold breeze. 'Our lord the Augustus Flavius Valerius Constantius has issued his commands for the forthcoming campaign against the barbarian Picts who invaded our province last summer.'

A shuffle ran through the assembled men, a low stir of whispered words. Castus turned to glare back over his shoulder.

'In ten days' time, a selected force will march for the north, to take the war to the territories of the enemy, punish them for their acts and demonstrate the power of Rome. Two cohorts of this legion have been designated to join the expedition.'

Once again the lines of the legion rippled, men muttering, others stretching up to catch the prefect's words. Only two cohorts. Castus set his jaw, gesturing with his staff for the men behind him to be silent.

'The First and Third Cohorts are to prepare themselves to depart with the field force,' the prefect cried, raising his voice to compete with the whining breeze. 'The others will remain here at Eboracum.'

Castus exhaled between his teeth, feeling the relief tiding through him, then the surge of anticipation. The men behind him fell into a hush. They knew, now, that the war would be theirs.

'Sixth Legion!' the prefect cried again, cutting off the groans of protest, the sighs of dismay from the other cohorts. 'Sixth Legion, remember your oath! I order every man of you to maintain wartime discipline, whether you are staying here or going north. The reputation of this proud legion is in the balance, and the emperor's eye is upon each of us! We must all be ready to serve, whatever our duty demands of us.'

He paused, letting the silence spread once more.

'Sixth Legion, are you ready for war?'

'*Ready*,' the cry came back. Again he shouted, and again the response. By the third cry, every man of the legion gave full voice.

'Sixth Legion: *dismissed*!'

Castus turned on his heel, nodded to Modestus, and ordered the century into march formation. As they passed him, Castus studied the men's faces. Six or seven months of training he had given them. Some of them looked glad, others fearful. But most just wore the mask of discipline. Castus hoped that would be enough.

And on the battlefield, he would know for sure.

PART THREE

CHAPTER XVII

They were burning the third village along the valley when they found the interpreter. Two soldiers brought him: a filthy hunched figure with a rope around his neck.

'We found him in a pit behind one of the houses, centurion,' they said. 'Tied up like an animal. Looks like a slave or something.'

Castus stood in the muddy central clearing of the village. Smoke swirled around him from the burning huts. He could hear pigs squealing, women crying, an old man pleading desperately. He looked down at the twisted figure kneeling before him.

The man had been mutilated, his hands, ears and nose cut off and the wounds seared with fire. Something done to his tongue as well – Castus did not want to look too closely at the ruined mouth, but the man was trying to speak and finding it difficult.

'Embr me, you ust,' he said, his head twitching. The two soldiers were gazing at him with expressions of fascinated disgust. 'Guo you! You'g centoo.'

'Caccumattus,' Castus said. 'That's his name. Get him water – run!'

He knelt down in the mud. The man stank – festering wounds, urine and shit. When the soldier came back with the waterskin Castus tipped it, holding the man's head so he could drink.

'What happened to you?' he said, low and urgent. 'What happened to my men?'

'In't trees,' the man said, gasping. He spoke more clearly now, but his tongue was ruined. 'Votadini all go. Picti come – make fight. No chance, centoo. All killed – c'd'n form lines. Me alone catched. Torture. Like play for them.'

Castus nodded. All this time and he had barely once thought of Caccumattus. In fact, he had assumed the interpreter had run when the century had been attacked by the Picts, or had joined the rebels. The thought shamed him now.

'Take him back to the tribune,' he ordered. 'Give him food if he'll take it. Not too much, or it'll kill him. And treat him gently, you bastards! He was an interpreter for the Roman army – allow him some dignity.'

The soldiers took the broken man away, and Castus glared at the village around him. Soldiers were running between the huts with firebrands, torching the thatch. Chickens scattered around them. Castus breathed in the smell of the burning. A dead man lay in the dirt only a few yards from him: no scarred and painted Pictish noble warrior, just a grey-haired villager. Castus thought back to his days as a fugitive, and the people in the hut settlement who had given him food. The innocent always suffered in war. But, no, he thought, somebody in this place had been holding the interpreter captive, even if they were gone now. Somebody here had been involved in the massacre of his men. He remembered what Caccumattus had said. *Torture. Like play to them.*

'Centurion! What do we do with the prisoners?'

'Chop off their fucking heads,' he said.

The soldier saluted and jogged away, drawing his sword.

'No, wait! Better idea – rope them together in a coffle and take them back to the camp.' He was forgetting himself. They needed captives to question – and slaves too. Already there were several hundred Picts and other Britons in the slave pens of the marching camp. They were supposed to be a lure, to draw the main Pictish force out to attack them. But so far there had been no sign of any organised enemy at all. Just these squalid little villages, most of them deserted. Old men, children and women in the rest. There was a word for this kind of war: *atrocitas*. It was grim work, but it was the only way to get at the enemy and draw them out to fight. This was the eighth village his cohort alone had destroyed since crossing the Wall, and the strain of it was showing on his men's faces. They were growing bored and brutal now. More importantly, they were getting careless.

Castus kicked a chicken out of his way, spat against the wall of a burning hut.

'Hornblower!' he shouted. 'Sound the assembly. We're finished here.'

The sun was low behind them as the cohort made their way back to the camp. They marched in open order, the centuries straggling down the valley following a dirt path that crossed and recrossed a narrow rushing brook. Between them, roped together, they herded their haul of prisoners. It was hot, the valley filled with tiny insects, and all the men were sweating.

'I had believed, centurion,' Diogenes said from the line, 'that this part of Britain was supposed to be perpetually cold and wet.' A few of the men around him laughed; they were used to the schoolteacher's curious asides.

'Whoever told you that?' Castus said over his shoulder.

'It's only what I read in the geographies of the ancients, centurion,' Diogenes replied. 'They all agree that in Britain, and especially the northern part, the sun is only seen for two or three hours a day, and the land constantly shrouded in thick mists. Also that the air and sea become thicker and more turgid the further north one goes.'

'They never came here then.'

'I suspect not. I am beginning to think that our ancient geographers had a lot of imagination, and not much else besides.'

Castus smiled. The men were not doing too badly after all, even with several days of burning and killing behind them. It had surprised him, in fact, how easily they had taken to the work. But most of them had seen the destruction wrought by the Picts on the land around Eboracum.

Now they climbed up out of the valley and crossed a rise, and the camp was before them. It lay on the level ground above the river; beyond were trees and the open slopes where the Pictish muster had been held the summer before. Somewhere to the right was the ford, and the low knoll with its ring of stone that Castus and his men had tried to defend. He could hardly bear to glance in that direction now. Five days they had been camped here, and he had not been able to steel himself to go and survey the scene of that terrible fight.

Cavalry piquets rode out to meet them, and the tribune at the head of the column called out the watchword. The air above the camp was misted with smoke from cooking fires, soft blue in the low evening light, and the high moors and mountains beyond were lit fiery orange and purple. Castus led his men up to the turf rampart and the palisade, then in through the open gateway. Brown leather tents stretched away in neat regular rows, horses tethered between the cavalry lines, carts and mules drawn up in the wagon park, and at the centre the huge white pavilions of the imperial party.

In the broad lane before the Sixth Legion lines Castus formed up his century and then dismissed them to their tents and cooking fires. Taking off his helmet, he swigged water from a skin, and then poured a little over his head and scrubbed it into his scalp. It was a sight to stir the heart, he thought as he blinked the water from his eyes: a Roman army in the field. Ten thousand men were camped here. Galerius had led more than double that number against the Persians, but Constantius's force looked more than enough to totally annihilate the Picts.

But Romans had been in this place before: the soldiers' entrenching mattocks had turned up corroded old coins and hobnails from hundred of years past. How many armies, Castus wondered, had marched into this land hoping to subdue its savage people? At least Constantius was not intending to conquer the place, or try and turn it into a Roman province. This was a punitive campaign, nothing more. A campaign of extermination, if it came to that. But first they had to get the Picts to face them in an open fight.

Forty days had passed since the army had departed Eboracum. They had marched north through Luguvalium, crossed the Wall at the fortress of Petrianis and moved into the territories of the Selgovae. The chiefs of that people had been quick to present themselves, quick to deny any role in the uprising – just a few hotheads among their youth, already punished. Constantius had ordered two thousand of their highest-ranking young men chained and sent back south, to the slave markets of the empire. It had seemed a cursory punishment to Castus, but the emperor hunted larger game.

The Votadini had been dealt with next. The old chief, Senomaglus, had ridden into the Roman camp beneath the Three Mountains, begging his loyalty to Rome, but Constantius had been unmoved. Senomaglus, his entire family and five hundred of his noblemen had been seized and sent to the imperial quarries, to break rocks until they died. Still the army had marched north. And once they had crossed the old grass-grown wall of Antoninus and moved into the lands of Picts, the real work of devastation had begun.

Castus sat by the fire as the evening sank into night, staring into the smoke at the darting insects that hovered around the flames. Being back in this place stirred strange memories and emotions. He remembered the meeting hut on the first night of the Pictish muster: the cup of foul beer they had given him to drink, and the scarred and barbaric chiefs standing up one by one to speak. Where were those chiefs now? Dead on the fields south of Eboracum, or up in the hills to the north with their assembled warriors, waiting to strike? He remembered his first sight of Cunomagla, as she had stood at the back of the gathering, proud and alone. How would she react, he wondered, to the Roman invasion? Would she surrender herself to the mercy of the emperor, like the Votadini chief? Castus knew she would not. The thought that he might have betrayed her trust twisted in his gut, but who would believe him now, a mere centurion, if he tried to claim that she was loyal to Rome? The possibility that she had tricked him, that Nigrinus was right and the uprising had been her doing, was still very real. He should not care about these things – he was back where he ought to be, in command of legionaries, with an army around him and a clear enemy somewhere ahead. But still his mind was shadowed by doubts.

Sitting back from the smoke, he listened to the nearest of his men, singing around their fire. From across the tent lines there was more music: a troop of Mauri was letting out a high wailing chant, beating hand drums and rattles. Then, in the distance, the roaring of the Alamanni from their own encampment near the imperial enclosure. And all around in the deep darkness, the silence of the mountains, the empty plains, the blackened, ravaged villages.

* * *

North again, the army spread out along the route of march in a column four miles long, following the track of an ancient road built by the legions in centuries past. At the vanguard rode the cavalry of the Equites Dalmatae and Equites Mauri, and behind them two cohorts of Legion I Minervia from the Rhine. Then came the commanders, the Augustus, his family and his staff, ringed by his elite bodyguard of Protectores, then the Praetorian Cohorts and a mounted guard of the Equites Scutarii. Following the emperor came the main legion force: detachments of VIII Augusta and XXII Primigenia; then II Augusta from the southern province of Britannia. The baggage train rolled after them, nearly two miles of carts and mules carrying tents and baggage, grain and water, and a full complement of siege artillery. With them went the slaves, and three hundred prisoners roped together and guarded by soldiers. The detachment of Legion VI Victrix brought up the rear, with the Equites Promoti as cavalry guard. And to either side of the march ranged the Alamannic warriors in loose order, with the horsemen of the Equites Batavi riding between them.

The army moved slowly, covering only twelve miles a day between camps. Castus was marching with his men at the rear of the column, and the air was thick with dust churned up by the men, wagons and horses ahead.

'Can't hardly breathe, or see,' Modestus said in a muffled voice. He had the dampened end of his scarf between his teeth.

'Get that rag out of your mouth, optio,' Castus growled.

Modestus spat the scarf from his mouth, making a more than usually sour face. 'Why do the German detachments always get to march at the front?' he said. 'It's our province, isn't it? We should be in the vanguard.'

'Got to earn it,' Castus told him. 'But don't worry – I'll make sure you're right up at the front when the Picts come down from the hills to chop us up.'

He had told the men about the Picts, and their habits. He was, after all, the closest the legion had to an expert. In particular, he had told them to avoid being captured at all costs – death would be far preferable to what the Picts did to their prisoners.

'How come you survived then, centurion?' one of the new men had asked. Stipo, the fullery assistant.

'My neck's too thick,' he told them. 'They'd blunt their blades trying to cut my head off.'

The men had laughed, nervously. Castus was glad that they were scared – they needed to be. This kind of warfare could too easily encourage a lack of caution. And he was determined that no men under his command would end up trapped in some ambush and slaughtered like his previous century. No – keep them nervous. Keep them alert. Let the Rhine detachments hold the vanguard if they wanted. Just keep the men together, Castus told himself, and deliver them safely to the battlefield.

By late afternoon the high black mountains filled the horizon to the north and west; the army crossed another river that flowed down out of the valley and built their entrenchments on the far bank. As the soldiers worked at the ditches they heard cheering from along the line of the fortification. A party of mounted men was circling the limits of the camp.

'There's the son of the Augustus!' Remigius said, standing at the lip of the trench. All along the line, soldiers were throwing their muddy arms up in salute. Castus frowned. Was it right to salute a mere tribune like an emperor, even if he was an emperor's son?

The cavalcade rode by, Constantine in the lead on his champing grey, dressed in a gilded cuirass and a flowing white cloak.

THE WAR AT THE EDGE OF THE WORLD

His head was bare, his long grave face set hard, and he ignored the salutations of the troops. Behind him was a heavy man with a big orange beard who wore a lot of gold.

'And that'll be our tame barbarian king,' Modestus sneered. 'What's he called? Krautus? Rackus?'

'Hrocus, I think,' said Diogenes, leaning on his mattock. 'His people were defeated on the Rhine five or six years back and he swore loyalty to Rome. Or to Constantius anyway.'

'Centurions!' a voice shouted. Victorinus, the tribune commanding the detachment of the Sixth, came strutting along the trench line, gesturing angrily. 'Get your men back to work! This isn't a pay parade!'

Castus saluted quickly, and gave his men an encouraging growl. But as he turned back to the trench he saw the figure riding at the back of Constantine's party, plainly dressed and unassuming. For a moment as he passed, the notary Nigrinus caught his eye and nodded in recognition. Then he was gone.

Thunder filled the sky at dusk, rolling in from the west. In the great marching camp the soldiers looked up apprehensively from their smoking fires between the tent lines and saw the lightning crackling and flickering over the dark peaks of the mountains. A gust of wind, heavy and charged, and then the rain came down, drumming off the tent leather and turning the ground to slippery mud.

What message was it, what omen? Castus considered it as he stood outside his tent, under the dripping hood of a cape. Jupiter the Thunderer, the lightning-hurler, was a friend of Rome. But an angry god all the same. Castus remembered the story of the emperor Carus, who had ruled back when he had been a boy: killed on campaign in Persia when his tent had been struck by lightning, or so the official version claimed. It was not wise to ignore divine warnings.

Hunching his shoulders, Castus made his way across the slippery turf to the southern perimeter of the camp, and the stretch of rampart allocated to his men. The barrier of sharpened stakes showed a jagged black outline with every flash of distant lightning.

Outside the stakes and the trench was utter darkness, filled with rushing rain. Castus stood and stared into it, letting his eyes trick him into seeing shapes moving out there. There were sentries standing six paces to his right and left, motionless in their capes and hoods, similarly gazing out into the night. The lightning glow flared off the tips of their spears. Castus paced slowly along the rampart.

'Centurion!' a voice said, one of the sentries at the rampart turning to salute. Castus recognised Diogenes' pinched face under the hood and helmet rim.

'Keep your eyes out there, not on me,' he growled. The former teacher nodded smartly and looked back across the jagged stakes.

'I don't believe there's anybody out there at all,' Diogenes said. 'Or for miles around either.'

'Maybe so. But barbarians are very illogical – you never know what they might do...'

'"They create a desolation, and they call it peace",' Diogenes intoned quietly.

'What's that?'

'It's from Tacitus. His account of the campaigns of Agricola, in this same country. I was thinking about it earlier today.'

Castus had never heard of Tacitus, or Agricola. But he was used to the schoolteacher's stories by now – all the things he had learned in his books.

'I rather wonder,' the man went on, 'what the people of this country must think of us. What do they tell themselves when they see a great fortress like this appearing overnight? Thousands of armed men, a city of tents, where there was only empty land...?' He turned again to gesture back at the camp, until Castus nudged him and pointed out into the darkness.

'Do they imagine,' Diogenes went on, 'that some race of terrible gods has appeared over the horizon, do you think?'

Castus shrugged. He had wondered similar things himself.

'Just keep your eyes open,' he said. 'The only terrible gods you need to worry about are me and the tribune.'

He stayed on the rampart for another two hours, pacing the line back and forth until Modestus came to relieve him. Then he made his way across the camp again towards the medical station; two of his men had been injured by a panicked horse earlier in the evening and he needed to check on them. The tent lines spread all around him in their regular rows. The fires were out now, damped by rain, and the only lights showed from the wagon park and the imperial enclosure at the heart of the camp. Castus steered a path in the shredded moonlight, alert to the sensations around him: the smell of wet horses from the cavalry lines, wood ash and tent leather; the stink of the latrine trenches; the peaty mud underfoot. He considered what Diogenes had said: truly the camp was like a city, spread here in the darkness of a wilderness. But it was his own city – the only place he could call home.

Sentries challenged him as he passed the looming tent that housed the standards of the legion detachments, and he called back the watchword. Skirting the edge of the imperial enclosure beyond, he turned into the narrower avenue leading to the medical station. Two soldiers came staggering in the other direction, drawing themselves up and saluting quickly as they saw him. Castus turned to watch them move away, and caught a gleam of light from one of the smaller pavilions at the edge of the imperial enclosure.

As he watched, the tent flap was flung aside and a figure stepped out, illuminated briefly. Castus recognised Valens, and was about to call out to his friend when another man appeared in the tent doorway. It was the notary Nigrinus, smiling and saying something to Valens, before stepping back inside the tent again. Castus stood motionless, watching from the shadows as his friend turned, threw his hood over his head and stalked away between the tent lines. Moments later, the departing figure was lost in the mist of falling rain.

CHAPTER XVIII

K neeling beside the path, Castus plucked a stem of long grass and put it between his teeth. Through the scrub and the trees he could see the village boundary, wattle fences, low stone walls, and the humped grey thatch of the huts beyond.

'What does it look like to you?' he said.

'Not much,' Modestus replied. The optio tipped back his head, nostrils tightened, as if he might be able to smell danger. 'No smoke from the huts. Reckon they're long gone, centurion. Cleared out, same as the rest. No sound of animals – must have taken them too.'

No sound of birds either, Castus thought. No crows screeching and flapping around the abandoned grain stores. He sucked on the grass stem for a moment, turning it between his teeth. Behind him, thirty men of his century were waiting on the path, sitting along the verge with a few sentries watching the approaches. After the night's rain the day was hot, still and sultry beneath a pale grey sky. Castus spat out the stem.

'Macrinus,' he called back down the track. The section leader nodded and came to join him at the head of the column. 'Take two men and move up one hundred paces to the edge of the village. When you reach the first fence branch off to the left and follow the boundary around. Keep quiet and keep your eyes open. Remigius: do the same, around to the right. If you

317

see anything or anyone give a shout then get back here quick.'

The two section leaders selected their men and moved off, walking slowly. Castus glanced at the scouts as they passed him. Macrinus and Remigius were in the lead, then the other five, with Diogenes lingering at the rear. They walked casually, spears across their shoulders.

'Stipo! You going for a stroll in the forum? Helmet! Shield!'

The young soldier muttered an apology, put his helmet on and slung the shield from his back. Some of the others did the same. The group of scouts tightened up slightly, appearing more alert. Still not alert enough, Castus thought as he watched them move up the path. He realised he was grinding his back teeth together. A low stir of muttered voices came from the men behind him, and he hissed for them to be silent.

Four hours had passed since they had left camp. Four hours of picking their way slowly through an empty countryside, crossing streams and cutting through thickets. They were supposed to be capturing prisoners for questioning, but every settlement they found had been cleared out. No people, no animals. Even the food stores removed or destroyed. There were other patrols out too; they had been scouring the land in a twenty-mile radius from the camp for days, but none had brought in anything. How long could they continue like this? How long, Castus thought, could the emperor lead his army through an abandoned wasteland, using up supplies, wearing out men, on these pointless forays? Would the whole campaign end in nothing?

He watched the scouts as they arrived at the village boundary and separated, moving to the right and left between the high bushes and scrubby trees. Behind him he could hear the other soldiers muttering again, relaxing into bored discomfort. He glanced at Modestus, but the optio was gazing away towards the horizon.

'Where are they, do you think?' Modestus said. 'Up there, in those hills?'

'Maybe closer,' Castus said quietly. For the last couple of hours he had felt a sensation of heat on the back of his neck, a tightening in his shoulders. The quiet of the land was unnerving, oppressive... maybe it was no more than that. Maybe no more than the pressure of keeping his men together, keeping them sharp and alert, when he knew as well as they did that this whole exercise could be pointless.

'Why all this waiting around?' a voice said from behind him somewhere, cutting through the low whispers. Placidus, the big Gaul. 'Ought to just pile in there, kick down the doors, torch the place then take the long way home. Fucking waste of our lives, this is—'

'Quiet!' Castus said in a harsh whisper. He saw Modestus grimacing, gesturing to the others.

Turning back to the village, Castus squinted into the haze. Was that a sound, just then? He could not be sure – the voices of the men had almost covered it. Surely a sound, he thought; maybe a stifled cry, a scrape of metal... His face was damp with sweat, his fists clenched.

'Did you hear something?' he asked the optio.

'What? No...' Modestus shrugged.

Imagination, maybe? There was no sign of the scouts now, the village silent and still. Nothing moved.

'Form the men up,' he said. 'Quietly – no horns. Marching order, but get them ready to fight if they need to.'

Modestus nodded quickly, frowning, and then hissed out the instructions. Clatter of kit, shields and spears, muffled curses. Too loud. Castus stayed kneeling, staring at the village. How stupid he would look if he was wrong – if the scouts were still picking their way around the boundary of an empty settlement, or maybe already at the far perimeter, sitting around eating apples... His head felt thick and hazy with dread and anticipation.

He got to his feet, stepped to the front of the column and gave the order to march. Behind him the regular crunch of boots on pathway dirt, the heat of men in armour, marching four abreast. He fought the temptation to double his pace, order them into a run. The sensation on his neck was like a fire burning at his back.

The path widened, and the village opened before him. The usual straggle of a dozen or so huts, ringed around by fences, animal pens between them and a broad dusty clearing in the middle with an old tree at the far end. All the hut doors closed. No sign of the scouting parties. Castus passed between the first couple of huts, flicking his eyes to left and right. He sensed the men behind him slowing and gathering closer as they marched, falling into step with a heavier tread.

Now they were into the central clearing. Wattle fences and low huts on all sides, the tree at the end, everything quiet. No point in secrecy now, Castus thought; he should recall the scouts. They must have got lost in the bushes somewhere...

'Cornicen,' he said, turning to the hornblower at his right shoulder, 'sound the...'

A brief flicker of movement from the animal pens caught his eye. A spearhead, glinting in the sun. Castus tensed, staring, and then heard the sudden shouts from behind him.

There was movement all around now, men leaping from the animal pens and appearing between the huts. A figure reared up at the far edge of the clearing, a scarred and painted warrior, spike-haired, raising a spear above his head and crying out.

'Shields!' Castus yelled, sweeping his sword from the scabbard. He could hear the panic behind him, the clattering confusion. Already the first javelins were arcing from the pens. Most fell short, but he heard one of them strike, then a high screech of pain.

Shield raised, sword in hand, Castus backed up until he met the man behind him. A barbed javelin head snicked off his shield rim and spun away. He glanced back over his shoulder quickly. Half the men were formed up behind their shields, but the rest clustered in packs or crouched on the ground, paralysed by shock as the javelins lanced and stabbed between them.

'Modestus! Form the men!' Castus yelled, and the words ripped at his throat. 'Double files – face out!' He pushed his way back, half turning, grabbing and shoving at shoulders and arms, at shields and helmets, trying to bully the men into formation. 'Optio to me!' he shouted. Something cracked off his helmet. A slingstone. They were aiming at him now.

For the first few moments of the attack the Picts had stayed behind cover, hurling their missiles from the pens and huts; now they saw the Romans bunching together they came out into the open, clambering across the walls and spilling from the doorways to shout and curse and brandish their spears and square-tipped swords. Castus reached the centre of the line and found Modestus pushing towards him. He grabbed the optio and pulled him close.

'We need to get amongst them,' he shouted. His words were punctuated by the rattle of stones and javelins on shields. 'Take the right wing. I'll take the left. At my command we charge in wedge formation. When we reach them, split into fours. Understand?'

Modestus nodded, white-faced.

The enemy warriors were moving closer, preparing to rush. Behind them, others continued the javelin barrage. Castus glanced around him: the century was formed into a tight knot now, a rough oval two deep behind locked shields. They had practised this formation scores of times on the drill field over the winter, but now it was real.

Raising his shield high, Castus pushed between the men to his left until the reached the front rank – they were packed too tight to throw javelins or darts. It would be a charge, or die slowly here. The Picts were only twenty paces away, daring themselves to attack. Castus felt his guts tighten, the lock of fear, the blood thick and heavy in his neck. A familiar dread – but he remembered the stone enclosure on the hillock, the tribesmen rushing at the walls… A sudden wave of anger ran through him, prickling across his scalp beneath the helmet's weight.

'At my command,' Castus shouted, 'form wedge and prepare to charge!'

He could hear the man beside him gagging. There was a sharp smell of urine. A flung javelin punched through his shield and hung there, swaying.

'Form… wedge!'

A quick glance behind: Modestus shoving his men into position. Most still had their spears, and the rest drew swords.

Unconquered Sun be with me now. Your light between us and evil.

'Charge!'

Castus launched himself forward as he shouted, shield up, sword low and level. *If they don't follow me I'm a dead man…* A roaring behind him, around him – his own men, following his lead. The noise powered him on, five running strides, then ten, the enemy massing to meet the charge. Castus ran at the warrior ahead of him, swerved at the last moment and slammed into the man to his left. The soldier behind him cut the first warrior down; the second fell to Castus's reaching blade.

'You're into them now, Victrix!' he heard himself shouting, his muscles of his neck bulging. 'Stick every mother's son! Hunt the bastards down!'

Running, striking to left and right, he was almost at the huts now. He slashed low, severed a man's tendons, and smashed him down with the shield boss. A sword swept the air beside his head. Turning on his heel, he cut high and felt his blade bite. Little sound now, only breath against his teeth, hollow battering of blades on shield boards, and the strange high clink and grate of metal.

A face appeared before him, familiar somehow – surprised, Castus recognised the dog-faced man that had wrestled him at the hill fort. He jinked left, and as the man hesitated he threw himself forward behind the shield. The collision punched the breath from his lungs, but he slammed Dog-face against the wall of a hut. Praying that someone was behind him watching his back, Castus angled his sword around the shield rim and drove the blade up under the man's ribs. A gush of blood across his sword-hand, and he let the man drop.

'Not so clever this time, eh?' he said.

Movement from his right as he turned, a grimacing warrior darting in from his unguarded side, driving a spear with both hands. Castus blocked, but too slow – the spearhead punched against the mail on his hip, the blow almost toppling him; then it grated downward and gashed his thigh. One cut hacked the spear aside; a backhand slash split the attacker's face.

For a moment he felt nothing. There was nobody around him now – just his own trail of destruction stretching behind him. Then he felt the lash of pain from his wound and stifled a cry, almost dropping to his knees. Hot blood poured down his leg, and he clamped his sword hand against the wound and sucked air into his lungs. Limping, glazed in the aftermath of the fight, Castus moved around the wall of the hut. Mailed figures ran between the animal pens, cutting down fugitives.

'Prisoners!' he called out through clenched teeth. 'We need prisoners!'

One of his soldiers was beside him, pointing. Castus limped after the man, trying to keep his head up. Between the stone walls they reached a wattle-walled pen at the rear of the village. Soldiers stood around, silent and gazing, and in the rutted mud and dung Castus saw the bodies of the scouting party.

Julius Stipo still had a startled look on his face, but his throat was slashed open to his spine. Macrinus lay beside him, his head severed and placed upon his chest. The third man had his mail dragged up around his shoulders and his stomach opened. All three had dark bloodstains between their legs.

Castus exhaled slowly. Behind him he could hear men dying, soldiers shouting.

'Cover them,' he said quietly to the man beside him, and then limped back between the huts.

In the central compound the prisoners had been herded together. Low-ranking fighters mostly, but a few painted warriors among them. As Castus watched he saw Placidus, the big Gaul, drag a prisoner to his knees and hack off his head with a single blow.

'Halt!' he shouted. 'Spare the rest. We need to take them back to camp.'

Placidus stared at him, his face boiling, the reddened sword in his hand. 'You saw what they did,' he said, raising the blade to point between the huts. 'They die! All of them!'

Castus glanced at the other soldiers, and saw the look in their eyes. Fierce, half sick, half excited. The killing frenzy still gripped them. Most were new recruits – men who had seen their homes and families destroyed by the Picts last summer.

The pain in his leg had shifted to a heavy throb, and his right boot was wet with blood, but Castus urged himself forward. He was still holding his drawn weapon.

'Sword down, Placidus,' he said. 'Remember your military oath. You're under orders.'

'*Orders*,' the Gaul sneered. 'And why should we obey you? You left your last century to be massacred, to save your own skin!' He grabbed another of the prisoners by the hair, pulling him close. 'I'm not taking any chances...'

Castus held his own blade low at his side. His blood ran cold with fury. Fear as well – but he would show neither. Some of the other men were backing away now, the fire dying from their eyes. All of them knew the punishment for mutiny.

Now only three paces separated Castus from the Gaul. Their gazes locked, and Castus tried to ignore the pain of his wound, tried not to blink. He heard Modestus's voice, quiet and firm.

'Step back, soldier. Your centurion's spoken.'

Placidus let his gaze drop. Then he turned away. Castus heard the sound of released breath.

'Get the prisoners secured,' he said. 'Where's Flaccus?'

'Here, centurion.' The standard-bearer appeared at his side, stone-faced and impassive.

'Report?'

'Three dead, centurion – that's the scouting party. Two badly wounded but walking. Ten or so minor wounds. Plus you...'

'This is nothing,' Castus told him, glancing down at his bloodsoaked leg. It could have been a lot worse. They had eight prisoners secured as well. Probably around a score of enemy dead. He wiped his face, and through a squint saw Remigius and the second scouting party coming in from the village boundary.

'Sorry, centurion,' Remigius said. 'They were all around us – we had to lie low, or they'd have killed us.'

Castus nodded, waving the man away. He noticed Diogenes trailing after his group leader with a look of shame on his face so intense Castus wanted to laugh.

Fear does many things to a man, he thought, but it seldom makes him brave.

They left the village burning behind them and marched back to the camp with the prisoners carrying the wrapped bodies of the slain legionaries. By the time they arrived back inside the ramparts Castus could no longer feel his right leg. He went to the medical station, but stayed only long enough for the wound to be cleaned, sutured and properly dressed. The cut was bloody but not deep, but his right hip was aching and livid with bruises where the spearpoint had punched into the mesh of mail and the padded vest beneath.

Back in the tent lines the men were singing. The patrol had brought back two sheep with them, and the men were feasting on roast mutton hot and greasy from the fire, telling exaggerated stories of the fight to their unlucky comrades who had remained behind at camp. Six months ago most of them had been farmers, labourers and townsmen; now they were soldiers, blooded in combat. Few grieved for the dead men; they had expected much worse, and felt the glory of survival.

Castus felt it too, although the delayed shock of what had happened was stronger. Perhaps they all had this same sensation, and covered it with the laughter and feasting of their brothers around the fires? For a terrible moment back in the village, as the column had broken apart and chaos had taken hold, he had feared total bloody ruin. When he thought about it now, he felt the sick clench of fear in his belly, the weakness in his limbs. But they had done well, they had held together. There would be no more mistakes now.

Placidus was more of a problem. His actions back at the village had been close to open mutiny; Castus could have had him flogged, could even have killed him right there and then. He had said as much to the big Gaul as soon as they were back in camp. Before the assembled men he had demoted Placidus to a common soldier and appointed another man, Attalus, as section leader in his place. Placidus could go and join Remigius's section – he would not be well liked there. But if his power and influence was dented, his threat remained. He was resentful now, vengeful. Castus knew he would have to watch his back from now on. The words the Gaul had spoken to him in the village still ached in his mind. Was that truly what they thought of him?

That evening, as he limped along the wall parapet cursing his bruised hip and the stinging wound in his thigh, Castus heard the first terrible screams drifting across the camp from the central enclosure. The sentries at the ramparts stiffened, glancing back over their shoulders; the men still lingering around the embers of the cooking fires muttered and made signs against evil. Eight times those wrenching howls rang out across the camp – once for each of the prisoners the patrol had brought in. Castus had heard those sounds before, and knew what they meant: the mangling of bodies; the defiling of flesh. The *quaestionarii* of the legions were both inventive and thorough. It was dishonourable, but they usually got results. Perhaps, he thought, the men that Placidus had executed were the lucky ones after all.

CHAPTER XIX

The night before the battle he dreamed of the dead. They were all around him, pressing close in darkness, and he shrank from their touch. He saw Marcellinus retching over his bowl of poison, Strabo stretching his neck to the butcher's knife. He saw Timotheus and Culchianus, their eyes filled with blood, Stipo the fullery assistant with his throat opened to his spine. He was cold, but pouring sweat as if he lay on the burning floor of a hypocaust.

Musk flooded over him, a thick and heady scent: Cunomagla appeared before his dreaming eyes now, splendid and terrible in her barbaric scar tattoos. *Why did you fail me?* Her voice low and hoarse, almost sorrowful. *You are a liar, like all Romans.*

He tried to speak, but his throat was locked. Then the heat was gone and a cool hand pressed his forehead. A soft voice, whispering to him. *Don't worry. You are a good man. You broke no vows.* He opened his eyes and saw Marcellina leaning over him, her face pale from shadow. He reached up to her...

'Centurion? Centurion!'

With a grunt and a jolt he was awake, sitting upright on his hard bed mat. The slave was shaking him by the ankle, and he gestured for the man to get out of the tent. Once he was alone he splashed his face with water from the jug and scrubbed his head with hard, stiff fingers. He seldom dreamed, and was glad of that. Dreams brought messages – from the gods, or from spirits. Or from the land of death. But already the sensations were leaving him, the images fading into the dull greyness of morning.

On his feet, he dressed and pulled his boots on, and then ducked out of the tent into the damp air. Greyness all around, the sun not yet risen, no trumpets to bring the soldiers to order but already activity filled the camp. Men stumbled in the half-dark, pulling on helmets and buckling belts. Others sat around the firepits, cursing and blowing, trying to coax a flame from a spark and a fistful of damp tinder. Horses kicked and snorted in the misty shadows.

Castus winged his arms, feeling the blood beginning to rush in his body. Standing, he ate a crust of dry bread, washing it down with sour watered wine, then the slave returned and helped him into his armour: the padded vest and mail coat; the plumed helmet. Pulling his belt tight and shrugging the sword baldric across his shoulder, Castus set off through the gloom of the waking camp. Then the first trumpet call rang out, booming brass through the mist.

The army had left their camp on the river the day before, flattening their ramparts and trenches and forming up for a rapid ten-mile march, following an old Roman road along the crest of a ridge that ran eastwards towards the coast. The prisoners had given the necessary information: the Pictish host was gathered in the wide river valley to the south-east, around one of their sacred sites.

Castus had learned of the strategy that evening, as his men had set up camp on the southern slope: with their march along the ridge, the Romans could threaten the enemy's line of retreat into the mountains, and stood poised to strike down into the valley at the fertile lands and villages further east. But the emperor had divided his army, with a light detachment supported by the Alamanni moving on ahead and making camp a mile further east, and the cavalry swinging around to the south and taking up a position screened by a lateral hill. The remaining force of four thousand infantry would appear a tempting target, but the Picts would need to ford the river at the foot of the slope and climb up through a crooked steep-sided defile to reach the heights. Before dark the scouts had returned, and reported the enemy camped on the far bank on the river, drinking and feasting, confident of victory. The trap was set and the bait laid.

Now Castus joined the group assembling around the standards: the centurions and tribunes of the cohorts, with the men gathered behind them. Smoke from the torches and braziers hung in the air, under the thin misty rain. The draco standards of the cohorts hung limp, but the *signa* of the centuries caught the gleam of the fires. All stood silent while the priests conducted the sacrifices, intoning prayers to Mars, Jupiter and the Unconquered Sun. Four thousand voices sounded the response, a strangely muffled rumble. Then the ranks of the officers and Praetorians parted, and a stooped figure in a dark purple cloak climbed onto the piled turf tribunal.

The emperor.

'Fellow soldiers,' he called, and his voice barely carried through the dawn murk. The ranks shifted, men moving closer. 'Fellow soldiers,' the emperor said again, more clearly, 'I need say few words to you. Out there are the hordes of our enemies, eager to throw themselves upon your swords. Do not disappoint them!'

Sudden laughter from the assembly, men flinging up their arms in salute. The emperor raised his hand, and then stifled a cough. His face was waxy grey in the low light.

'Remember...' he said, clasping his cloak to his neck, 'these are the savages who despoiled our province last year. Who burned our cities, our homes, raped our women, murdered our children...' He paused again, coughing into his fist. 'Show them no mercy! Let not one of them survive!'

The shout of acclaim was huge, echoing in the damp air. The soldiers surged forward, pushing against their officers, but the emperor was already clambering down from the tribunal, helped by his slaves. The moment of unity died into muttering, clattering of arms and shields, tramping of feet.

Castus turned and found Modestus behind him. The optio swung a quick salute.

'Century assembled, centurion! All present and ready for orders!'

'Form them up, optio. Wait for my command.'

The gathering of officers was breaking up now, individual tribunes gathering their centurions around them. Castus pushed through the throng until he stood with Valens and the others of the Sixth, formed in a rough circle around Tribune Victorinus.

'The surveyors have already marked out your start positions,' the tribune was saying. 'We form battle line across the head of the valley – the Sixth are on the left flank, with the First Minervia to our right. Form up in open order, two centuries deep. Keep the formation until the enemy get within five hundred paces, then at the signal retreat by line until you reach close order... At the second signal, discharge javelins, and the third advance by century. We'll have artillery and archers behind us throughout, but they'll have the ranges marked. Any questions?'

There were none. Castus felt Valens slapping him across the shoulders. His friend grinned, wolfish.

* * *

By daybreak the battle line was formed across the head of the valley, and the soldiers turned to the east and saluted the direction of the rising sun. The sun itself was invisible behind cloud – just a watery gleam low in the sky. Castus pulled his belts tight and squared his shoulders. On the march down from the camp his dream had returned to him: the faces of the dead. He closed his eyes and tried to banish the images from his mind.

To his left, the men of his century were waiting in position. A few of them swigged water, others talked in low nervous voices, others pissed where they stood. Behind him, Castus could hear Flaccus the standard-bearer whistling under his breath. They held the rear of the position; Valens's century was in front, but each rank of men stood six paces from the next. The formation was deep, spreading over the upper slopes of the valley, but would appear thinly stretched to the enemy.

And the enemy, Castus noticed, were already appearing. The narrow wooded defile leading up from the river opened out as it climbed, and the valley formed a shallow amphitheatre below the crest of the ridge with the slopes thick with thorny scrub. Already Pictish riders were cantering up from the throat of the defile, warriors on foot massing behind them, filling the lower end of the valley. Castus listened carefully, but could hear nothing; the damp morning air seemed to muffle all sounds. He saw Valens glance back at him from his position with the forward century.

A distant shout cut through the mist, then a chorus of yells. Figures ran across the open ground: archers and slingers in loose formation, pelting the gathering mass of the enemy and then running back. A low swell of noise came from the Picts, a wordless roar and a percussive rattle and clash of spear-butts on shields. The noise rolled across the hollow of the valley in waves.

How many of them now? Castus squinted, trying to count, dividing the horde up into sections and estimating their numbers as he had been taught. *Five thousand? Six?* Most were on foot, with a few carts heaving through the mass, nobles or chiefs brandishing spears. The details became clearer as they approached: now Castus could make out the high crests of their hair, the scars swirling over their naked limbs. The men beside him were beginning to shuffle, ducking their heads and edging their shields higher.

'Keep formation,' he called. 'Wait for them to come to us.'

There was a slight breeze now, stirring the bright tails of the draco standards. A good omen, Castus thought.

A sharp snapping sound from the rear, and a ballista bolt arced across the Roman lines and darted down into the forward ranks of the enemy. Ranging shot. A moment later, fifty catapults fired in unison; a volley of snaps and thuds, and the bolts flickered dark against the sky, then arced and fell. The Pictish mass shuddered under the impact, and a great groan went up from them.

Now they charge, Castus said under his breath.

But still the Picts hung back, massing in lines across the width of the valley. More of them came from the defile, pouring like liquid from the neck of a jug. The forward groups shouted and chanted, banging their weapons, taunting the Romans in their own tongue. Another volley of ballista bolts dropped into them, goading them, but still they did not break.

Castus glanced back towards the command position on the hillside, and saw the emperor's purple draco standard swirling and flapping around its shaft. A shout went up from the cohorts of VIII Augusta, holding the centre of the line: '*ROME AND VICTORY!*'

The shout spread through the flanking cohorts.

'*ROME AND VICTORY!*' Castus cried, and his men took up the shout. Spears drummed off shield rims all along the Roman line. Some of the Picts were climbing up the slopes of the valley to dart javelins, but the archers and slingers on the heights drove them back.

Now the trumpet signal rang out. Valens called out the order, and the forward century began edging backwards, closing up the ranks. Castus swung his arm, and the front three lines of his own men backed up. Slowly, steadily, the gaps between the ranks narrowed. A cheer went up from the Picts. Some of them were already dashing forward, flinging spears, thinking that their enemy was retreating. Those at the rear of the mass began to surge forward, ordered on by their chiefs.

'Steady,' Castus called. 'Hold steady... Back six paces...'

The leading century had already closed ranks, Valens's men locking their shields together; now, as the Picts began their charge, they found a solid mass of armoured men facing them, a wall of shields and levelled spears. Castus could see Modestus moving along the rear ranks, shoving the men into line with his staff.

'Ready javelins.'

Behind him he could still hear the thump and crack of the artillery; the sky overhead was stippled with arrows and ballista bolts.

'*Loose!*' he shouted, and as one the men of the front rank lunged forward and hurled their javelins. The missiles curved over the leading century and struck the face of the Pictish charge. At once the next rank stepped forward and threw: javelins clashed and shivered the air.

Castus stretched up, staring over the massed helmets of Valens's men. The enemy charge had faltered under the storm of missiles, great gaps torn in the Pictish mass. But others were pressing forward, stumbling over the fallen bodies. Now a volley of throwing darts followed the javelins, pelting sharp iron down into the enemy horde.

'Ready spears – prepare to advance!'

He heard the trumpet call even as he spoke, and Valens's cry of command at the same moment. The leading century seemed to rear up, massing towards the front, and then suddenly lurched into motion.

'Advance!'

Slow heavy movement, turf thick underfoot. Ahead, the noise of Valens's men smashing into the riven horde of the enemy. Screams, sudden and high-pitched, and the hollow thud of shields. Pacing forward, wanting to run, Castus glanced to his left, down the line of his front-rank men. Spears gripped, shields up, the line held steady.

He saw the first enemy bodies, left twisted and bleeding on the ground as the leading ranks stepped over and across them. One of his own men darted his spear down to stab at a fallen man as he advanced. Others did the same, spears rising and falling like darning needles.

Up ahead, the leading century was moving through the Picts like reapers through a wheatfield. Through the shouts, the screaming, Castus could clearly pick out the chop and suck of blades cutting flesh and hacking bone. Occasionally an enemy javelin would flicker across the wall of shields and into the ranks of the armoured men.

Cheering from the right. When he looked up again, Castus saw the first wave of cavalry crashing down the far slopes, towards the open flank of the massed enemy. He looked to the left, and there were the Alamanni pouring down the steep hillside above the defile, hollering their own barbaric war cries.

At the apex of the cavalry attack, galloping on his grey horse, was the tribune Constantine. Castus saw him clearly: the golden helmet with its feathered crest, the white cloak swinging behind him, his mouth open in a scream of joyous violence.

The cavalry struck, ripping into the Pictish flank. From his vantage point on the slope Castus saw a wave of panic pass through the mass of the enemy, warriors turning to flee from the horses, colliding and pressing together. Those who fled forward faced the advancing line of infantry, the impregnable shields and reaping blades. Others tried to retreat back into the defile, but it was already choked by fugitives. Carts and horses meshed in the rout, while the Alamanni swarmed down from the higher slopes.

The advance slowed, Valens and his men pushing against a bulwark of desperate, dying men. Swords still thundered against the pressing shields, javelins arced, but it was butcher's work now: the hollow of the valley was heaving with trapped Picts, cropped down on all sides, dying in a bloody morass.

Then, as Castus watched, he saw a knot of enemy warriors plunging forward towards the infantry lines, all of them scarred and painted nobles, screaming defiance. At their heart was a single battle cart, their leader standing high and proud, spear raised. Castus saw the long face and goatlike beard, the dyed mane of hair, and recognised Talorcagus, High King of the Picts. For a few heartbeats the warband pressed forward, until it appeared that they might breach the mob of their own panicked men. Then Valens yelled out the order to his troops: *Shield wall!* And like a ship caught in a storm wave, the chariot and the warriors surrounding it veered and tilted, capsizing into the surge of bodies. Castus stared as the king went down, Talorcagus toppling from his cart and falling into the melee.

He glanced around for the cornicen, and found him staring

dumbly forward at the massacre. He shook the man by the shoulder.

'On my command,' he said. 'Sound *charge*.'

'Great gods,' Diogenes said. 'This is a slaughteryard.'

Castus just nodded. They were picking their way back across the field of the battle, supervising a work detail retrieving the bodies of the Roman dead from among the slain. Behind him, he heard Diogenes cough, and then vomit noisily.

'Sorry, centurion.'

'Don't be. Happens to everyone, now and again.'

Rain was falling, the water mixing with the blood to form huge red lakes between the mounds of corpses. Castus felt his boots sinking into the mire, sucking with every step. All across the valley the dead were piled, some individually, others in great mounds where they had fallen fighting or trying to flee. Dead horses and shattered carts too. There were even more at the lower end of the valley, where hundreds had pressed together trying to enter the defile. There, the ground was invisible under bodies piled two and three deep. Some of the Picts had crawled under a thicket of thorn bushes to try and escape, but archers had surrounded the thicket and filled it with arrows until all were dead. Down the defile it was the same, where the Alamanni had come whooping and howling like hunters to spear the packed fugitives below. The slaughter stretched to the river ford, where the cavalry had pursued the fleeing Picts through the shallows.

'Are all battles like this, afterwards?' Diogenes asked, wiping his mouth.

'Sometimes.' Maybe Oxsa, Castus thought, although he had been unconscious and had not seen the full extent of it. Those

337

running skirmishes against the Carpi on the plains beyond the Danube had never resulted in such a massacre. The trapped Picts had died in such numbers it looked as though some god had destroyed them.

'I've read of battles often,' the schoolteacher said, 'but never expected anything like this. Truly an awesome and terrible sight.'

Castus grunted. Rainwater was running down his neck. To his left, two men of his century were moving through the corpses, methodically killing any Picts that remained alive. To his right he saw a dead man sprawled against a chariot wheel; the top of his skull had been sheared away, and wet brain matter spattered the spokes. Another man, his torso cleaved from shoulder to ribcage, his face oddly placid-looking. One Pict was sitting up, slumped with his legs stretched before him. His stomach was ripped open, and entrails pooled pink and grey between his thighs. Castus nudged the corpse's shoulder with his boot, and it rolled over backwards.

He knew the meaning of his dream now. The dead had returned to petition him for vengeance. They had got it, surely. The fury of battle had left him now, the killing rage of that last murderous charge across the valley, but Castus still felt the solid satisfaction of a job well done. Even so, there was a well of emptiness inside him. He and the men of his century had seen little real fighting, just killing; few of the Picts had put up any resistance to the charge, and those who had were easily despatched. Many had thrown aside their weapons and tried to surrender, but none had been spared. The Roman line had crossed the valley like an iron roller, crushing everything in its path.

Was that why he felt this hollowness? To watch a battle, but not truly participate, was hardly fulfilling. Then he remembered that other part of his dream: Cunomagla coming to him, accusing him. What did that signify?

338

He cleared his throat and spat. *Dreams!*

'What will they do with all these dead men?' Diogenes asked. 'Theirs, I mean?'

'Leave them to rot,' Castus said. 'They're food for the crows now.'

There was a mood of festival around the camp fires that evening. The victory had been total: fewer than a hundred Roman dead for thousands of the enemy slain. The troops had gathered around the imperial tribunal, and built a battle trophy of piled shields and weapons taken from the enemy chiefs. They had cheered the emperor as he had stood before them, shouting out his name and saluting him *imperator*. But they had cheered Constantine too, when the tribune had ridden back from the river ford at the head of his cavalry, his horse sprayed with blood to the withers. The victory belonged officially to the emperor, but in the hearts of the troops his son had taken the palm.

Out in the rain the pyres were still burning the bodies of the Roman dead. Castus stood beside the cooking fire, drinking beer from a wooden cup, listening to his men recount their tales of valour and destruction. He had been like that himself, he thought, when he had been a common soldier like them...

'Centurion Aurelius Castus?'

He turned, and saw two men in the white cloaks and uniforms of the Protectores, holding the hilts of their swords. One of them spoke again, in a heavy Germanic accent.

'You must come with us, centurion. Now, if you please.'

The German went before him, the second man behind, and they led Castus away through the camp, between the scattered fires.

'What's this about?' Castus asked. He did not expect a reply, and got none.

Out through the camp gates, they marched down the hillside towards the battle valley. Smoke from the funeral pyres hung in the rainy night air. On the slope where the imperial tribunal had been raised stood a large pavilion. Guards surrounded it – troopers of the Equites Scutarii, standing beside their horses. The Protectores led Castus through the guard lines and up to the door of the tent, and the German raised the flap and gestured for him to enter.

Warm light met him as he stepped inside, and the sweet stink of death. Oil lamps hung from tall stands around the leather tent walls. There were around a dozen men gathered in the smoky glow, and only half of them were still alive. Officers, mostly, with a few finely dressed civilians among them.

'Domini!' Castus cried, saluting, and jolted to attention, feet spread, thumbs hooked in his belt.

'You may relax,' said the notary, Nigrinus. 'This is not a formal occasion.' Castus was not at all surprised to find him here.

'This is the centurion I mentioned, who was held captive among the Picts,' the notary went on, addressing the gathering. 'He may be able to help us, I think.'

The six dead men were laid out on the floor of the tent, some still wrapped in bloodstained blankets. All of them were Pictish warriors; the scar patterns were livid on their greying flesh.

'These,' said a very fat man in a damask robe, flapping his palm at the corpses on the floor, 'are some of the bodies of the Pictish notables our scouts managed to recover from the field.' He had a high fluting voice. A eunuch, Castus realised. 'Study them, and see if you can identify any of them.'

340

Castus stepped closer to the row of corpses. The first was hard to recognise, as his face had been gouged almost entirely away. The ruined black features told him nothing, but the patterns etched onto the skin appeared familiar. Castus remembered the gathering in the meeting hut, the fug of smoke and sweat, the men gathered around the fire.

'This is one of their chiefs, I think,' he said.

'Name?' Nigrinus prompted. Castus shrugged and shook his head, and the notary scratched something on a waxed tablet. The others kept themselves away from the little man slightly, Castus noticed, even the senior officers. Almost as if they feared him. One of the civilians was wearing scent, or carrying a scented cloth perhaps – the floral aroma mixed with the cloying stink of dried blood.

The next two corpses were completely unidentifiable. Both warriors, faces contorted in death. Castus leaned across them, peering intently. Maybe he remembered them, maybe not. He shook his head again.

The fourth man he knew at once. The long goatlike face was crusted with blood, but there was no mistaking the stiff red mane of hair.

'This is their king. Talorcagus.'

'You're sure?' the eunuch asked eagerly. Castus nodded. A brief stir of pleasure and congratulation passed around the group of officers.

'These last two I don't know.'

'What about the king's nephew?' one of the tribunes snapped. 'Drustagnus, isn't it? Do you see him here?'

Castus looked again, then shook his head. 'No, dominus. He's not here.'

'Then he has escaped us!' another voice said. The group of officers jolted to attention suddenly, and some of the civilians made little gestures of salute. The tribune Constantine strode from the tent door and stood before them. His face was flushed, as if he had just been exercising, and he held a gold cup of wine. 'There was no way anyone could have slipped past my cavalry. Clearly this Drustagnus got clear before the rout began!'

'Indeed, dominus,' Nigrinus said, raising his stylus. 'And one more, of course, is missing. The woman who started this revolt. Cunomagla.'

Castus clenched his jaw, and tried not to show his discomfort. Constantine stepped forward and leaned over to gaze at the corpses laid on the floor.

'Such formidable warriors,' he said, 'stirred into hopeless rebellion by the wiles of a female...' For a moment he appeared almost sad, staring down at the bloodied face of the dead Pictish king. Then he straightened up.

'It is an unnatural thing,' he declared, his voice slurring slightly, 'when a woman gains primacy over a people! Nothing but evil can result from a woman's rule. Do you not agree, centurion?'

Castus stiffened his back. 'Of course, dominus,' he said.

Nigrinus gently cleared his throat, stepping forward with his tablet and stylus; the others officers moved aside. 'If I may, dominus?' he asked.

Constantine nodded.

'Some of the prisoners,' the notary continued, 'have suggested that their fugitive leaders may have taken refuge at a hill fort belonging to one of them. I believe this may be the same place that our centurion here was held captive...'

'Excellent!' Constantine declared. 'Then our centurion will go with the mounted scouts, find this place, and lead us to it.' He flung an arm across Castus's shoulders, squeezing tightly. Castus smelled the fumes of wine on his breath.

'We'll track this she-wolf to her lair,' he said. 'And when we find her, we'll put her to death!'

CHAPTER XX

Through dappled sunlight, the line of horsemen emerged from the trees and rode out onto an exposed spur of the hillside. The ground fell away sharply to their left, rocky outcrops showing between the thick heather and the trees, and below them the green flatlands spread north to the shore of the estuary. The water glittered in the noon sun. Above, to the right, the hillside rose steeply to a line of bare brown summits.

'Are you sure that's the place?' Victorinus asked, reining in his mount and pointing.

Castus nudged his horse closer to the tribune. He was still uncomfortable on horseback, and slid slightly in the saddle as he stretched up to stare along the line of the hills. Behind him, the six mounted scouts of the Equites Mauri scanned the slopes nervously.

'That's it,' Castus said. He had scouted several forts in the four days since the battle on the ridge. Most were little places with tumbled walls, clinging to the rocky summits above the valley, abandoned now. Once or twice Castus had almost believed he recognised the location – but this time he was sure. From the hillside spur he could make out the high stone buttress surrounding the lower enclosure, and the inner wall rising within. Squinting in the bright sun, he could even see the thatched roofs of the larger huts in the central enclosure. He felt a lurch in his blood. The last time he had seen this place, he had been a hunted fugitive. Now he had an army behind him. He remembered what he had said that night to Cunomagla. *If the gods allowed, I would be marching in their ranks.*

A thin trail of smoke rose against the sky. The fort, at least, was still occupied.

'All of the chiefs who've surrendered in the last few days are sure that Drustagnus has gathered a last warband,' Victorinus said. 'Probably only a few hundred men. We've got cavalry scouting all the valleys around here, so they shouldn't be able to slip away. It looks like a strong position, though. Direct assault along the ridge might be the only way to take it.'

Castus glanced at the tribune. Victorinus was a sober, soldierly officer, with a broad face and a big chin and very large, prominent teeth. The men of the cohort privately called him *the mule*. But Castus trusted him. He nodded.

'Tribune,' he said, 'I've been over the hill crest and along the valley at the far side. That was the way I came down when I escaped.' The horses shifted, twitching their ears. Victorinus motioned for him to continue.

'If a small party of men, a century or two,' Castus went on, 'got down into that valley, I think they could climb up to the walls undetected. If the defenders were distracted, they could get inside and open the gates...'

Victorinus frowned more deeply, running his tongue over his teeth. 'An artillery attack from the ridge to the north-west might be distraction enough,' he said. He fixed Castus with a narrow stare. 'You'd have to lead the assault party yourself, though. Do you think you could do it?'

'I think so, dominus.' Castus tried to recall the events of that night: his escape from the hut; the killing of Decentius and the wild scramble down over the walls and palisades; the race through the hills with the dogs behind him... He tried not to think of what had happened before that: his promise to Cunomagla. Was she really inside the fort now?

'I don't remember it too clearly,' he said. 'It was dark. Misty. But I'm sure I could find a way in.'

Victorinus nodded, satisfied. 'Think your men are up to it, centurion?'

'Yes, dominus. At every command we will be ready...'

The tribune stared up again at the walls of the fort on the hilltop. He bared his long teeth in a grimace. 'Incredible to think you were a captive in that place!' he said.

'Yes, dominus.'

'I admit, I can hardly imagine what it must have been like to be a prisoner of such savages.' He shook his head, hissing grimly. 'The indignities they must have forced on you...'

'Yes, dominus,' Castus said, reddening, but could not meet the tribune's eye.

'Look at those German cocksuckers!' Modestus laughed. 'Hey, Minervia!' he called out. 'Put some balls into it!'

All across the flank of the hill, the legionaries of I Minervia were toiling upwards, stripped to their tunics, lugging heavy baulks of shaped timber, rolls of cable and sheaves of iron-tipped bolts. Some hefted huge earthenware jars, carrying them carefully in rope slings. Castus paused to watch them; the line of men stretched away down the hill towards the marching camp in the valley below. Cavalry troopers stood guard all along the route.

'Let's go,' Castus said, and gestured on upwards. The men of his century straggled behind him, climbing up the steeper slope past the labouring legionaries. They were sweating in full equipment and armour; none carried spears or javelins, but every sixth man had a coil of rope and a hooked grapnel over his shoulder.

Reaching the crest of the ridge, Castus paused again, breathing hard. The engineers were at work here in the hot sun, piling together stones and turf to build artillery platforms. Along the ridge to the east the ground dipped, and then rose again, and there at the last summit Castus could see the fort. It appeared very close now, fewer than five hundred paces away, and very clear in the bright daylight. He could pick out the figures of men moving on the wall ramparts, gesticulating and waving spears.

'Why don't they try to escape?' Diogenes said, coming up behind him. 'They can surely see what's happening up here.'

'They must think they can hold out against us.'

'They've got a shock coming then!' called Modestus. The optio was bringing up the rear of the century, herding the last stragglers up onto the summit. 'They haven't seen what one of these bastards can do!' He gestured to the first of the artillery platforms, where the engineers were slotting and bolting the heavy timbers together, preparing the drums of cable that they would tighten into powerful torsion springs. Already the first of the massive long-armed *onager* catapults was taking shape. Further east, where the ground dipped, groups of soldiers from VIII Augusta were assembling the smaller bolt-throwing ballistae only a couple of hundred paces from the fort.

But those huge stone walls, cut into the hillside and lined with palisades, looked strong enough even to resist artillery. Maybe, Castus thought, the defenders were not so stupid after all.

'Could we not merely starve them out?' Diogenes asked, looking perplexed. 'Surely we'd need only to wait, and after a few days...'

'Where's the fun in that?' Castus said, and cuffed the teacher's shoulder. 'Anyway, there's no glory in it. Not the Roman way.'

Diogenes gave a resigned shrug. *'These are your arts, O Roman,'* he gravely intoned, *'to impose peace, spare the vanquished, and crush the proud... I suppose it must be so, then.'*

'Mule approaching,' Flaccus the *signifer* muttered under his breath.

'Dominus!' Castus cried, standing to attention as Victorinus strode towards them. The rest of the century shuffled into line behind him.

'Brothers,' the tribune said, 'the great work commences!' The rest of the assault party were coming up the hill now, led by Valens and the third centurion, a wiry African named Rogatianus, who had been promoted from Legion XXII Primigenia. The centurions gathered around Victorinus, giving their salutes.

The tribune showed his teeth as he squinted, pointing with his staff towards the fort. 'As you can see,' he said, 'the land falls away on both sides and to the rear. Once night falls, the artillery attack will begin on the north-west side, facing us here... They'll be using incendiary missiles, to set fires along the rampart there and among the huts in the lower enclosure behind it. Meanwhile, you'll drop down off the ridge to the south and circle around into the valley to the east...'

Castus sucked his lip, trying to judge the distances in his mind.

'Once you see the flames take hold,' the tribune went on, 'you'll climb up the far slope to the south-east rampart. Castus's century will lead. Once you reach the rampart, get inside as soon as you can...'

'What if they see us climbing the hill?' Valens asked.

'Then you'll have to fight your way in, and may the gods aid you in that. Hopefully the defenders will be distracted by the artillery attack. Once you're inside the lower enclosure, one group will circle around to the right and seize the main gate from the inside, over there at the north-east end of the fort. A storming party from the Eighth Augusta will be waiting outside. Give a single call on the horn, then open the gates and let them in. A second group will scale the inner wall and enter the upper enclosure, then circle around in the same way and secure the inner gate. It's vital that you do so – otherwise the storming party will be trapped between the two walls.'

'Oh, a simple exercise then,' Valens said. He glanced warily at Castus. 'Was this all Knucklehead's idea?'

'We've had patrols up and down the valley to the east all day,' Victorinus said, ignoring the remark, 'so it should be clear of hostiles, but once you're down there, keep silent and stay under cover until you're ready to begin the assault. When you see the first fires, get moving. The watchword is *Constantius Victor*... We've got four hours until dusk, and there's a work camp below the summit over there – rest your men and have them cook and eat. They won't get any more hot food until tomorrow.'

'Or until we breakfast with Father Hades!' Valens said.

Castus slept for two hours, lying on the springy turf with his cloak across his head, and woke suddenly with the sensation that somebody was looking at him. He threw the cloak aside and stared around him. The sun was already low, and long shadows stretched across the ridge. Against the lit western sky he could see the jutting catapult arms rising from the artillery platforms. Then he turned his head and saw the thick red features of Placidus as the soldier knelt beside him.

'Tribune wants to see you,' Placidus said. 'He said it's urgent... *centurion.*'

Scrambling to his feet, Castus rolled his cloak and slung it over his shoulder before following Placidus back up the slope towards the artillery positions. What did Victorinus want now? Had the plan been changed? The last shreds of disturbed sleep slipped from his mind as he toiled up onto the ridge.

The engineers were still making their final adjustments to the torsion ropes of the heavy catapults, and Castus paused a moment to watch them. Beside each machine were piled the big earthenware jars, still in their slings of plaited rope. Each would be filled with pitch, oil and sulphur, incendiaries ready to spill over the wooden ramparts of the enemy fort.

'Centurion Castus,' a voice called. Castus looked up; it was not Victorinus that had summoned him, he realised. His blood slowed, and he tried to keep his expression blank.

Nigrinus was flanked by two bodyguards, both almost as broad as Castus himself and dressed in the scale corselets of the Praetorian Cohorts. Compared to them, the notary appeared almost insubstantial, his head emerging from the folds of his moth-coloured cape like a mushroom. Placidus had fallen in behind him, smirking openly.

'Centurion,' Nigrinus said, drawing closer and dropping his voice. 'You are the only member of the assault party who can identify the barbarian leaders by sight. I mean Drustagnus and the woman Cunomagla. It's vital that you do so, and that you ensure they are... neutralised. By your own hand, if necessary. Do you understand?'

'I understand.'

'I've ordered one of your own men, here,' Nigrinus went on, pointing to the lurking Placidus, 'to stay close to you once you get inside the fort, and make sure you... do what's required.'

'I'm capable of ordering my own men. Dominus.'

'Yes, I'm sure,' the notary said with a thin flickering smile. 'Listen,' he said, leaning even closer until Castus could taste his breath. 'The emperor has placed great trust in you. If either of the barbarian leaders escape to rally further opposition elsewhere, the campaign could appear... less than entirely successful. So we need to make sure that there are no mistakes. I think we discussed your debt of loyalty before. This is your opportunity to pay it.'

With my life, he means, Castus thought. And if that failed, there was Placidus ready to finish the job. He smiled. In his mind he was taking that brown cape in his fist and twisting it into a throttling tourniquet around the man's neck.

'I'm very grateful, dominus,' he said, without warmth. Nigrinus too smiled. *We are neither of us fools*, he seemed to say.

'Remember. The emperor is relying on you.'

They waited, sitting on the hillside in the cover of a thorny thicket, until the sun had gone and dusk swelled from the valleys.

'Carry your shields on your backs,' he told them. 'Put your cloaks on over the top and pull the hoods up over your helmets.' He scratched up a clod of earth, then dashed water over it from his canteen. Rubbing his hands, he turned the dry earth to mud, and then smeared it over his face.

'Like that,' he said. 'All of you. There'll be some sharp eyes up in that fort, and they know this country well.'

Then they rose and moved, two scouts going ahead of them and a party of archers bringing up the rear. A few men slipped as they descended the slope. Muffled curses, the sound of a blow. The sky was still deep blue, but the ground ahead was dark, tangled with bushes and low rocks, threaded through with streams. From high above them, the men heard wailing voices and shouts from the fort. The cries of defiance.

An hour of scrambling and clambering in darkness, picking their way down the slope and along the narrow valley. Each man clung to the cloak of the man in front, alert for any sound or movement from the massed shadows on either side. Castus went in front, trying to make out the shapes of the scouts moving ahead of him. He remembered this valley – he had passed this way during his escape from the fort the summer before. The memory was uncomfortably clear now. Every rearing shape around him looked like a hunched dog, ready to spring. He splashed through a shallow stream, and his boots grated on the stones.

Finally the soldiers reached the slope on the far side of the valley and crouched, cloaks pulled around them. The fort was directly above them now, up the steep, rutted hillside. Castus could see little of the ground; all he remembered of it was a long reeling descent, tumbling and leaping. He looked around him at the grey shapes of his men hunched in the darkness. Modestus squatted nearby, with Flaccus at his side. Diogenes, with his hood almost completely covering his face. Placidus caught his eye, and creased his brow before turning away. How much, Castus wondered, had the notary offered to turn Placidus into his willing accomplice? A purse of gold, a guarantee of promotion? Or just a chance to avenge himself for past insults?

And perhaps Placidus was not the only one. Castus remembered seeing Valens leaving the notary's tent that rainy night. Was he too now an enemy? He glanced up towards the fort ramparts. If Cunomagla were in there, she would fight. Strange, Castus thought, that she had helped to save his life, when so many on his own side seemed determined to take it from him.

A moment later the first muffled thuds came from high on the ridge. From where they were waiting in the valley, Castus and his men could not see the great catapult arms swinging up and over, the slings whipping their missiles into high arcing flight. But as they stared up into the last glow of the western sky, they saw the dark shapes passing briefly, and then falling towards the fort. Castus knew the incendiary pots would be dropping onto the ramparts, shattering and spraying flammable liquid over the wooden palisades and the thatch of the huts in the lower enclosure.

'Won't be long now,' he said quietly.

Sure enough, the waiting soldiers soon saw the streaks of flame against the sky: burning bolts shot by the ballistae further down the slope to ignite the incendiary liquid. They sat, or squatted on their haunches, cloaks pulled around them, watching the sky and the dark loom of the hill above them, the ring of stone wall high on the brink. The smell of burning came to them, the distant crackle of fires, and then they saw the sparks showering upwards against the night sky in the billow of smoke.

'Form up,' Castus said. 'Pass the word along to Valens and Rogatianus.'

A rustle of low noise along the valley as two hundred legionaries rose and moved forward towards the slope, tightening belts and checking weapons, securing their cloaks to hide the gleam of their mail.

'Hook-men and archers after me,' Castus whispered to the men at his back. 'The rest, follow the man in front of you and keep silent. We'll reassemble below their wall.'

A figure stepped up close, dim in the shadow. Valens took his hand, clasping tightly. 'Good luck, brother,' he said quietly.

'Juno protect us, Father Mars guide us!' Castus saw the faint gleam of his teeth. They embraced fiercely and then moved apart, and the stir of sound died as the last men got into position.

'So,' Castus said. 'Let's begin.'

CHAPTER XXI

Scrambling, dragging himself up hand over hand, Castus tried to keep moving up the slope and not think about what might be waiting at the top. The hillside was far steeper than it had seemed when he had escaped from the fort, rutted with grassy hummocks, tangled with thorny bushes and studded with rocks and patches of loose stones. How had he not noticed that before? Cursing under his breath, dragging his cloak through the thorns, he forced himself on upwards. Behind him he could hear the men whispering, shields rattling, the bright clink of mail and weapons and the steady scrabbling thud of hobnailed boots.

When he glanced up quickly he saw the sky above the fort already dull orange with the fires and smoke from the far side. The wall and the palisade at the top were silhouetted solid black against the glow: how would they ever get over that? *Don't think*, he told himself. His hands and face were scratched, and his bruised hip ached with every heaving step upwards.

Then, suddenly, the ground levelled and the first massive stones of the wall were before him. He looked up and saw no enemy heads along the parapet. From inside the fort, he could hear men shouting, screams, the noise of panicking animals and the steady rushing crackle of the fire. Most of the defenders were surely trying to extinguish the blaze before it destroyed

355

their huts and defences – but sulphurous pitch burns hot and is hard to quench.

Castus threw his back to the wall. Other men were stumbling up around him now; he needed to wait until the main force was assembled before beginning the assault, if it were to stand any chance of succeeding. But more than half the men were still straggling around on the slope, clawing their way up in the dark. He gestured ferociously, cursing through his teeth. *Come on, come on…*

'Archers!' he hissed. 'Spread out along the wall and watch the parapet. Shoot anyone you see. Grapnels: get up here quick.'

More cursing and fumbling in the darkness. One of the men slipped and fell on his grapnel, crying out in pain. No point in silence now…

'On my command, throw together. As soon as you've got a firm hold, get up those ropes and start tearing down the parapets!'

Men spread out along the base of the wall. Valens came running up, panting breath, with most of his men clambering after him. Castus could wait no longer.

'Throw!'

Air whined as the iron hooks were whirled and slung, a score of ropes uncoiling upwards into the glow of the fires. Iron clinked on stone or wrenched against wood. The man nearest Castus, a lumpish slow-witted youth, slung his grapnel up and then stared dumbly as it thumped against the wooden parapet and tumbled back, almost hitting him as it fell.

'Give me that,' Castus snarled. The youth was already on his knees, groping in the grass, but Castus found the grapnel first and snatched it up. He gathered a coil of line, then whirled the grapnel and threw with all his strength. For a moment he saw the iron hook dark against the sky's glow, before it crossed the parapet and he started dragging on the rope until it ran taut.

Two tugs with his weight behind them: the grapnel held. All along the wall a web of ropes were pulled tight, men already scrambling upwards. Castus ran at the wall, feeding the rope between his hands and planting his boots against the rough stones. Muscles bunched, he started hauling himself up. He felt his own sixteen stone of weight, plus the weight of his mail and shield, stretching the rope. He feared that it would break, or the palisade collapse before he gained the top of the wall. Anyone up there with a spear, even a rock, could knock him down now... Grunting every breath, kicking his boots for grip against the wall, he dragged himself up hand over hand.

Then the rope ran horizontal, and the wooden stakes of the palisade were in front of him. He grabbed at them, vaulting across the summit and dropping into a crouch on the far side. In one motion he slung the shield from his back and drew his sword.

He was alone. First on the wall, and no sign of the defenders.

Then bodies crashed against the palisade, soldiers dragging themselves up and over onto the wall walk. In the space of six heartbeats there were a dozen up, then a score, some of them taking position with raised shields, others hacking and pulling at the palisade stakes, others leaning back over to help their comrades scramble in through the breaches.

Castus let out a long breath. The air inside the fort was fogged with smoke, the walls and huts lit by a dull orange glow. There was only a narrow space of ground on this side, between the outer rampart and the wall of upper compound, but it was mazed with animal pens and small thatched shelters. Castus heard a shout from his left, and saw men running between the pens.

'Shields up,' he shouted. 'Form a barrier along the rampart!'

Soldiers stepped in to either side of him, clattering their shields against his. Behind them, more men were climbing the wall, the space inside the shield wall crowding with armoured bodies. A flung javelin struck the shields, then another.

'Valens! Take your men and go for the gate. I'll take the inner wall.'

He saw his friend raise a fist, and then signal to his men; the ring of shields broke, Valens and his century veering off to the right along the line of the rampart. Castus stared across at the inner wall. It was over ten feet high, with another palisade at the top, but it sloped inwards from the base and the stones were worn and old. No time now to retrieve the grapnels and ropes.

'Modestus: take ten men and form testudo against the base of the wall. Ramped towards the top. Understand? The rest of you, stay close on me.'

Leaping down off the walkway, he jogged across the ground between the animal pens. Sounds of fighting to his right. Valens and his men had met the first wave of defenders. He glanced around, looking for Placidus, but there was no sign of him.

Suddenly a figure lurched up in front of him, a Pict with a tall ruff of hair. '*Ha!*' the man yelled, darting a spear at his face. Castus turned the blow with his shield and hacked the man down without breaking stride.

Modestus was shouting, pushing his group of men against the inner wall. They stumbled together, and then their raised shields rattled above their heads. There were figures moving along the higher parapet. Castus saw the shaved skulls, the matted hair-crests. A spear came down and struck one of the soldiers.

'Remigius, Attalus: form your men behind me,' Castus roared. 'We're going over that wall at a run – kill everyone that gets in your way!'

He felt the bunched strength in his arms, the force of the blood filling his head. The dim glow of the fires seemed as bright as daylight. Three running strides, and he launched himself up onto the ramp of locked and levelled shields.

For a moment they tilted, the men beneath gasping as they took his weight. Castus rolled, sliding on the slick boards; then he got his knees beneath him and managed to stand. A roar from Modestus, and he felt himself boosted upwards as the men heaved against the shields. Sword in hand, he took three long steps forward and snatched at the palisade above his head, dragging himself up onto the crest of the wall.

Thunder of boots on shield boards behind him. Remigius and Attalus leading their men up across the testudo. Castus raised his head over the palisade, but ducked immediately. A blade whirred above him, and he struck back with a wild swing. A crunch of bone, a scream. Then he vaulted the palisade and came down inside the upper enclosure, dropping into a fighting stance.

The sky beyond the far boundary was full of fire, and the shapes of running men threw mad distorted shadows through the smoke. Remigius scrambled across the palisade behind Castus, with three of his men following him.

But the defenders were already upon them: a pack of them, ten or fifteen, coming at a run with shields raised, darting their spears overhead. No time to form up. Castus charged at the first Pict, beat his spear aside and knocked him down with his shield. A second stabbed at him. Castus yelled, a full-throated roar, sliced through the shaft of the spear, and then hacked the man through the head on the backswing. From the corner of his eye he saw Remigius take on two warriors: the soldier lunged for the first, but the second cut low with a sword and sheared the blade through his leg.

Castus stepped back towards the palisade. Chaos of shouting down below: the testudo had buckled and collapsed, but soldiers were scrambling up with their bare hands now, or pushing each other up on their shoulders. Only six men inside the enclosure. Retreat? The thought died – no chance of getting out of here alive now.

Blades on all sides. Castus blocked a blow, turned the sword aside and slipped his own blade down it to shear off the attacker's knuckles. A spear jabbed at his shoulder, punching into the mail. Another thudded into his shield, splitting the boards. Feet braced, Castus felt an odd calm settling over him. He moved without thinking, fought without fear. All the men who had followed him over the wall were down and only he remained. *Move, block, cut.* A blade slashed his leg above the knee, but he barely felt it. *If I die here*, he thought. *If I die here…* Blood sprayed hot across his face.

Then the rush came from behind him, the chorus of shouts as Modestus and his men vaulted in across the wall and flung themselves into the fight. Castus took two long strides forward. Drove his levelled blade against the silhouette of a warrior and heard him shriek. Wheeled, slashed back. His sword sliced through a man's arm, and he saw blood jump in a black torrent.

'What took you?' he said, but it came out as a scream.

'Sorry, got into a scrum down there!' Modestus was laughing, his mouth bleeding.

Sound of a horn blast from the lower enclosure: Valens and his men had captured the outer gate. The defenders in the upper fort were hanging back now, hurling javelins from the weaving shadows. The air was full of drifting sparks and flecks of flame.

'Get to the inner gate!' Castus shouted. 'Form wedge and straight across the compound!'

They formed up around him as he moved, raised shields butting rim against rim, swords levelled. Castus set the pace, jogging, the knot of armoured men tight to either side. He had no real idea how many had followed Modestus over the wall – enough, he hoped. Ten paces, then fifteen, the defenders falling back before the moving wedge. A steady clatter and thunk of flung javelins against the wall of shields. With a jolt of surprise, Castus realised that the man to his right was Diogenes.

Staring over the upper rim of his shield, Castus could see the mass of men gathering around the upper gate. Warriors, all of them: Drustagnus's picked warband. And there with them, standing up on the low wall above, was Drustagnus himself. Castus recognised him at once: the flat scowling face, the crest of black curls. For a moment he thought the Pictish chief had recognised him too – but Drustagnus was calling to his warriors, screaming at them to turn and face the approaching enemies who had somehow forced their way into his fortress.

The gateway was a narrow stepped passage cut down through the rampart and the rock beneath, sealed with a gate and covered with a wooden platform. The passage was only wide enough for three men standing abreast; attacked from below, it would be almost impregnable. But from the upper fort it was no more than a culvert, a gap in the low wall.

The space between the gate and the moving wedge of Roman troops narrowed fast. A hedge of spears against them now, a rising wall of men.

'Double pace!' Castus shouted, his voice ringing between the close shields. '*Charge....!*'

The wedge drove into the thicket of spears at a run, crashing aside the first few warriors. The others gathered, crowding together. Four more paces and Castus ran his shield up against the pack of bodies. Diogenes was pressed against his side,

IAN ROSS

another soldier to his left. Together they shoved, sliding blades out between the shield rims. Spears jabbed and flickered above them.

A long moment of heaving, then the pack broke and Castus staggered forward, half tripping over a dead man. A sword clashed off the bowl of his helmet, and he felt the dizzying clamour of it in his skull.

Fighting all around now, the wedge splitting, the opening of the gate passage still blocked by a solid plug of enemy warriors. Castus hammered down an enemy shield, slammed his own into the man's chest and knocked him aside.

'Diogenes! Keep close behind me!'

Blood filled his left eye and he blinked it clear. He chopped down at an attacker, once and then twice; the warrior's sword broke near the hilt, and he hurled the shard at Castus's face. Another lunged forward from the press: one hammering blow shattered the man's shield, the next chopped into his shoulder.

The Pict buckled and fell, dragging Castus's arm down, the sword still firmly caught in his shoulder blade. Castus kicked at the dying man's chest, hauling on his sword hilt, but the weapon was trapped. He released it, got both hands behind his shield.

'Sword!' he yelled. 'Somebody get me a *fucking sword*!'

He swung the shield with both fists behind the boss, punching it against men to left and right. A blade struck the neckplate of his helmet and raked down his back, grating against the mail. The boards of his shield were split, and only the rawhide rim held it together. Then it was ripped from his grasp completely, and Castus saw a huge bare-chested warrior raising a spear to strike at him. For a heartbeat he stood, open-handed, open-mouthed. Then Diogenes darted in from his right and slashed the big Pict across the stretched muscles of his abdomen. The man crumpled, dropped the spear and fell back.

'Thanks,' Castus said, planting his boot on the chest of the corpse at his feet and hauling his weapon free.

Above him, on the wall, Drustagnus stood alone directing his warriors. Castus glanced up at him, then down at the mass of men still blocking the gate. He reached out his left hand, seized a Pict by the hair and dragged him close, hacking at his neck with the sword. Kicking the body away from him he pushed forward, barging the enemy aside with his shoulders. He could sense the fight ebbing from them now, the panic taking hold. Trapped in the narrow gate passage, they could already hear the Roman horns blaring from the lower enclosure. Castus raised his sword in a two-handed grip, feinting at the warriors in front of him, and they dropped and squirmed aside, writhing up out of the gate passage like snakes from a burning wheatfield.

'Modestus, get the gate open!' he cried, not even sure if Modestus was there. Then he was scrambling up onto the wall parapet. His left leg was pouring blood, the fabric of his breeches soaked black, and his head was still ringing from the blow to his helmet.

Drustagnus was only a few paces away, brandishing his spear at the men below him. Castus edged forward, crouching. He could take the man with a rush and a swift strike, but something stopped him. A heady rush of wild pride.

'Hey!' he called out. 'You know me?'

The Pictish chief turned quickly, swinging his spear down level in a boar-hunter's grip. No sign of recognition on his face; he just snarled and lunged. Castus slashed back, and his sword rang against the iron spearhead. Drustagnus stabbed again, breathing hard from his throat, and Castus stepped back and parried the blow. With the third lunge, Castus twisted to his right and grabbed at the spearshaft with his free hand. Drustagnus dragged back on the spear, but Castus was already inside his guard. For a moment they wrestled together, their weapons trapped between them. Castus felt the heat of the man's body close against him, smelled his breath and his sweat. Then he drew back his head and butted it forward into the Pict's face, heard bone and cartilage crunch under the iron rim of his helmet. The spear went up, and he levelled his blade and drove it in low. Drustagnus fell against him, choking blood.

A groan and crash of timbers from below the wall: the gate was open, and the red and white shields of VIII Augusta were pressing up through the stone passageway in testudo formation. '*Constantius Victor!*' shouted the men inside the gateway, '*Constantius Victor!*' And the troops surging in from the lower fort echoed it.

Castus shoved the body of the Pictish chief away from him. When he glanced over the palisade he saw troops spreading out across the enclosure of the lower fort, most of the huts down there burning and fugitives running between them. Already the bonds of discipline were slipping; Castus saw soldiers breaking their ranks, pursuing the screaming women, looting the huts even as flames boiled from the thatch above them. There was a smell like roasting pork, and his mouth flooded with saliva for a moment – then he saw the corpses burning in the animal pens, and his guts clenched and he spat.

He clambered down off the rampart walk, unlacing his helmet and dragging it off. His scalp and face were running with blood, and his body was aching, wounds starting to pulse pain. The upper fort was a maze of reeling shadows, running men and panicked animals.

'Modestus,' he called, seeing the optio jogging towards him, 'gather the men and get over to those huts at the far end. Flush out anyone you find.'

Modestus saluted quickly, and then cried out to the men of the Sixth still gathered around the gateway. The last Pictish defenders had been driven back now, and the troops coming up from the lower fort had herded them against the south-eastern rampart and had them surrounded. *Not my fight*, Castus thought. He waited until Modestus and his men had moved off, then he started across the compound towards the larger group of huts to his right. He realised he had dropped his helmet. No shield either, just the sword blunted and bloody in his grip.

As he approached the first of the larger huts, two soldiers reeled past him, and he heard a woman scream from the animal pens to his right. Fire flared beyond the parapet, blinding him for a moment, and he tripped over a body lying in the darkness. Down onto his knees, sprawling, from the corner of his eye he saw the figure of a man lunging at him from the hut doorway. He dropped and rolled. A blade bit the turf behind him.

'Sorry, centurion,' Placidus said. 'Thought you were a Pict. Nothing in that hut anyway – only some dead.'

Castus got to his feet. 'Get back over to the gate,' he said.

Placidus was circling away from him, sword in hand. Castus saw him smile and shake his head. 'I was ordered to keep an eye on you,' he said. 'Make sure everything goes as planned.'

Castus flexed his empty left hand. He raised the sword in his right, blade levelled. 'If you think you can kill me,' he said, 'come on and try it.'

The big Gaul drew up his lip in a snarl, and his face was vicious in the flickering firelight. He swung his sword up, but his arm was shaking.

'Coward,' Castus told him. 'You'd only attack me if my back was turned.'

Placidus let his sword drop, already edging away. 'We can settle this later,' he said, and gave a strained laugh. 'I want to get that barbarian bitch's head first!'

He turned and jogged towards the next hut. Cursing, Castus went after him. He was limping now, and Placidus was already at the hut door before Castus could catch up with him. The soldier took a step back, and kicked. Wood cracked; the door burst open.

A flung spear darted from the low opening and spitted Placidus through the throat.

For a moment the man stood with the spear through his neck. He made a wet coughing sound, and his knees buckled. He dropped heavily.

Castus limped towards the open doorway. A Pictish shield was lying on the ground, and he stooped and picked it up, holding it before him. Time slowed, the noise of the rout behind him fading in his ears. Carefully he stepped across Placidus's quivering corpse. Then he threw himself forward through the door of the hut.

The interior smelled of burning pitch and fresh blood. Two dead warriors on the floor, two flaming torches in the firepit. At the far side, half in shadow, Cunomagla stood with a heavy boar-spear raised to strike. Castus stepped to one side and got his back against the doorframe, the Pictish shield held up before him. Cunomagla's face hardened as she recognised him.

'You come back,' she said. 'Your gods are kind to you.'

Castus saw the boy, her son, clasped behind her. He watched the head of the spear, watched the woman's eyes.

'These your guards?' he said, motioning with his sword towards the dead men beside the firepit. Cunomagla did not shift her gaze.

'Drustagnus's men,' she said, gripping the spear firmly. 'He sent them to kill us, when he knew the fort would fall. But I was stronger than they.'

He could close with her in three strides, across the firepit and in under the reach of her spear. Castus tried to judge the angle, tried to guess his chances of catching the spear blow on the small shield he was carrying. But, yes, he thought, she was strong. And he was weakened by wounds, exhausted from the fight. Then there was the boy – even if he had only a knife, he could still be dangerous.

'You planned all this?' he said. 'The war. It was... your intention?'

Cunomagla smiled coldly, shaking her head. Her hair was dark bronze in the flickering light of the torches. 'No. I found out what happened after Drustagnus and your renegade murdered my husband, but then it was too late. So, I must follow fate's direction. Sometimes the gods sleep, and men make mistakes. When they wake we are punished.'

From the smoky compound outside Castus could hear his men calling to one another. Modestus's voice. They were getting closer.

'But now my son will be king,' Cunomagla said, and her arm tightened as she gripped the spear.

'If he lives.'

Three strides, Castus thought. Block the spear and charge into her, knock her down. He willed his body to move, but could not.

'Put down the weapon,' he said.

'You want to take me alive? Make a trophy of me, for your emperor? No.' The boy peered out from behind her, wide-eyed but defiant. 'So what will you do?' she asked. 'Kill me?'

'Once my men get here, I'll have to. Those are my orders.'

'And you Romans always follow your *orders*, yes?'

Castus heard a thud from above him: a burning torch tossed onto the thatch. Smoke was filling the interior of the hut.

'I gave you a knife once,' Cunomagla said.

'You did that.'

He took three breaths, trying not to cough. Her eyes held him, the spearhead unwavering. Then he lowered the shield and rolled his shoulder against the doorframe. As he ducked his head through the doorway he was tensing, expecting the bite of the iron spear in his spine. Out through the door, he stood up and stepped across Placidus's body. Three paces, then four. He tried to ease his shoulders out of their hunch.

'Nothing in there,' he called to Modestus. 'Move up to the next huts. Go!'

Diogenes came up beside him, with two canteens swinging from his shoulder. Castus took one of them and drank deeply, gulping the water down; then he poured the canteen over his head and washed the blood from his scalp and face. When he looked back towards the hut, the thatch was burning. No movement from inside.

'It's like the inferno of the Christians!' Diogenes said. Smoke all around them, fires and contorted bodies in the shadows. Castus nodded, washing the gore from his sword. He wiped the blade on the hem of his tunic and rammed it back into the scabbard. Pacing heavily, he crossed the compound. He felt nothing now, just a spreading numbness. No sense of time or place. But he realised the fear that had been eating away at him for months now: the thought that Cunomagla might have had a child by him. She had not. He was glad of that at least.

After a while he heard the shouts from the lower fort, and gazed into the reeling smoke. *Cavalry, they've got cavalry!*

Noise of neighing horses, beating hooves. Castus jerked into motion, snatching up a fallen javelin as he ran. The upper fort was clear now, but when he reached the ramparts he saw wild motion from the enclosure below. He ran along the wall and found a place where the palisades had been torn down.

Ponies were charging between the burning huts, released from some corral or pen at the far end of the lower fort. The soldiers who had scattered in terror were regrouping now, pulling back from the huts, readying spears. Then, as Castus stood on the wall with the javelin raised, he saw a figure ride out into the cleared space before the lower rampart. It was Cunomagla, riding bareback with her son seated in front her, brandishing the heavy spear over her head. He saw her strike down a fleeing soldier, and then drag back on the reins to turn the pony before the rampart.

'Throw!' somebody shouted. 'Kill her!'

Soldiers were closing in from all sides, shields up. In the ring of men Cunomagla turned the pony again, but there was no way out. For a moment she glanced up and saw Castus standing on the wall above her with his javelin aimed. She raised her spear in salute, and he saw her grinning in wild triumph.

Then she hauled on the reins again, kicking at the pony's flanks and charging it at the rampart. The palisades were gone, burned or broken, and beyond was only empty blackness. With a leap the pony was up onto the wall, Cunomagla turning to scream back at the soldiers; then she kicked again and the animal bolted forward, across the ruined palisade into the black gulf beyond.

For a heartbeat Castus saw her in the glow of the fires, her hair bright against the darkness. Then she fell and was gone.

The soldiers surged after her, dashing up into the breach and pelting spears and javelins down into the night.

'Why didn't you throw?' The same voice. Castus turned on his heel. Three paces away, the notary Nigrinus stood on the brink of the wall. He must have entered the fort with the first wave from the gates. Castus tightened his grip on the javelin, still holding it raised above his head, and for a moment the notary stared back at him, face blank with surprise. Then Castus eased his arm down, until the javelin head clinked on the stones of the wall.

Nigrinus smiled, raising an eyebrow. 'I think you missed your moment, centurion,' he said. Castus heard the crackle of the burning huts once more, the shouts and screams. He stepped down off the wall, and Nigrinus followed him.

'Well, she won't get very far,' the notary said, apparently quite calm now. 'If the fall didn't kill her, our troops outside the fort soon will. No matter... Did you find the other chief? Drustagnus?'

'I found him and I killed him,' Castus said without looking back.

'You did? Excellent! I'll mention it to my superiors and see you're rewarded.' Nigrinus was pacing close beside him. 'The slaughter here has been quite satisfactory. There's little chance these people will dare raise their heads against us again. I think,' he said, turning to address Castus directly, 'we might consider your debt paid in full. You have a rare talent for survival, it appears. But I'm sure if we never encounter each other again, we will both be pleased.'

'May the gods send us luck, then.'

'Now, tell me,' the notary said with sudden urgency, 'which of these huts was the home of the renegade, Decentius?'

Castus shrugged, scanning the fort enclosure. Away to his left, he saw the hut in which he had been held captive.

'That one.'

Nigrinus nodded and strode off without another word. Castus watched him go, until a swirl of smoke blotted the man out.

The notary would not find what he was looking for: the fire was spreading between the huts, and he would not have the chance to search more than one. Whatever compromising documents, whatever evidence of complicity the renegade might have left behind him would soon be lost to the flames. They were all the same, Castus thought. Nigrinus and Decentius, Drustagnus and Cunomagla. Even the emperor himself. All of them with their plans and schemes, all of them groping about in the shadowy mazes of conspiracy. If some lost and others won, what did it matter? It was the soldiers who paid in blood, the soldiers and the warriors, the civilians struck down and butchered in their thousands, the burnt homes and crops, the despoiled land.

The gods help us, Castus thought to himself. He could feel a strange punchy feeling rising from his chest, a quivering of nervous energy. Everything suddenly seemed absurd, hilarious. He threw back his head and laughed – laughed out loud until his eyes streamed. Pacing back towards the gateway, he was gulping air as the laughter heaved out of him.

The emperor had got what he wanted at least: a victorious war, far from the controlling influence of his imperial colleagues. And an army, welded to his cause by battle. To the cause of his son too.

And it was glorious, Castus told himself as he gasped for breath. This was what glory truly looked like: the corpses stacked in heaps, the fire and the slaughter. But he had survived. He had triumphed. The thought of that started him laughing again.

Over by the gateway the dead were lying thick. Castus saw one of them sprawled across his path, hardly more than a boy, fourteen or fifteen, with a sword still locked in his grip. He stepped across the body, waving to Valens and the others by the gate.

'Centurion...' Diogenes said, and then his eyes widened in sudden shock.

Castus jolted back into awareness, glancing around. He saw Valens take two running steps towards him, raising his sword.

'What...?' he said, startled. 'No... *You?*'

Then something hard and very heavy struck the back of his head and his legs were gone from beneath him. He was on the ground, hot blood gushing over his face. Shouts of rage, a scream.

'Little bastard was playing dead!'

Valens was standing over him. Castus tried to heave himself up, but the blood was pouring onto the ground beneath him.

'Well, he's dead for sure now...' he heard Valens say.

He opened his mouth, and it filled with blood. Then the tide of pain rushed over him, and he was lost beneath it.

CHAPTER XXII

'So, it looks like you're alive after all then.'

Castus opened his eyes with difficulty. The sunlight drove nails into the back of his skull. He was lying on his back, with a ceiling of tent leather above him, and Valens was sitting beside the bed on a folding stool, eating walnuts.

'You've been looking very like a corpse for a long time now, brother! We were about to break into the funeral fund on your behalf.'

'How long?' Castus managed to say. The words ground in his throat like boulders in a rushing stream.

'Ah, talking too now! Well, it's been over twenty days since you showed any signs of intelligence. Mind you, in your case that's a relative thing.'

Castus raised his top lip, but every movement of his face filled his head with fire. He resigned himself to enduring Valens's wit.

'Good thing you've got such a great solid head, though,' Valens went on, cracking nuts in his palm. 'Otherwise that Pictish lad would've taken the top of your skull off. As it is, you've just got a nice new scar to add to your collection. Shame, though – it's at the back. Everyone'll think you got it while you were running away! Ha ha!'

Rolling his neck slightly, Castus could feel the thick linen bound all around his head. When he closed his eyes he felt a plunging sensation, a rush of distorted memories. He had woken from a long aching dream: flames and smoke, thunderous noise, then lost muffled silence.

'Don't worry, though, you've got a good doctor looking after you. A freedman of the imperial household, sent by the emperor. He's been feeding you some Greek medicinal slop to dull the pain, so you're probably not feeling much.'

'What happened... after?'

'After the fight? Oh, you didn't miss anything good. We destroyed the fort and then marched up country for six days – you were slung in a baggage cart, but the rest of us had to walk. We got to the sea, built an altar to Neptune and sacrificed in thanks for a successful campaign, then turned around and headed back south. We're at Bremenium now, a day north of the Wall.'

The noise of the cracking walnuts was very loud, aching in Castus's ears. But Valens had a sober look on his face now, and he was leaning forward to speak more quietly.

'The emperor's sick. Worse, I mean. That doctor who's been treating you says there's some evil matter in his bowels, eating him from the inside. They've known about it for over a year, but there's no cure. And now he's *approaching the last crisis*. That was the phrase the doctor used anyway.'

Castus lay still for a while, digesting the news. It was nothing unexpected, he decided. When he opened his eyes he was surprised to see Valens still there.

'What about the Pict woman?' he asked, struggling to form the words. 'The one who jumped the rampart?'

'Oh, her? No idea. I didn't see it myself, but those idiots from the Eighth were saying it was magic. They didn't find any trace of her outside the wall anyway, so maybe she just vanished into the air! Or more likely made off to some dirty little cave in the mountains to hide out with her brat till we're gone. Rumour is she was a powerful witch, and beguiled men to do her bidding. Any ideas about that?'

'Nope.'

'Ah, well. She won't be troubling us again...'

Castus tried not to smile. Valens was getting up now, tossing aside his handful of nutshells. He paused, and then came back to stand beside the bed.

'Another thing,' he said, lifting a bundle from the floor. 'You may as well have this, now that you're alive again.'

Valens unwrapped the bundle, and placed something on Castus's chest.

'Awarded for valour, by order of the emperor. First over the enemy wall, and slew their chief in single combat, so they say. In the ancient days of glory you'd have won a golden crown and a lifetime's honour for it, but now you must be content with that bauble and double rations. Tribune Constantine presented it, and our mule-faced Victorinus accepted it on your behalf, since you looked so dead. Constantine says to tell you: *Don't lose it this time.*'

His friend left, the tent flap swinging shut behind him, and Castus lay in silence with his hands clasping the twisted ring of a gold torque.

A wet night in Eboracum, and in the fortress of the Sixth Legion the paved courtyard of the headquarters building was packed with men. Torches guttered in the mist, threading smoke through the massed soldiers and painting the wet stone of the porticos and the hulking legion basilica with a moving glow. There were men of all units, the Sixth and the other legion detachments, cavalrymen of the Mauri and Dalmatae, wild tribesmen of the Alamanni. All of them drawn by some uncanny impulse, some current of rumour and dread. Inside the basilica, in the shrine of the standards beneath the busts of ancient deified emperors and the great statue of Victory, the Augustus Flavius Constantius was dying.

Shouldering his way through the crowd at the gate, Castus pushed on through the throng filling the courtyard, Valens and Diogenes a few others close behind him. His head was still bandaged, and a sick dizziness still numbed his limbs, but he felt the strange energy of the gathering urging him forward. Men glanced back at him as he worked his bulk between them. Nobody knew what would happen. The air was charged with fear, anticipation, excitement, like the mood before a riot or a battle.

He reached the tall pillared entrance of the basilica, and saw the doorway blocked by Praetorians with locked shields, Protectores stationed behind them gripping the hilts of their swords. Castus looked back at the sea of men behind him, faces upturned beneath caps and helmets. Ripples of motion ran through the crowd, like shivers, although the night was warm. Here and there fights broke out, quickly quelled. Men shoved and jostled; others climbed up on the portico roofs.

Beside him, Castus saw Valens scrambling up onto the base of a pillar. The noise of the crowd was growing. He shuffled backwards until he felt one of the other pillars behind him, and then eased his swordbelt around and slipped the weapon up under his armpit where he could draw it quickly.

Now a great sigh came from the crowd, and they shifted forward. Castus leaned, peering upwards, and saw that a little fat man had appeared in one of the high arches of the basilica. The fat man raised his arms as the officers yelled for silence. The roar of voices died into a deep hush.

'Fellow soldiers!' the little man called out in a high cracked voice. It was the eunuch, Castus realised, who had been in the tent with the dead Pictish chiefs after the battle. A few harsh laughs came from the crowd.

'Fellow soldiers,' the eunuch cried again, raising his arms to the sky. 'The sacred soul of our emperor has ascended to the heavens!'

A vast moan came from the assembled men. A mass of booted feet scraped the paving stones. Some of the men at the back of crowd had already started shouting. The eunuch's voice rose to a high wail.

'Our beloved Augustus... Flavius... Valerius... Constantius... *has lived*!'

The chorus of shouts was growing, building into a chant, but Castus could not make out what the men were saying. The crowd seethed and surged.

'Brothers,' the eunuch went on, stirring the air with his palms, 'although this is a solemn day, it is also a joyous day, for now that our emperor stands beside the thrones of the gods, we can revere him as we revere the gods!'

With a shock, Castus made out what the crowd were chanting.

'*Constantine! Constantine! Constantine!*'

'... for his sublime virtues, his glorious victories against our savage enemies,' the eunuch went on, 'his tireless service to the state, and his piety toward the gods...'

'*Constantine! Constantine! Constantine!*' The chant was a pulse in the air, something almost physical. Castus saw scuffles breaking out, men knocked down and pummelled, other men raising their fists to the sky. He looked up at Valens, and saw his friend's face glowing with wild fervour.

'Constantine Augustus!' Valens cried, and the men nearby cheered. Castus remembered seeing him leaving the tent of the notary Nigrinus. How many others had the notary

377

spoken to? How many had he bribed? He touched the golden torque he wore around his neck. *For valour*, he thought. *For loyalty.*

Now the chant was joined by a stamp, a regular crashing beat of hobnailed boots on paving stones. From the far side of the courtyard a solid wedge of men was pushing through the crowd.

'Soldiers! Noble soldiers!' the eunuch cried, fanning the air with downward motions. 'This is not right! Remember your oath! The new Augustus must be Flavius Severus – it is imperial protocol! Soldiers: do not besmirch your victories with dishonour!'

Fierce shouts from below, a volley of wooden cups and broken tiles flung up at the eunuch. Even a javelin, rattling off the basilica wall. Who was Flavius Severus? For a moment Castus could not remember. Then it came to him: Severus Caesar, the junior emperor appointed by Diocletian the year before, as deputy and successor to Constantius. But Severus Caesar was far away in Italia, and Constantine was here, surrounded by his father's loyal troops...

The fat man retreated inside. Now Castus could see that the men pushing their way through the crowd were Germanic warriors of the Alamanni, with their king Hrocus at their head. Many of them carried shields, shoving the crowd aside as they came. Hrocus climbed onto the shoulders of his men, his beard flaming red in the torchlight.

'Constantine!' he cried out. 'Give us Constantine!'

With his back to the pillar and his hand on the hilt of his sword, Castus craned upwards and stared in through the door of the basilica. The wall of Praetorians was moving too now, driving the crowd back with their shields and spearshafts. Castus leaped up onto a pillar base beside Valens. Within the block of Praetorians he could make out the lone figure with a cloak pulled over his head.

Rufinius, Prefect of the Sixth Legion, was up in the arch of the basilica now, yelling at the riotous crowd.

'Men! Respect the wishes of the emperors! This is mutiny!'

'No! *Get down!*' the crowd cried in response. The tight mass of Alamanni had halted, and now the Praetorians were driving out from the basilica doors with Constantine between them. As the man passed, Castus saw his ruddy face and firm jutting jaw, his cheeks wet with tears. But was he smiling too? Castus blinked, and Constantine had moved on.

Out in the courtyard there was chaos, a milling riot of men pushing forward and back, screams, angry faces raised in the torchlight. Rufinius had given up trying to calm them. Now the Praetorians were leading a white horse from under the portico – where had that come from? – and helping Constantine to mount. The horse, terrified by the noise, champed and shied, rolling its eyes. All around there was struggle and confusion. Castus saw a body of men from the Rhine legions trying to forge their way through the cordon of guardsmen.

'Are they trying to murder him?' Diogenes called from behind the pillar. 'Should we... go and protect him?'

Castus shook his head. He was watching Constantine carefully: he was gesturing to the crowd, trying to wave them back, mopping his face with his free hand as if he were wiping away tears. Was this real, or theatre? Castus could not tell. But the violence in the courtyard was real enough. Soon there would be bloodshed.

'Constantine, we pray to you!' the Alamannic king bawled out in his bad Latin. 'You must be our leader! You must be our Augustus! The army lusts for your rule! The world awaits you!'

And now Constantine was down off the horse, a tumult of bodies all around him. A moment later and he appeared again, raised on the locked and levelled shields of Hrocus's warriors. Cheers rolled down from the men on the high porticos, and the courtyard echoed with shouts of acclamation. Even the Praetorians were cheering now, raising their palms in salute.

Swaying on the shields, Constantine struggled to stand upright, raising his face to the light. Hrocus, lifted on the shoulders of his men, seized a purple robe from the hands of a Praetorian and cast it around Constantine's shoulders; one of the Protectores raised a golden circlet on the tip of a spear, and another placed it on Constantine's head.

'Augustus!' the soldiers shouted, banging their weapons and stamping their feet. 'Invincible Augustus Constantine! The gods preserve you – your rule is our salvation!'

And still the chant went on.

'*CONSTANTINE! CONSTANTINE! CONSTANTINE!*'

'And *that*,' Valens said, leaning closer, his eyes alight with joy, 'is how we make emperors at the edge of the world!'

'Oh, no,' Diogenes called from behind the pillar. 'That is how we make *gods*.'

But Castus was still staring at the man raised on the shields. Constantine stood proudly now, the purple swathing his shoulders, his hawklike nose and firm chin shining in the torchlight. He raised an open palm, accepting the acclamation of the soldiers, and as he did so he turned and stared straight across the heads of the crowd to where Castus was standing.

Pushing himself away from the pillar, Castus threw up his hand, shouting into the roar of the crowd.

'Constantine Augustus! Invincible Emperor!'

CHAPTER XXIII

The sun was low and the breeze freshening as they approached the gates of the fortress. Castus could smell autumn in the air. Behind him on the road, the line of soldiers increased their pace with the promise of home.

'Close up,' Castus called over his shoulder, smacking his staff into his palm. 'Military step!'

A muffled grumble, but the men did as he ordered. All of them were tired and filthy from a day mending roads, but they were soldiers and not labourers. Castus heard the regular crunch of boots on gravel. Woodsmoke was rising from the furnaces of the bath-house inside the walls.

Two months had passed since the great imperial entourage had departed Eboracum, bearing their new-made emperor off to Gaul. The fortress had soon fallen back into those same slow regular routines that Castus had found when he had first arrived there, two years before. But he was glad of the routines now, happy to pass his days in simple duty. He was centurion of a frontier legion, even if he still wore the fine gold torque of valour around his neck. How long, he wondered, would he remain so content?

The Blue House had been rebuilt on its old foundations, down by the river. Afrodisia was there, and Castus had already paid her several visits. Perhaps he would go there again this evening, with Valens... He smiled at the thought, and felt a warmth in his limbs. For a moment he pictured himself in ten or fifteen years, retiring with honour from the legion, a fat purse of gold in his fist and a grant of land to farm, married to Afrodisia with a crowd of children already growing up around him. The thought pleased him.

No, he thought. Not me. He remembered Marcellina, the envoy's daughter; he often thought of her, and wondered what had happened to her. Married now, in some distant city. That was the way of civilians, after all: they wanted homes, families, security. But Castus was not a civilian, neither would he ever be.

He recalled the funeral ceremony for Constantius, Eboracum's last taste of imperial glory. The towering pyre built in the centre of the parade ground, three storeys high and taller than a house, the wood painted to look like marble, decked with garlands and hung with laurel wreaths. The linen-wrapped body of the old emperor had been placed at the top, under a canopy made to look like a temple pediment, and all the units of the army had marched around the pyre with reversed weapons.

Constantine had lit the pyre, of course. When the flames had risen to the top, an eagle had flown from the temple canopy, fluttering for a moment in the light and heat of the fire, the showering sparks, before vanishing into the night sky. The spirit of Constantius, so the orators said, released from his mortal flesh. Rain turned to steam in the heat of the burning pyre, and the massed soldiers had cried out their praises to the old emperor and the new.

Arma virumque cano... Castus thought. *Arms and the man I sing...* That was by Virgil – the greatest poet of Rome, so Diogenes claimed. Castus saw in his mind the word-symbols scratched onto his wax tablet: the writing exercises that the former schoolteacher made him perform during their secret tuition sessions. Just the simple stuff, Castus had told him. After all, even quite stupid people could read and write, so why should he not? He only needed enough skill to read a strength report or a watchword tablet, but the teacher insisted on starting with Virgil. Perhaps by spring, he had suggested, Castus would have mastered enough of reading and writing to get through the whole poem. Castus himself doubted that.

And by the spring, things could be different anyway. Already there were rumours, carried by the traders from Gaul, of new wars on the continent. The Franks had crossed the Rhine on plundering raids, and there was displeasure among the other emperors at Constantine's assumption of the imperial purple. The soldiers had made Constantine – would Constantine need his soldiers again? The tide of history and great events had rolled over Castus and then receded, but still he knew the fierce joy of battle, the longing for action.

But then he thought of that other woman: Cunomagla. The memory of her stirred his blood. He pictured her riding from the fallen fort with her spear in her hand, crying defiance to the soldiers. Rome had harried the north, but not conquered it, and Constantine had not been the only victor of the campaign. If Cunomagla survived, and he was certain that she had, then she would be the ruler, in her son's name, of whatever still remained of the nations of the Picts. As he marched in under the huge pitted arches of the gatehouse, Castus grinned to himself, though none of his men could see it. It would be a hard kind of ruling, but a noble one. In his heart he saluted her: a queen among her people, at the furthest edge of the world.

AUTHOR'S NOTE

Compared to the glories of the high empire, the days of Caesar and Augustus, Trajan and Marcus Aurelius, the later Roman world can seem a dark and mysterious place, lit only by the flames of violence and the passions of competing religions. But the early fourth century was an age of great drama, of towering personalities and warfare spanning the known world, a time of revolution when, in the space of a few short decades, the old certainties of the classical era were swept away as Constantine, and his adopted religion of Christianity, reshaped the empire and gave a new definition to much of the future of Europe.

There is a statue of the emperor in York today, outside the minster. A modern piece, it depicts Constantine seated rather pensively, gazing at a broken sword, but it marks the approximate position of the ancient *principia*, the headquarters building of the legionary fortress where he was first acclaimed by the army on 25 July AD 306. No source records Constantine being raised on a shield, but the practice was apparently established by the time his half-nephew Julian was similarly acclaimed just over half a century later; it was perhaps originally a Germanic custom, and as at least one Germanic king was present in York that day, I have chosen to imagine that the shield ritual began with Constantine himself.

Modern York is a medieval city, on Roman foundations. In this novel I have preferred the Roman name Eboracum, just as I have used the ancient rather than the modern names for other places. I have not been entirely consistent with this: Rome remains Rome, not Roma, and the Rhine and Danube rivers retain their familiar names. My intention was to use the term that best evokes the ancient past, with the fewest modern associations.

Our literary sources for this period are scarce, sometimes contradictory and often partisan: the churchmen Eusebius and Lactantius, eager to glorify their hero Constantine, together with later historians such as Zosimus, Eutropius and Aurelius Victor. Among the few contemporary writings are the series of panegyrics, speeches given in honour of the emperors themselves, and often in their presence, today known as the *Panegyrici Latini*. These are works of imperial propaganda, highly rhetorical and elaborate, but they preserve many details of the era otherwise lost to history.

One of these, *Panegyric VIII*, contains the first recorded mention of the people known as the Picts. Another (*Panegyric VI*) makes one of the few slight references to the campaign conducted in the north of Britain by Constantius, Constantine's father, shortly before his death in AD 306. Constantius did not, the orator claims, 'seek out British trophies, as commonly believed'; for this to need refuting in public, it must have been a rumour widely known. It would not be the first time, after all, and certainly not the last, that a war has been concocted to satisfy the desire for military glory; from that seed this story takes its root.

The Roman army of the early fourth century was in a period of transition. At its core was still the traditional legion of heavy infantry, officially about five to six thousand men strong, divided into ten cohorts, each cohort subdivided into six centuries. But most legions had been split up into several smaller detachments, and those that remained intact were much reduced in strength. The old century, commanded by a centurion and numbering around eighty men, may have shrunk to as little as half that number by the era of Diocletian.

Not only the size of the old legion had changed; the legionaries of the early fourth century also looked quite different from their forefathers. Gone were the familiar segmented iron body armour, short stabbing sword and rectangular shield of the age of Trajan. The tetrarchic soldier wore mail or scale armour, carried an oval shield and a long sword, and wore a long-sleeved tunic, boots and breeches, an appearance perhaps more suggestive of the medieval than the classical world.

Within two or three decades, this ancient military system would be overhauled once more, and a newly structured army rise from its ruins. Much about this process is still unclear, but I have preferred to assign the changes to the reforming Constantine rather than the traditionalist Diocletian.

If the Roman world of this era appears often misty, the lands that lay outside the imperial borders are almost entirely lost in fog. In particular, the north British people known to the Romans as the Picts have long been mysterious, their culture and society, their language, even their existence the subject of much academic and popular debate and controversy. My portrayal of the Picts and their culture in this novel is necessarily speculative, an imaginary hybrid of earlier Roman accounts of the northern Britons and descriptions from the early Middle Ages. I make no claims to veracity; while I have based my fiction on the fragments of fact wherever possible, my intention has been to try and show a society and a people that might plausibly have existed. No historian, I believe, could do more than that.

For a contextualising overview of the period, the relevant

chapters of David S. Potter's *The Roman Empire at Bay: AD 180–395* (2004) are both erudite and very readable. Bill Leadbetter's *Galerius and the Will of Diocletian* (2009), while often contentious, covers the complex period between the abdication of Diocletian and the rise of Constantine in considerable detail. *In Praise of Later Roman Emperors* (1994), edited by C. E. V. Nixon and Barbara S. Rodgers, is an invaluable compilation of the full texts and translations of the *Panegyrici Latini*, while Michael H. Dodgeon and Samuel N. C. Lieu's *The Roman Eastern Frontier and the Persian Wars, AD 226–363* (1991) contains the surviving documentary texts on the eastern campaign of AD 298 and the battle of Oxsa (often mistakenly referred to as the battle of Satala in modern works).

The later Roman military has received increasing study in recent decades. Pat Southern and Karen Dixon's *The Late Roman Army* (1996), and more academic monographs by Martinus J. Nicasie and Hugh Elton, have been joined by A. D. Lee's comprehensive *War in Late Antiquity: A Social History* (2007). Ross Cowan's forthcoming *Roman Legionary: AD 284–337*, part of the Osprey military history series, will doubtless offer a concise and accessible popular alternative, backed up by the latest research in the field.

Historical works on the Picts are rather more scarce. Nick Aitchison's *The Picts and the Scots at War* (2003) gathers a wealth of information from a wide range of sources, while James E. Fraser, in *From Caledonia to Pictland: Scotland to 795* (2009), gives one interpretation of the possible genesis and development of this elusive people.

Assembling the historical background for this story has taken nearly a decade of research, but without certain people this effort would not have borne fruit. My particular thanks go to my agent, Will Francis at Janklow & Nesbit, for his immediate and effective championing of the novel, and to Rosie de Courcy at Head of Zeus for being so enthusiastic about Castus and his adventures. I am also very grateful to David Breckon, who first read the manuscript, for his insightful and encouraging comments, and to the members of the Roman Army Talk online forum, whose collective knowledge has been a guide and an inspiration to me for many years as I picked my way across the dark terrain of the late Roman world.

ABOUT THE AUTHOR

IAN ROSS has been researching and writing about the later Roman world and its army for over a decade. He spent a year in Italy teaching English, but now lives in Bath.